Giorgio Faletti spent years as a successful comedian and singer/songwriter before a career as a writer. His first novel, *I Kill*, was an international sensation. His fifth novel, *I Am God*, was recently published to wide acclaim. He has been declared the best living Italian writer by *Corriere della Sera*, the most popular and highest-selling Italian newspaper.

Also by Giorgio Faletti

I Kill
I Am God
The Killer In My Eyes

The Pimp

Giorgio Faletti

Translated by Antony Shugaar

Constable & Robinson Ltd
55–56 Russell Square
London WC1B 4HP
www.constablerobinson.com

First published in Italy by Baldini Castoldi Dalai Editore S. P. A., Italy, 2010

First published in the UK by C&R Crime,
an imprint of Constable & Robinson Ltd, 2013

A copy of the British Library Cataloguing in
Publication data is available from the British Library

ISBN: 978-1-47210-809-8 (A-format paperback)
ISBN: 978-1-84901-999-6 (B-format paperback)
ISBN: 978-1-47210-477-9 (ebook)

Printed and bound by CPI Group (UK) Ltd, Croydon, CR0 4YY

1 3 5 7 9 10 8 6 4 2

To Marcella and Corrado,
who never left

Sure, let's eat it. —Adam and Eve

PROLOGUE

I'm Bravo. And I don't have a dick.

That could be my introduction. It doesn't change a thing that I go through life with a nickname instead of an official first and last name. You are who you are, whatever the bureaucratic trails that follow in your wake, like streamers from a carnival. My life wouldn't have been any better or worse, whatever name I gave with each handshake. The waves no higher or lower: the water just as choppy, the winds just as rough, the voyage every bit as daunting. Regret would be pointless. Being nameless just gave me an extra layer of shadow in which I could cloak myself: the fleeting glimpse of a face, a faint silhouette, nothing there, no one. I was what I was—so namelessness was exactly what I needed. Why add a clause or a rider?

As for that other anatomical detail, it's worth devoting a little time to the subject.

I wasn't born this way.

It's not like some doctor, presiding over my birth, stared in disbelief at my blank infant groin as I emerged from the maternal fissure, completely unequipped for life's principal task, or cast a baffled glance at my mother as she lay there, exhausted from the last grunting effort of giving birth. There was no doting sympathy for a child growing up with the burden of a distinctive handicap—distinctive, to say the least—a handicap likely to draw cruel mockery in the years to come. No tragic adolescent confessions, head bowed, gaze riveted on my shoes as if I were trying to read some higher meaning into my shoelaces.

No, when I came into the world I had all the right equipment, with everything in its place. Oh, I was equipped, all right, perhaps overequipped, in light of what happened later. Until things changed so radically one fine day, my equipment was the cause of plenty of trouble for a variety of adventuresome and reckless young (and not-so-young) ladies who wanted nothing more in life. I always figured that was their problem, not mine.

Until the day that one young lady's problem became my problem.

The how and the when and the why of the matter will never be subjected to the scrutiny of future historians. It was a simple case of the wrong person noticing the wrong thing at the wrong time. Guilty as charged, for whatever that's worth. I make a full admission, though I have no regrets. Our lives are what they are, and nothing more. Sometimes there's just no way—and no reason—to act any differently. Or if there was, I was oblivious to it. Now even the mere suggestion of a reason or motive would be just one more pin in a voodoo doll with my face on it.

One night—one of those turning points when your life changes course—someone was waiting for me, with a well-honed straight razor and a deep well of rage and sadism, ready to make me what I am today. He left me flat on my back, with a bloodstain spreading across my trousers; my voice waned to a whisper as the blossoming stain did my screaming for me. I was tossed out of the theater, kicked off

2

the stage and into the audience. Hurled back into the farthest row of seats, I would say. And yet the pain of that cut was nothing compared to the pain of the applause.

Until that day, I had paid lip service to love and enjoyed sex for my own personal pleasure. Now my condition meant I was no longer obliged to promise that love, because I was no longer capable of receiving its monetary equivalent in exchange. That is to say, sex.

A man's body held no appeal for me, and I no longer had anything to offer a woman.

Suddenly, peace reigned supreme. No more ups, no more downs, just flatland, stretching out. No more placid waters or stormy seas. Just the mocking irony of dead calm, the doldrums where sails neither belly nor rip. Now that I had no need to run, I had a chance to look around me and see how the world really works.

Love and sex.

Lies and illusions.

A moment of one, a moment of the other. Then off in search of the next stop, the next address jotted down with whatever comes to hand. Following your nose, your instincts, feeling your way. Blind, deaf, and mute, relying on a sense of touch and smell, the far reaches of instinct.

When I regained my sense of sight, my hearing, the ability to speak, I thought it over and understood.

I immediately accepted.

In the time that followed, I acted.

Since then, blood has been shed, a raw material that comes cheap everywhere around the world. People have died, and perhaps they were worth even less than the blood that was spilled. Some of those responsible for what was done to me have paid; others have gotten off scot-free.

3

Like everything that culminates in death, this too started out small.

It all began when I realized that there were women willing to sell their bodies for cash and there were men willing to spend their money to get their hands on those bodies.

It takes a healthy dose of greed or resentment or cynicism to work your way into the middle of that transaction.

I had all three.

April 1978

CHAPTER 1

When Daytona and I walk out onto the street, it's daybreak.

We stop on the sidewalk, a few feet apart, inhaling the cool morning air. Even in a big city, morning air gives the impression of purity. Actually, the breath that Milan exudes has halitosis, and both of us must have pretty bad morning breath ourselves. The only thing that's pure is the impression, but even that's something you can live on.

Daytona stretches his arms, yawns, twists both shoulders.

I thought I heard his spine crack, but maybe my ears are deceiving me. His face shows the signs of a night spent playing poker and snorting coke. He's pretty messed up. You can see the muscles tensing around his jaw. The double comb-over that covers up his bald spot like a clever bit of sleight of hand and hairspray has started to sag, slipping off to one side, like a hairy beret. His complexion is sallow, and he has dark circles around his eyes. His pencil mustache makes him look like one of those nasty, neurotic cartoon characters who wind up being funny in spite of themselves.

He lifts his hand in front of his face; pulls back his shirt cuff, begrimed by the night-long card game; and looks at the time.

"Jesus, it's almost six a.m."

7

Daytona says this as if it were a problem. As if it were a rarity for him still to be up and about at this hour of the morning. As if there were someone who cared what he did with his life, aside from himself and occasionally the police. He drops his arm and the watch vanishes beneath the cuff. That wristwatch is the source of his nickname. For years, he's worn a gold Paul Newman Daytona Rolex.

When he has the watch to wear.

It's a sartorial detail that makes it easy to tell Daytona's good times from his lean times. Just take a look at his left wrist. If there's no watch, it means he's pawned it. And if he's pawned it then it means that Daytona is hustling his heart out to get the watch out of hock. Without worrying much about what he has to do to lay hands on the money.

Well, this morning the watch is on his wrist and he's just spent the night balls-out, luck running high, winning hand after hand at poker. After last call, we stayed on in the private room of the Ascot Club, the room next to the bar. Him, Sergio Fanti, Godie, Matteo Sana aka Sanantonio, and me. Bonverde, the owner, went home with his wife, hard on the heels of the last spectator. On his way out, he told Giuliano, the manager, to close the place down and lock up. Without too much interest in what might happen after he walked out. We stayed on in the private room, breathing in the lingering aroma of decadent humanity, in the hay-scented dankness of wall-to-wall carpeting that hasn't been aired out for years. Someone put out the cards, packs of cigarettes, and a few yards of cocaine.

The hours sped past, the cigarettes and cards went around, and when the last snort of cocaine was just a distant memory, Daytona had become the unquestioned star of the evening's entertainment. The jackpot was four nines slapped down on

8

the table like a thunderbolt, dealing out death to a full house. Sweeping the pile of cash.

As if he'd just read my mind, Daytona turns to look at me.

"I was fucking lucky tonight. I needed that."

I smile, even though I try not to. I turn to look at the intermittent flow of morning traffic. Scattered cars move lazily along Via Monte Rosa. Inside the cars are frightened ghosts returning home and other ghosts, convinced that they're frightening, heading out for their daily damnation. As an impartial observer, I had the impression that Daytona had given the blindfolded goddess a name and address, with a few sleights of hand that were not entirely sportsmanlike. As far as I could tell, anyway. Not that it's any of my business. I don't gamble or play cards, so I don't win and I don't lose. I've always been the spectator who watches and minds his own business. Over time, this has evolved from a rule guiding my life to a pleasant routine. It's a better way to live and, in certain circles, it's a better way to stay alive.

I look back at him.

"Fucking lucky is right. How much did you win?"

Daytona scrutinizes my face in search of sarcasm. He's satisfied there is none, or maybe he chooses not to see it. He slips one hand into his pocket without pulling out his wad of cash, as if he can count the money by touch. I can almost see his fat hairy fingers rumpling the bills roughly, the way people do with money that's come easy.

"A million eight, more or less."

"Not bad."

"You said it. Yum, yum, yum, a rich pile of chips!"

He rubs his hands together with satisfaction, and it occurs to me that there are certain human beings who seem to be incapable of learning from past mistakes. I struggle to keep a

9

smile from spreading across my face again. One time, during a poker game with guys he completely outclassed, Daytona couldn't keep from repeating that gloating phrase, and he got punched in the eye by someone taller, stronger, and better armed than him. Of course, he had to take it without reacting. He went around for weeks with a black eye that made him look like a chubby, slightly melancholy Dalmatian. With a string of snickering mockery trailing behind him, like the long train of a wedding dress.

Behind us, the others emerge from the club.

They climb up the stairs under a sign that by night winks an invitation to step downstairs to the Ascot Club, the unrivaled temple of Milanese cabaret. The walls up and down the ramshackle staircase are lined with posters for the great talents that have passed through those walls, trodden that stage, looked up at those lights at the dawn of their careers. Every day, out on the street, by the front door, an illuminated billboard announces the names of the aspiring stars who will be appearing that night.

A marginal past, a glorious future, and a hopeful present. All gathered together under the old axiom that in Milan, late at night, after a certain hour, nobody's out and about but cops, artists, criminals, and whores.

The hard part has always been telling them apart.

Giuliano is the last to emerge. He lingers behind, locking a roll-down shutter that seals up the Ascot Club once and for all, protecting it from the contamination of daylight.

The others join us.

Godie sidles over to Daytona and places his index and middle fingers, open like scissors, on the side of his neck.

"Tac! Got you. You fumb duck."

Godie has a quaint and distinctive manner of speech and

10

behavior. He's a perfect distillation of the place, the time, and the people he frequents. It's a circle of people who express themselves with a language that attempts to be clearly recognizable, if not necessarily original. You need only invert the first consonants of certain words, so that the *black dog* becomes the *dack blog, good shit* becomes *shood git*, and *hard cash* becomes *card hash*. And *Diego*, his real name, turns into his nickname, *Godie*.

Il Godie, to be exact. *The one-and-only* Godie.

Simple, and possibly a little stupid. But people choose the medals that they pin on their own chest.

Daytona pulls Godie's hand away from his neck.

"You calling me a fumb duck? It's just that none of you know how to play cards. You, least of all."

Godie shoves his elbow.

"Aw, go fuck yourself. Remember, there was no one but me and the Cincinnati Kid in New Orleans."

The sense of humor is always the same, a bit repetitive, sometimes inspired by the cabaret artists who perform nightly at the Ascot, in other cases an inspiration from which they draw.

Giuliano catches up with us. Like me, he stayed out of the poker game. He just dabbled in the ancillary debauchery. I think he raked off some of the winnings in exchange for providing the club as a venue. As always, of course, that's none of my business.

"So, now what do we do?"

Sergio Fanti, average height, skinny, bald, with a prominent nose, looks at his watch. We all know by heart the words he's about to utter.

"I have exactly enough time to head home, take a quick shower, and head straight for the office."

11

Sergio is the only one of us who has a real job. He works in the fashion business and his rumpled but elegant suit confirms the fact. No one understands how he can reconcile his *noches de fuego* and rock 'n' roll with a serious business activity, but he seems to pull it off. The only evidence of his misdeeds are a pair of dark bags under his eyes the size of a B cup: he wears them like a trademark.

Matteo Sana yawns. Then he runs one hand over his unkempt beard, veined with tufts of white, like the hair on his head.

"I'm going to swing by Gattullo for a cappuccino."

Again, Godie scissors his two fingers into Matteo's neck. With an accent and voice so intensely Milanese that it verges on parody, he seconds the idea.

"Tac! I'm with you. I see you and raise you. A cappuccino and a pastry."

Giuliano looks at me and Daytona.

"You two coming with?"

Daytona taps the back of his left hand with his right index finger.

"I'll pass."

I shake my head.

"Ditto. I'm heading for my hut."

We watch the four of them walk off and head over to Sergio Fanti's BMW 528 — in the end, Fanti has given in. Godie flaps his arms and talks excitedly, the way he always does when he's a little high. They get in the car and, covered by the noise of the slamming car doors, the engine roars to life, puffing clouds of blue-gray exhaust out of the tailpipe. The car eases out of the parking spot and lurches off toward Piazza Buonarroti, in the direction of the Pasticceria Gattullo, the pastry shop and café at Porta Lodovica.

12

In my mind, I can see them stumbling into the café. In the time it takes them to drive over there, the place will have filled up with people ordering cappuccinos and pastries. Despite their stated intention of having cappuccinos and pastries themselves, they'll probably order three whiskeys and a Campari instead. A dozen heads will turn, up and down the counter. Then they'll all troop off to their respective apartments, and they'll each pop a Rohypnol to get to sleep, a way of counteracting the lingering effects of the cocaine and their accelerated pulses from the amphetamine with which the coke has surely been cut. The night is over, and that's how certain animals make their way back to their lairs.

Daytona and I are alone again, on the sidewalk.

"You know what would be the perfect way to top off a lucky night?"

"No."

But I do know, of course. I know perfectly. Still, I want to hear him say it.

Daytona looks at me, his comb-over this way and that and his eyes glistening to the extent that they can after a sleepless night. Then he tips his head toward a point on the other side of the street.

"A trip through the Northwest Passage with that pine fiece of ass."

I smile, this time without having to conceal it.

Across the street from the Ascot Club is a big office building, the Milan headquarters of Costa Britain Shipping. It's four stories tall and it takes up a good portion of the block—from the corner of Via Tempesta stretching past us all the way to Piazzale Lotto. Reinforced concrete, aluminum, steel, and sheet glass. And overhead lights always on, illuminating ceilings and empty desks, to remind everyone

13

that in this city, even when people are at home sleeping, someone is thinking about work.

A group of people have just stepped out of the glass doors. Cleaning women. They've emptied the trash cans, vacuumed the wall-to-wall carpeting, and scrubbed the bathrooms, hard laborers of the night who've toiled till now so that the hard laborers of the daytime will find a nice clean workplace when they arrive. A couple of them hurry off immediately, heading for bed or breakfast. The other cleaning women have stopped to talk, perhaps experiencing the same sensation that we had: at this time of the morning, the air is worth breathing. One of them has stepped aside to light a cigarette, and stands slightly separated from the group. She's tall and slender, and her shapeless smock is incapable of concealing a certain attractiveness. Her hair is long and brunette and her face is fair and luminous.

And resigned.

I tip my head in her direction.

"That one?"

"Yup. Nice dish."

I look at Daytona, who's already experiencing a movie in his head. Not a movie that they'd be able to show in any of the better movie theaters along the Corso Vittorio.

"How much is she worth, to you?"

"A C-note, if she's willing."

A hundred thousand lire would buy a nice pair of shoes, with prices these days. And these days are getting very pricey.

"Two hundred, and she'll do it."

Daytona stares, eyes wide. He's not doubting my statement, he's doubting the price.

"Christ, two C-notes."

"A hundred and fifty for her, and fifty for me."

"You piece of shit."

I look at him scornfully, as if he were a newly landed immigrant with a cheap suitcase.

"It's six in the morning, you're all alone, you're an ugly troll, and that's a damn good-looking young woman."

He hesitates. Maybe he can't tell whether I'm serious or I'm joking.

I strike the fatal blow.

"You just won a million eight. That leaves you with a million six."

"Okay. Let's see what you can do."

I turn my back on him and walk away. Now it's his turn to sit and watch. I cross the street and approach the girl, who's smoking her cigarette, purse slung over one shoulder, eyeing me, evaluating me as I draw nearer. She's much cuter up close. Actually, she's quite pretty. Her eyes are light hazel, with a hint of sadness, maybe from seeing too much of life on the outskirts of the big city; they're eyes that have yearned for things she's never been able to afford.

I smile.

"*Ciao*. Happen to have a light?"

She swings her purse around, rummages in it, and pulls out a plastic cigarette lighter. She must be new to the job. Her hands aren't roughened and reddened from ammonia and chores, at home and elsewhere. From the way she looks at me I can tell that she knows that getting a light for my cigarette was just an excuse. And not a very original one, I have to admit.

I pull out my pack of Marlboros and light one up. I poke my finger through the cloud of smoke to point at the office building behind her.

"You work here?"

She bobs her head vaguely.

"Cleaning woman. If you call that a job, then sure, I work here."

"What's your name?"

"Carla."

"All right, Carla. Can I ask a personal question?"

She silently assents. She's curious. That means she's smart.

"How much money do you make a month?"

She studies me, waiting to hear where I want to take this. There's no fear in her eyes, and I like that.

"A hundred eighty."

"Feel like making a hundred fifty in a couple of hours?"

She understands immediately. I brace myself for a slap that doesn't come. Which is already significant. Maybe she's familiar with propositions of this kind. Maybe she has a special need for money right now. Maybe, in a flash, she has simply glimpsed a way out of the misery of the city's outskirts, frozen foods, clothing purchased off the rack in a UPIM department store. There are countless possibilities, and I don't care about any of them.

There is only one thing left to clear up, so she asks.

"With who?"

I jerk my head sideways at a point behind me. She identifies Daytona on the other side of the street. Then she turns her gaze back to me, with a hint of disappointment in her eyes. She drops her gaze and stares at the sidewalk, before answering.

"He's no Robert Redford."

I put on an innocent expression, the way you do when something is patently obvious.

"Yeah, if he was I wouldn't be here talking to you."

She looks over at the other women, clustering a short distance away as if waiting for her. Since the two of us began our conversation, they've been studying us, silently surmising. An occasional giggle, a few sidelong glances. A few of those glances may have contained a hint of envy. Carla looks back at me, a note of defiance in her hazel eyes.

She speaks in a low voice, as if her lips were uttering a furtive thought. She suggests an alternative.

"If it was you, I'd do it for free . . ."

I lightly shake my head, firmly cordoning off that line of inquiry.

"I'm out of the question."

She needs to understand.

"Is it that you don't like me, or do you just not like women?"

"Neither one. Let's just say that in this particular circumstance I'm a middleman."

Carla says nothing. I sense that she's weighing the pros and cons. I don't have the impression that it's a question of morality, just of convenience. Maybe she comes from one of those families in which the father is the proprietor of everything that's in the house, daughters included. Maybe it's just a matter of setting a fair price for something she usually has to give up without being asked. Or maybe those are all just fantasies I'm spinning in my mind and, as is so often the case, the truth is completely different. No one can say what's really going on in people's minds.

And sometimes all that matters is what people decide to do.

Carla nods her head.

"Tell him to wait for me out front of the Alemagna, on Via Monte Bianco. I'll be there in a couple of minutes."

I point to Daytona's orange Porsche. It's an old model, a used car with dimmed status. Most of the status remained in the hands of the original owner, who is certainly now driving the latest model. But for people like Daytona and the people he frequents that car remains a glittering trinket, a badge of honor.

"That's his car."

"All right."

While we talk, her fellow workers move off down the sidewalk. Carla seems relieved. She won't have to come up with an explanation right now. I feel certain that by tomorrow she'll have something ready. Cash and a sense of guilt are two excellent incentives for ingenious falsehood.

"Just a piece of advice."

"Yes?"

"Have him buy you a cup of coffee and don't get in the car unless you have the money safe in your purse."

She looks at me with a smile that's not exactly a smile.

"Is that how it's done?"

"Yes, that's how it's done."

I turn to go and my gaze settles on Daytona, waiting expectantly on the other side of the street. I cross the street and walk over to him. He saw the exchange, though he couldn't tell what we were saying, just like Carla's fellow cleaning women. As I approach him, I discard the cigarette and exhale the last lungful of smoke into the general haze of Milanese smog.

"Well?"

"Wait for her in front of the Alemagna. She'll see you there."

18

"How much?"

"A hundred and fifty, like I said."

"Shit."

Maybe Daytona can't believe his ears and meant to express his astonishment. Or else he was hoping for a discount. He long ago stopped believing in his own personal allure.

"And fifty for me."

I hold out a hand toward him, palm upward. He understands and reaches into his pocket. Then he hands me a wrinkled, rumpled bill, crumpled up the way you do with money you earn without lifting a finger. Only, this time, I'm the one who earned it. Without cheating. It's the oldest game in the world, and I know all the rules. Daytona knows the rules too, but he won't stoop to play by them. He likes to have someone to play for him. And like lots of others I've met, he's willing to pay for that service.

As I slip the money into my jacket pocket, he gives me a hard, meaningful stare.

"No kidding around, Bravo."

I shrug my shoulders.

"You know I don't kid around."

Daytona heads over to his Porsche, pulls the door open, gets in, and starts the engine. He waits for traffic to pass, and roars off toward Piazzale Lotto. At the green traffic light, his brake lights blink on, and then he vanishes in a right-hand turn, accelerating toward a dubious tryst.

I stand alone on the sidewalk.

I slide my hand into my jacket pocket, find my car keys, and walk toward my car, a dark blue Innocenti Mini, parked a short distance away.

I get into my nondescript little car. On my left I see Carla walking fast, heading for her appointment. She spots me and looks sharply down at the sidewalk ahead of her. Good luck, sweetheart. A month's salary for two hours of work isn't a bad deal, if you're adaptable. And she clearly knows how to adapt. For me, it's been nothing more than an idle game, because I usually work with contacts and negotiations at quite a different level. I don't think twice about the damage caused by what I just did and what I do on a regular basis.

The laws that govern society are a line drawn in the dirt by a fairly unsteady hand. Some cross that line, others respect it. I believe that I float a hairsbreadth above that line, never setting foot on either side of it. I don't worry about it, because the world I live in doesn't worry about it.

Like it or not, that's who I am.

CHAPTER 2

If it was you, I'd do it for free . . .

The girl's words ring in my ears as I zip along the Nuova Vigevanese, heading for home. I can see her eyes. To rid myself of sounds and visions and desires, I cover them with Daytona's mottled red face and all the predictable words he will grunt as he takes her to bed. I picture her, hastily peeled of clothes like an orange by his pudgy hands, the white flesh of his fingers dotted with dense black hair. I know the impatient way he must have pulled down his trousers and shoved her head between his legs. I know what'll happen afterward, or maybe what's already happened. Sex the way sex happens, dulled by the effects of the cocaine, the girl's indifference, the shabby anonymity of the motel.

But Daytona's not the kind of guy who notices certain things. He lacks the sheer power to be a predatory animal, and the girl is no shy antelope, for that matter. It's nothing but a transaction, a contract involving an offer of consideration and a delivery of goods. There are people who care more about the anticipation of the act than its actual performance. This is one of those cases. In other ways, for other reasons, the same thing applies to me.

A traffic light blinks from yellow to red; I come to a stop and light a cigarette. While we were pretending to live the

21

good life, for the rest of the world a Sunday turned into a Monday. All around me, morning traffic is beginning to weave itself into a tangle that half an hour from now, more or less, will harden into an inextricable knot. But by then I'll be safely hidden at home. There's nothing glamorous about being a creature of the night, there's no glory to it. Sometimes it's all deception and fabrication, because darkness blends everything together, beliefs indistinguishable from truths. Documentaries show us scenes of lions feasting on prey while packs of hyenas circle, waiting to fight over the remains. As often as not, it was the hyenas that actually brought down the kill. The lion showed up afterward and by the law of kings took first choice without lifting a paw, forcing the ones who did the dirty work to settle for his leftovers. That image is projected into the real world, upside down, making it hard to tell who's the lion and who's the hyena.

Alongside me, in a gleaming new Mercedes, some guy opens his mouth in an involuntary yawn.

I focus, trying to make out which kind of animal he is.

He doesn't have the wrecked facial features of a sleepless all-nighter; rather, his face bears the stamp of an alarm clock that always rings too soon. An ordinary everyman, classifiable as a "not-not." He's not young and he's not old, not handsome and not ugly, not rich and not poor. And so on and so forth. He's probably got a wife and kids at home, and he bought himself a Mercedes because he'd made up his mind that life owed him one, the same way that, sometimes, he'll buy a few hours with one of the girls that I handle. He must be a small businessman; he probably owns one of those warehouses that snake along the road leading to Vigevano. In his warehouse, maybe they machine-tool structural aluminum or they sell footwear at cost.

22

The traffic light turns green and simultaneously a horn honks behind me. So predictable that I don't even waste a go-fuck-yourself. The sky has veered from colorless to blue and with the sunlight the shadows have put in an appearance. Other shadows are vanishing. It's the law of the city and its daily buzzing drone, rising and falling according to the time of day. For those who can't stand that drone, it's almost time to cover your ears and burrow your head under the pillow.

When I reach the intersection at the Metro stop, I take a right, follow the service road for a short distance, and then turn into the Quartiere Tessera, where I live. The quarter is filled with five-story apartment buildings, sheathed in dark brown tile, wedged inside a metal fence to convey the idea of order and ownership. Between one building and the next, open spaces covered with sickly grass and the occasional pine tree or maple serve as vegetation. The buildings belong to the RAS insurance company. They're just part of the reserve fund of real estate holdings that all insurance companies are required to establish by law. Before long, when the buildings start to deteriorate and maintenance costs rise to levels that become a drag on the balance sheet, the company will sell them. Then we'll see which tenants were born to be homeowners and which will just spend a lifetime paying rent and be forced to migrate to some other part of town.

For the most part, the apartments are occupied by commuters, men dressed in suits they bought in a department store somewhere, with shirt collars always a shade too loose or a little too tight; men who go to work every morning, leaving behind a wife who's always a day older when they come home at night; men who never know or wonder what made her age that day. I have to say that in my comings and goings I've run into more than one married woman who looked at me with interest and sent me a glance of urgent and unmistakable SOS. I've always lowered my gaze and walked on by. I have nothing to offer and nothing to receive. This place and this life make colors wither and it does no good to mix gray with gray. It might come out darker or lighter, but all you're ever going to get is more gray.

I steer the car deftly into one of the herringbone parking spots, a space that another car has just vacated. The man driving away is young, but he already has an air of resignation. His expression turns him into a living, breathing white flag of surrender. It's incredible to see how fast some people give up. They're not losers, they're people who never even put up a fight. And that gives them starring roles in something much worse than mere defeat.

I know lots of people like that.

There are times I think I see one every time I look in the mirror. I swing open the car door, get out, and lock this cloud of all-nighter depression inside my parked Mini. I turn and head for home, walking with one shoulder practically brushing the enclosure wall.

On my left, two hundred yards farther on, is public housing. That's another world, fly-by-night and sedentary at the same time. Rough and continuously evolving. A patchwork of people live there, factory workers and small-time crooks, undifferentiated manpower that feeds into a larger and more complicated system. Fleeting instants of glory, a bundle of easy cash that gets shown off at the local bar along with a new car, and then a couple of Carabinieri squad cars pull up early the next morning. Plenty of room in jail for another inmate, plenty of room in society for another criminal. Come to think of it, it's just another way of commuting.

The topography of the Milanese hinterland tells us that we're in Via Fratelli Rosselli, number 4. I say that I'm in the place that I call home for a few hours every day. On the far side of the yard, there's a lady walking her dog. The dog is a German shepherd, and he runs out and back and leaps happily around his yawning owner. The animal seems to have a higher opinion of that green space fertilized by smog than most of the residents.

I swing open the glass front door and climb the steps to the second floor without meeting a soul. I insert my key in the keyhole, click the lock open, and a voice catches me off guard.

"The click of the lock of a man returning home sounds different from the click of a man going out for the day."

I turn and the silhouette of Lucio emerges from the doorway across the landing. The direction of his gaze is slightly off-kilter with respect to where I'm standing. He's wearing a pair of black sunglasses. I know that when he's alone he doesn't wear them, but a blind man's understandable sense of modesty demands that he cover his eyes, veiled with an unsettling white film, when someone else is around.

I sketch out a smile that he can't see, only hear.

"You've got the ears of a cat."

"I've got the ears of a musician. Keys are one of my fields of expertise."

He hastens to disavow the joke.

"Questionable wisecrack. I could never do stand-up. I'm afraid I'm going to have to settle for being the Italian Stevie Wonder."

Lucio plays acoustic guitar, and he's incredibly good at it. In my apartment I often hear him practicing. That sinuous musical instrument, broad-hipped, accommodating, and

25

womanly, represents his emancipation from darkness, his personal freedom. He gets by pretty well with his music. He alternates periods of playing in clubs in the Brera district with stretches of playing in the city subways. I imagine he does it to create a sort of variation between day and night, since as far as he's concerned it's all just permanent nighttime. He could have more if he wanted, but he's satisfied with what he's got. I've never asked and he's never told me. For every man alive there's a part of life that lies within the sacred boundaries of his own fucking business. The hardest thing to understand, for every individual, is just how big that area is.

"You want a cup of coffee?"

I stand there, motionless, with the door open. He shrugs his shoulders.

"Wipe that doubtful expression off your face. I know it's there. Nobody can refuse to join you for a cup of coffee. This time is no exception. I can't see a reason it would be."

Lucio inserted a brief pause before uttering that last phrase, and he emphasized it ever so slightly with his voice. A self-deprecating irony is, I think, just one more of the screens he sets up between himself and a world that is invisible to him. Putting himself on an equal footing; making sure that he can't be seen by a world he can't see.

"Sure, let's have that coffee. You're such a pain in the ass."

He hears my door click shut again and my footsteps coming across the landing. He swings his door open a little wider and steps back from the threshold to let me by.

"And you're an ungrateful turd. I'm going to make you a shitty cup of coffee, just to teach you a lesson."

We walk into his apartment. No concession has been made to the visual. The fabrics were all chosen for their tactile qualities and the colors are haphazard at best. Not the furniture. When we first met, a year ago, Lucio told me that he took that apartment because the layout was very similar to the place he used to live. The furniture was arranged exactly the way it was in the other place, and the routes through the apartment were memorized without difficulty.

Or almost.

As he likes to say, in his situation, there's always an almost.

I go to the table next to the French doors. I look out the curtainless windows. The woman with the German shepherd is gone. There's no one in the street.

We're alone, outside and in.

Lucio moves as if he can see, in his little private domain, free of corners and sharp edges. He vanishes into the small galley kitchen, and I hear him clattering around, with the cabinet doors and the espresso pot. His words drift out to me as I take a seat.

"Here's an easy one, since you haven't slept all night."

"Shoot."

"*Agriculture in remote Chinese dynasty*. Three and four equals seven."

It's a cryptic clue. You've got to work from that definition to find two words that, when joined together, create a third word that is the sum of their letters. For this one, I don't even have to think it over for a second.

"*Agriculture in remote Chinese dynasty*: Far Ming. Farming."

This time, I'm the one who can hear the smile in his voice, even without seeing it.

"Well, that one really was *too* easy. Or else I have to say Bravo because it's your name and because you deserve it."

27

It's a routine that we've developed over the months, the two of us. We invent and trade cryptic clues instead of confiding in each other. Someday, one of us will invent an especially intricate clue and the other one will guess it. Maybe that day we'll be able to say that we're friends. But for now, we're just a couple of people well aware that we're only sharing a couple of hours of prison yard time.

The coffee announces its arrival with the throaty gurgling sound of the espresso pot. Lucio emerges from his little kitchen carrying a pair of mismatched demitasse cups and a sugar bowl. I don't help him because I know he wouldn't want me to. All the confirmation I need is the fact that he's never asked.

He sets them down on the table and vanishes again. When he comes back he's carrying a two-cup espresso pot and a couple of demitasse spoons. He sets them on the table too, and then sits down across from me.

"All right, Hazel. Go ahead and pour the coffee."

"Is that a cryptic clue?"

"No, it's an order."

This is the one concession that Lucio makes to his blindness. I'm no longer doing him a favor, I'm performing a task. I pour coffee into the two cups, then I add sugar. Two spoonfuls for him, half a spoonful for me. I set his cup in front of him, making sure he knows where it is from the sound. He extends his hand, grips the cup by the handle, and savors it unhurriedly, while I empty mine in two gulps, even though it's scalding hot. That's why Godie calls me Asbestos Mouth, for once without relying on the relentless fishtailing zigzags of his personal jargon.

I light a cigarette. Lucio smells the smoke. He turns his head to a point that my bad habit has identified for him.

"Marlboro?"

"Yes."

"That's what I used to smoke. But I quit."

He takes his last sip of coffee.

"You might not believe it, but there's no pleasure in smoking a cigarette if you can't see the smoke pouring out of your mouth. Evidently there's a bigger aesthetic component to bad habits than you might think."

Once again, his voice is veiled in a layer of irony.

"That could be a cure for smoking. Take someone and blindfold them until they lose the urge."

He smiles.

"Or until they have to get plastic surgery to fix the nose they've scorched by trying to light cigarettes with their disposable lighter."

His smile broadens at the idea. Then a mental connection makes him change the subject.

"Speaking of blindfolds, apparently on Sunday Lady Luck lifted the rag over her eyes and cast a glance in our direction."

"How so?"

"Down at Michele's bar, the one next to the church, somebody bought a lottery ticket that won 490 million lire."

"Fuck. Nice win. Do they know who it was?"

Lucio moves confidently and well in all the public places he frequents. Because of his physical handicap and his personality, he manages to win people's trust. And so they tell him things.

"Not for sure, but there are a few clues. There's a guy, name of Remo Frontini, hard worker, decent fellow, lives over in the public housing project. I think he works in a factory. He's got a boy, a kid about eight, and I give him guitar lessons for

29

a pittance, because he has a gift and because music is a good way to keep him off the streets. You've probably seen him leaving my apartment, I'd imagine."

In fact, I never have, but that hardly seems material to the purpose of the story. Lucio continues without waiting for an answer. He probably thinks the same thing.

"I have to say that what little he pays me comes in when it comes in, if you take my meaning."

"That's mighty good of you."

"Yes, it is. But that's not the point."

He breaks off for a minute—I imagine so he can rethink what he's about to say and make sure of the conclusions he's drawn.

"Yesterday he came by with his son and he was almost giddy—very talkative. Unusual thing for him; he doesn't usually talk much. He assured me that before long he'd pay all his back fees, and that from now on he'd pay on time. He even asked me what the best make would be if he decided to buy his son a new guitar."

After another brief pause, Lucio concludes this little personal investigation of his.

"Throw in the fact that Frontini frequents Michele's bar and that every week he plays the Totocalcio soccer lottery, and the facts speak for themselves."

I think it over. Maybe for just a second too long.

"When something changes your life, it's always difficult to conceal it."

Lucio lowers his head. The register of his voice drops by a tone or two.

"I don't know why, but it strikes me that these words are more about you than our lucky lottery winner."

I get to my feet and leave this statement hanging in the

30

air before it can find the strength to turn into a full-fledged curiosity and therefore a question.

"*Time to go*, Lucio," I sing out in playful English.

He understands and lightens up.

"Anybody who can turn his hand to farming after an all-nighter deserves the bed that awaits him."

I head for the door.

"Thanks for the hospitality. You certainly are a man who keeps his promises."

The question I'm expecting comes just as I'm pulling the door open to leave.

"Which is to say?"

"That was one shitty cup of coffee."

I swing the door shut behind mc on his laughter, cross the landing, and a second later I'm home, in a six-hundred-square-foot apartment that's the mirror image of Lucio's. Just a few short steps, but it's another world. Here you see colors, posters on the walls, books on a bookshelf, green plants.

A television set.

I take off my jacket and toss it on the couch. I empty my pockets and lay their contents on top of the chest of drawers. Cigarettes, wallet, pager, the rumpled money I pried out of Daytona. A blinking red light on the phone tells me there are messages on my answering machine. I push play, and as I unbutton my shirt I listen to the rushing hiss of the rewinding tape.

Then, the voices.

Beep. A euphoric voice.

"Ciao, *Bravo, it's Barbara. I'm on the French Riviera. The yacht is fantastic and this guy is so nice. He wants me to stay a couple more days, so I told him you could talk to him about terms. Thanks. Kisses, tall dark and handsome."*

Beep. A cracking, damaged voice.

"This is Lorella. I need to work. I really really do. I'm desperate. I just don't know where to turn anymore. Please, call me."

Beep. A voice hidden in tears.

"Bravo, it's Laura. Something terrible has happened. I went out with Tulip. I couldn't tell him no and he beat me up again. I'm afraid. One of these days that guy's going to kill me. When you hear this message, call me. I don't care what time it is. Talk to you soon."

My shirt flies over to join my jacket on the couch. The cleaning woman can take care of putting them away. I move from the living room and head down the hallway to the doors of my bedroom and bathroom.

As I walk, I kick off my shoes and reflect.

Barbara is an incredible young woman. Infatuated with the big city, head over heels in love with the good life, and pragmatic in a way that's typical of someone who got only one gift from destiny: a spectacular physical appearance. We understand each other because we're very similar in certain ways. We have an agreement and we get along fine.

Lorella is a pretty girl. I gave her work for a while, until I found out that she was a drug addict. The people who call me, with the prices they pay, have a right to certain standards, and I can't afford to send them women with holes in their arms, strung out on heroin. I didn't even try to get her off drugs. I just dropped her, on the spot. I've watched girls like her slide downhill at alarming speed, and wind up behind Piazzale Lotto selling mouth, pussy, and asshole—a package deal for ten thousand lire. A waste of time, not worth the phone call.

The situation with Laura is quite another matter, far more

delicate. She works as a fashion model, at a level that's not stratospheric but regular and reliable, and she rounds out her paycheck with other, more discreet earnings, thanks to my management. One night we went out together to the Ascot, and that's where Salvatore Menno, aka Tulip, first saw her. They call him Tulip because in the winter, at Piazzale Brescia, he has a flower stand; in the summer it becomes a watermelon kiosk. That's just a cover for his operations. Actually, he's a hoodlum, a thug and a gangster in the orbit of Tano Casale, a mid-level boss who went head-to-head with Turatello and Vallanzasca for control of Milan. That asshole paid for one night with her, and then he started demanding a relationship free of charge, and immediately after that, he expected her to be faithful to him. The next step was when he started beating her up. Laura is just a woman like any other, and I don't care about her as a person. But she's a spectacular earner, and I can't afford to have her face covered with bruises.

I open the bathroom door and walk over to the toilet. I pass the mirror above the sink without glancing at myself. I undo my trousers and lower them, along with my underpants. I sit on the toilet and piss. For reasons entirely out of my control, in the past I've had to undergo surgical procedures that mean I can no longer pee standing up. Now I pee like a woman. Now I wipe myself with toilet paper after peeing, almost the same as a woman.

I'm thinking about how to solve the problem of Laura and Tulip without getting either one of us killed. As I'm brushing my teeth, an idea occurs to me. I'll have to have a talk with Tano Casale and propose a trade.

On the one hand, this thought worries me; on the other hand, it gives me a slight sense of relief. If I play my cards right and if that guy can be taken at his word the way I think he can, it could work out just fine. At last, an extra little crumb of good luck would really help me out.

I walk out of the bathroom and into my bedroom. When I wake up, I'll have a lot of things to do. I finish undressing. I take a Valium and wash it down with a gulp of water from the bottle I always keep on my night table.

I stretch out, pull the covers up, turn out the light, and wait for my body and the sleeping pill to drag me down for a few hours into the darkness where Lucio spends all his time.

CHAPTER 3

I open my eyes.

I switch on the light on my night table and look at the time. The angle of the hands on my clock tells me it's five thirty. The sheets are almost as taut as if I hadn't slept at all. I slept without dreaming, and waking up was a painless birth back into the world.

It's strange how sometimes, when your mind is in cahoots with the dark, it's capable of catalyzing ugly memories and turning them into nightmares.

The things I've carried with me over the years are archived in a part of my brain, hidden behind the conscious screen of acts and words. When I'm asleep, if those things come back to me, there's no escaping them. I lie there, helpless, nailed to the spot, a prisoner of what my mind spits out. Today, however, the keeper of bad dreams seems to have forgotten that I exist, and I've emerged intact.

I swing my legs over the side of the bed and sit up, just long enough to let my life swim back into coherence and my thoughts return to the present. I stand up and walk across the wall-to-wall carpeting and make my way to my galley kitchen where, unlike Lucio, I can see what's in the cabinets. Strangely, I sometimes bump my head against them; Lucio never does.

35

From outside, the daylight of a late spring afternoon filters through the blinds.

My shirt and jacket aren't lying on the couch anymore. The dirty plates and glasses are no longer in the kitchen sink. The ashtrays have been emptied and washed and are drying on the counter. Signora Argenti, my diminutive cleaning woman, came in to take care of the apartment and its occupant as I slept.

I rummage around in the kitchen assembling a loaded espresso pot. While I wait for the Moka Express and the gas burner to work their magic, I go over and turn on the radio. As if by tacit agreement with my neighbor, I also prefer it to television. With him, it's because he can't see it; with me, it's because as often as not I prefer not to. The voice of the newscaster fills the room.

. . . referring to the Red Brigades' communiqué number six, delivered two days ago to the newspaper La Repubblica, *and announcing that after a lengthy interrogation the prisoner Aldo Moro has been sentenced to death, President Giovanni Leone urged, with words of . . .*

I switch to another radio station. I'll never know the words that followed. The voice is replaced by a piece of rock music that I can't quite recognize but that I'm happy to take in place of the other. There are times when I can't stand hearing about loneliness, and the story of that man is full of it. The photographs of his detention, his forlorn face, his death sentence, all make me think that, when you live with the suspicion that you're surrounded by nothingness, there's almost always something or someone ready and willing to convert that suspicion to certainty. I wonder if he thought the same thing while the vast world that he once had at his fingertips shrank to the few dozen square feet of a tiny cubicle.

I go back to the stove, where only the confidential burbling of an espresso pot awaits me, along with the occasional puff of steam, signifying nothing. I pour out the coffee and take a sip. The pager sitting on the hall chest emits a sound that we can quantify onomatopoeically as a beep. For my own convenience, I subscribe to a phone paging service. It's a little expensive but it more than pays for itself. Every time the device emits its signal, it means that the switchboard at the Eurocheck service to which I subscribe has taken a call for me.

I go over to the telephone and dial the number. The operator's remote, slightly mechanical voice answers. Without saying hello I give him my identity.

"This is Bravo. Code 1182."

"Good evening. You are requested to call this number: 02 67859. There's no name with that."

"Thanks."

"Thank you, sir."

The switchboard operator goes back to being hypothetical. I jot down the number on a pad of notepaper next to the machine. I don't recognize it. I know by heart nearly all the numbers I need, but this one is completely foreign to me. The fact that the person didn't leave his name is fairly normal. Not everyone is interested in scattering evidence in all directions when they're procuring prostitutes. After a couple of rings, a male voice answers, not young, but clear and vigorous.

"Hello?"

"I was just told to call this number."

"Is this Bravo?"

"Yes."

"A friend we have in common told me about you."

"Is he more your friend or my friend?"

"Well, he's enough of a friend to ask you to provide him with the services of two girls at a time whenever he comes north from Rome. And enough of a friend to assure me of your discretion and the quality of your taste."

I know the person he's talking about. One of the wealthiest antiques dealers in the Italian capital, who has a passion for three-ways and for women who take money for sex. I have no idea who I'm talking to, but I doubt that he'd tell me over the telephone.

"What can I do for you?"

"It would be a pleasure to meet one of the girls you work with."

"Just one?"

There's a hint of amusement in his voice when he answers. And a light sigh of regret.

"Yes, I'm afraid. I can't perform the way I did when I was younger."

"Tonight?"

"No, tomorrow morning. I like a happy wake-up."

"Any preferences?"

He decides to toss the dice and see what number comes up.

"My friend told me that you don't usually spring nasty surprises on him. But he was especially satisfied with someone named Laura. Does that check out?"

My silence is taken as confirmation.

"Fine. That's who I want. As an incentive, let me tell you that money is not a problem."

That's good news. And I need some good news, considering the phone call I'm going to have to make a little later.

"Where and when?"

"I'm at the Hotel Gallia, room 605. Nine o'clock would be fine. I'll leave word at the reception desk to let anyone who asks for me come upstairs."

I freeze and say nothing. He understands and reassures me.

"I'm in a business suite. I have a direct line. If it can be of any assistance to you, call the hotel and have them put you through to my room. Do it now, if you like."

I don't know who the man I'm talking to is, but he definitely has brains. And money. He's someone who knows how the world works and how much money you have to spend to make it work the way it ought to. Those two aspects of his personality arouse a feeling of unquestioned esteem in me.

"Agreed then, nine tomorrow morning. The person will be paid one million lire by you. In cash."

"That's a lot of money."

"When you see the girl, you can decide whether or not she's worth it."

This time there's a pause on the other end of the line. Then a clarification, in a slightly more authoritative tone. In fact, a great deal more authoritative.

"Let me remind you that this could be the beginning of a long and satisfying relationship for both of us."

"Naturally. That's why I'm happy to give you the right to check out the merchandise."

The tone becomes conversational, as before.

"Very good. It's been a pleasure."

"It's been a pleasure for me too. Talk to you soon."

I hang up. Now it's time to make the second call, much more demanding. I dial Laura's number. The voice that hastily responds is that of a person waiting by the phone.

A frightened person.

"Hello."

"Hi, Laura, this is Bravo."

Her relief at hearing my voice comes surging through the phone line.

"At last. Where the hell have you been?"

I let a second or two pass before I answer. That silence ought to let her know that where the hell I've been is none of her business. So I add no further explanations.

"I heard your message. What happened?"

"What happened is, that man is insane. Now he wants to stick me in an apartment, where I can watch television and wait for him. When I said no, he hit me."

Without prompting, Laura takes care of my main worry. "He didn't leave any marks, but he hurt me just the same."

Good. Her face is intact. And all the rest, maybe. When a horse throws you, the best thing is to get right back in the saddle. Now the problem is to make her see it.

"I have some interesting new projects. Important ones. You feel up to doing some work?"

"Have you lost your mind? If he catches me going out with somebody there's going to be a murder. He's not normal. You should have seen his eyes."

None of that comes as a surprise. I've heard that Tulip has more than one screw loose. I know a couple of people who have seen him lose his temper, and they are willing to confirm that he's not normal. Other people who wound up in that situation aren't around anymore to confirm anything. Anyway, that's what I've heard. But certain chatter, in certain cases and with certain people, generally has a fairly high percentage in terms of reliability.

"Don't worry, I'll take care of everything."

"But how?"

But how? Good question . . . With a little brains and a lot of luck, I hope.

"I know someone who can give me a hand."

"Are you sure you know what you're doing?"

"Absolutely."

Absolutely not.

"I'm afraid, Bravo."

And who wouldn't be, when it comes to certain people?

"There's no reason to be afraid. Everything is going to turn out fine."

I can't say whether the silence I receive as a reply means hope or mistrust. I intervene with a suggestion that refers to a familiar setting, and therefore to the usual nightlife and the usual mood.

"Why don't you meet me at the Ascot around eleven? I need to talk to you about something that might be of interest."

"Today's Monday. It's closed."

"No. There's a really great group of mimes from the BBC, the Silly Dilly M. This was the only date they could make. The Ascot skipped its day off just to book them."

Another brief pause to think, and then she gives in.

"All right, I'll see you there. At eleven."

"Okay, see you later. *Ciao*."

Her voice vanishes into the phone line and is sealed in place by the receiver. With a demitasse in hand I go back to my little galley kitchen to pour the rest of the coffee, which has cooled off in the meantime. I light a cigarette and then my bladder urges me into the bathroom. This business with Tulip is definitely the last thing I need. But here it is, and I can't pretend it's not happening. I could say to hell with it and leave Laura to her fate as an unwilling concubine. But every

41

arrangement is propped up by a certain degree of credibility, and no matter how questionable and compromised mine might be, I can't afford to lose it.

I sit on the toilet, close to the window. Next to the toilet, on top of the wicker laundry hamper, lies a copy of *La Settimana Enigmistica*, the puzzler's weekly, with a ballpoint pen next to it. I pick it up and look at the picture of Dustin Hoffman smiling up at me in black and white from the little panel on the cover. Then I smile too, in spite of myself. Every time I read the slogan emblazoned on the masthead I remember Beefsteak, one of the idlers who spends his evenings at the Ascot, the occasional dispenser of devastating lightning-bolt wisecracks, usually absolutely pitiless. One time, when he was in the control booth watching a truly dreadful impersonator doing an audition, he issued a verdict in his nonchalant voice that branded that aspiring artist for the rest of his days.

"This guy is just like *La Settimana Enigmistica*. He boasts no fewer than 206 unsuccessful attempted imitations."

I open the little pulp stock magazine and I'm presented with the Page of the Sphinx and a cryptic clue.

Outlaw leader managing money (7)

I give myself a second to think. Maybe more than a second. Word puzzles excite me and relax me. Sometimes the solution comes immediately, sometimes it never does. Like everything else in life. Life has made the enigma, the puzzle, the mystery, its underlying concept. In this case, intuition flashes into the darkness after a few seconds.

To outlaw is to ban. A leader could be a king. Managing money, I suppose, could be described as banking. Ban + king = Banking.

I put down the magazine and stand up. This insignificant achievement has put me in a good mood. In the mirror over the bathroom sink, there's my face, punctual as ever. A dark man, with long wavy hair and black eyes. Handsome, they say. Once, in a rumpled bed, a woman with soft breasts and fragrant skin told me: "With eyes like that, you can get into hot water every day. There'll always be a woman to get you out of trouble."

I was so young and hungry for certainty that I accepted the fact that that unimaginative woman had recycled a phrase from a Brigitte Bardot movie to pay me a compliment. No question, she achieved her objective: I don't even remember her name, but I remember what she said to me. Too bad that when I did get into hot water, she wasn't around. None of the women were.

I wet my face and start soaping my cheeks with the shaving brush. The faint scent of menthol wafts over me in waves of cool freshness, reddening my eyes. Without warning, like all memories, a character comes to mind, a character I invented when I was a little boy watching the town barber lathering a client's face with his shaving brush until he was half covered by that foamy white stuff that reminded me of whipped cream. I wonder what ever happened to my poor Foam Man. I wonder whether in all these years he ever discovered whether under that mound of insubstantial whiteness there really was such a thing as a face.

I, on the other hand, know that I have one. I found that out far too young. That's always been my problem.

I start to shave.

The razor blade slices swaths of reality through my childhood games and I find myself smooth-cheeked, gazing at myself with eyes made adult by the passage of time, by my

43

own personal choices and by choices that were forced upon me. The kind of choices that age you fastest, deep inside.

I turn on the shower, and while I wait for the flow of water to heat up, I try to think of a new cryptic clue for Lucio. As I step into the spray, the stable-like enclosure of the shower stall gives me a Eureka moment.

Here it is, the new enigma.

Forms of luck: horses that come in first, gold mines, or where a losing team is sent after the game (7, 7, 3, 7)

That means that the solution is composed of four words. Two seven-letter words; then one three-letter word, followed by another seven-letter word. It isn't hard, and I imagine he'll solve it right away, even though apparently easy challenges often conceal tangled welters of complication.

I take a sponge off the counter, squeeze some body wash onto it, and start to soap up. I prefer to wash myself through the mediation of this inanimate object, as if avoiding the contact of human hands on the body could change something. Sometimes a minor mania can forestall a major problem.

If it was you, I'd do it for free . . .

The girl reappears in a flash before my mind's eye. Her words never really went away. I imagine her body, slender and strong beneath her clothing. I feel her breast, firm in my cupped hand. The smell of soap brings to mind other scents, the sublime aroma of sex, its taste a mixture of sickly sweetness and rust, before and after the fury. Desire surges implacably, running its slimy soft fingers over my belly. I start to massage my groin, and in exchange I get only a confirmation that becomes harder to accept with every day that passes. I do it faster and faster, as if to erase myself or to reconstruct myself, until my heart begins to race and I let myself slip to the floor, beneath the spray that jets down indifferently from above. I lie there, waiting for a conclusion that will never come, welcoming as a benediction the mingling of the shower water with the one and only ejaculation still allowed me: the slow drip of tears.

CHAPTER 4

I stop my car on Via Monte Rosa, a hundred meters or so from the brightly lit entrance of the Ascot Club.

I light a cigarette and sit smoking in the car, trying to clear my head and draw a few conclusions about my own evening's headlines.

When I left my apartment, back in Cesano Boscone, I walked over to Via Turati and into what they call Michele's bar. I've been there once or twice, to buy a pack of cigarettes or to grab an espresso, but I can't claim to be a regular client. So I don't know anyone there and no one knows me.

The bar, practically empty, was a single large open space, with a rectangular floor plan and two plate-glass windows in the long wall, looking out onto the street. On the left is the space set aside for the soccer lottery ticket counter and all the posters proclaiming the glories of soccer and the glorious future that the SISAL lottery offers you. In the middle is the bar, arranged perpendicular so as to split the space into two sections. Facing it, a few little café tables and chairs with plastic backs, exactly the kind you'd expect in a place like this. On either side, the multicolored masses of a pinball machine and a jukebox.

On the wall opposite the entrance is a door. I knew there was a backroom where people played cards. Gin rummy, for the most part, at decidedly affordable stakes. Anyone who could afford to play for more robust stakes was certainly not going to come lose money in Michele's. They would frequent certain illegal open-air gambling dens, informal casinos on the street that aren't very hard to find in Milan.

I stepped up to the cash register and stood there, waiting. A tall skinny guy, with a gray cast to his complexion and an air of annoyance, finished serving an espresso and then came over to find out what I wanted. No greeting, no smile.

"What'll it be?"

"A pack of Marlboros and a piece of information."

In places like this, the second part of that request tends to make people a little wary. The man behind the counter was no exception to that rule, so he took his time with the first part. He turned around and extracted a pack of cigarettes from the rack on the wall and put it down in front of me.

Then he gave me a quizzical glance.

"What information would you be looking for?"

"I need the address of a guy named Remo Frontini. I know this is his usual café."

I laid a fifty-thousand-lira bill on the counter. And I flashed a half smile that was meant to stand in for human fellowship.

"Considering that times are hard all over, you can keep the change."

He eyed my face, my clothing, and my smile, calculating just how dangerous I might be to him and why. Then he threw the fifty-thousand-lira note into the equation. When he was done evaluating the various factors, he decided it wasn't worth ratcheting up from annoyance to full-blown hostility. He reached out a hand and made the money vanish.

47

He pointed to the street outside and muttered under his breath, "Second door on the left, number ten. Above the grocery store."

I nodded my thanks and left the bar. I walked at just the right speed, hunting for the address and the right words at the same time. The way I put the proposal would be crucial to the success of this first approach. I skimmed past the subsidized housing, surrounded on both sides by parked cars. Here, too, numbers. Fiats: 124, 127, 128, with the occasional luxury of a 131 and, as exotic touches, here and there an Opel or a Renault, until I found the number plate marked ten. I walked up to a row of buzzers, where I found the name I was looking for. There was no lock on the street door. I mused that probably even the tenants had no idea how long the lock had been missing and how long it would be until it was replaced. So much the better. I hate to telegraph my arrival by ringing the downstairs doorbell. I went in and walked up the stairs to the third floor, where another name plate told me I was standing in front of the right door.

I rang the doorbell and got lucky. He opened the door himself. He had a smile on his face, and he was still talking to someone inside, but when he caught a glimpse of me both smile and words faded from his lips. He was a little taller than average, with a normal build, an unguarded facial expression, and the uncertain glance of someone who's experiencing something that's much bigger than him. Through that half-open door, I could see an apartment inhabited by people of modest means, with run-of-the-mill furniture and the smell of fried foods in the air, along with the unmistakable odor of the monthly struggle to make ends meet. If what I'd heard about the winning lottery ticket was true, I could see at first glance what 490 million lire would mean in a place like that.

"Good evening. Are you by any chance Signore Frontini?"

"Yes, I am."

"I'm a neighbor of yours. I live here in the Quartiere Tessera. Do you have a minute to talk?"

He courteously opened the door to let me in. I raised one hand to decline the offer.

"You're too kind. If you don't mind, I'd prefer that we talk alone."

Without a word, letting the curiosity on his face serve as a reply, Remo Frontini stepped out onto the landing, pulling the door behind him and leaving it just slightly ajar.

The ball was in my court. And I had to haul back and throw it straight and hard if I wanted to win the kewpie doll.

"Signore Remo, let me come straight to the heart of the matter. I have the impression that you've had a stroke of good luck recently. A huge stroke of good luck."

The curiosity on his face was instantly replaced by alarm. He squinted and turned wary.

"Wait a minute: who are you and who told you . . ."

I interrupted him, sketching out a reassuring gesture.

"Don't worry. I'm not a problem. If anything, you can think of me as another stroke of good luck, Signore Frontini."

I paused.

"Let's just say, ten million lire more than what is already due to you. Which rounds out to a nice fat half a billion lire."

When the word *billion* jumped in right after the word *million*, it had a satisfying effect. And the sight of him standing there, listening to what I had to say instead of kicking my ass down the stairs, confirmed that the rumors I had heard were true.

Which was lucky for him and, I hoped, for me.

Little by little, winning him over despite his reluctance

and assuring him that no one needed to know about it but the two of us, I managed to get him to admit that he was the one with the winning lottery ticket. The most important thing, to my relief, was that he hadn't turned it in yet; it was tucked away in a safe-deposit box while he tried to figure out what to do next. I explained what I wanted from him, how it would be to his advantage, and just how we'd work the deal. I made him understand that I represented certain people who were known for being extremely grateful and generous with those who did them favors, or else deeply resentful toward those who refused. In the end, I could see that he was willing to accept my proposal, more out of fear of the consequences than greed.

"All right, if you say that's the way things really are . . ."

I gave him my very sunniest smile, the one that over time had won me the charms of many women and a razor blade.

"Of course that's the way things really stand. You're running absolutely no risk. You'll have a great deal to gain and nothing to lose."

I extended my hand. He gripped it. Not one hundred percent convinced, but still, he shook my hand.

"You'll see that you made the right choice. You'll have no reason to regret it."

I took a step toward the stairs, a signal that our brief business meeting was over.

"I'll be in touch with you. For now, have a good evening."

"And good evening to you, Signore . . ."

I flashed him another smile.

"Everyone calls me Bravo. Why don't you do the same?"

He turned and went back into the apartment. As I headed downstairs, I heard a woman's voice from inside.

"Remo, who was that?"

The door swung shut before I could hear the answer. I found myself back in the street, inhaling the air of a warm spring evening, the kind that puts you at peace with the world. I went back to my car, feeling what the television news anchors describe as cautiously optimistic. Driving at a leisurely pace, I made it into the Brera neighborhood where, for an aperitif, I was forced to drive around looking for a place to park until I'd worked up an appetite. At last, I made it to a restaurant that I frequented, both for pleasure and for public relations. The Torre Pendente, in that period, was a very popular little place, where the Milan that goes out at night meets to begin the evening. The Milan that goes to Courmayeur, Santa Margherita, Portofino, and so on, with a long list of etceteras. All of them expensive little etceteras. People from the world of fashion, businesspeople, night owls, shitheads. All jumbled together in a way that makes it hard to tell which category any particular individual fits into. Here I saw a couple of girls I work with, one of them out for dinner with a date I had set her up with. I saw a couple of others I'd like to work with. I greeted friends, male and female, many of whom were faces with absolutely no names for me. I made one phone call to further Barbara's economic interests and another to lay out the rest of the operation I was getting under way with Remo Frontini.

Finally I ate dinner, just trying to kill time until my appointment with Laura.

And now I'm here, crushing my cigarette with the heel of my shoe and locking my miserable little loser car. Aside from the occasional concession to the importance of façade, that is to say personal grooming and apparel suitable for appearing in certain social circles, my life is usually lived behind the scenes. Milan is a city that by night offers many

51

hiding places in spite of the neon, the bright lights, and the blinking signs. The more light there is, the more shadow becomes available. And I've always been particularly good at moving in those shadows.

I'm outside the front door of the Ascot Club and I'm about to take the stairs when a Ferrari 308 GTB, so red it could piss off a bull and an army of wage slaves, pulls up alongside me. The man behind the wheel gestures to me with one hand. I walk over and he leans across to push open the passenger door. I get in, sit down, and seal our conversation behind the thump of a panel of elegantly shaped metal.

"*Ciao*, Bravo."

"Hey, Micky. How's it hanging?"

"Sometimes to the right, other times to the left. As usual."

I take in the handsome blond young man dressed in Armani sitting in the driver's seat. Micky is about thirty and he's at the top of his game. He leads a pretty good life, spending time with the kind of women who are willing to pay for his expensive bad habits and the kind of people who allow him to set aside a little something for the future, without putting too fine a point on the various whys and for whoms. He was on the other end of one of the two phone calls I made from the restaurant.

By the orange glow of the streetlights, he looks even blonder and more tan. He comes right to the point, and I swerve to accommodate.

"What can I do for you?"

"I need to talk to Tano Casale."

Among Micky's many jobs, he drums up business for the gambling dens that the mob boss sets up and moves around with great cunning, popping up here and there around the city and the greater metropolitan area. Micky looks out at the street and a couple who are just slipping into the Ascot. He waits until they have disappeared from sight, as if they might have overheard what he was about to say.

"When?"

"Tonight."

"Why?"

"I have an opportunity that might interest him."

He turns wary.

"Bravo, this had better not be bullshit."

"Oh, it's not. Take my word for it. You'll see: he'll be grateful that you and I both thought of him."

He thinks for a minute. Then he decides that I'm trustworthy and gives me this one chance.

"All right. But I have to make a phone call first."

I nod.

"Of course."

Micky looks at his watch, which is obviously gold and authentic. And I have to guess that, unlike Daytona, he has more than one.

"I'll meet you out here in an hour. If you don't see me, it means I can't arrange it for tonight. In that case, I'll let you know when it's possible."

"Roger. May the Force be with you."

I get out of the car and start toward the entrance of the club. The roar of the Ferrari's eight cylinders accompanies me part of the way as the car screeches away, leaving ten thousand lire worth of rubber on the asphalt and the sound of the money spent reverberating in the air.

I start down the stairs, and after a fairly short number of steps I'm in a cellar that has covered itself with glory by producing nearly all the big names in popular cabaret entertainment in northern Italy. Just past the entrance there's a little salon, bounded on the left by the coat check, with cheap wall-to-wall carpeting, sofas, and lights, an area dedicated to killing time, where the usual clientele gathers to drink and smoke. In spite of the purposely drab aesthetics and a sense of institutional shabbiness, there's a certain dose of magic in the air, a feeling of potential success, real success, the kind that can change your life without warning. It's no secret that television and film producers in search of new talent come here first. For many, working at the Ascot will be the end of the road, but for a few others it's only the beginning. Afterward, it becomes a difficult bond to break. There are evenings when the club becomes such a gathering place for famous comedians and hit singers, aside from the young actors and comics on the playbill, that if a bomb went off in that musty cellar, it would take out half the theater people in our laughable country.

This is one of those evenings. The little room at the bottom of the stairs is full. The reputation of the Silly Dilly M. has attracted a big crowd, including a number of well-known show business professionals, here to satisfy their curiosity and to win the right to criticize after the show.

There's a line outside the cloakroom. The couple I saw coming in earlier is lingering to admire the posters tacked to the walls. Maybe they're here from outside of Milan and they're a little dazzled to be breathing the same oxygen as celebrities they've seen on television.

I say hello to a few people, I let others say hello to me, and in the meantime I let my gaze roam the room until I spot her. Laura's sitting on a couch, talking with a young man. If the experience with Tulip undermined her morale, it did nothing to dim her beauty. She looks like a young girl. She's dressed in relaxed clothing, with a pair of jeans and a white blouse under a casual jacket made of dark blue canvas that doesn't concede much to the fashion of the Year of Our Lord 1978. Her hair is mahogany brown, pulled back in a ponytail, and her candid, open face looks out on the world through a pair of eyes so intensely blue that they'd make a cornflower jealous.

That's what I'd say if I were a man who was in love with her. But all I am is a man who sells her, and so my words, because of the way things are, are of a different nature.

The man who's talking with her is Giorgio Fieschi, a cabaret artist who's been appearing at the Ascot since the start of the season. He's a dark young man with a clean face, and he's almost as naïve as he is talented. He showed up, new in town, asking to audition, and that very same evening he was the star of a stunning debut performance. Bonverde, who is sharp-eyed and farsighted, hired him on the spot. The audience took to him immediately. The veterans of the Ascot, all from Milan, welcomed him with a certain arrogance and from the very first day targeted him with a veiled ostracism. I can't say whether he's realized it yet, but when he finally does I hope he understands that their attitude is dictated by fear of his talent, not any actual superiority. I hope he figures it out soon. Unfortunately, the climb to the top demands a thick skin and a grim determination that this overgrown boy doesn't have yet.

I draw closer and find that there's a certain look in Laura's eyes and the same look in his. I know all too well the way sex leaps from eye to eye to fail to see that this is something very different. I know that what I have in front of me is not just male and female, but a man and a woman. And it seems to me that I can hear the sound of violins in the background, along with a faint stench of trouble.

I grab a chair right across from them, certain that I'm interrupting something.

"Hey, lovely people, how's it going?"

The two of them don't answer quickly enough. Piero, a waiter with a very professional manner, materializes suddenly beside the table and warns Giorgio that he's on in just a few minutes. The first half of the evening's show will consist of the acts of a few of the young artists in the Ascot's usual repertory, while the second half of the show will feature the evening's star attraction, the British mimes.

The budding cabaret star smiles. The smile spreads all the way into his eyes. I believe that what the rest of the world considers to be work, he looks upon as pure unadulterated fun.

"Okay, it's time. See you afterward, Laura?"

"Sure, I'll be in the club, watching your show."

Knowing that she'll be in the crowd tonight seems to give him pleasure. To judge from appearances, a great deal of pleasure.

"Good. I'm trying out a new skit tonight."

The young man stands up and walks briskly away and up a few steps, vanishing through a door on the left that leads to the backstage area and the control booth.

Laura and I are left alone together. I try to catch her eye, but she's not eager to meet my gaze. The sound of violins has died away; all that remains in the air is the smell of trouble. She stands up, smoothing the wrinkles out of her jacket. It strikes me that her concern about her dire situation has softened considerably. I don't know to what extent I should attribute that to my reassurances earlier that afternoon and to what extent it's due to the man she just met this evening.

She beats me to the punch.

56

"Do you mind if we talk later? I want to see that guy's show. I've heard he's really good."

"Sure, I'll come with you."

We get to our feet and follow the same path that Giorgio took just a few minutes earlier. Only where he went backstage, we continue straight, passing by the bar where two other cabaret artists on the bill this week sit drinking. Bonverdc is standing next to the bar, in the throes of his distinctive personal style of gesticulation, chatting with a famous tennis player who spends a lot of time at the club whenever he's in Milan.

At the end of a short hallway is the door that leads into the cramped and crowded little theater. We pass through that door and find ourselves in the dim half-light, standing against the wall just to the left of the door. To our right is the mini-amphitheater, packed with people. The fact that they scheduled Giorgio Fieschi for tonight must mean that he's making a name for himself in the world of Milanese comedy.

As if these thoughts of mine had summoned him from behind the scenes, Giorgio appcars from behind the black drapery that serves as both backdrop and curtain and makes his entrance onstage. There's virtually no applause but you can detect a quickening sense of expectation. He starts the show by tossing off a few good offhand wisecracks about current events, the way they all do to break the ice. He follows that with fifteen minutes or so of excellent stock material that I've heard before, and the audience really starts warming up. Then he begins talking about himself, saying that he was born into a big family, that hc had a lot of brothers, and that he hasn't had an easy life. At this point, I expect one of those routines that churns out a tragicomic elegy to poverty. Instead he surprises me and everyone in the audience, by suddenly changing his voice and mouthing the subdued and emphatic tones of a child.

. . . Oh yes, I come from a really big family. I remember in the mornings we always woke up at dawn and as soon as we were awake we said good morning all around, we'd say: buon giorno, *Aldo*, buon giorno, *Glauco*, buon giorno, *Ugo*, buon giorno, *Silvio*, buon giorno, *Sergio*, buon giorno, *Giorgio*, buon giorno, *Amilcare*, buon giorno, *Gaspare*, buon giorno, *Anselmo*, buon giorno, *Massimo* . . .

With each greeting and name Giorgio swivels his head, changes voice, intonation, and facial expression. The audience has the impression that on the stage before them, they really are seeing all those people interacting. After a pause he turns to the audience.

Around eleven thirty, we'd go out to begin the hard work of tilling the fields. At noon our mama would call us for the simple good food of our midday meal and we'd sit down around the table thanking the good Lord for that day's gifts and then buon appetito, *Aldo*, buon appetito, *Glauco*, buon appetito, *Ugo*, buon appetito, *Silvio*, buon appetito, *Sergio*, buon appetito, *Giorgio*, buon appetito, *Amilcare*, buon appetito, *Gaspare*, buon appetito, *Anselmo*, buon appetito, *Massimo* . . .

He offers the spectators a gesture of resignation and then, in a slightly more adult voice:

I've never tasted a spoonful of hot soup in my life!

Then he returns to the world of his character.

And then, when evening came, weary but happy, we'd go to bed after brushing our teeth and, before falling asleep . . .

By now the audience knows what's coming and starts repeating along with him:

. . . buona notte, *Aldo*, buona notte, *Glauco*, buona notte,

Ugo, buona notte, *Silvio*, buona notte, *Sergio*, buona notte, *Giorgio*, buona notte, *Amilcare*, buona notte, *Gaspare*, buona notte, *Anselmo*, buona notte, *Massimo . . . And then we'd close our eyes and fall into a peaceful sleep . . .*

Another pause for effect.

. . . around four in the morning.

Someone slips involuntarily into the kind of laughter that you simply can't stop, the kind that has the power to spread to everyone else in the room, the kind that only talent—true talent—can trigger. Giorgio continues.

One Sunday morning, the day on which we gave thanks for our good lives, we were in the courtyard of our farmhouse, and we were playing soccer, passing the ball from one to another and saying grazie, *Aldo*, grazie, *Glauco*, grazie, *Ugo*, grazie, *Silvio*, grazie, *Sergio*, grazie, *Giorgio*, grazie, *Amilcare*, grazie, *Gaspare*, grazie, *Anselmo*, grazie, *Massimo . . .*

He breaks off and appears to look into the distance on his right.

At a certain point we saw someone come slowly down the hill, heading in our direction. As he drew closer we realized that he was the midwife's husband, a man who knows us all perfectly well because he practically watched us come into the world. So we lined up, along the fenceposts, thinking that when he passed by he'd greet us one by one, by our names. But instead, when he came even with us, he smiled, waved his hand, and called out "Hi, everybody" and continued on his way . . .

Giorgio pauses again, looking around with an expression of baffled bewilderment. Then he speaks in a forlorn voice.

. . . having ruined our childhood.

The audience sits in silence for a moment before it clicks.

59

Then comes the wave of applause, warm with empathy and tenderness, prompted by his surreal sense of humor and the sheer virtuosity of his monologue. Seated next to me in the dark, Laura claps, her eyes glistening, tears of laughter sliding down her cheeks. Giorgio Fieschi must be one good perfomer if he can make someone forget about the existence of a creature like Tulip.

I look at my watch. In just a few minutes I have an appointment to meet Micky, outside in the street. I drag Laura out of the theater. I want her to be able to see me and hear me clearly. As we close the door behind us, surging applause still echoes in the air.

I move Laura back against the wall. I speak to her in an undertone but emphatically. I'm no actor, but I can play my part when it's necessary.

"Listen to me. I do something for you, you do something for me. I have a meeting in just a little while that should solve your problem once and for all. And you have an appointment tomorrow morning at nine o'clock, at the Hotel Gallia, room 605, with a very refined and courteous gentleman who, if you're willing, wants nothing better than to hand you a million lire."

Laura looks at me. I look back at her and there are no violins in the air, just the rumbling of thunder.

"Tell me that you understand and that the answer is yes."

She makes the tiniest movement of her head, as if to nod yes.

"Should I consider that to be the yes I'm looking for?"

At last, Laura accepts that she is what she always has been.

"I understand. Hotel Gallia, room 605, at nine o'clock."

"Excellent."

I relax. I smile at her and authorize a distraction, one that I would guess she was planning to enjoy in any case.

"Have all the fun you want fucking your little cabaret artist, but tomorrow morning you have to give that gentleman the time of his life."

I leave her waiting, alone, though I feel sure that she won't be alone for long. I climb back upstairs to the street, slithering out without a word to anyone. Actually, I'm fifteen minutes early, but I was dying for a cigarette to make up for the sense of envy that other people's talent and success have always aroused in me. I wait under the glow of the streetlights, studied with some curiosity by a pair of hookers competing for the few passing cars. Then, from around the corner of Via Silva, preceded by the grumbling of the engine, Micky's Ferrari emerges. As before, he pulls up next to me and waves for me to get in. I open the door and take a seat on the cream Connolly leather upholstery.

"So, are we going?"

He confirms with his voice and his head.

"Yes."

He takes off while I'm still pulling the door shut. Instinctively I wonder whether this is the last ride I'll take in any car as I set off for an appointment with a businessman said to have been responsible for a series of unmarked graves scattered through the vast amount of cement that's been poured in this city.

CHAPTER 5

Micky threads his Ferrari through the evening traffic without any pointlessly showy acrobatics. He makes a U-turn, takes Via Tempesta as far as Piazzale Zavattari, and then turns onto the outer ring road. Now we're roaring through Piazza Bolivar, and where we're heading is a complete mystery to me. He has chosen silence as the distinctive feature of our journey together and I go along with his choice. For that matter, what is there for us to say to each other that we don't already both know? In two very different ways, we're the same person, even though physically we're two different chessmen.

In spite of the most impassioned pleadings of counsel for the defense, a couple of pawns, I'd have to add.

We drive on, roaring through a city part of which is sound asleep while another is just getting dressed and made up for a gala banquet of bad habits and vice. Every night can be considered a special occasion, until a midnight finally rolls around when everyone will realize that none of those nights was special at all.

And that's not going to be a midnight to look forward to.

We stop at a red light, next to a newsstand. Posters cover the little shack, announcing the lead stories of the newspapers and magazines: the ongoing and hopeless saga of Aldo Moro, the trial of the founders of the Red Brigades, *UFO Robot Grendizer*, Loredana Bertè and her latest love affair, the FIFA World Cup on its way, Juventus and Torino F.C., *TV Sorrisi e Canzoni*, the troubles of Italian president Giovanni Leone.

All these different stories intertwined on the same wall, in the same world, in the same life. And I don't give a damn about any of it or any of thcm. Maybe that's because first and foremost I don't give a damn about myself. I turn my head to look at Micky. I wonder if he ever thinks about it. I wonder if he ever asks questions, or if he's just pure instinct. Fast cars, fast trips, fast love affairs. And time, capable of outstripping the fastest speed there is, time, which kills you quickly because there's no memory that can remember every instant.

Micky mistakes my glance for impatience.

"It's going to take us a little while to get there. We have to go all the way out to Opera."

I dismiss with a nonchalant gesture all my thoughts of just a few seconds ago.

"Don't sweat it. There's no hurry. We have all the time we need."

I turn my head to watch the road.

All the time we need . . .

Lucio would appreciate the irony. How much time do you need, anyway? Now that I know who I am, I'd prefer not to know it. Memory is the only way of being sure you've even lived. But I don't remember, so I won't be remembered.

Micky turns right, leaving Viale Liguria and heading for the on-ramp of the Milan–Genoa superhighway. He asks me if I want to snort a line of cocaine. I shake my head no. He pulls a solid-gold contraption out of his pocket, a tiny container that dispenses one snort at a time. He sticks it up his nostril and inhales powerfully. He does the same thing with the other nostril. Then he snaps it shut and shakes it before putting it away, ready for the next snort.

He turns toward me, gives me a look, and comments: "Good shit."

I have no difficulty taking him at his word. People like him always have the best of everything.

As soon as we're on the bypass for Assago, the speed begins to increase and the Ferrari's eight cylinders start to suck gasoline and give back power. The way mechanical objects work is a game I like, an honest game. I give and I get. Cocaine is a fraud: it leaves people exactly as they are and tricks them into thinking they're different.

We curve onto the beltway and the speed increases even more.

I'm not afraid. I'm not afraid of dying, to be specific. I've already suffered that misfortune. A fatal crash in a car rocketing along at 125 mph would be nothing more than a formal certification of the fact, a red wax seal on a letter that's already been written and signed.

We take the Vigentina–Val Tidone exit. Before entering Opera we take a right. A short time later our trip is over. Micky decelerates and steers the Ferrari left onto an unpaved lane that intersects with the asphalt road. I can hear the tires crunching over the gravel and, because of the car's stiff suspension, I can feel every bump and pothole in my spine. We rumble through a couple of curves, and after a short straightaway we see a warehouse and a parking lot cluttered with the decrepit automotive carcasses of a scrapyard. The area is surrounded by a hurricane fence. A few well-meaning streetlights do their best to scatter a little light.

We pull up to a gate. It's closed. Micky flashes his brights and immediately, on the other side of the fence, the silhouette of a man emerges from the dim shadows. He walks toward us and the twin cones of the headlights reveal a short, powerful individual wearing work pants and a denim jacket, peering with light-dazzled eyes through the mesh of the gate.

He recognizes the car and starts swinging the gate open. We drive past him and through the gate. We continue along the road that leads to the warehouse, past stacks of flattened automobiles, cubist shapes, lifeless relics. A series of totems erected at the cost of a chain of human and mechanical sacrifices, though there's no one around who seems willing to worship them.

Micky stops in a clearing where a number of other cars are already parked. In the first row I see a shiny new Porsche and, parked next to it, in all its tawdry desolation, Daytona's old orange Porsche. Speak of the devil. As if he were declaring: This is what I am and this is what I wish I could be. Then there are a couple of Mercedes-Benzes, a 240 and a Pagoda, a BMW 733i, and a string of other cars of various makes and models and engine displacements. All of them intact, motionless, and gleaming, as if to mock the crushed automotive carcasses that surround them. There's a sense of rust and melancholy in the air that only failure can convey.

I kick myself for the asshole I am.

I'm here for other reasons and to run other risks. I have no time for dreary animistic reveries.

If I make one false move tonight, I could wind up looking like one of these stripped automobiles, just waiting to be handed over to the tender loving care of the crusher.

Micky gets out of the car and I follow suit. I follow him

65

toward the building on our left. We walk along the outside wall of the structure for a certain distance in the inadequate light of the overhead lamps. We walk around the far corner, and on our left we see a sliding metal door. There's a man standing guard. Having heard our footsteps, he's already walking toward us. He's a completely different-looking type from the squat guy at the gate. He's dressed in a dark brown suit and has the appearance of a man who would ring a doorbell and pull a trigger with the same unruffled calm: maybe the trigger of the gun sticking out of his belt, visible through his unbuttoned suit jacket.

When he recognizes Micky, he relaxes slightly.

Without a word of greeting, my friend comes right to the point.

"We have an appointment with Tano."

The guy looks me up and down before deciding that my escort is reference enough for my admission. Then he jerks his head toward the interior and opens the smaller door carved out of the sliding metal door.

We walk through the door and suddenly we're in another world. On the side of the warehouse we've just walked into, we're surrounded by all the equipment and machinery needed for the operations of the ostensible host company. Workbenches, metal presses, lathes, and other heavy machinery I couldn't identify. In front of us are the glass doors of a painting department. There's a diffuse odor of solvents, milled metal, and lubricant. I wouldn't be a bit surprised if this shop was used not only to scrap cars with regulation certificates of demolition but also to modify the appearance of vehicles of much murkier provenance.

But the real surprise comes with what we see on the opposite side of the interior space. Under the lights hanging down from the ceiling and on a modular wooden floor is a genuine miniature casino. There's an American-style roulette wheel with a croupier, a long craps table, and another table where a number of people are sitting, both men and women, playing what looks to me like blackjack. I think I catch a glimpse of Daytona's double comb-over, among the card players. There's even a little bar, with a man and a blond woman leaning against it, waiting for their drinks. Three men dressed in dark suits mingle silently with the crowd, keeping an eye on everything that's going on.

When Tano Casale does something, he does it right. I'm pretty sure that tomorrow morning, none of what I'm looking at will be here to greet the light of day. The tables will be broken down, the green felt and the black curtains covering the high windows of the warehouse will all be gone. There'll be nothing but a warehouse full of people cutting metal with oxyacetylene blowtorches, hammering, and waving paint spray guns and airbrushes. But tonight there's still plenty of time for anyone who wants to hunt for a lucky card or a winning number. They just have to pay their dues, winning occasionally and losing almost inevitably, as required by the rules of the game.

I follow Micky as he walks across the warehouse floor, heading for a door that looks like it leads to an office. Before we have a chance to knock on the door, it swings open and a man walks out. His face is swollen, and a stream of blood is pouring out of his nose. He's doing his best to stop the blood with a pocket handkerchief. Another man with a powerful physique and a face that's probably seen more than one bout in a boxing ring holds him firmly by the arm, pushing him along toward the exit and concealing him from the view of the other players.

Micky knocks twice on the doorjamb, and then walks through the door, which has been left wide open. I follow him through. Inside we see two men. One is sitting down at a desk piled high with paperwork and the other is on his feet, leaning against a zinc filing cabinet.

The one sitting down is Tano Casale.

He looks to be about forty-five, with slicked-back hair. There are a few streaks of gray around his temples, and not a trace of gray in his thick, dark mustache. His eyes are determined but his right eyebrow, crisscrossed by a small scar, gives him a slightly quizzical look. His big hands resting on the desktop convey an idea of strength and of a person who knows how to use it.

He sees us walk in and nods hello to Micky. The nod is followed by a smile that says the boss likes Micky. My friend must be a reliable worker and a good earner. What I hear about Tano Casale is that he's a man of his word and that he recognizes and rewards merit.

"*Ciao*, blondie."

"*Ciao*, Tano."

Micky, for all his airs as a man of the world, is intimidated. He points to me.

"This is Bravo, the person I mentioned on the phone."

Only then does Tano seem to notice my presence. He looks me up and down without a word and his face hardens.

"Bravo? What kind of a fucking name is Bravo?"

A voice emerges from my memory and echoes in my head. It sounds like sandpaper on rust.

. . . hold still, youngster, don't give me trouble. If you make this easy on me, I'll make it easy on you and try not to make it hurt too bad. Understand? That's it, don't squirm. Bravo!

I shrug my shoulders.

"Maybe it's not a name, maybe it's just an involuntary shout of approval I get from people."

Tano bursts out laughing.

"Nice answer, kid—bravo!"

"You see? You said it, I didn't."

Maybe my ready wit has made a good impression on him, or maybe not. Still, when the smile fades he looks at me differently. He waves me over and points to the steel and Formica chair in front of his desk. Micky can tell he's no longer needed, and he leaves before anyone has to ask him to. The other man remains standing, on my left. Maybe he's trying to intimidate me, but I ignore him.

Tano offers me a thoughtful tone of voice and a piece of flattery.

"All kidding aside, I've heard good things about you. You've put together your little network, you seem to know what you're doing, and, best of all, you seem to respect boundaries."

He points to the door that the guy with the nosebleed walked through a little while ago.

"Not like some people, who think they're smarter than me and come to my casino and try to sneak in some late bets under my nose. You wouldn't believe how stupid some people can be."

He pauses.

"But don't let's talk about disagreeable things. Micky tells me you have a deal for me."

"More than a deal; I'd say a trade."

"I'm listening."

I stall for time and light a cigarette. Then I sweep my hand in a gesture that includes everything that's happening in the warehouse.

"I'd have to imagine that with all this money coming in, the biggest problem you have is how to spend it."

Tano smiles like a cat thinking about mice.

"We always know what to do with our money."

I nod agreeably and continue. And I wonder if he'd have the same purr in his voice and glint in his eye if he were telling someone to cut my throat.

"All the same, sometimes it's good to make things a little easier on yourself. I have the name and address of a guy who just hit the jackpot on the soccer lottery and won himself 490 million lire. He's willing to sell this winning lottery ticket for a modest gratuity of ten million lire."

Just to forestall any misunderstanding, I volunteer the terms I have in mind.

"I wouldn't touch a cent of it. I promised him that money as an incentive and because he strikes me as an honest person. And, most important of all, a reasonable person."

I'm sure that Tano understands exactly what I'm driving at, but he wants to hear it from me.

"Go on."

"Oh, I don't think there are any difficulties from that point on. If you buy the winning ticket, you have a certain sum of money in hand that you can spend without having to worry. Moreover, it would be tax exempt, since it's winnings from a state-run lottery."

Tano Casale looks in my direction, but I'm pretty sure he doesn't even see me. Then he turns his head to meet the gaze of the man standing next to the filing cabinet. In exchange he receives a look of circumspect approval, confirming a decision that he's actually already made internally. He addresses me once again in an untroubled voice.

"This we could do. We'd have to look at just how, but this is something we could do."

After a pause he turns to the second part of the matter.

"Now what about you? What do you get out of this?"

"I just get to keep doing my job without a major headache. There's a problem between Laura, one of my girls, and one of your men."

At this point, everything happens very quickly. The guy standing next to the filing cabinet, a man of average height with bulging eyes and a mouth with a nasty sneer, grabs me by my jacket lapels and heaves me up out of my seat. I find myself shoved against the wall, his deranged eyes about a foot from mine, and his breath, which hardly reeks of violets, hissing his cold fury. I'm not all that surprised. This is fairly ordinary behavior from Salvatore Menno, aka Tulip.

His boss, from behind the desk, intervenes.

"Salvatore, leave him alone."

My aggressor ignores him and smashes me against the wall once or twice.

"You nasty goddamn pimp, what the fuck do you want here?"

Any fuck you've got, I reply instinctively, in my head.

This last would have prompted a round of applause from Lucio, if he ever knew. But I don't think that Tulip would get the joke. Even if he knew, I still think he'd miss the point.

Tano Casale stands up suddenly from his chair. He doesn't yell, but it's worse than if he had.

"I told you to let him go. Go back to where you were."

Even a psychopath like Tulip shits his pants when Tano Casale speaks in that tone of voice. I can feel the vise grip loosen and I'm free. He walks backward, with my death still dancing in his eyes, until he's standing next to the filing cabinet again.

I move away from the wall, doing my best to straighten my jacket.

I ignore my adversary and I speak to Tano. With a cool calm that's nothing like what I'm feeling inside.

"Since the hen that squawks is the one that laid the egg, at this point I hardly think I need to name names. Laura is a girl who works for me and your man wants to force her to be part of his harem."

Instinctively, Tulip takes another step toward me. Tano halts him with a wave of his hand. The only way left for Tulip to let off steam is with words, and he speaks them with flecks of whitish foam speckling the corners of his mouth.

"Laura's a whore, and you're making a living off her pussy."

"That may be. But she's a whore with free will, and she can be a whore when and with whomever she pleases. No matter what she does, she's the one who decides. I don't impose, I simply propose, without duress and, above all, without fists."

The threat comes as no surprise.

"I'll have your hands cut off at the wrist."

I turn to look at him, and I stare him straight in the eye.

"So you're too scared to do your own hand-cutting in person these days?"

Tano's voice, slightly raised, cuts sharply through this little exchange of compliments.

"That's enough! And I mean both of you!"

He goes back and sits down at his desk. He speaks to Tulip without looking him in the face.

"Salvo, go in the other room and see if everything's under control."

That request is tantamount to a get-the-fuck-out-of-here, loud and clear. Reluctantly, Menno heads for the door, covering his humiliation with a dignified, unhurried pace. Just before he walks through the door, he gives me a look that contains a complete road map of his intentions. I know that he's not likely to get over this particular humiliation anytime soon and that, in any case, I've just made an enemy for life.

Oh well, nobody lives forever.

Now Tano and I are alone. I go back to my chair. He puts his hands behind his head and draws his own conclusions.

"So, for you this Laura's freedom is worth all that money."

"That's right."

He looks at me as if he were seeing me for the first time.

"You're a smart guy. You're no chicken. From the way you talk, I can tell you're educated. You have a nice appearance. Are you ambitious, too?"

This sounds like the preamble to a job offer. Which I tactfully do my best to avoid.

"Sometimes ambition can take you on some strange rides, in the backs of certain cars and inside certain coffins. Plus, I'm allergic to flowers."

Tano Casale bursts out laughing.

"And you're a philosopher too. Happiness comes to him who settles for less."

This time I put a ceremonious smirk on my face.

"Or you could put it another way. He who is happy to settle for less lives well and much longer."

The man sitting across the desk from me seems satisfied, both with me and with the turn of events.

"Outstanding. I guarantee that Salvo won't bother your girl anymore. As for the rest of it, give me the time to put together the money and then we'll complete this operation. I'd be just as happy if it was you supervising it, even though, for obvious reasons, I'd assign a trusted colleague to work alongside you."

I pull a ballpoint pen out of a cup and jot down the phone number of the answering service I use on a notepad lying on the desk. I push it across the desk to him.

"You can get in touch with me any time of the day or night at this number."

Tano stands up. This signals an unspoken dismissal. I stand up too and reach out to grip the hand he extends to me.

"Now, if you want to go take a stroll around the room in there, I'll have them give you a handful of chips, just so you can't say we sent you away empty-handed."

I put another aspect of my life onto the scale.

"Thanks. But I don't gamble."

"Smart boy. There are plenty smarter ways to burn up your money."

We emerge from the office and into the warehouse. While I was busy negotiating with Tano Casale and getting myself beaten up by Tulip, more people have shown up. Now the roulette table is almost completely concealed by the crowd of male and female players clustering around it. For the same reason, I can barely see the craps table, and I notice that they've set up another blackjack table. This line of business must bring in a fortune. A safe and risk-free source of revenue, every night on earth that God grants us. The world is teeming with people willing to lose the deed to their house at a roulette table. Moreover, in the specific case in question, alongside the sheer thrill of gambling is the added charge of doing so in a way that's against the law. Though I'm pretty

74

sure that Tano, as far as that goes, has arranged for all the necessary protections.

Everything that needs to be said between us has been said. The boss waves his hand good-bye and goes over to Menno, who's facing the croupier at the head of the roulette table. I see Micky excuse himself from his conversation with an elegant laughing blond woman; he leaves her and walks over to them. They chat. Then my blond friend heads in my direction, while the other two leave through a door in the far wall, followed by a third man who must be their bodyguard.

"What the fuck are you doing here?"

The voice, with a heavy Milanese accent, comes out of nowhere. A second later I'm looking at Daytona, large as life, wiping his face with a handkerchief. He must be on a bad losing streak. When he's sweating at the card table it means that the goddess of fortune has taken off her blindfold, but only to hand it to him so he can mop his brow.

I doubt it would be wise to tell him the real reason for my presence at the Township of Opera Scrapyard Casino. I come up with a wisecrack, just to take his eye off the ball.

"I dropped by to make sure you didn't gamble away your underwear, too."

"Then you got here too late. I lost my undies a while ago, along with everything else."

To judge from his red face, he must have dropped quite a bundle. But I don't think he's hit bottom yet. I can see the watch is still there on his wrist.

As we are exchanging these wisecracks, Micky comes over to join us. He and Daytona know each other, though it's not like they're so fond of each other that they're about to jump up and do the flamenco on one of the tables. In fact,

75

Micky talks to me and ignores Daytona entirely, as if I were there alone.

"Everything okay?"

"Everything's okay. I want to thank you."

"For what? When you want to leave, let me know."

Daytona is an openly avowed loser, with regularly thwarted ambitions of moving up to the next level. He saw the scene with the blond woman. He knows that Micky is one of Tano's favorites, so he unfurls the servile tone of voice he uses when he wants to ingratiate himself with someone.

"If you want to stay here, I'll be glad to drive Bravo back."

Micky looks at him and then looks at me. He cocks an eyebrow.

"Is that a problem for you? I have something to do and it would sure help me out."

"No problem."

"Great. See you around."

He leaves us and swoops back down on his prey. When all is said and done, this too is a fair game. I give and in exchange I am given. The young man is offering for sale exactly what that blond woman wants. Events will determine whether the price was too high or too low. And in the final analysis, as always, it's their own fucking problem.

Daytona rubs his hands together, with the crafty look of somebody who's just pulled off a considerable public relations coup.

"So, shall we go?"

I head out the door I came in by. He follows me with his swaggering gait, belly protruding from the dark blue jacket that once fit him. We get outside and the guard standing watch observes us as we pass by him, without changing expression and without offering a greeting.

After we walk a few steps together, Daytona utters a phrase in a low voice, to keep from being overheard.

"With all the money we left on the table, he could at least have said *buona notte*."

I stop and give him a look.

"Don't try to drag me into a first person plural that has nothing to do with me. With all the money that *you* left on the table, is what you mean."

Daytona's face lights up, as if he'd suddenly remembered something.

"Speaking of money . . ."

He pauses to unlock the Porsche. He gets in and waits until I'm sitting beside him before he continues.

"You remember that pine fiece of ass that I took upstairs this morning, the one we picked up in front of the Ascot and that thanks to you cost me a bundle of cash?"

The one that we *picked up?*

That's what I think, but I say nothing and wait. Daytona continues, working himself up. "A fantastic body. A figure to knock your eyes out. A couple of tits straight out of science fiction and an ass that talks, eloquently. In fact, if I'm not mistaken, her ass has even given a few interviews."

He starts the engine. He puts the car in gear and pulls out toward the front gate.

"If you want to give her a whirl, believe me, you won't regret it. She already told me that if I want to see her again I'll have to up the rate, so she can go fuck herself as far as I'm concerned. But I think that she'd be willing to give you a discount. Wait a minute . . ."

He slips two fingers into the breast pocket of his jacket and extends a little sheet of paper folded in half to me.

"Here, she even gave me her phone number. Give her a

call, take some good advice from a miserable idiot like me."

I unfold the wrinkled little piece of paper and look at it. In the half-light inside the car I can just make out a number written in a feminine hand. I crumple it up and drop it into the ashtray. Daytona observes and objects.

"You know, you're making a mistake. That girl is first-class."

I dismiss the subject with a few words, and I hope they're definitive.

"I know plenty of first-class girls. One more won't change my life."

All the same, as we pull out of the gate, I feel a strange sense of annoyance at Daytona's appraisals of the girl. And as we bounce along the unpaved road on our way back to blacktop, I find myself thinking that our Carla turned out to be a quick study. Then, for the rest of the trip, in spite of my driver's senseless chatter, I can see her face before me and in my mind I hear those words over and over.

If it was you, I'd do it for free . . .

CHAPTER 6

The taxi comes to a halt near the front door of the Ascot Club and my stomach is doing somersaults. The cabbie, a hippyish-looking guy with long hair and a reddish beard you'd expect to see on a hobo, has a face that reminds me of Chewbacca, the hairy first mate from *Star Wars*. I couldn't say whether the Wookiee drove his spaceships the same way. But one thing I can say is that we definitely made at least two or three leaps into hyperspace on the journey from Piazza Napoli to here.

I give him the fee he demands even though, as usual, the total doesn't seem to square with the readout on the meter. There are taxi drivers in Milan who'd be willing to ask you for a special late-night supplemental fee in the middle of the day just because you're wearing sunglasses, and charge you extra for luggage just because you've got a wallet in your back pocket. I watch him pull out safe and sound, even though I feel like telling him to go fuck himself.

But it's a nice evening, I've just solved a problem, I'm alone, and I'm in precisely the right mood for being alone.

Just a short while before, after we entered the city of Milan and as we were driving along Via Giambellino, Daytona suddenly stopped his freewheeling talk of women, cars, and the large amounts of money that are always just about to come to him. Today he's expecting a payment from a certain Rondano, his insurance agent, to be specific.

I knew what he was thinking and the question that was spinning in his head. It's just that I expected it much earlier. At last he opened up, in a seemingly careless voice, continuing to watch the street with a zeal that seemed perhaps excessive.

"That's a nice thing Tano Casale's put together, eh? He must pull money out of that place hand over fist."

"Yeah."

I'm all laconic, he's finally explicit.

"Do you have any deals under way?"

"I'd have to say no."

"You know, I saw you come out of his office with him and I thought . . ."

I interrupted. Sliding into a jocular scolding tone just so I could steer the conversation away from thin ice.

"Daytona, don't do too much thinking. Extensive experience shows that it's not something you're particularly good at."

If Daytona gets it into his head that I have connections with Tano, I'll never get him off my back. His attitude with Micky told me everything I needed to know. He took the dressing-down with some resentment.

"Ah, go yuck fourself. If that's your way of trying to tell me it's none of my business, then you can just keep your own . . ."

Yes, I'll keep my own secret forever.

I felt like answering him in the Italian voice of Greta Garbo. Instead, I decided to minimize and change the subject with a plausible explanation, to keep him from sticking his nose in my business in the future. Most of all, I was sick of being questioned.

"I had an errand to do. I was there as a messenger, nothing more. Once I delivered the message, the relationship was over. No deals under way, as you put it."

Whether or not that convinced him, the topic was closed. And with it, any interest Daytona might have had in me. Which was certainly one of the reasons he offered to drive me back to town in the first place.

This time, when he asks the next question, he turns to look at me.

"Where did you park your car?"

"At the Ascot."

Standard expression of disappointment.

"Do you mind if I leave you at the taxi stand, down at the end of this street? I have to be someplace and I'm already running late."

As long as I've known him, Daytona almost always has to be someplace. I'm pretty sure that these aren't places where anybody does anything commendable. One of these days he'll go directly from one of those places to a high-security prison without even transitioning through the street, as Godie would say. Placing his index and middle fingers on the victim's throat like a pair of scissors.

Tac! Got you! You have the right to remain silent.

I wave a hand dismissively.

"Don't worry about it, drop me off wherever you want."

"Bravo, you're a friend."

A friend. I feel like laughing out loud. After a certain time of night and a certain threshold of alcohol and cocaine, it's the easiest thing in the world to find friends in Milan. You wind up in certain clubs, hanging out with a crowd that, taken all together, accounts for seven hundred years in prison, tossing around the word *friend*, distilled directly from the coca leaf.

81

In reality, nobody's anyone's friend, not even their own. So it's the commonest thing imaginable, the next morning, for someone to wake up with a terrifyingly ugly woman asleep next to him and not even remember her name. She's just anyone, a woman picked up at random, out of desperation, when loneliness and booze conspire to shut your eyes tighter than a roll-down security shutter.

I got out of Daytona's Porsche and I headed over to the column of two or three taxis waiting hopefully in line, without realizing I was about to step into the *Millennium Falcon*. Which by now must have reached Warp Nine and must be hurtling past the San Siro Stadium on its way out of town.

I'm just about to pull open the driver's side door of my Mini when I see Giorgio Fieschi walk out of the club along with a pair of fellow actors. I hear their laughter as they climb into a green Renault R4 and head off in the direction of Piazza Buonarroti, away from where I'm standing. I envy them. They're young and they're talented. I hope they understand that this means they have the world in the palms of their hands. At the same time, I turn my mind with pleasure to Laura and her sense of duty. Her current crush on the cabaret artist has been filed away for later, with reference to her appointment tomorrow morning. In part because 70 percent of a million isn't a bad fee for one hour's work.

The rest is my commission.

I slip my key into the lock. Someone comes up next to me. I hear the voice, I recognize the face, and I see the gun — all at the same moment. But Tulip's expression is the single most significant factor, the one that puts the worst light on the likely outcome of the night.

"*Ciao*, pimp. As you can see, we meet again."

82

I know why he's here. And the fact that he's here means that his sense of thug's honor is much stronger than his fear of his boss. I forced him to submit to a humiliation that he can't get out of his mind. Right this second, Laura and Tano mean nothing to him. This is between him and me. Nothing I could do or say would change the situation.

So I say nothing and look at him.

He's unruffled. He's past his anger: it's been replaced by the calm of determination. And I consider that to be a very negative additional wrinkle.

"What's the matter, you swallow your tongue? How come?"

Out of the blue, in the silence of the street, a backhanded slap cracks out as it makes contact with my right cheek with the power of a gunshot. My ear starts whistling. A constellation of tiny yellow dots begins bobbing in front of my eyes like so many gnats.

"Just wanted to show you that I still have the courage to come take care of a piece of shit like you in person. Get moving."

He waves his pistol in the direction of Piazzale Lotto. I get moving, looking around me without seeming to. But he notices.

"There's nobody around, you little pussy. Don't worry. It's just you and me."

He's right. The show at the Ascot has been over for a while and the parking lot is practically empty. This evening not even the two streetwalkers who usually loiter around near the club are out. Which I don't like. Which I don't like one little bit.

We reach a Citroën CX, oversize and slightly decrepit. Still keeping a safe distance, he rummages through his jacket pockets and then places the keys on the roof of the car.

"Here, you drive. Smooth as silk, and no funny business."

I pick up the keys, get behind the wheel, and start the engine. I look over and he's sitting next to me. Tulip's years of experience ensure that in all these various movements, the muzzle of the pistol has been invariably trained on my belly.

I sit in silence and wait.

"Take the Nuova Vigevanese."

I pull out of the parking lot and drive in the direction he indicated. I wonder whether the expression on my face resembles that of Aldo Moro, in the photograph that has been published repeatedly in the newspapers over the past few weeks. I can't expect to be the subject of *the intense concern of the entire nation*, nor can I expect a single word of intercession from anyone on earth. I don't even think I deserve either concern or words of intercession. Unless there's a miracle, I'm about to vanish into thin air and no one will ever come looking for me, since no one gives a crap what becomes of me.

We drive on in silence. The only thing I could try would be if we happen to cross paths with a police car. Still, I'm afraid that wouldn't make much of a difference, as far as my abductor is concerned. From what I know about him and what I've been able to see with my own eyes, he must not be entirely right in the head. If he's decided to cross the line and disobey a direct order from Tano, it means nothing can stop him now.

As if he'd just read my mind, he breaks the silence.

"Tano told me to leave the girl alone. He didn't say anything about you."

"I've got a deal pending with your boss and this will screw it up. He's not going to like that."

He smiles. It's a twisted grimace I would have been just as happy not to see.

"Nothing's going to happen to that deal. You're going to write down the name and the address of that guy, I'm going to take the paper you write it on to Tano, and everything's going to be fine."

"Now why would I do that? No matter what I do, you're going to kill me anyway."

"I'll tell you why. You can avoid dying in a pretty unpleasant manner. I've got plenty of time. I can shoot you in the knee and wait. Then I can shoot you in the other knee, and then in the shoulder, and so on. Or else with a single shot blow off all your equipment. I've heard that it hurts like hell to be shot in the balls."

I sit in silence. My thoughts wander off in another direction. Now I'm no longer in the car, I'm elsewhere, with other men like Tulip, men with the same intentions, men with the same indifference.

A long long time ago.

"Too bad, boy, that you don't seem to know how to keep your dick in your pants. Sometimes when you zip up afterward you could get it caught: accidents will happen . . ."

Tulip's voice brings me back to the car. He thinks that I'm dreaming up a way of screwing him and he decides to share the possible consequences.

"Let's say by chance you were to decide to give me the wrong name and address, well, you'd better not. I'll find out if you have a girlfriend, a buddy, or a dog. Any creature on this earth that you care about. And then I'll kill them too."

I don't have the slightest doubt that he'll keep his word. Which persuades me once and for all that Salvatore Menno is a psychopath. My mind plays Laura's face back to me as she gazes entranced at Giorgio Fieschi; Lucio's expression, perennially rapt in his blindness; the cryptic clue that I left for him before leaving—I'll never know if he solved it.

In the meantime, as we continue along Via Lorenteggio, we've passed the intersection with Via Primaticcio. The road widens into the Vigevanese, with two lanes running in each direction. Along the highway are all-night gas stations, two-bit whores, industrial sheds, cars parked along the service road. A young man is standing next to the service window of an all-night pharmacy. No question: he's a junkie buying a syringe to shoot up. But at this particular instant, the fate of some drug addict is the least of my concerns, if I might ever have cared. At least he has the good luck to have a choice in how he dies.

"Keep going straight through Trezzano, then I'll tell you."

The car travels on. The handgun is still aimed straight at my belly. I keep my eyes on the road; Tulip watches me and smiles. We pass through the Quartiere Tessera. This is a departure without a return trip, and I'm surprised to find that I feel no nostalgia whatsoever. Doubt floats spontaneously to the surface: Is that all there is? Nothing more? Are these the wonders that we were promised, is this the beauty of the world, is this the life that was worth living? I struggle to find a meaning to things, any meaning at all, as I pass one nameless place where I live and continue on to another nameless place where I'm going to take a gunshot to the head.

Trezzano streams past in a flash, like all moments just before dying. Now we're out in the country and the streetlights are just a memory. Out here there are no concessions. The open road accepts only the beams of the headlights.

"Turn right."

86

The muzzle of the pistol points me toward a secondary road. I slow down and steer the car down a strip of asphalt running through the countryside. I keep driving until it turns into a dirt lane. We continue along it, skirting a quarry at a certain point, until we reach a wide place in the road, surrounded by trees and bushes.

"Stop here and get out."

I stop the car and swing the door open. The ground underfoot is hard and uneven. The air is damp and I can smell wet grass. This would have been the perfect night to be alone, and I was in the mood for it, too. But there's no time. There's never enough time. And now Tulip is already on my side of the car, surrounded by the reddish halo of the taillights. The handgun hasn't shifted a millimeter. Nor have his intentions, I decide. He takes a few steps back and points to the car.

"Open the trunk."

I do as he says. Inside, amid the clutter, is a shovel. For a fraction of a second I tell myself to go for it. But the son of a bitch has more experience in this kind of thing than I do. In my life, I've always been on the wrong end of the gun or the knife.

Which teaches you nothing, except to be afraid.

His voice erases any clever ideas before they have a chance to take shape.

"Pick it up and step away."

I take two steps backward, pathetic with my shovel in my hand. I watch as he steps over to the trunk and rummages around inside. When he pulls out his hand it's holding a flashlight.

"Turn off the headlights."

A few seconds later we're in the dark, with the luminous beam of the flashlight as the only barrier between us and the night. I see the beam move and uncover a path through the greenery.

"Over that way."

I start walking. I don't know where we are, but my captor looks like he feels right at home here. I can imagine that all around us, under a yard or so of dirt, there must be buried any number of bodies that experienced a journey just like my own. I walk as best I can, feeling the bushes cut my hands, with nothing to guide me but the flashlight beam, flattening my shadow over the underbrush.

At last we come to a point that Tulip must have defined in his head with a single word: here. There's a little grass clearing, just big enough for the purpose he has in mind. I see the light move away and shift to my left. The voice emerges from the darkness immediately behind it. There's an unmistakable note of derision dripping from the words now.

"Dig. Even though your nice suit will get a little wrinkled. If you want, when you're done, I'll send it to the cleaners."

I start digging so I don't have to hear him laugh. And so I can think. I know that where my hopes for survival are concerned there's a big fat zero. All the same, I don't want to let this asshole just win without putting up a fight. It can't be a jerk like Tulip who finally rubs me off the list. The only opportunity I'll have to try anything will be when he asks me to write down a name and an address. Maybe he'll be distracted or maybe he might slip and fall, maybe . . .

Or maybe what I learned in school is true. Hope is just the last item in Pandora's box, all I have left.

Little by little, my legs are standing in a hole that grows steadily deeper. The sweat pours off my forehead and trickles down my back. My hands start to hurt. I stand up and lean on the shovel, gripping the handle tightly.

"What's the matter? Don't you have the strength? You already tired, jerk-off?"

I'm about to tell him to go fuck himself. I'm about to lift the shovel and lunge at him, because by now the anger is more powerful than any instinct for self-preservation. Then something happens.

In the silence, one after another, three smothered noises, in rapid succession.

Pfft . . . pfft . . . pfft . . .

The flashlight suddenly jumps into the air, spinning around in a couple of luminous somersaults before falling to earth. I hear the sound of branches rustling as a body falls into the bushes. I think I hear light footsteps. But that must be nothing more than an impression because they vanish immediately.

Then silence.

Time keelhauls me and what happens meanwhile is: nothing. No more voice, no more orders. Only the half-beam of the flashlight on the ground where it's fallen, illuminating the base of a shrub. I walk over, pick it up, and swing the shaft of light around me.

Tulip is flat on his back, as if nailed to a cross, a short distance away. His eyes are open, staring straight up. He seems to be looking at the hole that just opened up in the middle of his forehead. There are two other holes in his chest, from which a bloodstain is beginning to spread.

It dawns on me what's happened. I instinctively take a step backward and I switch off the flashlight. If whoever shot that son of a bitch decides that I'm just as much of a son of a bitch, I have no desire to help them shoot me by offering a light source. That is, if they intend to do any more shooting. I wait a little longer, and then I decide that it's time to leave. I turn the flashlight back on, I pick up the shovel, and I retrace my route along the trail, doing my best not to lose my way. After a while, I see the beam reflected off the hood of the CX. I decide the best thing I can do is put a little distance between me and this fucked-up place. I get in the car, start the engine, do a three-point turn, and drive back to the main road. I meet no cars coming in the opposite direction along the way. Now that the the worst is over, an anxiety attack sweeps over me. My hands start trembling and no matter how hard I try, I can't master the shaking. I don't waste a lot of time trying to figure out what just happened. For now, I'm just happy to be alive. Thanks to someone I don't know, the man who was about to kill me can be buried in my place in the hole I dug for him.

But I won't be doing the burying, that's for sure.

I drive back onto the road, take a left, and drive calmly back to Milan. I have to get rid of this car as quickly as I can. I wouldn't want to run into a police car, the kind that's never around when you need them, and have the cops stop me driving a car I could never explain away. A car that belongs to a man who's going to be found, sooner or later, with three bullet holes in his body.

I reach Piazza Frattini and dump the CX in a cross street of Via d'Alviano. It's at a decent distance from the Ascot but still close enough that I can walk to the club without having to catch a taxi. It's just incredible what good memories certain taxi drivers who work the night shift seem to have. Before I leave, I carefully wipe off all the parts that I've touched. The steering wheel, the gearshift, the door, the shovel, the trunk.

Then I start walking.

My sense of agitation has subsided, but the danger that I just narrowly escaped has sapped all my energy. I suddenly feel exhausted. As if for my entire life up till now I had done hard physical labor without ever being able to rest. I keep walking at the pace that I'm able to keep up, mulling over the events that have brought me here, walking alone through the streets of Milan dressed in dirt-caked clothing. I keep asking myself questions and I can't come up with a satisfactory answer to any of them. I don't keep count of the steps, or the time. Only the exhaustion. And I've even lost track of that when I turn the corner of Via Tempesta and find myself outside the Ascot Club. It's locked up tight and all the lights are out, but to my eyes it's as spectacularly glorious as all of Las Vegas.

I head for the Mini. Standing next to the car is a woman, her back turned toward me. She's smoking a cigarette and looks familiar. I stop to look at her, thinking that it's too late even for a poor and obstinate streetwalker. Just then, she turns around and I recognize her.

It's Carla.

My surprise manages to overcome the exhaustion that's twisting my shoulders, legs, and stomach.

I walk over to her. She sees me, throws the cigarette butt to the ground, and launches the last puff of smoke out into the night. She comes toward me. Her face is as beautiful as I remembered it. She's wearing a short jacket over a light dress and she moves with the natural elegance of a feline.

I hadn't noticed her walk the other time. Or maybe I was too busy trying to show off in front of Daytona to notice it. Step by step, her eyes emerge from the dim light. She holds them level, meeting my gaze, even though when she finally speaks there's a note of embarrassment in her voice. And an exquisitely feminine form of caution and shame at being in my presence, at a place like that at that hour of the morning.

"*Ciao.*"

"*Ciao.* What are you doing here?"

"I've been waiting for you."

"You've been waiting for me?"

"That's right."

"Why?"

She tosses her head in the direction of the office building where, behind the lit-up windows, her coworkers are laboring with mops and rags.

"I was at work. When I got here I saw your car. Then I kept watching it out the window, hoping that you'd come get it. At a certain point I couldn't help it anymore. I took off my smock, I walked out of there, and I came down here."

I'm having a hard time focusing on her face. My stomach feels as if it's full of sawdust and my body by this point is just a pile of firewood. And yet, all the same, what strikes me about her is a form of womanliness I've never encountered before.

I feel bad and I feel as if I'm being attacked. So I'm a little harsh with her.

"What do you want from me?"

She looks away as she talks to me.

"I'm sick of my life. I'm sick of breaking my back for a couple of lire. I'm sick of seeing women all around me who've grown old without ever being young. I'm sick of having to fuck my boss to keep my job or having to fuck my landlord to cover the rent."

I take a deep breath. This confession falls onto the pavement with the sound of tinkling coins. I don't know why, but I know that this is an important moment. Our two lives are intertwining and I feel like an idiot because I'm so tired that I can hardly utter anything more than monosyllabic grunts.

"And so?"

She looks me straight in the eye again. Her embarrassment and caution have vanished.

"Your proposition yesterday morning . . ."

A short pause, as if to give me time to remember.

"Yes?"

"Your friend told me that you're someone who knows what he's doing. That you have a nice network. I'd like you to make me part of the network and help me to make a lot of money."

I'm standing in front of her and it's as if I'm slowly watching her vanish into the distance. My head is exploding and I feel as if my legs are hollow inside. The question that I ask may come as a surprise to her.

"Do you have a driver's license?"

"Yes."

I stick my hands into my pockets and then I hold out my car keys to her. I can't imagine what my face looks like as I tell her, with the thin thread of a voice that I can still muster, what I want from her.

"Drive me home, please. I don't want to faint behind the wheel."

CHAPTER 7

The last thing I see are headlights.

The light disappears suddenly, along with my breath. Then a rough canvas bag over my head, shoving, yanking, a callused hand pushing me into a car. From then on it's only sounds. Bumping and jouncing, the clicking of vibrations and the roar of the engine in the dark. The heavy breathing of more than one man. Then the car stops and the whole thing happens in reverse. This time it's to get out of the car, but it's still yanking and jerking and shoving and a callused hand

the same one?

pulling me out and I'm unable to breathe because now two hands

the same ones?

are throttling my neck and forcing me down onto my knees. And the voice comes out of the void and . . .

I wake up with a jolt.

I'm in bed, naked, and I can feel that the sheets are drenched with sweat. Maybe it's not only sweat, but I pay no attention to that detail. My head is doing its best to get my thoughts into some kind of order. Unfortunately, with the return of some semblance of order comes memory as well. Tulip, the trip to the outskirts of the city, those three pistol shots smothered by the silencer, the bloodstain on his shirt, his eyes staring glassy in the darkness. And after that, Carla's eyes, docile while she looked at me, rebellious while she was speaking to me, and careful while she was driving and listening to the directions to my house.

I can't imagine what her eyes were like as she watched me emerge from my clothing.

As soon as we got home, walking as best I could, I went into my bedroom and collapsed onto the bed, fully dressed. I fell asleep instantly. She must have undressed me. I can well imagine her surprise. Maybe she leaped backward when she slipped off my underwear. A reflexive act of horror, a switchblade jab to the stomach, the kind of thing that the mind combines to form a new memory.

I stand up, yank the sheet off the bed, and wrap myself in it like a toga, ready for my twenty-three stab wounds. I walk into the bathroom, lock the door behind me, lower myself onto the pot, and let go of everything I've got inside. When I think of the fact that right now I ought to be lying motionless a yard deep in the ground with a bullet lodged in my head, even pissing and shitting can become a hymn to life.

I step into the shower and carefully soap every square inch of my body to remove all traces of last night. I don't know who shot Tulip and I don't even bother to venture a name. I'd need to search through too long a list of people who might have it in for that murderous psychotic. The thing I can't figure out, no matter how hard I try, is why the same guy didn't shoot me too.

I slip into my bathrobe and notice as I step out of the shower that my clothing is piled in a heap next to the laundry hamper. I'll have to get rid of it. Washing it might be enough, but it's a risk I'd rather avoid. I don't want to be found walking around in clothes that might contain traces of dirt from a place where the police have just found a dead body with three bullet holes in it.

I step out of the bathroom with my hair still wet, walk up the hallway, and emerge into the living room. Carla's on my right, lying down on the sofa. She's asleep, fully dressed, her legs tucked up, one arm wedged under one of the little throw pillows. She's removed her jacket and wrapped it around her shoulders as a blanket. Her shoes lie neatly on the floor. She's breathing lightly, despite her uncomfortable position. Her face is beautiful; her complexion is fair, even without her eyes to illuminate it.

I run my gaze around the room.

On the chest of drawers next to the television set is everything I had in my pockets. Cigarettes, lighter, wallet, money clip and wad of bills, pager—almost exactly the way I arrange them before I undress, in practically the same order. The wall clock says it's noon. The red light on the phone is blinking to tell me there are messages on my answering machine.

Later for them.

When my eyes swing back around to Carla, she's awake and looking at me. I made no noise walking on the carpeted floor. Evidently my simple presence was enough to awaken her. She remains curled up, in anticipation and in self-defense. She speaks without moving.

"Sorry."

"About what?"

"For taking off your clothes. I didn't—"

I break in, brusquely and dismissively filing the case away for good.

"It's not a problem. Do you want some coffee?"

She studies me, carefully. Then she swivels to a sitting position, in a rather graceful manner.

"Do you want to talk about it?"

I shake my head slightly, and as I do, in spite of myself, I can feel my jaw muscles tightening. "No."

I walk past her and head into the small galley kitchen. Her voice follows me.

"That thingy made a noise once or twice."

I accept the information without comment. I presume that the thingy in question is my pager. It can wait too. Right now, I don't feel like getting back in touch with the world. I'm still alive and I'm at home, with one of the few people on earth who knows about my condition. I feel strangely at ease. That's a feeling that I should enjoy as a gift of chance. I doubt that heaven would go to that much trouble on my behalf.

While I'm preparing the espresso maker, her voice comes looking for me again.

"You know, I don't even know what to call you."

"Bravo."

"That's a strange name."

"In fact, it's not my name at all. But that's what everyone calls me."

"You must have a name of your own."

"A name doesn't mean a thing. Even Shakespeare said so. You can just call me Bravo like everybody else."

"Exactly where did you get this nickname?"

Understand? That's it, don't squirm. Bravo!

I shrug my shoulders, as if she could see me.

"It's just one of those things you get stuck with for no reason. I don't even remember how it happened."

I turn around to put the espresso pot on the burner and I see that she's standing in the door watching me. Her footsteps, like mine, made no noise. But I didn't perceive her presence behind me.

"Can I help you?"

"No, take it easy. Have a seat. There's barely room for one person in here."

I watch her as she goes over and sits in one of the four chairs around the small circular table by the window. I think back to her outburst that morning, when we met outside the Ascot. I wonder how much determination and how much emotion there was behind her words. The first quality makes a person act, the second makes them cut and run. You have to work out the proportion of one and the other. And there's only one way to do it. I lean against the doorjamb and ask her.

"Are you still determined to do what you asked me this morning?"

"Yes."

"It's not a road you can't come back from. But if you do, you'll be bringing some unpleasant memories with you."

She instinctively shakes her head.

"That's something to worry about in the future. Anything would be better than the present."

From the stove I hear the steaming gargle of the espresso pot. I swivel around and turn off the gas. I pick up the demitasses and the sugar bowl and set them down on the table. Then I step back into the galley kitchen and reappear with the pot of coffee. She watches as I pour the espresso into the little cups. An intense gaze, which would wind up who knows where if she allowed it to roam.

"Why do you do it?"

"For the same reason you've decided to work with me. For money."

She takes a sip of coffee without adding sugar. Then she sets the demitasse back down on the table, running her hand underneath to make sure there are no drops clinging to the bottom.

"I don't think it's that simple. In my case, sure, because I intend to use what God gave me to get out of this shitty life."

She pauses, and in the interval she allows herself a little extra time to size me up. Then she continues, as if she were thinking aloud.

"You don't strike me as somebody who came from the poorer part of town, from the outskirts. I can spot people like you. You speak without an accent. You have nice manners, I'd even say elegant. You have books on your shelves that don't strike me as the pulp porn that my brother reads."

From the tension in her voice I can tell that she's having a hard time not referring to what she found out about me when she slipped off my underwear.

"In other words, you don't seem like what you are."

"No. I am: one hundred percent."

I finish my cup of coffee before going on.

"The men who use my services are usually afraid and in a hurry. They're far too busy running a company, a bank, or a political party. These are lines of work that completely devour your free time. What they're afraid of, on the other hand, is the idea of hearing someone say to their face the one syllable they're least willing to hear: no."

I go over to get my cigarettes from the top of the chest of drawers. I light one.

"I remove that fear and I give them that time. My girls are a reliable *yes*, satisfied and accommodating. A smiling island that has no name and won't remember any."

I emit a puff of smoke into the room, and it mingles with words that are equally unsubstantial.

"Sometimes these men have a wife they no longer love and who perhaps no longer loves them. They have children they see when they get a chance. They have families that are weak but armor-plated by plenty of money."

At last I pull my greedy little rabbit out of the hat.

"But, as in all armor, there's a chink in theirs. I identify that chink; I widen it until it becomes a fissure, and then a wide-open door."

I sit down again. She catches me off guard with a sidetrack.

"In Spanish, *bravo* means courageous."

"I know that."

"And are you?"

I think back to a grave I dug but didn't occupy. To the way I felt at that moment. I smile faintly, not at her, but at myself.

"It doesn't take any particular courage to do what I do. Nothing really to be proud of. In the final analysis, the satisfaction I get is a very modest sense of power."

We exchange a glance, and then we both look away at the same time, with the precision of a couple of experienced dancers. We sit in silence for a few seconds. Each of us has something different in our heads, both springing from the same subject.

Her voice brings us both back to practical considerations.

"Could I take a shower?"

"Of course. If you like, I think I have some casual clothes a friend of mine left in the apartment. She left them here one day when she got changed, just before an appointment. I had them cleaned and she never came by to pick them up. They ought to be just your size. They're in the armoire at the end of the hall."

She stands up and it's a parade that seems to end too soon. I imagine her body under the cheap dress she's wearing. I remember what Daytona said, when we were leaving the gambling den in Opera.

A fantastic body. A figure to knock your eyes out. A couple of tits straight out of science fiction and an ass that talks, eloquently . . .

She takes a couple of steps down the hallway. Then she turns around.

"Are you coming? I assume you'd want to check out the merchandise."

I sit on the chair and look at her. Something moves inside me. Something that's digging, looking for a way out that it can find only at the cost of my life. In my case, anger is the only outlet for desire. I want to hurt her, but I can't do it. All I can do is give a slight jab, to remind her that she's already been a whore, already worked for me.

"There's no need. My friend gave me excellent references on your work."

She gets the point and nods. Then she turns and disappears down the hall, leaving me alone. Unfortunately, what she aroused in me she doesn't take with her. It sits there inside me, carving me inside and nourishing itself on my breath.

I light another cigarette.

Then I call the Eurocheck switchboard. They tell me to call the phone number 02 212121, without a name. I recognize it and know that it's not a phone number at all. It's just a signal, a sort of message. And in my mind, I'm replacing every one of those digits with a dollar sign.

I dial a number that I've memorized. In this case, no address books or sheets of paper or memos. Nothing that can be read. The mind is the best instance of something that can't

101

be read. With the face, it's a little more challenging but you can get to it, in time.

The person at the other end of the line picks up almost instantly.

"Hello."

"This is Bravo."

My client's voice is direct and flat, accustomed to giving orders.

"I need three girls."

No chitchat. I know perfectly well that the man on the other end of the line looks down on me for the work I do. I believe that he must assume that, to the exact same extent, I look down on him for what he's asking me to do for him. Neither of us cares. Each of us has something the other one needs. In his case, money. In my case, beautiful women who can keep a secret. I give and I get. Everything works smoothly if it's a fair game.

"When?"

"Tomorrow, in the early afternoon. Let's say around three o'clock. They'll be picked up the same way as the other times. They'll have to spend the night and be completely open to anything. Do you think that three million lire apiece will persuade them to be sufficiently compliant?"

I keep myself from whistling. Considering that I have the girls on a 70-30 split, that means there's 2.7 million lire in some anonymous bank account that's ready and eager to hop into my pockets.

"Oh, absolutely. Do you want the same girls?"

"Yes. They were perfect. If I remember correctly they were—"

I break in before he can speak.

"No names over the phone. Mine is sufficient."

The voice concedes something that perhaps in another context would have prompted quite a different reaction.

"As you think best."

"Very good. I'll arrange to supply you with what you need."

I hang up. I don't need anything else. I know the address, even though it's my policy to forget an address as soon as I've used it. I sit back down, to smoke and think back to my one *non*-meeting with Lorenzo Bonifaci.

I was sitting at a table with two girls, Jane and Hanneke. Two models, one American, the other Dutch. They had traveled to the Bel Paese wearing patched jeans, seeking their fortunes in the world of fashion. After various vicissitudes they found me. I don't know if I could be considered a fortune, but I was something very close to it, in practical terms. They had family, back in the Netherlands and Tennessee, who were living much better now, thanks to that meeting. It might not have been *Miracle in Milan*, but it was certainly a piece of dumb luck.

All around us, inevitable signs of summer, were the characters and the tourists of the eastern stretch of the Italian Riviera, the faces that populate the Covo di Nord Est in Santa Margherita and the Carillon in Paraggi, where we were sitting.

The food was good, the wine was cold, and the girls were pretty and high-class. I was thinking to myself that at times fate offered me some very nice palliatives. A man had come over discreetly and was now standing by our table.

"Are you Mister Bravo?"

He spoke Italian with a slight British accent, which justified that *mister*.

"Yes. Can I help you?"

"If I'm not intruding, I wonder if I could speak with you."

He smiled at the girls and then turned to me once again.

"Alone."

That impeccable gentleman in a dark blue linen suit smelled of Eau Sauvage and money. The cologne was French. As for the other scent, any currency was eminently acceptable.

I presented a guileless face of pure innocence to my two friends.

"Girls, why don't you go check your makeup while we're waiting for dessert?"

Hanneke and Jane understood that they were to leave the table so that we could put them at the center of attention. They got up and headed off toward the bathroom. The man sat down in the chair left vacant by the American girl.

"My name is Gabriel Lincoln and I work closely with a person who isn't here now, but who was when you and the girls came in."

I looked at the man with the pale skin and the fine hair, waiting for the rest.

"This person was particularly impressed by the attractiveness of your two friends. Right now he's on board his yacht, which is moored just across the way, and he'd be very pleased, after dinner, to invite you all over to enjoy a glass of champagne."

"Could I know just who this person is?"

I'd spoken low and slow on the last three words, just to make it perfectly clear that I found mysteries to be annoying, not alluring. With a half smile, he launched the missile. Which completely demolished my little red wagon.

"Does the name Lorenzo Bonifaci mean anything to you?"

I'll say it meant something to me. It meant steel and glossy

104

magazines and banks and a few gazillion lire. But it also meant direct, behind-the-scenes power and, save for a few isolated episodes, a quiet life out of the spotlight, a name that never appeared in the gossip sheets. Just having been in the same place at the same time as him could be considered a privilege.

"Certainly. I need no further elucidations."

"Then you'll come?"

"Mr. Lincoln, I think we can both consider ourselves men of the world. Am I in any way out of line or offensive when I venture to say that my presence might be considered unnecessary?"

"Neither out of line nor offensive. Quite simply a display of savoir-faire which would be viewed in the most favorable of lights."

"Well, just consider my two young friends to be on board the yacht as we speak, champagne glasses in hand."

And their panties around their ankles . . .

For obvious reasons, I chose not to actually utter this last thought. He looked at me with some curiosity but then slid into a moment of awkwardness.

"I imagine, from the things I've heard about you, that there might be a financial consideration to discuss. I want to assure you—"

I held up my hand to stop him.

"No need for assurances. Please consider this visit aboard the yacht, especially when prefaced by such a courteous invitation, as my own personal gift to Dottore Bonifaci."

Lincoln ducked his head to express his appreciation and pleasure.

"This gift, as you call it, will be most welcome. May I beg to hope that it will be accompanied by your two friends' complete and absolute discretion? Concerning your own discretion, I have no cause for concern, I feel certain."

"My friends aren't stupid. They know they'd have everything to lose and nothing to gain."

In the meantime, the girls had come back from the bathroom. Lincoln moved off, to give me a chance to bring them up to date on the latest developments of the evening. I explained the situation to them and assured them that I would take care of their fee in person after they had performed their services. I'd never given them the short end of the stick before, and they saw no reason not to trust me that time as well.

I waved Gabriel Lincoln over, and he joined us. I got to my feet and the girls followed my lead.

"Mr. Lincoln, may I introduce Hanneke and Jane? They would be delighted to accept your invitation."

I held out my business card, with my phone numbers on it.

"You can reach me at any of these numbers, if the experience meets with approval."

The man solemnly slipped it into his pocket. I believe that he would have worn the same expression if it had been the business card of a Greek shipbuilder.

"One last thing."

"Yes?"

"What brand of champagne will I be missing?"

"It's usually Cristal."

"A pity. I'll try to get over it."

With a smile of amusement, Gabriel Lincoln walked the girls to the front door. I was left sitting alone, surrounded by music, with a good feeling about the future.

To celebrate, I ordered a bottle of Cristal.

About a month later, I was contacted again by Lincoln,

who gave me a number to call whenever I received a message, via pager, asking me to call 02 212121. To my enormous surprise, the voice I found myself dealing with was Bonifaci's. He always remained nothing more than a voice on the phone to me. Those above a certain level use people like me for their own pleasure, but they are certainly not eager to see us socially. Which was fine with me, considering the very comfortable ratio of effort to profit.

My pager beeps.

The usual transaction with the switchboard. With the new development that this time the operator on duty is a woman. I immediately recognize the phone number I'm told to call. It's a direct line to room 605 at the Hotel Gallia. I dial it with a sense of foreboding. When the phone is answered, I recognize the voice. It doesn't sound happy.

"Hello?"

"This is Bravo."

"I thought you were a man of your word."

"In fact, I am."

"Well, the same can't be said of your little friend, if you still consider her one."

"May I ask what happened?"

"I can tell you what *didn't* happen. She didn't show up."

Shit.

"I apologize on her behalf."

"Apology accepted, Signore Bravo. But relationship over."

"Allow me to make up for it. I'll send you—"

The voice breaks in, without any possibility of response.

"I warned you."

Then the line goes dead. I can hardly blame him. No one can appreciate more keenly than I how frustrating an unsatisfied desire can be. I wonder what could have happened. Laura's not the kind of girl to miss an appointment. Or at least, she never has been before. The one thing I know for certain is that this isn't the result of any surprises on Tulip's part, God rest his miserable soul.

What now?

A couple of filthy words are spinning around in my head as I dial Laura's phone number. I can't wait to drop them on her. The phone rings and rings but no one answers. Not even the answering machine clicks on.

I hang up and listen to my own answering machine. The tape winds back with a short whining clatter. Then come the voices.

Beep.

"Bravo, it's Cindy. I'm finally back. I arrived yesterday. America is nice but by now I feel as if I'm Italian. When can I see you? I have so much to tell you. I bet you do too. I've done some accounting and I feel like getting back to work. Give me a call as soon as you hear this message."

Beep.

"It's Barbara. Vacation's over. I'm back in Milan. Do you have anything equally interesting for me? Kisses to you, you fantastic man."

Beep.

"It's Laura. Call me."

"*Call me* my ass, you stupid bitch."

The thought escaped me aloud, instinctively, in a hiss. I hear an amused comment in response.

"Is that how you'll treat me, when I leave a message on your answering machine?"

I turn around and there, standing in front of me, is Carla. She found the clothes I told her about and now she's

108

completely changed, however casual her clothes might be. It's another world, another story, another movie.

Another woman.

She's wearing a pair of jeans and has a pair of light-colored suede *campero* boots on her feet. A light blue T-shirt and a canvas jacket the same color as her boots. Her wet hair is combed back and her eyes stand out like colorful handkerchiefs lying on the snow.

"I feel like a cowboy. How do I look?"

I stand there speechless, without answering her question. I'm only causing myself pain, but I can't do anything else. I'm just captivated by the thought of what she'll look like after a hairdresser, a makeup artist, and a designer have done some work on her. The minute I utter these thoughts in my mind, I realize I'm hopelessly lost.

CHAPTER 8

We step out onto the landing and I pull the door shut behind us. As soon as my door closes, the one across the landing clicks and swings open. The figure of Lucio appears between door and doorjamb.

"Winners, placers, and showers."

Carla is baffled. I smile. It's the solution to the cryptic clue that I wrote on a slip of paper and slid under Lucio's door, yesterday.

Forms of luck: horses that come in first, gold mines, or where a losing team is sent after the game (7, 7, 3, 7)

Winners, placers, and showers, in fact. As in "win, place, or show." A horse that comes in first is a winner, a placer mine is a kind of gold mine, and a losing team is sent to the showers. But a horse that comes in second is a placer, and a horse that comes in third is a shower. I knew that Chico, the young man who takes Lucio to work and back home every day, would find it and read it to him. And that he'd solve it. It wasn't even all that hard. I decide that at this point it's incumbent upon me to make introductions.

"Carla, this is my neighbor, Lucio."

She looks at me, her brow furrowed. I wave a hand in

front of my eyes, to let her know that Lucio is blind. He steps out of the door, his dark glasses now completely justified, and takes a step toward us on the landing.

"Lucio, the young lady who's with me is named Carla."

He extends his hand.

"*Ciao*, Carla. I'm afraid you'll have to shake my hand, otherwise I might wind up looking like I'm playing blind man's bluff."

Lucio's sense of humor is capable of resolving any awkward situation. In fact, the sticky moment passes and Carla shakes his hand. He holds hers longer than necessary.

"Nice skin, Carla. If it's the same all over your body, your boyfriend is a lucky guy."

Carla laughs. I can see that Lucio is pleased with his little triumph. I'm happy for him. We're three people lost in a stormy sea and the landing is our raft. I think that we're all well aware of the fact, each in his or her own way.

And each of us tries to battle the gales with the few tattered sails available.

Lucio turns toward me, his head just slightly out of alignment. He looks as if he's hoping to get me into trouble.

"Now I've come up with one for you. It's a bear."

"Let me have it."

"*Everyone was in debt—that's permitted (seven)*. You might want to look at it written down, rather than rely on pronunciation. Though I didn't, obviously."

I repeat the puzzle in a low voice, to make sure I know it by heart. If my friend tells me that it's a bear, I'm pretty sure it won't be easy to solve. But he didn't say it was a monster, so it's not as bad as it could be.

I smack his arm with my hand, in a sign of farewell.

"*Ciao*, Lucio. I'm afraid we have to go."

He pretends to take offense and he strikes up a little melodrama.

"Fine, fine. Just leave me here to brood over my grief, without so much as a cryptic clue to solve."

I start downstairs and toss a challenge back over my shoulder to him.

"I've got a stumper all ready for you."

"Go ahead."

"Why do you persist in trying to be a musician, when you're obviously not cut out for it?"

His words waft down to me when I'm already on the second landing down.

"Bravo, spending time with you is like sitting on a sea urchin, and you have the ear of Beethoven in his later years. Carla . . ."

She is a few steps ahead of me, and she stops when she hears her name. She looks up toward the voice that is echoing down the stairwell.

"Yes?"

"If you'd like to get a better understanding of Bravo's cultural poverty this evening, just tell him to take you to Byblos, in Brera. That's where I play."

Carla catches the ball on the first bounce and joins in the game.

"Nothing on earth could make me miss it. I'll force him to go, at gunpoint, if necessary."

"Very good. I have a hunch you have more than one kind of weapon at your disposal."

Carla seems to enjoy trading wisecracks with Lucio. And so does he. I'm so used to it that it's nothing more to me than a small everyday pleasure. I push open the glass door and we walk out onto the street. There are parked cars. There

112

are children playing. Some of them have unlikely English names, like Richard or Elisabeth, followed by surnames that are so Italian that they cut off any international aspirations the moment you hear them. A number of people, male and female, watch us go by with the curiosity of those who don't know but would give anything to find out.

I decide that Carla has figured out everything at first glance.

"It doesn't strike me that you socialize much around here."

"I'm afraid I don't."

We walk around the corner of the building and head for the front gate, leaving behind us the whispers of the Quartiere Tessera.

"Bravo, what was that thing about the winners and the showers? And the other thing, the crypt—"

She stops short. I come to her rescue and complete the phrase for her.

"Cryptic clues."

While we walk to the Mini I tell her about the routine that Lucio and I have developed of challenging each other to solve word puzzles. I explain the various kinds of puzzles to her and the verbal mechanism involved in solving cryptic clues. The whole time she listens raptly. Maybe she's trying to impress my explanation on her memory.

As we talk, we get into the car and I start the engine.

"What was the one he just asked you?"

"*Everyone was in debt—that's permitted.* The answer is one word of seven letters."

She sits there, pensive, and looks around while I pull onto Via Vigevanese, heading for Milan. The light of day has changed the appearance of the houses, the industrial

113

sheds, the people. The dark streetlights are intruders in this panorama. There's traffic and there's life, exactly what I was about to lose last night, when I drove this road in the opposite direction with a man gripping a gun sitting next to me. I was sure it was going to be my last trip anywhere.

Those three puffs of air were all that was needed to change everything.

Pfft . . . pfft . . . pfft . . .

The sound of nothing really, three flaps of a wing that turned the universe upside down. I am here, I'm alive, I'm breathing, I'm driving my car with a pretty young woman sitting next to me, armed with nothing but her determination. Someone else died the death that he had meant for me, may he roast in hell. All I need to know now is why. That's the cryptic clue I want to solve: the motive. But I have no definition, no number of letters, unless *mors tua vita mea* — your death is my life — is the universal solution.

"Where are we going?"

"To take a spin through Fairyland. And to obtain some enchantments that expire at midnight."

I smile at her, with mysterious complicity. Or at least that's what I think I'm doing. With Carla I'm losing many of my bedrock certainties. She's about to answer me when the pager beeps from my belt.

After a hundred yards or so, I slow down and brake to a halt next to a phone booth. Carla says nothing but keeps turning her head to look around, perhaps wondering what magic spell it could be that just transformed the world she lives in.

"I have to make a phone call."

I step out of the car after providing an explanation to someone who hadn't asked for one. I walk into the phone

114

booth and slide the token into the slot, which gulps it down its metal throat. I dial the reliable number. They tell me that Laura was looking for me.

Her of all people. Speak of a whore and you hear the click of stiletto heels.

I slip in a second token and it seems as if everything is moving in slow motion, with the rage that's building inside me. I carve the numbers into the dial. Laura answers almost immediately.

"Hello?"

"It's Bravo. Well?"

"Well what?"

The sheer incongruity of this response makes me snap. So when I reply it's not in veiled or allusive terms.

"Tell me something, you idiot, have you lost your goddamned mind? Weren't you supposed to be at the Hotel Gallia at nine o'clock this morning? Why didn't you show up? You made me look like a complete asshole in front of somebody who could have been a gold mine."

She hesitates, unsure exactly what to say to me. Then, whatever it is, she decides that she has to tell me in person.

"Bravo, I need to see you."

Her judicious tone fails to calm my nerves. Not after what just happened.

"I think so too. I need to see you, *now*. And I hope you have a pretty damn persuasive explanation."

"Where?"

"I'll be at your front door in just a few minutes."

A pause. Then a voice edged with anxiety.

"Bravo, I'd really prefer to meet someplace else."

I'd tell her to go fuck herself for the bitch that she is, but I can't. Not right now, anyway. Laura is one of the three girls, together with Barbara and Cindy, that Bonifaci requested for his nine-million-lire evening.

I take a deep breath before I speak.

"I'm going to get my hair done by Alex, a hairdresser across from the Stazione Centrale. You know him?"

"At the Jean Louis David salon?"

"Yes."

"Of course I know him."

"That's not far from your house. Next to the salon is a bar. I'll wait for you in the back room. In twenty minutes."

"Fine. I'll be there."

I go back to the car, get in, and slam the door behind me a little harder than normal. Carla looks at me and understands from my expression that my mood has changed.

"Something wrong?"

"Nothing that can't be taken care of with a nice fat 'go fuck yourself.'"

I put the car in gear and slip back out into the flow of traffic. Carla decides that silence is the balm that will let me settle down. That is clearly to her credit and it raises her standing in my estimation.

The whole thing with Laura has really pissed me off. In my relationships with the girls who work for me, there have never been elements of constraint or extortion, just total clarity. They work with me by their own free choice and they are free to do as they like, but they can't abuse that freedom and make a fool out of me. In this case I gave but I was given nothing in return: the game is no longer fair. Maybe Tulip knew what he was doing when he smacked her around.

Still, by the time we get to Via Vittor Pisani my anger has boiled down a little bit. Just a bit, though, I decide. I guess it's wrong to make Carla the scapegoat for another person's faults. I find an unoccupied parking spot just fifty yards from where we're going. In Milan, in this neighborhood and at this time of day, that's a gift of the gods.

We get out of the car.

Carla glances at me with some curiosity. This must not be a part of the city that she spends much time in.

"Where are we going?"

"You'll see."

I start off and she follows me on the first leg of this trip through a world of enchantment, which in this specific case is the salon of a beautician and hairdresser. When we walk into Alex's shop, it's packed as usual. There are lights, scents, women under hair dryers. Young men and women in black uniforms move soundlessly across the glossy floor. This place must make more money than the casino in Opera, even though I can't imagine Tano Casale cutting anyone's hair. Their throat, sure, but not their hair. Carla is attracted and at the same time perhaps a bit intimidated. I don't imagine that a place like this—where a shampoo and a permanent cost more than she gets paid for a week's work—is something she's accustomed to.

Alex, who's busy advising a young man on the best way to waste time on a matron whose face looks like a hen has been walking on it, sees me, and his face lights up. He tells the young man to wait, leaves the woman to her fate, and walks over to us. He's a tall, skinny man, with the little remaining hair on his head chopped very short, indifferent to a case of incipient baldness that's already as bad as it's likely to get. He's a likable guy. He knows how to treat people and how to do his job. It's no accident that he's one of the most sought-after hairdressers and makeup artists in the worlds of television, fashion, and advertising. And

117

even though he's no male model, he's very successful with women.

"*Ciao*, Bravo. It's about time you showed up here. Shall we give a trim to that bush you have on your head?"

"No, I'm not here for my hair. I need you to be in top form today."

"I'm always in top form."

At this point it strikes me that it's time to tell my companion just what's happening. Even though she must already have guessed, because her eyes are sparkling.

"Carla, let me introduce you to Alex, who's about to turn you into a goddess."

At last I explain to Alex the reason for our presence in his salon.

"You need to take good care of this young lady. Use all the tools in your tool kit—money is no object—and lavish your talent on her."

Ever since my friend came over to speak with us, he's clearly been evaluating Carla. Perhaps, just out of professional habit, he'd already been considering how to cut this diamond in the rough. Now that he knows he's about to be given a free hand with her, he seems to be intrigued by the challenge that I've just issued.

For him, this too is a cryptic clue.

I've been filed away for later. I no longer exist. Alex's mind is already humming with activity, summoning all his experience and all his imagination for the job. He reaches a hand out to Carla.

"Come on. Let's see what we can do."

He drags her away without so much as a glance at me. As Carla moves off, she turns to look back at me with a puzzled expression. I make a meaningful gesture with my hands, as if to recommend that she relax, but also signaling my helplessness in the face of Alex's creative fury.

I'm left standing alone.

I leave the shop. Behind me, photographs taped to the shop windows show models, both male and female, pouting for the camera in their new hairdos. It's a few dozen steps to the neighboring bar. It's a newly renovated place, with some aspirations to architectural style, but made ordinary and nondescript by an excess of mirrors and chrome. At lunchtime they serve hot and cold lunches to the neighborhood office workers. The rush has ended and the place is only sparsely populated. Men and women with all the trappings of executives, running a little behind schedule, indulge in a coffee or a snack.

A waitress takes her own sweet time before bestowing the privilege of her attention on me, which is as meager as her charms. I've finished my coffee and I'm smoking my second cigarette when Laura shows up. When she walks in, a hush falls over the café. It's fleeting, almost imperceptible, but significant. She's dressed in an understated manner: a pair of jeans, a blouse, the same jacket she had on last night. Still, she's stunning, and she captures people's eyes and imaginations. The few women present look at her with envy, while all the men reserve their envy for me. I could eliminate that envy by standing up and saying just a few words. *If you like her and you want her, and of course if you can afford her, step right up: I'm the man to see.*

But I stay where I am and I watch Laura as she pulls back the chair across from me.

"*Ciao*, Bravo."

I don't even give her a chance to sit all the way down before I launch into her.

119

"Well? And don't answer 'Well what?' again or I'll have to throw acid in your face."

She takes off her dark glasses. Her eyes look drawn, as if she hadn't gotten much sleep last night. Whether that's because she cried all night or fucked someone all night, I don't give a damn. What I care about is that she was supposed to fuck someone this morning and that she failed to.

"But didn't you see the television news today, at one o'clock?"

"No. Should I have?"

She lowers her voice a little.

"Tulip was found murdered, near a quarry, on the far side of Trezzano. Three bullet holes from a handgun . . ."

She leaves the sentence open-ended and looks at me. I realize the question that's lurking in her eyes, and at the exact same time I feel like upending the table onto her. Now I understand why she didn't want me to come to her house.

She's afraid of me.

"Laura, have you lost your mind? Do you think that I did it?"

"You told me that you were going to take care of things with him. And this morning they find him, murdered. What else would I think?"

"Did you talk to anyone about this?"

"No."

"Ah, good. Don't say a word. I took care of the situation between you and Menno by setting up an agreement with someone who has the authority to order him to stop bothering you. And it cost me quite a bit of money. That's all. I didn't even know that he had been killed."

The lie floats across the table, lightly, with a muffled sound.

Pfft . . . pfft . . . pfft . . .

Laura believes me and looks relieved. I lay it on a little thicker.

"We've known each other a long time. We've done a lot of good work together. Do I strike you as the kind of person who goes around shooting people? Have you ever seen me carrying a weapon?"

Laura seems entirely reassured. Now she feels that in some sense she has to answer for what she thought.

"No, of course not. But put yourself in my shoes. When I saw that report on TV, I—"

But it's not over. There's something else she needs to answer for.

"You saw the news report at one o'clock. You had an appointment at the Gallia at nine o'clock this morning. So Tulip's murder had nothing at all to do with your decision not to go."

Laura lowers her eyes. When she looks up, they're glistening with repressed tears. She sits there for a few seconds, without speaking, as if searching for the right words. When she does, they surprise me.

"Bravo, I'm twenty-six years old and I'm a whore."

She raises a hand to halt any objection I might make.

"You can call me whatever you want. There are plenty of words to make it seem a little less harsh. *Hostess, escort, arm candy*. But the facts don't change. I am and I remain a whore. And after some more time goes by, I'm going to wake up one day and discover I've become an old whore. I just don't want my life to end that way."

I put a halt to this headlong race along what appears to be the road to Damascus.

"Does that cabaret artist, Giorgio Fieschi, have anything to do with all this?"

That name falls between us like a bomb devastating its target. Laura sniffs and rummages through her purse for a Kleenex. She blows her nose, which gives her an excuse not to look me in the eye.

"Yes, he does."

No, please, Laura, I beg of you. Don't play the role of the whore who's been seduced and redeemed. Not here, not now . . .

I keep my thoughts to myself. I wait for the rest. Because the rest is coming without fail.

"I spent last night with him. Nothing like this has ever happened to me before. So beautiful and so unexpected, I mean. It made it clear to me that I want to try something different, I want to stop living this way."

Laura has butterflies wheeling in her eyes.

"Bravo, I think I'm in love."

I feel like leaping to my feet and screaming.

In order to get a criminal psychotic who was ruining your life off your back, I came this close to being murdered last night. And while I was literally digging my own grave, you were screwing that little punk cabaret artist. And now you tell me that you think you're in love? I'd at least like you to be sure about it, considering what it's cost me so far . . .

But I neither leap to my feet nor do I begin shouting or, for that matter, beating her black-and-blue. Instead I remain seated, motionless, and I'm deeply impressed with this display of self-control. It's not much satisfaction, but it's the one thing I can cling to in this bleak moment. As I regain control over my temper, I'm surprised to find myself remembering the sound of that young man's laughter as he left the Ascot last night with his group of friends. They were young and talented, which made them the kings of the world.

I look at Laura and I can see she's lost in her dream, a dream that like all dreams will eventually fade in the light of dawn. Suddenly, everything strikes me as cruel and endearing and ridiculous, all at the same time.

And I see the solution to Lucio's cryptic clue.

Everyone was in debt—that's permitted (7)

Allowed . . .

A smile appears on my lips.

"That's fine, Laura. Have it your way."

"What?"

"You heard me loud and clear. Follow the path you've chosen. Your life belongs to you and so on and so forth, as they say in the movies."

"You're not mad at me?"

"Would it matter if I was?"

"Bravo, I—"

"I don't think there's anything more to say. If you change your mind, you know how to find me. Just try to be happy."

That's what they say in the movies, along with all the other clichés. But it strikes me as pointless to emphasize it again. Laura puts her sunglasses back on and stands up. I can hear a note of relief in her voice, relief interwoven with good intentions.

"*Ciao*, Bravo. Thanks."

"*Ciao*, Laura. Take it easy."

I watch her as she leaves, and I have plenty of company. At the same time, I flip through my mental Rolodex of all the girls I know, trying to figure out which one would be her ideal replacement for the job at Bonifaci's house. Once she's walked out the door, I toss a handful of change on the

123

table—the price of an espresso and a small additional tip. I walk out of the bar and the end of one relationship and into the beauty salon and the beginning of another. I'm not sure what to expect from Carla and what to expect from myself. I've always navigated by sight, and once again I'm going to have to rely on my instincts.

When I walk back into Alex's shop, the young men and women are all busy serving the customers who are occupying the chairs in front of the mirrors. Neither Alex nor Carla are anywhere to be seen in the main area of the salon. I take a seat and wait, smoking cigarettes and leafing through magazines filled with the love affairs of actresses and actors. Some of the faces I see pictured in the magazines belong to people I've met in this shop. I know that some of the stories are completely invented. I have my doubts about the others. After about half an hour, Alex's voice draws me away from an article that was doing its best to palm off a female singer's comfortable shirt as a maternity smock.

"All done. You be the judge."

I stand up and turn around.

When I see her, I think to myself that before leaving the shop I really should have said a final farewell to Carla, because I was never going to see her again. The person in front of me is someone entirely different and entirely new, so luminous that she outshines the spotlights that the interior decorator has scattered throughout the salon. Her hair, dyed honey blond and cut short, frames a face that has now become the only possible setting in which to admire those jewel-like eyes. Her gaze makes you yearn to know the magic word that will unlock the world behind those eyes. As I watch her, I'm like a glider launched into flight through a turbulent sky dotted with air pockets. I think too many different things,

124

and all at the same time. I decide to focus my attention on just one thing: the easiest, the most certain, and therefore the most despicable. At once an evasion and a solution to a problem. Now there's one thing I know for sure: I've found the woman who can take Laura's place at the appointment tomorrow.

CHAPTER 9

I don't know what I'm going to do with it, but one thing is certain: I've created a memory for myself today. I find myself thinking about it again as we walk out of Bargagli, loaded down with bags and boxes. There's a glow inside Carla that she shares with the world. She's filled with a magnificent excitement. That excitement is clearly contagious, to judge from the glances of the people we meet. The eyes of the men, as they mentally strip off all the new clothing I just bought her, are a promising indicator, for now and for the future. The things you can read in men's eyes, in this kind of situation, are a pretty good thermometer reading of a woman's potential. I had an excellent confirmation of this approach just a few hours ago, when Laura walked into the bar. I have the same confirmation now with Carla, in case I need it. As for myself, I find myself watching my behavior as if from some external vantage point: observing the way I walk and the things I do. I can see that I'm wary, uncertain about what to expect from this woman who's walking beside me as we stroll along Corso Vittorio Emanuele, leaving a wake of perfume behind her that erases everything else she's been in her life. And everything that *I've* been in my life up till now.

Carla turns to look at me, with those eyes that are a twin incitement to crime.

"I really feel like Cinderella."

"Not anymore. You're going to the Prince's ball."

I haven't explained to her yet that actually the Fairy Godmother is going to be played by a son of a bitch; that Prince Charming's ball has been canceled, so she'll be going to a sumptuous villa outside Lesmo to do dances of quite a different sort—not the waltz, anyway. Still, she asked me to make her what she's going to be and to help her do what she's going to do, even though I haven't been able to shake a certain uneasiness ever since she did.

I'm not accustomed to certain complications. I'm more accustomed to clear-cut situations.

This dramatic piece of self-mockery, which would have overjoyed Lucio, makes me smile. Carla assumes that my smile is meant for her. She smiles back at me and catches me off guard.

"You spent a lot of money on all these gifts."

In order to get us both back home safe and sound, I decide that I should make one thing very clear, so we can both keep our feet on the ground.

"I'm not accustomed to giving gifts. This is just an advance against your future emoluments."

Carla looks at me in surprise, and then bursts out laughing.

"Emolu . . . what?"

"It means earnings."

"Professor, what kind of words do you use? You make me feel like a donkey. Maybe I ought to read some of your books myself."

I feel like explaining to her that books are a curse, actually. Optimists believe that reading books helps them fight their ignorance, while realists are certain of only one thing, that books give them proof of their ignorance. The measurement of what people don't know is actually the only true way of telling them apart. Age, money, and appearance mean nothing. The real difference is there.

Life depends on the things you know.

My pager distracts me from my ambitions as a tutor and mentor, alerting me to the fact that I need to make a phone call. I leave Carla to window-shop and I walk over to a phone booth. I drop in a token and I call the switchboard number.

In exchange, I'm given another phone number, without a name to go with it. When I call, the voice that answers is impersonal and detached, and in the background I hear a faint clatter of dishes and the hum of a crowd.

"Bar La Torre."

"Bravo speaking. I was told to call this number."

"Hold on."

The sound of a receiver set down on a counter. The steps of someone approaching. Then a voice I know comes out of the phone.

"Bravo?"

"Yes."

"It's Tano."

I should have guessed that that man would never give me a private number to call. The place he's talking to me from now must be one of the many public safe houses from which he conducts his business.

"Speak to me."

"I'll be ready for that operation we discussed starting tomorrow."

"Very good. It might be for the day after tomorrow. I'll talk to the person and let you know."

"Where are you going to be tonight?"

"I'm having dinner at the Ricovero Attrezzi, a restaurant on Via—"

"Yeah, I know the place. One of my men will get in touch with you to work out the details."

"How will I recognize him?"

"He'll recognize you."

"All right."

A pause on the other end of the line. Then the tone of voice I know changes almost imperceptibly. I don't know if it's done intentionally or not, but it seems just a shade more menacing.

"Bravo, did you hear about Salvo?"

Hear about him? I actually watched as he . . .

"Yes. Nasty story."

"Yeah. It really was a nasty story."

Another pause.

"You don't have anything you want to tell me?"

"No."

The third pause doesn't promise anything good. Nor do the words that come after it.

"Okay. We'll talk about it later."

"Fine. Whenever you like."

A click from the other end of the line tells me that the conversation is over for now. When the time comes, however, it'll resume and I'll have to explain a thing or two to Tano Casale. From what I know about the way the world works, I doubt that Tulip's death has chipped away much at Tano's emotions. But Tulip was one of his men, and according to the rules of a certain milieu, whoever killed Tulip has disrespected Tano. And no boss can afford to put up with that, whatever the motive.

I take advantage of the phone to call Barbara and Cindy

and invite them to dinner. I tell them to meet us at the restaurant, and that it's a special occasion. I do my best to keep my mind off it, but when I get back to Carla the whole thing with Tulip must still be showing on my face.

"Something wrong? Bad news?"

I try to go back to the state of mind I was in just a short while ago. I don't know how successfully, but that's the hand I'm playing. Carla understands and agrees to play along.

"Not at all. Now that you're stunning and enviably elegant, let me show you off a little. I'm going to take you out to dinner with two girls you should get to know."

"Do they work for you?"

"Yes. Tomorrow they're going to a party with some very important people."

I look at her and I wait a beat. Everyone has a right to a drumroll now and then.

"And you're going with them."

Carla looks up at me with a jerk.

"Me? Tomorrow?"

Suddenly the smile is gone. Cinderella is going to have to go back to doing work that involves getting her hands dirty. It seems odd to me that someone who agreed to go to bed with Daytona for a few bucks should have a problem with this, but the world is a strange place. And it's the people in it that make it so strange.

I confirm it.

"Yes, tomorrow. If it matters to you, it'll put 2.1 million lire in your pocket."

"Shit."

In that instinctive exclamation I can hear all the years of ramshackle housing—the truly old houses of old Milan, not the ones that have been renovated to create romantic apartments for the wealthy in the quaint old parts of the city. I can sense a world in which rent and utilities come due every month promptly, while paychecks are far less predictable. Expenses that drive the poor inexorably out of the center of the city and into the outskirts, crossing the boundary between living life and merely scraping by.

I've never cared much about all this. But it's different with Carla. I don't know why, and I'd just as soon not ask. Maybe I'm just a sick individual and my few emotional attachments suffer from the same sickness.

Lucio, Carla, me.

Three human beings who are going to spend the rest of the time remaining to them destroying and reconstructing themselves, day by day, until one day they find themselves in pieces on the ground, without the strength or the will to put those pieces back together. As we walk to the car, I abandon those thoughts and continue Carla's education. It's better for her to know what's going to be awaiting her and how she's going to have to behave.

"Tomorrow night you're going to be in a very delicate situation. There are going to be very important men there, maybe people whose pictures you've seen in the newspaper. But as far as you're concerned, they have to remain perfect strangers, before and after you meet them. Is that clear?"

She nods her head.

"The foundation of my business is the fact that I've always been able to guarantee the people who work with me absolute discretion. That means that in a certain milieu, word of mouth brings me customers. Reputation means money. For you and for me."

This little speech was necessary. Just like others that I'd deliver later, much cruder and more laden with details. For

131

the moment, I've done my best to use language that wouldn't make her feel like too much of a whore. The relationship with the work she'd be doing, as Laura taught me, is a personal matter. My job ends outside the bedroom door.

If for no other reason than that, inside, I wouldn't have a lot to offer.

She seems to be lost in thought. She's staring into the middle distance, and I have no idea what she's actually visualizing. If what I'm seeing on her face is hesitation, it would probably be better to clear things up immediately, before it's too late.

"Are you having second thoughts? Changing your mind?"

Carla looks at me in that way she has, which creates a new vacuum inside me every time.

"No, I'm not having second thoughts. It's just that I'm discovering a new and unexpected world, Bravo. It's not clean, it's not honest, and it's totally unjustified. I'll earn in one night what I used to earn in a year. And I'm sick and tired of resoled shoes, of hairdressers in fourth-floor walk-ups, of living in a building where the smell of cooking seems to have seeped into the plaster."

In her voice I can sense all of those things. I feel as if I can see them and smell them as she speaks.

"I want a real home, nice clothes, a car, and some things I can rely on. I don't care what I have to give in exchange. My dreams, if there are any, can come later. For now, there's nothing but bare necessities and things I want to forget. And I intend to wipe them out, all of them, one by one."

She smiles. But there's no happiness on her lips, only bitter traces of regret.

"Today, thanks to you, I learned three things. The first thing is that I can be beautiful too. The second thing is that, for better or worse, I can decide how to live my life. The third thing . . ."

She falls silent. I push to know more. Not out of curiosity, just a strange and sadistic form of personal euthanasia.

"The third thing?"

She smiles in a different way and steps close to me. She sets all her bags down on the sidewalk. She stands back up and in her high heels she's almost as tall as me. She tilts her face up, throws her arms around my neck, and places her lips on mine. She closes her eyes as she does it. She stays there, motionless, forever. Then she pulls away and time resumes flowing normally.

"The third thing, if you don't mind, I'll keep to myself for right now."

She picks up the bags again and starts off, leaving me rooted to the sidewalk, alone in a way I hadn't thought possible. I catch up with her, because I can't do anything else. We walk in silence, side by side, looking at the world while the world looks back, until we reach my car. I open the trunk and add the bags and packages to the ones already stowed away. If I consider myself as a businessman, I can just think of this as an investment for the future.

We get in the car and we pull away from the Galleria del Corso and the Crota Piemunteisa, a bar where I once ate about two metric tons of frankfurter and sauerkraut sandwiches, when I first came to Milan. Not because I was a snob, but because other people were snubbing me.

Just to lighten the atmosphere, I steer the conversation onto more worldly topics.

"Are you hungry?"

"Starving. Where are we going to eat?"

"In one of the restaurants that I find it necessary to

frequent, from time to time. We have an appointment there with Cindy and Barbara, the girls I told you about."

She instinctively asks the question.

"Is it expensive?"

She said it in such an apprehensive tone of voice that this time I'm the one who bursts out laughing.

"Don't worry about it. It's my treat. Moreover, I herewith authorize you to assume that the days of packing a sandwich before you leave the house are over."

I give her time to metabolize what I just told her. It's important that she believe. Confidence in the future makes your eyes shine, and it gives you a certain strength. Carla needs that strength right now the way she needs oxygen. Confidence is allure and allure is power.

And power equals money.

I talk to her about practical things to erase memories and ward off sadness.

"It seems to me that you no longer want to go home. Until you find a better place to live, you could stay at the residence in Piazzale Principessa Clotilde. It's very popular with models these days. It's a good showcase for the work we have to do."

I forestall any further financial analysis.

"And don't ask me how much it costs. I guarantee that you'll be able to afford it."

She looks at me. I can't decipher her expression.

"Can I stay at your house again tonight?"

Perhaps I wait a little longer than I need to before answering. And maybe I ask the wrong question.

"What for?"

"No reason. I just don't feel like being alone. Too many things have happened, and all too quickly."

I'm surprised to hear my voice giving permission for something I would never have allowed any other person in any other case.

"All right. Tomorrow, while you're working, I'll find you a place to stay."

Carla relaxes and smiles.

"I'm hungry and tonight, since it's on you, I want to have a feast. You know I've never tasted champagne?"

We laugh heartily at the thought and it occurs to me that to someone watching us from outside we must look like an ordinary couple, our car full of packages, heading home after an afternoon shopping spree. What we really are is tucked away deep inside, and we have the whole evening ahead of us to avoid thinking about it. Meanwhile, an oddly indulgent traffic flow has allowed us to move quickly down Via Ripamonti and to drive past the intersection with Via Antonini. We keep driving and take a left turn. A short distance later we're parked outside a renovated farmhouse where a sign confirms that we have arrived at the restaurant called Ricovero Attrezzi — the Toolshed. The cars parked in the dim light are nearly all powerful and expensive. I can guess that later this evening some of these cars are likely to be pulling into the parking lot of a casino somewhere outside the town of Opera. Or maybe they'll be parking at the Charly Max or they might be double-parked outside Nepentha, with a lavish tip left to the attendant to make sure the car's parked properly as soon as a space opens up. I slip my pathetic little Mini between a couple of grown-up cars, handing a thousand lire to Nino, the parking attendant, so he'll keep an eye on it.

We walk into the place, and Carla stops just inside the door. Her entrance was like tossing a bowling ball at a cluster of pins. I don't know if it was a strike, but she definitely knocked down quite a few. Within a couple of seconds dozens of eyes swivel to stare at her.

I'm used to it.

But she isn't.

I take her arm and I can feel that she's slightly tense. I smile at her and she can sense the amusement in my voice.

"It's all just like I told you it would be, isn't it? You just have to get used to it. Come on. Barbara and Cindy are already here."

The girls are sitting in a small room in the back, visible at a diagonal angle from the front door. I walk ahead of Carla. Passing by sharp glances and silverware, we make our way through the main dining room of the restaurant, furnished in a style that matches the age and nature of the building. Wood, amber lights, slightly rough plaster in a light yellow hue, oaken tables. As in all fashionable restaurants, the food is no good at all and the prices are astronomical. This is the magic of Milan by night, mysterious alchemies that transform lousy food into solid gold. Maybe many years ago this really was a toolshed, but whoever renovated it turned it into a shed where they hang rich people out to dry. Actually, now that I think about it, many of those rich people really are nothing but tools. So in a way, its original purpose has been preserved.

As we walk over to the table, I can see Cindy and Barbara unstitch the clothes on Carla's back and count the money in her purse.

By the time we sit down, she's already been identified and cataloged as a dangerous rival, although neither of them would admit it, even under torture. But in this case the point of reference is me, and none of them have ever had any reason to complain, about their pride or their pocketbooks. Of course, certain minor jealousies can be tolerated, especially if there's caviar and champagne to go with them.

I make the introductions.

"Carla, meet Cindy and Barbara."

Barbara is a brunette, a daughter of the Mediterranean, with dark eyes and an olive complexion. She is self-possessed, with a magnificent figure and a cheerful temperament. Cindy is the diametric opposite. She's tall and slender, with nice curves where it counts, fair-skinned, with a blond pageboy and blue eyes. She's a little neurotic and slightly introverted but, I am told, just unbelievable between the sheets.

Voice of the people, voice of Eros itself.

The two girls both look at me with a very similar expression, tacitly asking the same question. I assuage their concern and curiosity by completing the introductions.

"Girls, this is Carla. From now on, she's working with us."

They're evidently relieved, to some extent. This means that the conversation can at least be freewheeling, no matter what there might be to say. There's no time to add anything more. A waiter promptly shows up at our table bearing four leather folders containing our menus. Before he leaves, I order mineral water and a bottle of champagne, as promised. Carla watches what the other girls do and behaves accordingly. I look around at the three women's faces as they immerse themselves in the reading of the menu to determine whether to order fish or fowl. Restaurants are one of the few places where it's possible to establish with confidence whether it's one thing or the other.

While the girls study the menu, I study the dining room. There are a couple of television personalities, a few leading celebrities of the Milanese milieu, and lots of people I don't recognize, possibly provincials who've made the long journey into the city just to see and be seen.

At the far end of the room are two women, alone, eating dinner. One of them has her back to me. The other has salt-and-pepper hair. She's pretty, a very attractive forty-five-year-old, nicely attired in a dark outfit that must have cost a fortune. Her complexion speaks eloquently of beauty masks and Caribbean sunlight. Her name is Margherita Boni and I know her very well. The name means a husband who's almost always away for work and a huge amount of money to spend on her pastimes. She nods her head in my direction and swivels her gaze toward the door of the bathroom, on the wall to the right of where I'm sitting. Then she stands up, picks up a clutch bag from the chair next to hers, crosses the room, and slips into the restroom.

"Order whatever you like, just no onions and no garlic. I want your breath to be sweet as a rose tomorrow. When I get back I'll explain everything you need to know. Order me a steak, blood rare, and a salad."

I stand up and I join Margherita in the bathroom. She's waiting for me in front of the bathroom sinks, checking her makeup, which has absolutely no need of a touch-up. I doubt that she invited me there to snort a line of coke. She knows I never touch the stuff. I find out the real reason immediately, and it's exactly what I thought.

"Who is that girl?"

I understand exactly who she means, but I'm feeling lively this evening and I sense that my prey is about to walk into the trap. And the trap is poised to snap shut on her checking account.

"What girl?"

"Don't act stupid. The girl who walked in the front door with you."

I move over next to her and start washing my hands. Our conversation continues between our reflected images in the mirror.

"Her name is Carla."

"I want her."

Margherita is a lesbian and on more than one occasion I've supplied her with the toys she requires to satisfy this innocent diversity of hers. There are plenty of girls in my network who are AC/DC, or, as we say in Italian, who run on both sail and steam. But where Carla is concerned, we haven't yet established how far she's willing to go.

I let my uncertainty become hers.

"She's a new girl and I don't know her well enough to be sure. What about Barbara, the brunette: Don't you like her? She's bisexual."

"The other two are local talent and nothing more. They're pretty, but it's stamped on their faces just what they are. Carla's a dream, and I want her to come true."

Now the preliminaries are over. It's time to talk business.

"If I can swing it, she'll cost you."

"Has money ever been a problem?"

"I'd have to say no."

"Very good. I'll wait to hear from you at the usual number."

She picks up her clutch bag from the bathroom counter and leaves, while I remain behind to consider my expression in the mirror.

It's the eternal conflict between having and being.

Some time ago somebody heavily curtailed my possibility of being. What remains to me is the possibility of having. Which is a pretty miserable surrogate, unless you own half

139

the world. But even in that case, sooner or later you'll wind up running into the person who owns the other half, and then things turn ugly. I feel like I'm the owner of that thin line that marks the boundary, and nothing more, for now.

Sooner or later I'll have everything I'm looking for, and when that happens, I can go back to being, to some extent.

I dry my hands and toss the hand towel into a burnished metal receptacle. In one corner of the bathroom is a phone for clients to use. I slip a token into the slot and dial Remo Frontini's number. I looked him up in the phone book and committed the number to memory, the way I have all the others.

He picks up on the third ring.

"Hello?"

"Signore Frontini?"

He must be unaccustomed to being addressed in those terms, because his answer, when it comes, is a little hesitant.

"Yes. Who's this?"

"This is Bravo, your neighbor. We talked the other evening, do you remember?"

"Yes, of course."

"Excellent. I just wanted to let you know that the transaction we discussed can be completed the day after tomorrow. Does that work for you?"

There's a hesitation. A long pause. I think I must have ruined this decent man's sleep, involving him in something that he feels is much bigger than him. He must be frightened for his part, especially because I went a little heavy on the threat that pulling out might have some unpleasant consequences.

I do my best to reassure him.

"Don't worry about a thing. It's going to go smoothly and

you're going to be a person with no more uncertainties in life."

"Okay. What do I have to do?"

"Around eleven o'clock you'll be outside the bank where you have your safe-deposit box, with a photocopy of the winning lottery ticket to prove that you actually have it. In exchange, you'll be given the money we agreed upon. Once you've made sure that it's the correct amount, you'll go into the bank, you'll place the money in the safe-deposit box, and only then will you take the original ticket and hand it over to me. Do you think that this procedure ensures your safety?"

The voice that comes through the receiver after due consideration strikes me as relieved. Maybe he too had been trying to think of a way to make sure he couldn't be made the victim of some unpleasant machinations, and this solution is probably better than anything he was able to come up with.

"It seems good to me. The bank is the Credito Romagnolo, on Via Roma, in Cesano Boscone."

I'm about to hang up, but then I decide that I still owe him a little advice, whether or not he can make use of it.

"Just one more thing, Signore Frontini."

"Yes?"

"You know, a fortune has rained down on you out of a clear blue sky. Do your best not to ruin it for yourself. Take it easy with the money. Don't change your life from one day to the next. Just go on living the same way for a while, let the world forget about things, and then move away, maybe to another city if you can. That sum of money can be a nice gift for you and your wife, but it can also mean a very nice future for your children."

There's a brief, silent moment of thought on the other end of the line.

"I think I understand."

"I hope you do. Have a good evening, Signore Frontini. Sleep tight. You're going to be a wealthy man very soon."

As I hang up, a fleck of remorse arrives to flap its black wings over my certainties. It's not something that happens very often, but this man has won my sympathy from the minute I met him, in all his disarming humanity. I feel as if I'm standing surety for him with myself and with the others, guaranteeing that nothing's going to go horribly wrong.

I leave the bathroom and return to the table. Here I'm greeted by the awkward gazes of the three young women and the smirking expression of the man sitting with them in my chair. He's a guy of average height, skinny, with a dark shirt and jacket that both need dry cleaning and pressing. His skin is slightly pockmarked by adolescent acne, he has an aquiline nose, and his broad, thin mouth needs only the hint of a smile to resemble the Jolly Joker. I know him very well, too, for a couple of reasons.

The first is the work that I do for a living; the second is the work that he does.

He's Stefano Milla, a detective working out of the police station on Via Fatebenefratelli.

CHAPTER 10

When we get to Byblos, Lucio is already performing.

He's wearing his sunglasses and his hair is unkempt as usual. He's sitting on a stool in the middle of a raised dais, his back to the wall, under an array of spotlights that he can't see. I've always wondered whether the lighting of a stage is designed to put the star at the center of attention or whether it actually serves to keep him from seeing whether the room is empty or full. I imagine, as a person who lives in a reassuring penumbra, that both options can be a source of considerable anxiety. In any case, Lucio is the least likely person on earth to help me solve this riddle. I would guess that his relationship with his audience is much more olfactory than visual.

On the floor behind him is a stand with a classical Spanish guitar perched on it. What he's holding in his lap right now is a Martin acoustic, on which he's playing a very commendable personal version of Traffic's "John Barleycorn."

Lucio plays very well; he has both technique and heart. Although he doesn't have a standard voice, it can transmit the kind of feeling that in a club like this one silences the noises in the room.

To keep from making noise during the performance, Carla and I stand by the bar until the performer is done with the song and has received the applause he deserves. Then we head for an empty table more or less in the middle of the room, the boundary between people who are there to listen to music and people who are there to drink and talk about everything without realizing that they're actually talking about nothing.

I check with Carla.

"Is this table okay with you?"

She simply nods her head and sits down. Her eyes are focused on the stage. It's clear that she loves music. I saw the expression with which she listened to the piece while we were waiting at the counter.

Without a word, Lucio replaces his acoustic guitar with the classical Spanish guitar and begins a piece by José Feliciano entitled "La Entrada de Bilbao." The notes emerge and ricochet as Lucio's fingers pinch and torment the nylon and copper of the guitar strings. I sit, relaxed, waiting to order my drink. I listen to the music, I look at Carla, and I do my best to put some order into everything that happened at the restaurant.

The club vanishes, along with the music and all the spectators.

I'd known Stefano Milla for a long time. My relationship was not one of friendship but merely a professional collaboration, if I can use the term. The kind of collaboration that could take place between someone like me and a policeman willing to turn a blind eye. And willing, when necessary, to put in a good word so that someone else might turn an equally blind eye. Not necessarily true corruption, just a very handy seat belt in case of a head-on collision. Which could never have been truly dangerous for either of us, because I always drove at very slow speeds. In exchange I would let him have a small bundle of cash from time to time so that he could pay for whatever his vices were — or else I let him have an evening with one of my girls.

I could never tell which of the two expense accounts pleased him more.

But finding him right in front of me at the Ricovero Attrezzi was a surprise. Which I did my best to conceal as I walked toward the table.

Milla was on his feet.

"I need to talk with you. What do you say we step outside for a couple of minutes?"

The tone of voice warned me that I hadn't pulled a Jolly Joker out of the deck this time.

"That'll be fine."

Carla shot me a glance that contained more than one question mark. I reassured her with a quick facial expression. Then I excused myself from the table and followed the back of my visitor's neck to the front door.

In the half-light of the parking lot we walked a short distance to make sure we weren't within earshot of the attendant, who was leaning against the wall on our right, smoking a cigarette. Once we'd come even with my car, Milla told me what he wanted.

"There's something you and I need to do together."

"What?"

"You know better than I do. All I'm supposed to do is guard a briefcase and make sure that a certain envelope makes it safe and sound to its intended destination."

That caught me off guard. It never occurred to me that Stefano Milla might be on Tano Casale's payroll, nor would I have expected him to admit it so openly.

Perhaps all this appeared on my face. The policeman must have taken my bafflement for a judgment of his actions.

145

He ventured into one of those unsolicited self-justifications that do nothing more than to tell you what an unpleasant traveling companion a guilty conscience must be on certain stretches of highway.

"Don't act surprised, Bravo. And don't you dare lecture me. You're the last person on earth to even think of preaching."

I shrugged a shoulder and lit a cigarette.

"What you do is none of my business. I'm not looking for trouble and I don't want to make trouble for anyone else."

"Ah, outstanding. A wise policy. So, what do we do?"

"Meet me the day after tomorrow at eleven o'clock in the morning on Via Roma, in Cesano Boscone, outside the branch office of the Credito Romagnolo."

"That's it?"

"That's it. I need to see somebody and then you can hand over what you're supposed to hand over. Anything else?"

He waited before answering. I realized that he wasn't hesitating, just studying me. Or the expression I'd be wearing after the question he was about to ask.

"There might be something else. Did you hear about what happened to Salvatore Menno?"

This was the second person who had mentioned his name to me that same evening, and with practically the same words. It was just that I couldn't quite determine in what capacity Milla was approaching the topic. Was he asking me about it as a representative of the law or as a man who has let personal self-interest drag him over to the opposite side? I looked up to sniff the air, and I didn't like the scent I picked up one little bit.

"Sure. It was on TV."

"I heard that recently you and he had had some disagreements."

146

A derisive voice came charging through my memories and echoed in my head, as if Tulip were standing in front of me, instead of Milla.

"Dig. Even though your nice suit will get a little wrinkled. If you want, when you're done, I'll send it to the cleaners."

And then those muffled noises

Pfft . . . pfft . . . pfft . . .

that traded life for death, one in place of the other, like pieces on a checkerboard.

"That guy was a psychotic bastard. I don't know who knocked him off, but whoever it was probably had a perfectly good motive."

"I can agree with you on that point."

Milla stopped for a second. When he went on, his pockmarked face in the half-light made his words even less reassuring.

"But the same way that certain rumors reached my ears, they might make their way to the person who's investigating his murder."

Whichever side of the law that person might be on, I thought.

The idea of getting heat from both the cops and Tano Casale wasn't at all comforting. I kept it vague and uttered a half-truth, which as such offered me only partial security.

"I didn't have anything to do with it."

"That's something that only you and Tulip know. And unfortunately he's not around anymore to confirm what you say."

"So what do you recommend I do?"

"Out of the fondness I feel for you, I recommend that you have an alibi for last night that'll hold up."

Carla's voice caught us both by surprise.

147

"Oh, he has a perfectly good alibi."

We both turned around and there she was, in front of us, lovely and distinct despite the dim light. She must have an internal light source that she carries with her, to make her eyes stand out like that.

She drew closer and stood at my side.

"We were together last night. All night long."

Milla studied her for a little while before saying anything. In his tone of voice, I could hear the proper consideration for Carla's words and appearance.

"Signorina, if it should prove to be necessary and you are willing to swear to that in front of a judge, there won't be any problems for Bravo."

"Of course I'm willing."

"Very good."

Milla raised an arm and lifted his cuff to check the time.

"I'm afraid I'm going to have to take my leave of this enchanting company. As for you, Signorina . . . ?"

"Carla. Carla Bonelli."

"There are people who would really be willing to kill to have a guarantor like you. *Arrivederci*."

Without waiting for any response to his farewell, he turned on his heel and headed off toward a cluster of cars parked along the side of the road, under the streetlights. After taking a few steps, he stopped, turned back to look at us, and stamped our travel documents with a single phrase.

"Sometimes, only the stupid and the innocent lack an alibi."

Then he left and was transformed into, progressively, the noise of a car door slamming and the same car's engine moving away into the distance. Carla and I were left alone, surrounded by shiny cars and murky situations.

148

She could cast a little light on one or two of those situations.

"There are two things I want you to tell me."

With a watchful expression Carla waited in silence until I was finished.

"One: Why did you follow me? Two: Why did you lie?"

A hint of defiance appeared in her voice, and I couldn't say whether it was intentional.

"I followed you because I don't like that guy. I lied because I do like you. And I trust you."

I thought it was best to remind her of the way matters really stood. With determined precision. Not out of honesty, but out of squalid self-interest.

"This is a case of murder."

In return, she replied with equally determined precision. Without any alternative: black or white.

"Did you do it?"

I declared my true color.

"No."

"You see? So there's no problem with saying that we spent the night together."

She turned on her heel and walked without haste toward the front door of the restaurant, from which poured a light ill suited to chase away certain shadows. I caught up with her and walked by her side, and in that short distance, for the first time in my life, I felt as if I were part of something. I thought about the psychologist who worked with me for a certain period of time after my accident. At the time, he didn't do me a bit of good, because all I wanted was to run away. I wondered what help he could give me now that my urge to flee had vanished as if by magic.

We went back to the table, where Cindy and Barbara were

finishing their first course. The champagne was already half consumed. My steak was cold and the salad had withered from the vinegar. What remained of Carla's risotto *alla milanese* had congealed into a dense yellow clump.

Cindy, who knows Stefano, lifted her light blue eyes in my direction. Her American accent turned her pasta with tomato and basil just a shade less Italian.

"Problems?"

I smiled at her, just as false as Judas Iscariot.

"Not even half a problem."

Barbara dabbed at the corners of her mouth with her napkin.

"So, are you going to tell us what this important thing is?"

I sat down and leaned toward them, lowering my voice slightly.

"Tomorrow you have an engagement in a place you and Cindy have already been. In Lesmo, at the villa of Lorenzo Bonifaci."

I gave Carla time to take in that name. The expression on her face confirmed that she knew him and that it had made a big impression on her.

"I need you to be ready at three o'clock tomorrow afternoon in Piazza San Babila, with everything you need to spend the night. A car will pick you up and take you to where you're going. The terms are excellent: three million lire apiece. The people ought to be the same as last time, because they specifically requested you."

"What about Laura?"

"She doesn't work with us anymore. She chose another path."

To keep from muddying the water, I stopped myself before telling them that Laura had opted for love. I didn't

150

want to trigger any mysterious mental mechanisms, which can be especially unpredictable in women. I doubted that Cindy and Barbara cared much about the subject, but Carla was still a mystery to me and I had to protect her.

From herself, for me.

"So I've been forced to choose one myself. Carla will replace her. Much better, I think. This is her first job, so I'm counting on you to work with her to make her feel comfortable."

Barbara started laughing. She smothered her hilarity in her napkin.

Carla turned a little edgy.

"What are you laughing about?"

Barbara waved one hand in the air, dismissively.

"Nothing, nothing. It's just that there was one guy, last time, who was crazy about the service entrance, if you know what I mean. I'm just warning you, in case you get him."

As a joke, it would have been in poor taste, to say the least, but it was no joke. It was the truth, the naked truth, and this was the only way to deal with it. I looked at Carla, to see how she responded. She took her time, looking first at one woman and then the other.

"Do you do it?"

Cindy answered for both of them.

"No violence and no whips, but other than that, for this much money, the sky's the limit."

Carla nodded her head ever so slightly. One small nod for a woman, one giant step for her earning potential and for mine.

"Then it's fine with me."

She drank the rest of the champagne in her glass, then held the empty glass out to me.

"This is good. Can I have a little more?"

151

*

The thunderous applause at the end of Lucio's performance brings me back to Byblos and wipes out the rest of an evening spent with three beautiful girls, trying my best to persuade them to become colleagues, since the word *friends* is always such a challenge.

Then the spotlight on the stage dims and is replaced by the general lighting in the room. The club's stereo system starts playing recorded music, perhaps a few decibels louder than necessary. The show is over. Lucio stands up from his stool and is immediately joined by a technician who helps him put his guitars away and step down from the stage.

Carla turns to look at me.

"I like the way he plays."

I don't have time to comment before a waiter comes over and we order two drinks at random, drinks we don't especially want. Like an old-fashioned gentleman, I lean over to light the cigarette that Carla has placed between her lips. Then I lay a hand on her shoulder.

"Excuse me for a moment."

I make my way through and around the tables and go over to where Lucio is sitting. I toss him the solution to that afternoon's cryptic clue as a token of my presence.

"Allowed. You have to see it written, not spoken out loud, as you pointed out."

At the sound of my voice, Lucio turns in my direction, without the slightest surprise.

"I knew you'd solve it. It's almost no fun anymore with you."

He bends over and checks to make sure that his guitar cases are securely fastened shut. Like all musicians, he lavishes maniacal care on his instruments. A considerable

152

portion of his personal wealth and affection are bound up in those two rigid cases.

"Have you been here long?"

"No, unfortunately we only got here in time to hear the last two songs."

"We?"

"Carla's here with me."

"She is?"

Those two words contain a great many more. An entire world. Perhaps Lucio is trying to imagine the face of a woman whose voice he has heard, but nothing more.

"The girl with the skin that smells so good."

I smile. Maybe I was right when I thought what I did about Lucio's senses. If one fails, the other four rise to the challenge.

"You wouldn't recognize her now. We've added a very nice perfume."

"French?"

"I know it's good. I didn't check its passport."

"Idiot. I'm friends with an idiot."

Lucio stands up and reaches out one hand to grab my arm. He finds me and entrusts himself to me.

"There are only two ways for you to redeem yourself in my eyes."

"How?"

"First, get me a pair of my own that work. Then take me to say hello to that divine creature."

Sometimes I catch myself thinking that if Lucio had kept his sight, the world would have lost his marvelous and bitter sense of humor. But given the terms of the exchange, I think he would gladly have refrained from sharing that gift of his with the rest of humanity.

I lead him to the table where Carla is waiting for us. Lucio reaches around for a chair.

"*Ciao*, Lucio. You were fantastic."

"*Ciao*, girl. Bravo was right."

"When he said you weren't fantastic?"

"No. He doesn't know a fucking thing about music. But he does know a thing or two about perfume. The perfume you're wearing is outstanding."

"He bought it for me, along with a number of other things."

While they're talking, I look around, astonished not to see Chico, the young man who usually takes Lucio back and forth between home and work.

"Isn't your alter ego here tonight?"

My friend puts on a pose with gesture and voice, speaking in a slight falsetto.

"My chauffeur, you mean? No, I gave him an evening to himself."

"So who's taking you home tonight?"

Lucio turns serious.

"Chico brought me here tonight, but he can't drive me home. So the owner of the club said he'd give me a ride."

Carla beats me to it.

"Come with us."

I chime in with a favorable opinion, though I point out a couple of difficulties.

"You'll have to put up with some discomfort. The car is packed with bags and packages, but we'll dig out a space for you."

"Fine. I'll take up no more room than a herring. Am I okay as I am, or would you prefer me smoked?"

Carla laughs and we all stand up. We tell the owner of the club about the change in plans; he seems relieved not to have to drive all the way to Cesano Boscone at that time of night. Since Lucio is scheduled to play at the same club tomorrow night, he entrusts the owner with his guitars, asking him to lock the room where he'll be storing the instruments.

We walk out of the club, leaving the customers and staff dealing with the tail end of the dwindling Milanese nightlife. We walk to the car and a few minutes later we're three different people traveling down the same road. The whole way, I drive and smoke in silence. I listen as my two passengers talk about music, after Carla has finished an excited description of her afternoon's shopping.

The nighttime traffic opens its arms to us, the street signs show us the way, and sooner than I expected, the Mini is parked outside the apartment building. We gather our bags and packages and, in spite of the fact that our arms are full and we're all laughing, I manage to direct Lucio to the front door, open the glass doors, and we all make our way upstairs to the landing.

I open my front door and we finally set down our packages, not heavy but costly, on the floor. The voice catches me by surprise before I can switch on the light.

"You want a cup of coffee?"

I turn and see Lucio standing in the door of his apartment.

Carla and I turn to look at each other. We both know perfectly well that the cup of coffee is strictly a pretext. The aim, and it's hardly concealed, is to dilute his loneliness with a few spoonfuls of sugar. If I were anyone else but who I am, I'd be in a hurry to get Carla alone. But at times you don't have the luxury of a choice, in life. The only thing you're allowed is to choose who you're going to share your cage with.

"Let's have a cup of coffee."

We join him in his apartment across the landing. When he hears us come in, Lucio reaches out a hand to switch on the lights. I feel a twinge in my heart at the thought that he's doing it just for us. His electric bills must be low. Carla looks around, without bothering to conceal her curiosity. She observes the unadorned walls and the mismatched colors, and perhaps she's drawing the same conclusions I came to, long ago. Every decision in this apartment was made on the basis of functionality and the elimination of corners and edges. The aesthetic side of things is a luxury that Lucio has been obliged to renounce. And like any luxury, it turns out to be unnecessary.

Our host heads for his tiny kitchen.

"You two sit down while I make the coffee."

Carla blocks his path.

"No, I'll do it."

"But . . ."

"No ifs, ands, or buts. You worked this evening, and I've just been enjoying myself all day long. Sit down and let me serve you. For once, it's my choice whether to serve, and that's a new experience for me."

Lucio gives up and sits down at the table. Carla vanishes into the tiny kitchen and we listen as she rummages through the cabinets in search of the Moka pot and the necessary materials. I'm still standing in the middle of the room, next to a credenza with cabinet doors and drawers. On the counter is a telephone, a radio, and a glass container with some keys, a few sheets of paper, and some coins.

Next to them are some pictures. I look at them closely and I see that one of them depicts Lucio, a few years younger, with some other young men onstage. They're posing like the musicians they are and all around them are musical instruments, microphones, and amplifiers. On the bass drum is written the name of the band, in Gothic letters: *Les Misérables*.

"You never told me you played in a band."

"How do you know about that?"

"There's some pictures here, on the dresser."

My friend resolves the minor mystery.

"I showed them to Chico, before we went out. He forgot to put them back. I'll have to get a new butler."

"How long did it last? The band, I mean."

Lucio smirks.

"Not long. We kept it up for a while, but we were good, we weren't great. And the other guys in the band had some projects in mind that had nothing to do with music."

"What about you?"

For the first time since I've known him, he allows regret to appear on his face.

"I went on playing on my own, but without the necessary drive. When those pictures were taken, even if you can't tell, my eyes were already practically shot."

I look back at the pictures. Lucio is the only one who isn't smiling. I put them back on the dresser and I go back to sit at the table, across from him.

"Bravo, can I ask you a question?"

"Naturally."

"You know what I do for a living. Now you've even had a glimpse into my past. What line of work are you in?"

It's already hard to describe it in general. It's very difficult to do so in particular with someone as sharp as Lucio.

"Shall we just say that I'm a businessman?"

He smiles and concedes.

"I have the feeling that, if I were to ask what kind of business, you might not give me an exhaustive answer."

157

I minimize with my tone of voice, since he can't see my instinctive gestures.

"Business is all the same. It all has one single objective, to take home money. And whatever is limited to making money isn't worth our consideration."

Carla shows up with the coffee to interrupt this moment of intimacy. She has certainly heard what we said but says nothing about either of the two topics. She sets a demitasse on the table in front of each of us. Then she goes back into the kitchen to get her cup and the sugar.

"How about you, Carla? What kind of work do you do?"

Carla comes back, puts the sugar bowl and the little spoons on the tabletop, and sits down between us, her demitasse in hand. I serve the sugar, as usual. Two spoonfuls for Lucio, half a spoonful for me. Carla takes hers bitter.

"Until yesterday I worked for a cleaning service. Now I'm looking around for something else."

"You, a cleaning woman? With that scent? I can't believe it."

"But it's true. Or rather, it was true."

The coffee, hot and aromatic, silences us for a little while. We sit saying nothing, under the light pouring down from above, each of us rapt in imagining what our lives would have been like if things had gone differently. Constructing a fictitious and illusory alternative reality, which as such cannot be any sweeter.

Lucio is the first to break the silence.

"Carla, can I touch your face?"

She has to stop and think about that question, apparently. I have plenty of time to light a cigarette before she answers.

But there is no uncertainty in her voice when she does.

"Sure."

She stands up and walks around the table to where Lucio is sitting. He senses her presence and stands up. He raises his hands and slowly runs the tips of his fingers over her face. He runs his fingers through her hair, over her forehead, down the bridge of her nose, and surveys her skin. He explores her with the care and curiosity of an expert deciphering an antique document.

"My God, you're beautiful."

Pain appears on Carla's face, after a long journey from some faraway place. She turns to look at me with a question in her eyes. I nod my assent.

Then she takes Lucio's hands and places them on her breasts. She moves them slowly, to acquaint him with that part of her body as well. Then she draws close to him and kisses him. At first, she simply places her lips on his and then pulls back. An exchange of breath and nothing more. After a moment's hesitation, as weightless as air, Carla leans back toward him and the kiss becomes real, a kiss of tongues and saliva, the only pen and ink in which a man and a woman can write a perfect message of love.

Carla pulls away again, steps back, and takes Lucio by the hand. Without a word, she moves off with him, leading him down the hallway to a door, which I assume leads into the bedroom.

I'm left sitting alone.

In a way that now seems limitless.

I finish my cigarette and light another, before going in. When I walk into the bedroom, it's lit only by the glow that arrives from the living room, making its way down the short hallway.

I take a seat on a chair against the wall across from the bed, and I watch Lucio and Carla make love. Without noticing it, all three of us slip into an enchanted, provisional evening where nothing belongs to anyone. The two nude bodies on the bed twist and writhe, offering each other every sort of venom and its exact antidote. I sit there watching, trying to absorb oxygen from their exhalations, like a plant. Immobile, like a marble statue, in the presence of a sexual act performed by someone who can't see it, doing it in place of someone who will never do it again.

CHAPTER 11

At noon, when I wake up, Carla's still sleeping.

I hadn't locked the apartment door, though I assumed that she would stay at Lucio's until morning. Instead, sometime during the night, I felt her slip into the bed without a word. She turned her back to me and sought contact with my body. I dropped back into slumber, as if having her sleep at my side was something normal.

I turn on the lamp on my nightstand and look at her. She's stretched out on her side, naked, her body only partly covered by the sheets. I reach out a hand and caress her skin, following the gentle line of her side. Sighing, she turns over, offering me the loveliness of her breast. Then she wraps her arms around my neck and, without opening her eyes, buries her face in the hollow of my shoulder.

Her breath is warm and scented with sleep.

"Bravo . . ."

I don't know if that's my name or an approval of the quality of my caress. I opt for the first instance.

"What is it?"

"Everything's nice with you."

I know these words. I've heard them before, many different times. But only once before this did they come to me in this way, ready to be accepted and with the possibility of hurting me. Another time, in another place, when I was a different man from who I am now. And the woman who spoke these words to me was a different woman.

When we both lived in the illusion that we were better people than we actually were.

Still, there are moments you don't forget, and Carla just gave me one, whatever the nature of the hour that this second concludes. I don't know what the future marked by the hour that follows will hold, but I do know it's a threshold beyond which I'll only be able to foget and look for substitutes.

Not right away, though.

"I've got things to do. And so do you."

"Yes, I know."

"We can talk about it later."

"Okay."

She releases me and lies back on the pillow, still with her eyes closed. Perhaps that's why I survive and manage to make it out of bed intact, and perhaps that's why I'm able to hurl my useless body into the shower, with the impulse to scrub myself until I take all my skin off.

I spend a long time in the bathroom, shaving and thinking. The whole thing that happened with Tulip keeps spinning in my head. I'm reasonably certain that I did everything carefully and right and that I left no traces of my presence. Moreover, the fact that nobody saw us when he walked me to his car outside the Ascot, which was shitty luck at the time, is now another detail in my favor. That's as far as the police are concerned, if they're somehow able to track me down. Where Tano is concerned, things get just a shade more complicated. His methods might be rather more unorthodox, if he did decide to dig into the matter. I wonder to what extent I'd be believable if I was just to tell him the raw, unvarnished truth.

162

Sometimes, only the stupid and the innocent lack an alibi . . .

As I'm patting aftershave onto my face, my eye happens to fall on the copy of *La Settimana Enigmistica* sitting on the laundry hamper. I catch myself smiling at the thought of how much those brainteasers are like life itself, in aesthetic terms as well.

When you're born, it's really the luck of the draw. The page you wind up on is a matter of dumb chance. From then on, it's all black-and-white, blank spaces you need to clear of unknown factors, letters ready for any handwriting at all, each letter in its little square, each with the conceit of self-importance. Only to realize in time that it means nothing without all the other letters.

When all is said and done, this is what we are: horizontals and verticals. A simple series of attitudes and positions, words that intersect—down and across—as we walk, sleep, play, make love, come home with the shakes, fall into bed with a fever. Until one day it all evens out and it dawns on us that the puzzle, the puzzle that we've all been working so long and so hard to solve, will never be solved.

The rest of time becomes a long horizontal line.

I hear someone knocking at the bathroom door.

The robes of Zarathustra melt away and I find myself wrapped in my old terry cloth bathrobe, with Carla distorted by the pebbled glass of the bathroom door, asking if she can come in.

"Come on in."

Her head pokes around the frame of the door, held slightly ajar. Her eyes are made of the blond wood from the Tree of the Knowledge of Good and Evil.

"I made some pasta, if you're hungry."

I had absolutely no idea there was anything edible in my apartment. The only thing I make on my stove here is coffee. I hope she didn't make pasta with espresso.

"Like with what?"

"With what little I could find. Oil, salt, a can of peeled tomatoes. Your pantry wasn't exactly well stocked."

"Just give me a second."

I wait for her to walk away down the hallway before I come out. I open the closet door and pull out a pair of slacks and a shirt. I go into the bedroom, where the bed has been made, with sheets and blanket pulled so tightly into place you could bounce a coin off them.

I close the door and get dressed.

She's already seen me naked once and we both bear the consequences.

When I get to the living room, Carla is wearing nothing but the shirt I wore yesterday. On her, it looks something like an evening gown. She's sitting at the table with a bowl of spaghetti in front of her. Another bowl is sitting across from her, at what she has chosen as my place at the table.

I sit down and sample a forkful.

"Good."

I mean it. The pasta is really good.

Carla smiles at me.

"Not as good as dinner last night."

"Maybe not. But it has the flavor of something new. I don't think I've ever eaten at home in my life."

"I've never eaten anywhere else."

These two simple phrases tell more about our lives than long conversations could. We go on eating without speaking, certain of each other's presence. Neither of us makes any reference to last night or what happened with Lucio.

164

I finish my bowl of pasta first, and once she's done eating I stand up.

"I'll do the dishes. You go get ready."

"Okay."

She stands up too and vanishes down the little corridor. I stack the dishes in the sink, leaving them to the tender care of the cleaning woman. I light a cigarette, without giving in to the siren song of a cup of coffee. In part because I don't feel like making it.

While Carla takes a shower and gets ready to be as spectacular as she needs to be, I take care of a little business. I arrange appointments for a couple of my old clients, docile, trouble-free, who ask for nothing more than a little of the company that they don't seem able to procure for themselves. A reliable arrangement, for them and for yours truly. Thirty percent of me is extremely sympathetic. The remaining 70 percent is a matter involving the men in question, their conscience, and the girls.

Beep.

My pocket butler alerts me to the fact that someone wants me. I retrieve from the Eurocheck switchboard a phone number without a name, a call from the usual unknown john. I return the call. A male voice, slightly hesitant, answers the phone, with a faint foreign accent I can't place. I introduce myself according to the well-tested formula. In practical terms, it's as if I were pulling open the curtain.

"I received a call from this phone number."

"Are you Bravo?"

"I certainly am. What can I do for you?"

"I got your number from a friend. He told me that you're a trustworthy and very reliable person."

Very kind of him, but that's not enough. One or

165

two references are necessary, when possible, in cases like this.

"May I ask the name of your friend?"

"Dr. Larsson."

I remember the name. He's a Swedish plastic surgeon who comes to Milan on a fairly regular basis and has a certain predilection for the company of women. Accompanied by various forms and quantities of smoke and powder. He's a fan of Betsy, a stunning Jamaican girl. Standard procedure for a Scandinavian. I doubt that he used full anesthesia when he operated on her. All the same, I decide to lay a little trap for my potential client, just to be safe.

"Ah, of course, Dr. Larsson. One of the finest dentists in Göteborg."

My interlocutor fails to realize that the mistake is intentional. But he immediately corrects me and passes the test.

"No, you must be confused. Dr. Larsson is a surgeon and his practice is in Stockholm."

"Of course. So silly of me. How can I be of service?"

"Well, I was just wondering if . . ."

Many of my clients are shy and hesitant at their first contact. I wait while he tries to find the right words. As far as finding courage is concerned, that's either there or it isn't. In any case, he manages to come up with a reasonable facsimile.

"I was wondering if you could supply me with very young girls."

"All the girls who work with me are young."

The voice on the other end of the line shifts from uncertain to allusive.

"No, I'm talking about very, very young girls . . ."

His voice trails off and I finish the sentence for myself. Then I act accordingly. My moral fabric is pretty accommodating,

166

but there are still a few things too big to slip through its holes. I hiss like a serpent as I respond. I imagine that it's the only language that bastard will understand.

"Listen to me, you son of a bitch, and listen good. I don't know who you are, but I know who I am. If you ever dare to call me again for your filthy pursuits, I'll track you down and break your arms and legs. And don't you even think of asking around for what you're looking for here in Milan. I'd find out about it, and you'd receive the exact same treatment. Have I made myself clear?"

"Yes, but I—"

I don't give him a chance to finish.

"*Yes, but I* my ass! You just go fuck yourself, you piece of shit."

I slam the receiver down onto the hook with such violence that at first I'm afraid that I broke it. I take a sheet of paper and a ballpoint pen and I take note of the number that I just called. The first chance I get, I'll slip it to Milla with an urgent request to look into the case.

Carla's voice comes as an unexpected plot twist.

"I'm ready."

I turn around and I'm struck. Struck by what I couldn't say. I'm not sure I could come up with the words.

Carla is wearing one of the dresses she bought yesterday, something soft and dove gray, and it goes perfectly with her eyes. Over it she's wearing a jacket with a jacquard pattern, against a background the same color as her dress. Her shoes, even though the heels are not dizzyingly high, elevate her until she could touch the summit of K2.

She makes a show turn, smiling, allowing herself the hint of vanity that she richly deserves.

"How do I look?"

"You're stunning."

Carla turns serious.

"I always want to look this way for you."

She looks at me and draws closer until she has pressed her body up against mine. Then her arms slither around my neck and we kiss. Her tongue tastes of strawberry toothpaste and something else I can't remember. Suddenly I find myself in front of an open door, but no matter how hard I try I could never walk through it. All the same, I don't move, returning that kiss as if it were the first or the last one of my life. Afterward, we stand, arms wrapped around each other. She rests her head on my shoulder.

"Bravo . . ."

"Yes?"

"However this turns out, thank you."

I pull her away from me. I raise one arm to check the time. When I speak, the voice that comes out isn't entirely mine.

"It's late and we need to get going. It can take a while to get from here to San Babila, if the traffic's bad."

"Yes, I understand."

She looks disappointed. I'm certainly pissed off. At myself, at her, at Lucio, at our stupid puzzles, at our foolish and grandiose games, at the whole world. We leave the apartment and head for the car. Enough things have happened that I need to think about, enough things that are hard to put into words. That's why we both lack words right now, why we're both so afraid.

I get to the car, I open the trunk, and I put Carla's suitcase in. Then we get into the car and I put the key into the ignition. I turn it and the engine starts up. I slip the gearshift into reverse but I don't pull out of the parking spot. I turn off the engine and look around. The steering wheel, the seats, the floor mats, the objects in the shelf under the dashboard and in the backseat. Everything's the same as it was yesterday. Still, there's something that just doesn't seem right. Lucio would chuckle with joy if I told him that I was experiencing a *déjà pas vu* and it would seem like the solution to one of our cryptic clues. But here there are no words to decipher or jump over or somersault through. There's nothing but this strange feeling that I can't pin down.

"Is something wrong?"

"No, everything's fine."

I start the engine again and I pull out of the parking space. I must not have been all that convincing in my reply. The whole way to Piazza San Babila, as I go over the importance and exclusivity of the place to which Carla is going to be admitted for the umpteenth time, she keeps looking at me as if she were trying to decipher through my gestures and words a more complex message concealed behind them.

When we reach the center of Milan, Barbara is already there, standing outside of the Bar Gin Rosa, with a small overnight bag on the sidewalk at her feet. I pull up next to her and, as I open the door for Carla, a taxi pulls up behind us. The passenger door swings open and out come Cindy's long legs, followed by Cindy. She gets out and comes over, carrying a Vuitton travel bag. Tall, beautiful, and without boundaries. Otherwise how could she ever afford that travel bag and the designer clothes she's wearing? She steps up and joins the group.

She smiles, thrilled with life.

"That taxi driver wasn't half bad. A good-looking boy, no question about it. He didn't charge me for the ride. I gave him my phone number. If he calls me, I might not make *him* pay for the ride, either."

Barbara laughs but Carla seems rapt, distracted. Maybe she's thinking back to the words she said when we met for the first time.

If it was you, I'd do it for free . . .

Maybe, but there's no way of finding out.

A cluster of beautiful girls at this level can hardly pass unnoticed. The problem is that I'm not going unnoticed either, and that's something I don't especially appreciate. I'm eager to get out of here at my earliest possible opportunity. I'm eager to be left alone with my car.

"So long, girls. Break a leg. Let me know when you get home."

I acknowledge Barbara's and Cindy's farewells and I ignore Carla's lingering gaze, which follows me as I get back into my car.

I take advantage of the green traffic light and turn up Corso Venezia heading toward Corso Buenos Aires.

The afternoon stretches out before me, long and full of questions. I've decided that this is the right time to go to the Cinema Argentina, located very imaginatively in Piazza Argentina. In a movie house that has seen better days, they show film series of various genres: science fiction, horror movies, Westerns, and tributes to this or that famous actor, changing the featured films on an almost daily basis.

The perfect place to kill a couple of hours.

As I make my way through the heavy Milan traffic I keep looking around the interior of the car, because that odd sensation I'd filed away during the drive in from Cesano has come back, stronger than ever. When I get close to the movie house, I look for a parking place. When I find it, I turn off the engine and light a cigarette. As soon as I exhale the first mouthful of smoke, I realize.

There's nothing new in the car, but something old is missing.

The smell of cigarette smoke.

I pull open the glove compartment in front of the passenger seat and I decide that it won't do me any harm to do what I'm about to do, since there's no one around to witness it. I'll look like a senile old man to myself and nobody else. I pull out the registration booklet and I yank the lever that pops the hood. I go around to the front of the car, lift the hood, and prop it into place with the hinged rod, as instructed by the manual. Then I compare the serial number on the frame with the number in the registration booklet.

My senility vanishes instantly, replaced by the feeling that I've been a dope. The two numbers don't match up. I check them twice, but they remain alphanumerical sequences that fail to coincide, like the same sentence in two different languages.

I don't know what to think.

Usually, in cases like this, I simply don't think. This is a technique I use when I can't manage to solve a cryptic clue. I take a break, I do something else, I wait for the part of my brain that's out of my control to do the work on its own. And the solution, sooner or later, is a flash of lightning that's followed by a stream of *Well, of course!*'s and *Why didn't I think of that earlier?*'s.

"Hey, dickhead, does this strike you as a good place to change your oil?"

I turn toward the voice and there, within arm's reach, is Daytona. He came up behind me along the sidewalk on my right. Immersed as I was in my own small mystery, I'd neither seen him nor heard him. He's wearing, in impeccable style, a wrecked face and his usual dark blue, eminently rumpled three-piece suit.

I quickly hide the registration booklet that I'm still holding.

"There's a sound I don't like. I'm afraid it might be the timing belt."

Daytona flashes me one of his smirky smiles, the kind that make him look like a character out of cartoons. He points to my car, without the slightest idea that there has been no noise at all and that the timing belt is in tip-top shape.

"It's high time you decided to get yourself a decent ride instead of this ramshackle jalopy. You're someone who ought to drive a custom-built vehicle, not a car about the size of a nostril."

I pull the hood prop out of its socket and lay it down. Then I slam the hood.

"When you make up your mind to sell it, I could buy your Porsche, as long as it hasn't fallen under the jurisdiction of the Commission for Historic Preservation."

Cut to the quick, Daytona immediately treats me like the snob he is.

"Mine is a machine for aristocrats. You lack the necessary touch of class. If a plebeian like you ever got behind the wheel, as soon as you turned the key in the ignition it would explode."

I decide to skip the banter: this repartee could go on forever without resolution. I trot out a bit of conventional conversational boilerplate.

"What are you doing around here? I thought at this time of day you'd still be sleeping."

Daytona points in a direction that could mean virtually anyplace in the city.

"I wish I *was* still asleep. I had work to do: a business meeting in a street right around the corner. A very interesting project."

I've always had a hard time combining the word *work* with the figure of Daytona, who leads such an unhealthy life that his face is often the color of an ice smoothie from the Viel fruit bar. Various flavors, either banana or strawberry, depending on the day. To avoid saying something unpleasant, I bring up my own personal program for the afternoon.

"I'm going to the Cinema Argentina."

"People who don't have anything useful to do. That's who goes to the movies in the afternoon."

Stung, I respond to the provocation with my finest sarcastic tone of rebuttal.

"And just what important appointments do you have today?"

"None at all. In fact I'm coming with you to the movies. What are they showing today?"

"I haven't the slightest idea. But walk with me for half a block and we can find out."

We head for the box office. I would rather have spent the time alone, but I couldn't find a believable reason to reject his company and his conversation. I pray that at least during the movie he'll shut up. If he doesn't, at least I'll have a good reason to ask him to pipe down.

Once we're outside the theater, the posters tell us that there's a retrospective of films starring Paul Newman, and that today's feature is *The Sting*. He looks at me, doubtfully.

"I haven't seen it. Have you?"

I shrug my shoulders. One film's as good as another, as far as I'm concerned. I just came here to kill a couple of hours in a quiet out-of-the-way place, minding my own business.

"Yeah, I've seen it, but I'd be glad to watch it again."

We're in luck. As we walk in, the signal on the device hanging on the wall above the cash register that indicates the first half of the film is being shown blinks on. When we buy our tickets, the cashier confirms that the movie just started a few seconds ago.

We walk into a room upholstered in shadow.

As for seating, we have the luxury of choosing at will. There might be ten people, certainly no more, in the theater. Guiding ourselves by the light flickering off the screen, we make our way to a couple of seats halfway up the aisle.

Daytona gets comfortable to my left and launches into a learned disquisition on the movie. One of those essays that will be carved into stone in the shrines of international filmmaking.

"Robert Redford's good."

I'm afraid there's going to be more, but Daytona lapses into silence, and after a few minutes I'm overjoyed. His head slumps forward, his upper lip hangs freely, and his comb-over dangles pathetically into the void. He falls asleep, snoring softly like an enormous well-fed cat.

I lean back in my seat, I watch what's happening on the screen, and I think. The two heroes of the story, dressed to the nines as you'd expect for a couple of Hollywood stars of their wattage, try to pull a con on a major boss of the Chicago underworld of the thirties. The fictitious tale of those two con artists blends with my own life and somewhere, in some corner of my brain, I have an intuition.

More than an intuition, a notion. But I immediately elevate it to the rank of an idea.

I get out of my seat and head for the exit, leaving Daytona to slumber in the arms of Morpheus—or Murf the Surf, as one of the cabaret artists of the Ascot likes to say. I reach the lobby, where there's a pay phone in a corner. I can't remember the number I need and I'm forced to look it up in the phone book.

I drop a phone token into the slot and my voice is authorized to travel across town.

My friend answers with a booming Lombard accent, after a long succession of rings.

"Hello, who's this?"

"Pino, it's Bravo."

"Bravo, bravo, I applaud the way you jack off all day. Where have you been all this time?"

Pino is a little bit of a talker, but he's a respectable, decent person and a wizard in his profession. His wife is an outstanding cook, and his daughter is an unsightly toad. We see even less of each other than we used to, and our friendship almost came to an end entirely when I realized that they were trying to set me up with her. And that the daughter was delighted at the prospect.

"I've been out of town. I've been really busy lately."

"I'm going to pretend I believe you. What are you calling about?"

"There's something I need. And I need it by tomorrow morning, at the latest."

"What do you take me for, the Wizard of Oz?"

Stung where he lives, Pino raises his voice. All of which is predictable and factored in, knowing Pino. I can see him in my mind's eye, skinny and short, in a wife-beater, hanging on to the phone on the hallway wall, standing up slightly on tiptoe as he shouts this last phrase into the receiver.

I flatter him, trying to manipulate him by appealing to his self-regard.

175

"No, just a wizard, nothing more. You could be from anywhere."

"So what do you need?"

I tell him what I'm looking for. He expresses a predictable concern about my request.

"You're going to get yourself into trouble. You'll never get away with it."

"I don't have to get away with anything. I just want it for a kind of a prank."

"You know, there are pranks that'll get you express admission to San Vittore Prison."

I can't tell him that that's exactly what I'm hoping for.

"Take it easy. No trouble, for me or for you. So?"

He seems to ponder timing and logistics. Then he gives in.

"I can do it. Come by tomorrow morning after nine o'clock. But be aware: this is going to cost you real money."

"What kind of money do you call real?"

"A rock."

"Shit. A rock. You're not the Wizard of Oz. You're John Dillinger."

"Okay, then find someone else."

"No, no, we've got a deal for one million lire. See you tomorrow morning."

"You staying for lunch?"

"No, I can't. Some other time."

"Okay, see you tomorrow."

I hang up the phone and go back into the theater. Daytona is still slumped over, fast asleep. He's only moved his head slightly. I'm willing to bet that he won't wake up at all until the lights come back on. Which is exactly what happens, after Paul Newman and Robert Redford have successfully ripped off the unpleasant and wicked Doyle Lonnegan.

176

He blinks open his eyes and looks around with the expression of someone who doesn't know where they are or how they got there.

Then he remembers and ventures a reckless bluff.

"That was a great movie."

I decide to dig a little deeper. In fact, I respond in kind, just for the pleasure of leading him out of the movie theater and into the deep grass. I'm a little giddy over the idea I've had, and leading Daytona around by the nose is my idea of fun.

"I love it. The scene with Robert Redford on horseback was fantastic."

He falls for it. And comes off looking like an asshole.

"Yeah. I told you that guy was a hell of an actor."

In the meantime, we've gotten to our feet and we're walking up the aisle. I shove him from behind.

"Oh, go take a shit somewhere. There wasn't a scene with a horse. You slept like a log through the whole movie."

He makes a pathetic attempt to justify himself, his eyes bloodshot.

"I'm just a little worn-out. I haven't gotten much sleep lately. I've got some pretty challenging projects on the front burner."

I decide to skip asking what kind of projects they might be. I feel fairly certain that if word were to spread, it would result in a squad car pulling up outside of a certain local institution that Pino mentioned just a few minutes ago. That's the way Daytona is: take him or leave him. And in fact, many men and women prefer to leave him.

We walk out into the lobby and he spots the phone.

"Can you wait a second? I've got to call a guy."

I step outside, smoke a cigarette, and watch the city go by,

177

already poised for rush hour, but ignoring me, Daytona, and anyone else who wastes time, tires, and shoe leather on the sidewalks and the streets.

My friend walks out of the Cinema Argentina looking a little troubled, a little worried, to judge from his familiar features.

"What's wrong?"

"What's wrong is that I'm in big trouble. This evening I have to be in two places at the same time. And I can't afford not to show up in either place. Especially not in one of the places."

He looks around, as if the world around him might be about to offer a solution. Which is what happens, but not to my personal satisfaction. At all.

"But you could go to the other place for me."

"Are you crazy?"

"It's no big thing. I just have to make a delivery over near where you live."

"A delivery? You've lost your mind. I'm not working as a courier for any type of shit you may be handling. Not for you, not for anyone."

He pretends to take offense.

"Who do you take me for? It's not drugs. I don't deal in that line of work."

He rummages around in his jacket and pulls out a fat envelope from an inside pocket. He steps closer to me and cracks it open so that I can see what's inside, but it's covered by our bodies. It's full of 100,000-lira bills.

"I'm supposed to give this money to the guys I owe it to, at midnight. They're coming from out of town and if I don't show up, they're going to get pissed off. And when these guys get pissed off it's not a pretty sight to see."

A guy walks toward us and Daytona, in an excess of caution, slips the envelope back into his jacket pocket. The man walks past, completely indifferent to us. We're left standing there, face-to-face.

I look at him. He looks at me.

"Come on, just do me this favor. I guarantee there's no rip-off involved."

It's starting to look like my main job is being a money transporter. Tonight for Daytona, tomorrow for Tano Casale.

"All right. Where do I have to go?"

"Outside of Trezzano, along the road to Vigevano. There's a restaurant called La Pergola. At twelve thirty a.m. in the parking lot. I'll tell them you're going to be there instead of me. As soon as they get there, you give them the envelope and then leave."

I lower my head, still undecided. When I raise my eyes to look at Daytona, he's pulled the envelope back out and he's licking the flap to seal it. He hands it to me.

"Nice show of trust."

"I'm putting several million lire into your hands. If you don't think that's a sign of trust . . ."

I take the envelope and stick it into my jacket pocket.

"Okay. But I'm going to remind you that you owe me one."

"I have an elephant's memory, I won't forget."

I mock him. He deserves it and he owes me.

"You keep on eating the way you do and you'll have an elephant's figure, my friend."

We shake hands and I head for the Mini, which awaits me with its mystery still unresolved.

While waiting for my intuition to suggest a specific

direction, I get in the car and start circling around the city, in a series of automotive waltzes.

I swing by the Duomo, to listen to the endlessly evolving conversations of a group of people who never seem to move away from the front doors of La Rinascente department store. Then I drop by the Bar Jamaica and drink a beer with a bunch of demented artists, as funny as they are funny-looking. I have dinner at the Torre Pendente, where I see people and I pick up a couple of jobs for my girls, followed by a quick hop over to the Budineria, the Irish tavern near Via Chiesa Rossa.

At last I find myself sitting in a parking lot outside of town, in a suspicious vehicle, with my pockets full of money that doesn't belong to me, waiting for the people it does belong to to come along and collect it. The restaurant is closed and I'm all alone in this unpaved area by the main road. The cars that race past give me a gift of light but snatch it back just a few seconds later, hurtling along so that they can play the same trick on someone farther down the road.

I sit and smoke and think.

My life has changed in the past few days. Carla, Tulip, Lucio, Daytona: one new face and other, familiar faces, but with new expressions. Death, emerging out of the darkness and bringing darkness with it. Life, which perhaps still exists.

Thoughts, thoughts, thoughts . . .

Meanwhile, time is passing and no one's showing up.

My watch says it's a quarter past one. Daytona's debt to me is increasing exponentially. At two o'clock I decide that the price has risen above its market quote so I mentally tell them to go fuck themselves.

I start the car and head for home, which is luckily very close; otherwise I'd have to charge an annoyance bonus for every additional kilometer, aside from the standard rate for oil and gas.

When I get back to my apartment, I undress and toss the envelope onto the chest of drawers, next to the telephone. Then a thought occurs to me. Tomorrow morning I'm going to have to give Pino one million lire. It goes without saying that I'll have to pay him in cash, because it's always a bad idea to give certain people checks. I have some cash hidden in my apartment, in a secure place I built for myself. But I don't want to dig into my personal reserve for emergency situations. Ever since I put the money away, I've forced myself to pretend it doesn't exist.

I decide to use the money in the envelope, which will save me a trip to the bank before going to see Pino. It's partly for convenience, and partly because sitting there like an idiot waiting for some assholes who never showed up is still making my balls spin in annoyance and frustration. If Daytona has the nerve to get mad because I opened the envelope, I'll bitch-slap him around the Milan beltway.

I pick up the envelope, slip my pinky into the little opening at the corner of the flap, and run it the length of the crease. The envelope rips open raggedly and part of what's inside falls with a rustling sound on top of the chest of drawers. I stand there like an idiot, staring openmouthed at something I can't believe I'm really seeing. The envelope is full of strips of newspaper, cut into the exact size of a 100,000-lira bill.

CHAPTER 12

I'm parked on Via Roma, outside a nondescript bank branch office, sitting in my mystery car. This morning I got up early and left the apartment without even showering and shaving. I decided that the people I was going to meet would have to accept me, unkempt as I am.

When I walked out my door onto the landing, I ran into Lucio with his white cane and dark glasses, climbing the last flight of stairs. He reached the landing and stopped. The sound of my door opening and then closing alerted him to my presence.

"You're an early riser."

"So are you, I'd have to say."

He put one hand in his pocket and pulled out his house key. Feeling the door, he inserted it into the lock.

"I had a session in a recording studio at the Castle of Carimate, last night. It went on longer than we expected and I just slept there. This morning I took the only ride coming back. Practically at dawn, as you can see."

He opened the door and put the key back in his pocket.

"I came up with a new one for you."

I had neither interest nor time for cryptic clues. I tried to tell him that in a way that wouldn't offend him.

"I'm sorry, this is a bad time for it, Lucio. I've really got to make tracks."

He refused to take no for an answer.

"It's always a good time to give your brain a workout. This one's easy. Listen: *Starlets going incognito in an opera libretto* (four plus six equals ten). Memorized?"

"Memorized."

I started downstairs but his voice stopped me.

"Bravo, just one thing."

"Tell me."

"Thanks for the other night. With Carla, I mean. I don't know what the relationship is between the two of you, but I'm pretty sure that I owe you for what happened."

For an instant the sight of their bodies on the bed appeared before my eyes, blotting out everything else. Then I became myself again.

"Everything's fine, music man. Now I've really got to go."

I heard his door swing shut while I was descending the last flight of steps. I did everything I needed to do as quickly as possible, with the aid of mercifully light morning traffic: bank, one million lire from the teller, then at top speed to Pino's house, in Cormano. I picked up the product of his craftsmanship, slaloming to avoid the fond glances of his daughter, his invitations, and his good advice, the fruit of age-old wisdom that never kept him from spending various stretches in state prison.

Now I'm a man waiting for someone to show up, and hoping that it turns out differently than last night.

A light green Simca 1000 passes me and pulls in a few slots ahead. A few seconds later Remo Frontini gets out. He's wearing a dark blue jacket that's seen better days and a pair of trousers that scream discount store from a mile away. I get out of my car and walk toward him. It's evident from his appearance that he didn't get much sleep last night. For different reasons, I'm in the exact same condition. This strange assonance increases my fondness for him, and therefore my concern for his well-being. Maybe it's because of a certain irritated and instinctive attraction that honesty seems to exert upon people like me.

"*Buon giorno*, Signore Frontini."

"I hope it is a good day."

"It will be. Don't worry. Trust me."

Maybe he assumes that he has no reason to do so and that's the reason for his uneasiness. Awkwardly, with the general attitude of someone who can't wait for it all to be over, he rummages in his pocket and extracts a sheet of paper folded in half, in letter format.

"Here's what you asked me to bring."

I open it and check the photocopy. It's clear and legible. I pull a newspaper clipping with the numbers of the winning ticket out of my pocket, check it, and recheck it. These numbers at least coincide.

"Excellent. Now all we have to do is wait."

He doesn't ask who we're waiting for.

I offer him a Marlboro. He refuses the cigarette with a simple swivel of the head. I light one up and smoke without even tasting the smoke. What happened last night left a bad taste in my mouth. Not feeling entirely in charge of my life is something I'm not used to. I sense a looming threat of some kind, something coming, and I can't tell what it is or where it's coming from. It's not a particularly enjoyable state of mind, because however hard I try, I can't find even the beginnings of an explanation.

The strips of newspaper in the envelope can mean only one thing, at first glance: Daytona wanted to rip off his creditors and he decided to use me as the courier and maybe as the scapegoat. All the same, it strikes me as such a stupid plan that even the atrophied brain of that chimp should have been able to glimpse its limitations. The fact that those guys didn't show up at the appointment is something I can't seem to place. Was it a stroke of good luck for me, or was it a signal that the explanation should be sought elsewhere? The problem is that I don't have the faintest idea of where that elsewhere might be.

Then there's the detail, anything but minor, of the serial number on the chassis of my car. This isn't one of those innocuous puzzler's skirmishes between me and Lucio. One of those nameless instincts that make you guess the winning horse or avoid the losing one suggests to me that this is anything but a simple matter. This is a much more complicated puzzle, filled with numbers and letters I can't put together.

Hard as I try, I can't figure it out. And when I can't figure something out I feel like a fool, and that makes me mad.

I see a cream Alfa Romeo Giulietta approach from the right and I recognize Stefano Milla behind the wheel. He parks a fair distance away from us. Since he doesn't get out, I go over to him. He's sitting in the car, smoking and waiting for me. I pull open the passenger-side door and get in. No greetings. He reaches into the backseat and picks up a saddle-brown Naugahyde valise. He lays it in my lap.

"Delivery completed."

"Aren't you coming?"

Milla shakes his head.

"I'd just as soon that guy didn't see me. I'm only an escort.

Tano told me that you're in charge on this one. With all the honor and all the risks."

Experience tells me very clearly just what the scope of the risks and the honor might be. I take the briefcase, get out of the Alfa, and go back to Frontini, who seems more nervous than ever. I invite him to step into my car and sit next to me. I crane my neck to make sure there's no one around, then I open the briefcase and show him what's inside.

"Here you go."

I could never describe that man's expression. It wasn't greed, it was astonishment. It was the face of a little boy gazing at a pirate's treasure trove, staring at something he thought could only exist in the imagination, never in reality. There's the certainty of a new and unexpected way of life in that briefcase, and I look at him and feel happy for him.

"Go ahead and count. There should be fifty bundles of ten million lire each. A total of five hundred million lire. That's exactly how much money we agreed on."

I set the briefcase in his lap.

"Take all the time you need."

He rummages through the money long enough to count the bills in three or four bundles chosen at random and then counts to make sure there are fifty bundles. Then he closes the top and makes sure that the locks click shut.

"It looks like it's all here."

"Perfect. Now you go get that lottery ticket."

I feel it's my duty to let him know that the risks and the honor that Milla mentioned a few minutes ago involve not only me, but him as well. Experience has taught me that you can never be too careful, even though I've broken this rule of mine several times already with Frontini.

"I want to make one thing very clear. I know that it's not

186

really necessary, but I feel obliged to emphasize that if you pull any funny business at all, of any kind, the consequences could be very unpleasant."

To my surprise, he smiles.

"At this point, if I hadn't figured that out, I really would be an idiot."

Then he gets out of the car, with his briefcase full of joy in one hand. When he's out of the car he leans over, rests his arm on the car door, and sticks his head in through the open window.

"I don't need to go get it."

He sticks his hand into the inside breast pocket of his jacket and pulls out an envelope. The same gesture that Daytona made, the day before, with his little Trojan horse full of cut-up newspaper. But performed by a different man. A very different man.

"Here's the lottery ticket."

I open the envelope and check it against my newspaper clipping and the photocopy. Everything matches up: date, scores, validation strips, number of the lottery office. I look at him and this time I'm the one who's caught off guard. Remo Frontini smiles at me again.

"Bravo, I think that I'm a decent person. And whatever you might think of yourself, I'm pretty sure you're a decent person too. I want to thank you for your advice, and if you don't mind, I'd like to give you a piece of advice myself."

"Go ahead."

"It's the exact opposite of the advice that you gave me. I'm going to wait before I change the way I live. I think you should change the way you live as soon as you can. You deserve better. Have a good day."

Before I have a chance to answer, he stands up and strides

off at a brisk pace toward the bank, to tuck his little nest egg away from prying eyes and clawing fingers. I sit there alone, with my envelope in my hands.

This is an unexpected piece of luck. I can do what I planned out without haste. From my inside jacket pocket I extract the fruit of Pino's recent labors. Pino is one of the best counterfeiters around. I commissioned him to make a fake lottery ticket. It would certainly never pass the scrutiny of the experts in the verification office set up by SISAL, but it's just the thing to make Tano Casale believe he's holding the winning ticket in his hands. If he tries to collect his winnings tomorrow morning, then it's quite likely that tomorrow night I'll be at the bottom of the Ticino River with a rock tied to my ankles, learning to speak Trout. But I'm counting on his greed to make sure that doesn't happen. I have an idea to suggest to him that ought to cover my ass for a little while.

Just enough time . . .

I slip the bogus lottery ticket into the envelope and a second later Milla materializes next to my window, on the driver's side.

"Everything okay?"

"Everything's okay."

I hand him the envelope I'm holding.

"Here. You need to deliver this to Tano."

"You're going to deliver it in person. He told me that he'd like to speak to you. So I think you'd better come with me."

His Jolly Joker face pops out of a chaotic deck of cards, and this time there's no smile. His tone of voice suggests that he wouldn't want to be in my shoes. The fact is, I would just as soon not be in my shoes myself. He can't know that this is just one more unknowable factor tossed onto the pile of unknowable factors.

"All right. You lead the way. I'll follow you."

He walks off and a few minutes later his car drives past mine. I pull out of the parking lot and I follow his Giulietta. Because of the various traffic lights, we're almost separated more than once as we're leaving Cesano.

I look at the back of Milla's neck as he drives ahead of me. I don't know what I can expect from him. Before this, I thought of him as a protector of sorts—whatever a partnership of that kind is worth in a world where at the slightest whiff of trouble everybody's willing to toss their mother and grandmother overboard into the salty sea. Now that he's shown his true colors and made it clear that he's one of Tano's men, I have no doubt whose side he'd be on if push came to shove. What I can't quite figure out is how deeply he's involved, and therefore how far he'd be willing to go.

We pull onto the beltway around Milan not far from my house and we head south. My car struggles to keep pace with the Alfa Romeo. The two lottery tickets are like anvils in my pockets. If for some reason that I don't dare to imagine Tano Casale decides to have me searched, my plunge into the waters of the Ticino might be moved up to this evening.

I try to get my mind off the subject, and I think about Carla.

The fact that at this very moment she might be in bed with one or more men makes me neither jealous nor depressed. The day that a straight razor steered me once and for all away from certain activities, in a certain sense it also cut me loose from the corresponding emotions. Not the urge. That's still there. As a way to compensate for a desire that can be piercing and painful at times, an impulse that can never again be satisfied, women have become an instrument of communication with the world of men.

Women on one side, men on the other.

And me in the middle, still scarred by the aftermath of my own perineal urethrostomy, the operation that affords me a less chaotic relationship with my body when I experience the very human need to piss.

Carla is one of the few people on earth who knows about that. And who understands. I guessed that when she asked permission to make love with Lucio and at the same time offered it to me as a gift. I had further confirmation later, when I felt her slipping into bed next to me and then seeking physical contact.

Milla's car takes the Opera exit. I instinctively guess that we're going to the industrial shed with the car crusher where Micky took me. The one that turns into a gambling den at night. The picture in my mind of a rock tied around my ankles as I sink into the dark waters of the Ticino is replaced with one of my body jammed into a junked car and then crushed into a cube. These aren't pretty thoughts to have as one's traveling companion, especially on a nice sunny day that, as Lucio Battisti once sang, conjures up salt spray and your laughter.

Instead, the Giulietta continues straight along the road, and a few kilometers farther on turns right onto a narrow lane that ends a few hundred meters later in the parking lot of a trattoria. The building is low, with windows protected by iron grillwork with some degree of artistic aspiration. The walls, which must once have been brick red, are now a faded pink, stained and discolored by the elements. In the back is a pergola with an enormous wisteria spreading overhead. In the summer, this must be the garden for outdoor dining.

We park among the few other cars in the lot, get out, and

without a word we head for a small wooden door, beneath a sign that touts Jole's home cooking. Inside, the windows provide little light for the few diners, so there are several electric lights burning. A listless waiter doesn't even bother to glance in our direction, while a blond matron, corpulent and perspiring—maybe she's the Jole mentioned on the sign—can be glimpsed through an open door, working in the steam and smoke of the kitchen.

Milla strides without hesitation toward a hallway that leads to a secluded private dining room, where we find Tano Casale and his bodyguard sitting at the only occupied table. We walk over to the table. The boss is eating a bowl of spaghetti. His underling, who's dressed in the same suit as the first time I saw him, is in the throes of a noisy battle with a bowl of minestrone.

Tano points to the chair across from him without speaking. As I take a seat, he gestures to Milla and the man sitting to his right. The guy stands up without a word, and he and the policeman vanish into the large dining room.

We're alone. I can't figure out if that's a good sign or a bad one.

"You want something to eat? The carbonara here is fantastic."

"No, I'm not really hungry."

He swallows his mouthful of food with a gulp, wipes his mouth with his napkin, and extends an open hand across the table.

"I think you have something that belongs to me."

I pull the envelope out of my pocket and hand it to him. He opens the envelope and pulls out the lottery ticket. He stares at it for a long time. Maybe he finds it difficult to believe that he bought this meaningless little rectangle for a huge chunk of cash. Then he looks up at me again with an undefinable expression on his face.

"You're a smart boy, Francesco Marcona, born in Sellano, in the province of Perugia, in November 1943, to Alfonso and Marisa Giusti, who later emigrated to Australia. You are certainly one smart boy. I think you've blazed a trail, with this clever ploy you've come up with."

He smiles at the look of surprise on my face.

"Did you think that I'd let you run this thing without getting a little information about you? Otherwise, what good is it to me to have a police detective on my payroll?"

I take the facts at face value.

"That's understandable."

Tano takes another look at the lottery ticket. Then he puts it down on the table in front of him, as if to keep an eye on it.

He speaks to me in that voice that I know.

"We still have that minor matter of Salvo's death. I want you to tell me what you know, so I can watch you while you tell me."

On the exterior I seem relaxed. Inside, I'm anything but.

"I don't know anything about that. The night it happened I was with a girl."

He eyes me intently. As far as he's concerned, I'm not done talking.

Only the stupid and the innocent lack an alibi . . .

I lean my elbows on the table and stretch my neck in his direction.

"Tano, if you don't mind my being charitable toward myself, I've always been more of a diplomat than a man of action. I've never owned a gun and I never expect to. When I had trouble with Menno, I came to you and I did my best to resolve it as a business transaction. Peaceful, easygoing, profitable for both sides. You've got the evidence of that right in front of you."

I point to the lottery ticket, in order to emphasize the concept and prepare the ground for what I'm about to say.

"And as far as I'm concerned, we can continue along that path. If you're interested, I have another proposal that could let you double your money in just one hour's time."

A light glitters in his eyes. He's done with his spaghetti, but his appetite for this new opportunity has just been aroused. After all, I've earned just a crumb of credibility by now. Tano takes a sip of his wine.

"I'm listening."

"Among your many clients, would you happen to have anyone who works for a bank? Someone who has a bad gambling habit, maybe someone who owes you a lot of money?"

I see that he's curious to hear how this story turns out.

"Maybe I do. Go on."

Doing my best to be as persuasive as possible, I explain my new idea. It's a shade riskier than the one that procured him a 490-million-lira lottery ticket, a little more complex to put into action, a bit more of the sort of thing that only real men with hairy balls would take on. I emphasize the fact, instead of trying to skirt around it. However powerful he's become, however cunning he may be, Tano is still fundamentally a street crook, a guy who's made his way through life with all the tools that physical courage and a lack of scruples have made available to him. His temperament remains that of a man who accepts challenges.

And that's exactly what he does.

"It could work. Jesus, it could actually work."

He smiles and throws back the rest of his wine in a single

193

gulp, a little giddy and a little arrogant at the prospect that my words have opened to him.

"I really feel like sticking it up those bastards' asses. Four hundred and ninety million cocks up their asses."

When he's done turning the idea over, he remembers about me.

"Do you want to be involved in this thing?"

I shake my head.

"I told you before. I'm not a man of action. I'm a small fish, and that's all I ever want to be."

Tano shoots back with an expression that seems to be carved out of pure relentlessness.

"I'm afraid you're going to have to get a little bigger this time, youngster."

He stares at me with his dark eyes, deep pools of a certain benevolence. Real or put on, I couldn't say.

"I like you, Bravo. I want you to take care of this. You've got a first-class head on your shoulders."

"Thanks very much. But I'd really rather keep it right there, firmly attached. That's why I bowed out of this one."

"In the world we live in, you can't always sit out every dance."

As if to say: You're in, boy, up to your neck. And there's no kidding around.

I look at him. Being dragged into this pool of venom is exactly what I set out to accomplish. But I couldn't make it obvious that that's what I wanted. I wanted him to insist on it. In spite of everything, I haven't been able to eliminate the last little shadow of doubt. I'm afraid that when you're dealing with someone with his mind-set, you're not likely to eliminate suspicion entirely. But he clearly likes me, and that's a big step forward.

He leans toward me ever so slightly.

"Are you up to this?"

I lower my head and pretend to ponder the question, as if I were still unsure. Then I look up, suddenly confident.

"I can do it."

"Do you have the right men? People you trust?"

"Yes. I know just the right people. Determined and discreet, when necessary."

He relaxes. He fails to notice that I just did the same thing.

"Then you take care of them. I'll see to that other detail."

I add a few words that signal my consent.

"Then we're agreed. I'll get busy and I'll let you know when I'm ready."

"That's fine. While you're here, are you sure you don't want something to eat?"

This is either an invitation or a dismissal, and it's up to me to choose which. I prefer to have the session end there, awaiting further developments.

I stand up.

"Thanks, but I really have to go."

"Whatever you say."

I leave the private dining room where I just pulled a potentially fatal con job on a very dangerous individual, happy to do so without a bodyguard or a gun at my back. In the big dining room I notice his henchman sitting in silence on a chair. Maybe he's thinking that his minestrone must be cold by now. Maybe he's not thinking a thing and is just waiting for orders from the guy who does his thinking for him.

I don't say anything to him and he doesn't say anything to me.

Stefano Milla has the receiver of a phone with a click-counter glued to the side of his head, next to the cash register. He waves good-bye with his free hand. I wave back, relieved I don't have to talk to him. We wouldn't have a thing to say to each other. That fine thread connecting us—a thread of complicity based on a sense of fun more than anything else— has snapped. He's been playing both ends against the middle for so long that he's become too twisted for my tastes. I walk out and take a deep breath.

Outside, the sun is shining brashly and the sky, swept clean of clouds by a light breeze that's sprung up out of the north, is a shade of blue that only spring can paint it. As I walk to my Mini I regret that I'm not in the mood to appreciate it.

Too many things have happened, and all at the same time.

The death of Tulip, the arrival of Carla in my life, the chassis number of my car, Tano Casale with his voice that I know and his counterfeit lottery ticket. And then there are the bundles of newspaper strips that Daytona gave me—I intend to ask him for an explanation the minute I can get my hands on a telephone or wrapped around his neck.

I head back toward Milan, toward home. I need to lie down for a few hours and vegetate with the television turned on, in the shadows. Try to establish a little order in this panorama of chaos. Make a few phone calls, while I wait to hear from the girls.

I retrace the route I followed to get here. When you're thinking about other things, certain trips really seem short, unless your thoughts are obsessively focused on the destination.

Which isn't the case right now.

Before long, I'm back in Cesano. At this time of the afternoon there are plenty of empty parking spaces. I get out of my car, walk around the shrill games the kids are playing

196

on the lawn, and let the gazes of a couple of mothers slide off my back and onto the ground.

A few more moments and I lock the world outside my front door, taking with me only the bare necessities to keep at bay the things that are chasing me. The apartment smells of soap and disinfectant and the wooden roller blinds are lowered halfway. Signora Argenti must have come to put the house in order, an order that I sense I'll soon disrupt.

The minute I walk in the door, I pick up the phone and dial a number, hoping that the person I'm calling is in his office. For once, he answers the phone himself.

"Biondi here. Who's calling?"

"Ugo, it's Bravo."

"I'm busy right now. Tell me quick."

From his slightly disheveled tone of voice, I'm guessing he's entertaining one of his special clients, and she may be sitting astride him right now.

"I need permission to get in to see Carmine."

"When?"

"As soon as possible."

"This isn't a very good time to visit prisoners in San Vittore."

"I can imagine. But I have to see him."

"Okay. I'll call you as soon as I know something."

I don't even have time to say good-bye before the line goes dead.

With the receiver still in my hand, I see in my mind's eye a man's face in a prison visiting room, behind glass. Each time his expression is a little deader, a little more defeated. The idea I'm going to suggest to him may rekindle a bit of life in his features.

Then I go back to considering my own position. I'm doing

197

the twist in a minefield. If I make just one false step, there'll be nothing left of me but shredded flesh.

I hang up the phone very delicately, as if it, too, were mined.

I take the lottery ticket of my dreams out of my inside jacket pocket and toss the jacket onto the couch. I slip off my loafers and walk into my bedroom. I conceal the ticket in my hiding place. Then I turn on the television. The screen flickers to life as I'm stretching out on the bed.

I don't even get a chance to lay my head on the pillow.

The TV's turned to RAI One, which is broadcasting a special edition of the national news. The face of news anchor Bruno Vespa is deadpan, his voice is inexorable, while he reads through a news report that Paolo Frajese has just handed him.

". . . and now, we have confirmation that the member of parliament for the Christian Democratic Party Mattia Sangiorgi, the younger brother of Senator Amedeo Sangiorgi, is also believed to be one of the victims of the multiple homicide committed at the villa of Lorenzo Bonifaci, who was also found dead. We do not yet know the names of the other victims or any other details concerning this horrible massacre, but early leaks from the investigators seem to indicate that no one in the villa escaped alive, even the security personnel, well-trained and competent men that the financier had hired to ensure the safety of himself and his guests, evidently and unfortunately in vain. Let's go to our reporter in Lesmo, near Monza, outside the villa where the massacre took place."

The scene of the news studio is replaced by live images from an exterior camera. The face of the correspondent appears in the foreground, and in the background is a front gate framed by two redbrick columns. A wall, behind which you can see tall trees, extends in both directions, enclosing the grounds of the estate.

The camera shows a squad car parked next to the gate, keeping out the crowd of television and newspaper journalists milling around in search of news.

I don't even hear the reporter's words.

Suddenly I find myself breathing heavy air that smells distinctly unhealthy, as if an evil cloud had permeated every square inch of my bedroom. Sitting there faceless and voiceless, I inspect images I can't see and voices I can't hear, with only one certainty burned in my mind.

My own time, the time I knew, the time in which I moved, is over forever.

CHAPTER 13

The doorbell rings with the roar of an explosion, blowing into a million tiny fragments the moment in which I was hiding. I turn off the television set and get up with the sensation that the legs I'm moving don't actually belong to me. I walk to the door, confident that when I open it I'll see Lucio asking me the solution to my latest puzzle attack and offering to make me a cup of coffee.

Instead, the serious face of Stefano Milla appears before me. With him are two uniformed policemen. One has a dog on a leash, a mongrel that must be part German shepherd. The detective has a neutral expression that in this context comes off as highly professional. At this particular moment I don't have full control of my facial expression. In a few short seconds we're looking at each other again, but now we're two different people. I'm the one who opened my apartment door and got a nasty surprise and he's an officer of the law.

He sticks a hand in his pocket, pulls out a sheet of paper, and hands it to me.

"*Ciao*, Bravo. I'm afraid you're going to have to let us come in. We have a search warrant."

I don't even bother to check the document. I'm sure it's all according to regulation. He strides briskly ahead through the heavily trampled field of formalities.

"You have the right to request the presence of a lawyer during this search. Do you intend to call someone?"

I shake my head and step aside to let them in. Milla walks past me and the two police officers follow close behind him. They stop in the middle of the living room, looking around, wordlessly surveying the room. The dog is calm, and at the order of its policeman handler it sits on the wall-to-wall carpeting.

"You can help us speed up the process. Do you have a storage facility in the basement or attic?"

"No."

"Do you have weapons or drugs in the house?"

"No."

"Do you have a safe?"

I catch myself smiling, disconsolately. I wave one hand eloquently in the air.

"What would I put in a safe?"

I notice that one of the policemen bursts out laughing. He turns away to conceal the fact. Milla doesn't notice and he addresses his men with all the official pomp that his rank confers upon him.

"All right. Proceed."

Without a word, the two policemen spring into action and disappear down the hall. One thought in my mind follows them with a certain degree of apprehension. I'm finally going to have a chance to see if my secret hiding place, which I've always thought was so clever, will stand up to a thorough police search.

Milla has a doleful expression on his face. How sincere it is I couldn't say.

"I'm sorry. I'm afraid your apartment's going to be a bit of a mess when we're done."

"Do I have a choice?"

"I don't think you do."

Resignedly, I go over to the couch and take a seat and wait. Stefano starts rummaging through my dresser drawers. I don't know what to expect from him. Without a doubt, I have a certain privileged advantage in this situation, because to some extent I know about the skeletons in his closet. Can I make tactical use of that? Actually, I doubt it, since talking about Tano Casale and him would mean talking about Tano Casale and *me*.

Maybe Stefano's thinking the same thing, because the whole time that he's working busily between the living room and the tiny kitchen, rummaging and burrowing, our eyes never meet and we never say a word. I believe that the presence of the two police officers in the other rooms is a valid deterrent to any form of communication.

The search seems to last for an eternity. They literally turn the place inside out, pulling out drawers, checking every piece of paper, pulling paintings off the wall, removing the upholstery from the couch, the cases from the cushions and pillows.

In the end, all three of them are standing in the middle of the room. Three men, to say nothing of the dog, as Jerome K. Jerome put it in the title of his novel. Except that this story isn't particularly funny and the boat is springing leaks all over.

Milla looks at me.

"Everything seems okay here. But we're not done yet. You're going to have to come with us."

"Am I under arrest?"

"If you were, you'd already be on the road with handcuffs on your wrists. They just need some information at headquarters."

I stand up from the chair I've been sitting on since he kicked me off the sofa. I pick up my jacket and grab my shoes.

"Then let's get going."

We walk out onto the landing and in a couple of minutes we're at the bottom of the stairs. There's nobody outside. I try to count in my mind how many pairs of eyes are probably watching from the windows and how many *I always suspected that he*'s are wafting up toward the ceilings. Suddenly I understand that I don't give a damn after all. It's just curiosity piled on curiosity, suppositions added to suppositions.

Outside the gate, a police squad car and a truck from the K9 unit are waiting.

The dog disappears with a leap into the back of the K9 truck and I'm ushered toward the Alfa Romeo patrol car. The officer opens the right-side door for me and Milla goes around and gets in on the other side. Once we're all aboard, the car pulls out, without the indignity of the siren, leaving behind us that portion of the world of honest folks who'll never take a trip like the one I'm on.

The car runs through the streets of Milan. Outside there are sounds and noises. Inside there is nothing but silence. Milla and I are seated side by side and we absorb the jolts of the asphalt without looking at each other. Each of us would pay a considerable sum of money to know the other one's thoughts. Each of us would lie if we were asked what we were thinking.

The trip ends at the police station on Via Fatebenefratelli. We drive through the front gate and park in the middle of the courtyard. We get out and walk to a staircase straight ahead of us. Two flights of beat-up old stone stairs and a wall of flaking plaster, then a corridor that echoes our footsteps. Finally, a wooden door.

Milla knocks, and when he hears from the other side of the door the magic word that authorizes him to do so, he turns the handle and creates a void where there once was a door. I walk into an office that smacks of police even if you just suddenly found yourself there, without going through the front door. It's the mismatched furniture and the paper on the desk and the halfhearted paintings on the walls. But especially the faces of the two men sitting in the room. One guy, around thirty, with a dark, mature face, long hair, and a scraggly beard, is sitting in a chair with armrests, in the left-hand corner. He's dressed in an ordinary manner, which in the street might even help him blend in. In this room, he looks like a plainclothes officer or a member of the intelligence services—you could spot him from a plane.

Milla addresses the man sitting behind the desk.

"*Buon giorno*, Mr. Chief Inspector. This is the person in question. As for the other matter, negative."

"Fine. You can go."

While the detective leaves the room, the chief inspector points me to a chair across from him.

"Take a seat."

I comply with his command and we sit facing each other. The chief inspector is older than the other man in the room and is dressed much more formally, with a light blue shirt, a gray three-piece suit, and a tie that should trigger an automatic warrant for his arrest. His hair is short and chestnut brown, his face is lean, and his gaze is enigmatic behind the lenses of his glasses.

I look at him and wait.

"I'm Chief Inspector Vincenzo Giovannone, just to introduce myself."

He says nothing about the other guy, the pale man sitting wordless in his chair. A man with no identity or position. In my mind he immediately becomes the Nameless One.

The chief inspector opens a file that's lying in front of him on his desk.

"Are you Francesco Marcona, also known by the nickname Bravo?"

"Yes."

"I see that you were arrested once for exploitation of prostitution."

Predictable. The waltz begins the way these dances always do. I follow the steps, though I have the feeling that from a certain point on it's going to become necessary to improvise.

"Then you must also see that I was released and there wasn't even an indictment, much less a trial."

"Right."

Giovannone finally looks up from the file. He shoots me a direct glance. His eyes are light-colored and sharp. They're the eyes of a man who knows what he's doing.

"Do you know three young women named, respectively, Cindy Jameson, Barbara Marrano, and Laura Torchio?"

"Yes."

"Were you aware of the fact that last night they were in Lorenzo Bonifaci's villa, in Lesmo, outside of Monza?"

I have a strong presentiment that sweeps over my head and stomach at the same time. The unpleasant sensation of falling that I sometimes get in dreams takes hold of me. There's something grotesque and wrong about this list of names. I took Carla to Piazza San Babila myself. True, I didn't wait around to make sure that Bonifaci's car and driver showed up to get the girls and take them to their appointment, but the presence of Cindy and Barbara in that horrible place ought to mean that she had been there too.

How the hell did Laura get dragged into this?

The chief inspector's harsh tone of voice drags me headlong out of my thoughts.

"Well, were you aware of it or not?"

"Yes. I know that they were invited to a party there."

Despite my best efforts, my voice is different this time. It's the voice of a man who's run out of wisecracks. The chief inspector notices.

He bears in on me.

"Did you know that all three of them were murdered?"

I nod my head affirmatively.

"Yes. Or I guess I should say I had assumed so. When the police came to my apartment, I was watching the television news. There was a special report about what had happened in Bonifaci's villa."

"Then let's talk about him. Did you know Lorenzo Bonifaci?"

"Not in person. What I mean is that I never met him in the flesh. I only spoke to him on the phone."

The chief inspector puts on a look of astonishment, which strikes me as a piece of contrived mockery.

"They tell me he was a fairly reserved and discreet gentleman. Practically impossible to get in touch with. How on earth did he come to have a direct relationship with someone like you?"

I swallow the intentional provocation of the *someone like you*. I make a vague gesture and do my best to accompany it with an innocent tone of voice.

"I know a lot of people in Milan. Especially in the field of fashion. When he has guests over, he calls me to send over a few girls, runway models and cover girls, to make his parties a little more decorative."

"Parties or orgies?"

"I wouldn't know that. I've never been to one."

Chief Inspector Giovannone suddenly springs a new topic on me.

"Did you know a certain Salvatore Menno, an ex-con also known by the nickname Tulip?"

"Yes."

"Did you know that he was also found dead, with three bullet holes in his body from a handgun, in a quarry not far from Trezzano?"

I'll say I knew that.

Pfft . . . pfft . . . pfft . . .

"I read about it in the newspaper."

"In what context did you make his acquaintance?"

"I met him on several occasions at the Ascot Club, on Via Monte Rosa. We had no relationship, except for the fact that now and then we were clients of the same club. Later on I had a disagreement with him over the fact that he was courting a friend of mine with excessive intensity."

"And what's the name of this friend of yours?"

"Laura Torchio."

"Ah."

This tiny monosyllabic word is suddenly as long as a novel and packed with far more information. Bad information. The chief inspector stands up and walks over to the window. He stands there in silence, looking out. When he finally does speak to me, he's shifted from the formal *lei* to the informal *tu*. In Italian, theoretically, that should be friendlier, but the way he uses it, it sounds more like a threat.

"You see, Bravo, there are certain elements in this network of acquaintances that strike me as rather odd."

I can hear him walking up and down behind me. I resist the temptation to turn around to look at him.

"The people you know have a disturbing habit of winding up dead. A man with whom you had a disagreement, as you put it, is found shot to death. The same thing happens to three girls who are friends of yours, as well as a powerful financier with whom you're in regular contact, in a villa where a full-fledged mass murder takes place."

I understand that the knockout punch is about to arrive. And it does.

"The odd thing is that the gun that killed Salvatore Menno turns out to have been one of the weapons used in the murders at the Bonifaci residence. Do you have any idea of how such a thing could have happened?"

He's not really expecting an answer to his question. Or, in any case, there's not any answer I can give him that the chief inspector is willing to believe, except for a full and unconditional confession. It's just a piece of information that he spits in my face because he wants to see how I react. He's putting me on notice that since a ballistics report was delivered in record time, I'm a prime suspect in this case.

"Absolutely not."

Giovannone comes back and sits down across from me. Throughout the interrogation, the Nameless One hasn't changed position or expression.

"Can you tell me where you spent yesterday evening and last night, up until this morning?"

"I had dinner at the Torre Pendente, on Via Ravello. Then I swung by the Budineria, on Via Chiesa Rossa. Then, around midnight, I went home and stayed there until this morning."

I make no reference to what happened with Daytona and the money I was supposed to deliver. An annoying thought has insinuated itself into my brain. A woodworm that gathers power and energy from the words that Stefano Milla tossed out the other night during our conversation.

Only the stupid and the innocent lack an alibi.

My alibi for the night that Tulip was killed had been Carla, and now she's vanished into thin air. And I also have no alibi for the night of the massacre, because I was sitting like an idiot in my car, waiting for a group of strangers to show up— a group of strangers who never came to pick up an envelope full of bundles of newspaper.

"Is there anyone who can verify what you've just told me?"

Christ, no, there isn't. Even Lucio was out. He was in a recording studio at the Castle of Carimate, playing his god-damned guitars. I can feel a rage of unknown origin choking off my breath.

"No."

My answer is brusque and rude.

"That *no* may cost you dearly. And the way you said it, even more."

The detective plays the role of an angry man. I really am angry. I look at him, and for once I ask the questions.

"Am I under arrest? Should I call a lawyer?"

"No, you're not under arrest. Any stupid first-year law student would have you out in an hour, with the evidence I have at this point."

I relax and start to rib him a little.

"Then am I free to go?"

"Sure. But you don't mind if we try a little paraffin glove on you for size, do you?"

Now he's toying with me. And he doesn't even bother to conceal the fact. He knows perfectly well that all you have to do is scrub your hands and you've eliminated all traces of molecular particles. He's just trying to bust my chops and remind me that he has the whip hand. He hasn't made any reference to it, but I feel certain that he knows the precise nature of my relationship with Laura, Cindy, Barbara, and all the other girls. The police have a profound contempt for everyone involved in a certain kind of trafficking, no matter how high the level. Except when they can use their power to rake off a little extra for themselves, the way Stefano Milla does.

"Go right ahead. I've never fired a gun in my life."

"There are people who've never shot a gun, and they're still guiltier than the guy who pulled the trigger."

Giovannone pauses. When he speaks again, his voice is dripping with contempt.

"You're a piece of shit who makes a living off the flesh of girls who are stupid enough to believe you and trust you. You're nothing but a jerk-off who lacks the courage to go any further. How to put it: the smallest possible result with the smallest possible risk. If sheer squalor were against the law, I could get you a life sentence without parole."

He smiles at me. Only with his lips, though.

"This time I'm afraid you may have overstepped your bounds and planted your foot right in the middle of a pile of shit the size of all Lombardy. With all the things that are already going on, you haven't the faintest idea of the tornado that this latest twist has unleashed. And I'm certain that one way or another you're involved."

He takes a second to wipe the smile off his face.

"If it's true, we'll find out. I guarantee you that in that

210

case, many long years in prison will no longer be a fanciful hypothesis, but a fragrant reality that I'll bite into with all the gusto of fresh bread."

He pushes a button on his telephone.

After a second or two the door swings open and a uniformed officer comes in.

"Alfio, accompany the gentleman to the laboratory. And please extend our apologies if the paraffin glove we're going to ask him to wear doesn't go with his lovely designer suit."

I hoist my ass up off the seat before he can figure out a way to make it turn into an electric chair. Then I follow the policeman out of the room. As I leave without so much as a word from either of the two, I do have the slight satisfaction of seeing the Nameless One getting up. At least I now know that he possesses some motor function. I'm also certain that he wasn't just there to complete his training.

By the time I leave the police station, after a lengthy litany of chop-busting over attitudes and acts, it's eight o'clock. The city that awaits me is no longer the city of the day before, when I still believed that the shadow behind the lights was a more than adequate hiding place. I do my best to be realistic with myself. I'm neck-deep in shit. And the worst thing about it all is the sensation that the shit is rising.

I head off on foot toward Piazza San Marco, where I know there's a taxi stand. There's a sense of impending doom in the air, something I never noticed before because I've always slept through my days and at night I frequented a world that was impermeable to anything other than the relentless pursuit of pleasure. Every step is a thought, a question without an answer, a new version of a grim foreboding.

I realize that I'm hungry. I haven't had a bite to eat all day long: my urgent errands before the exchange with Frontini,

211

the conversation with Tano Casale, the discovery of the mass killing, the arrival of the police.

So many things, so little time. And what little time there is is rapidly dwindling, I'm pretty sure.

I walk past a newsstand that's closing for the night. Newspapers must have sold like hotcakes today. I buy one of the last remaining copies of *La Notte*, an afternoon paper that has devoted practically the entire issue to the *Massacre of Lesmo*, as the front-page headline screams. I duck into a restaurant and take a table, after carefully scoping the place out to make sure there's no one I know. I have no interest in absorbing the river of bullshit that certain people spew from their mouths when they're trying to be interesting or funny.

While waiting for the waiter, I open the newspaper. The article alludes to a great deal more than it states, which means the journalist must have made some daring leaps based on the scanty information in his possession. Which was basically the names of the victims. Lorenzo Bonifaci, financier; Mattia Sangiorgi, Christian Democratic member of parliament; Ercole Soderini, wealthy builder, with accompanying stock photos.

Next come the names of the three girls, but among them Carla's name stubbornly refuses to appear. I pause to admire the reporter's deftness at leaving the field wide open to the reader's imagination when it comes to the possible significance of the presence of three men and three women, while never actually making any explicit statements that might justify a libel suit.

The security staff is given short shrift. The paper doesn't even mention their names. Maybe it's an oversight, maybe it's to keep from tainting them by association with the rest of the squalid story.

Finally, the article gives plenty of space to the larger picture of what Italy's going through right now, speculating on a possible link between the Moro kidnapping, the ongoing trial of Red Brigades founder Renato Curcio and his comrades, and this new bloody mass murder, for which there have so far been no claims of responsibility.

If there had been one, if this murder appeared to be related to a terrorist movement, I wouldn't have had such an easy time getting out of the police station. When there's even a hint of suspected subversion, the police are happy to trample rules and procedures underfoot.

I sit thinking in the restaurant, rereading the piece once or twice, as if the facts might change, and eating food that I ingest as a form of nutrition without ever getting a clear sense of its flavor. Two questions keep pounding in my brain.

Why Laura and not Carla?

Why an envelope full of slips of newspaper instead of money?

The answers fail to surface. What comes instead is the check, even though I hadn't asked for it. The restaurant is closing. It's not one of those places that's willing to provide food and hospitality until late, like almost all the other restaurants in this part of town.

I find myself back in the street, where nothing has changed: outside or inside of me. There's just one addition to the equation: now I'm determined to get to the bottom of this, before someone else does it for me and establishes appearances in the place of facts.

I head for the nearest taxi stand. Next to it is a phone booth. I step in, slide a token into the slot, and dial Daytona's number. At this time of evening, there's even a chance of catching him at home. The phone rings and rings but no one picks up.

I catch a cab and tell the driver to take me to the Ascot Club.

The cabbie says nothing and neither do I: a perfect driver and a perfect passenger. He delivers me to my destination with only one statement: the fare for the ride.

Via Monte Rosa is experiencing one of its ordinary nights: traffic, parked cars, women loitering in the street. I take up a position in the shade of a tree at the corner of Via Tempesta, with a clear view of both the front door of the Ascot and the entrance to the Costa Britain office building.

I don't know how long I'm going to have to wait, but I certainly don't feel like waiting in the company of one of the nosy regulars at the Ascot Club.

By now, everyone knows what happened. The ones who knew Laura, Cindy, and Barbara and who knew about their ties to me would be willing to kill, so to speak, to get some firsthand information on the case. Even though the show doesn't start until eleven and it's unlikely I'd run into anyone before then, I still prefer to lurk in the shadows. It's always been my guiding rule in life, though I can't say it's done me a lot of good.

I pace and smoke as I wait, until my patience is finally rewarded. I see two women walking in my direction on the far side of the street. When they come more or less even with me, they cross over to my side of the street, and as they pass I recognize one of them. It's the cleaning woman who looked at me with a face full of assumptions, the morning I first approached Carla.

I step up and address them.

They're two women of ordinary appearance, the same

height and impossible to place in terms of age, maybe made slightly more attractive in the half-light. They look so much alike they could easily be sisters. Or maybe they're just born losers and that hallmark creates a resemblance that's stronger than blood. They come to a halt and stand side by side, with the suspicion stamped on their faces that I've probably just taken them for prostitutes.

I speak to the familiar face.

"Excuse me, do you mind if I ask you a question?"

"Go right ahead."

"Do you do the cleaning at the Costa offices?"

"Yes."

"There's a girl who works with you, a certain Carla Bonelli. You wouldn't happen to have her address and phone number by any chance, would you?"

The two women exchange a glance. Then the one I first spoke to answers for the pair of them.

"What was the name you just said?"

"Carla Bonelli."

The reply comes immediately, without hesitation.

"There's no girl by that name working with us."

I don't know how big the plot of ground is that I'm standing on, but I can definitely feel it shrinking beneath my feet.

"Are you sure? She's a tall girl, with chestnut hair and hazel eyes. I saw her leave work with you, a few days ago."

"Sure, I remember that girl. But she was standing in the street by the front door when we left work, she was never inside with us. And I remember you, too. Forgive me, but we just assumed that the girl was one of those women and that you were . . ."

She catches herself before telling me what she thought I

was. And I see how things actually went. I never did actually see Carla come out the door with the others. Daytona was the one who pointed her out to me, outside the Costa offices. He was the one who challenged me to pick her up, knowing that I'd eagerly take the bait.

I turn my back on the two women and leave, without thanking them or saying good-bye. Who the fuck cares. I have something more important to do right now. I walk briskly toward the taxi stand in Piazza Amendola. I can feel the impelling need, as tight around me as if I were wearing a straitjacket, to have a little talk with Paolo Boccoli, better known by his nickname, Daytona.

CHAPTER 14

Daytona's mother lives in the Isola district, on Via Confalonieri, near the Stecca degli Artigiani. As I walk through the park on my way to her house, I wonder whether I'm doing something incredibly stupid. That's certainly a possibility I can't rule out, but when you're drowning, even a sponge bobbing on the surface starts to look a lot like a lifesaver.

Last night I covered half of Milan, dropping into the all the places my friend usually spends his evenings, but without success. At Le Scimmie, on the Navigli, I ran into Matteo Sana and Godie, but when they saw me they reacted in a way that frankly surprised me. Instead of hurrying me into a dark, quiet corner where they could hammer my balls with question after question, they just pretended they hadn't seen me at all. That allowed me to gauge my current position. Now I'm someone it's best not to be seen talking to. In this specific case, it might just be better that way. I took a look around the crowded club, trying to catch a glimpse of Daytona's head with its distinctive double comb-over.

I didn't find him.

I figured there were plenty of places he could be: at Tano's gambling den or someplace where they let you lose all your money, or else in bed with some hooker. Or else up in some hovel, like a giant treacherous rat, gnawing away at his piece of hard cheese, waiting for the storm to blow over.

In any case, all of those places are either unidentifiable or unreachable.

In the taxi that took me home, I remembered the words that Daytona spoke in an almost identical situation, and that gave me an idea. A pathetic, desperate, miserable idea, but it was the only one I had. Now here I am, with an oversize leather-bound desk diary under my arm and a heavy manila business envelope, which, as fate would have it, is stuffed with bundles of neatly clipped pages from a newspaper. As I was filling the envelope, I couldn't help but smile, thinking that this could be a case of *sartor resartus*—the clipper reclipped.

Lucio would have been proud of me for that one.

But I didn't feel like telling him about my troubles in order to collect the prize.

I find myself outside the street door of an ordinary apartment building, clearly the product of some public housing project. This is where Daytona's mother lives, and she's the only hope left to me in my quest to track him down. That piece of shit actually has a pretty close relationship with the woman who brought his unkempt bundle of loserdom into the world, as so often seems to be the case with certifiable whoremongers like him. If he's pulled something big and decided to lie low for a while, his mother is the one person who certainly knows where he is. And before long, with a sliver of good luck and plenty of my good old-fashioned shameless impudence, I hope to find out for myself.

I step up to the intercom and press the buzzer that's marked boccoli-crippa. Time passes as I imagine her dragging her feet down a hallway on a couple of felt pads to keep from

218

dulling the shine of the wax. The voice that comes out of the speaker is warm and pleasant.

"Yes?"

I cross my fingers and announce myself.

"*Buon giorno, Signora.* My name is Rondano, I'm Paolo's insurance agent. I can't find him at his apartment. Would he happen to be here, by any chance?"

"No, he's out of town for a few days, for work."

Just as I expected. That poor woman is the only person in the city of Milan who could mention her son and the idea of work in the same breath. If it's true that a son can always pull the wool over his mother's eyes, Daytona's pulled the entire sheep.

"That's what I guessed. I just happened to be in the neighborhood, and since I have some documents for him to sign, I thought I'd stop by and drop them off with you. It's for a claim settlement. If you'll open the door for me, I can leave them with you. That way, when he gets back he can sign them right away. The quicker he gets them to me, the quicker I can get him his money."

She's stumped. I can tell from the long silence that follows my words. At last, her fear of interfering with her son's interests or even getting him mad at her wins out over her inborn caution.

"Third floor."

The door clicks open with a harsh, metallic sound. The word *money* is a jimmy that can force open many doors, both physical and mental. I climb the drab steps, inhaling air that reeks of cooking and bleach. It's not a very appetizing medley. But I'm not here to buy an apartment, just to steal some information.

Daytona's mother is waiting for me at the door. She's a

woman of average height, with a weary face and a vulnerable air about her. She's wearing an apron over a housedress. Maybe when I rang she was making something to eat, more out of habit than hunger. From what little I know of her life, the only good thing that ever happened to her was that her husband, who treated her like a dog, died at an early age. Unfortunately fate took its revenge by presenting her with a son like Daytona, who calls her *la me mameta* and who must be personally responsible for half the white hairs on her head.

There are some people who never seem to catch a break.

She greets me with that same lovely voice, but over the intercom it had made me imagine a very different appearance. Fantasy on the radio, reality on TV.

"Buon giorno."

"Buon giorno, Signora . . ."

"Crippa, Teresa."

In spite of my current frame of mind, I'm touched by a twinge of tenderness at this introduction. As if I were a census taker, she gives me surname, comma, followed by Christian name. I extend a hand with my very sunniest smile. She clasps my hand with some hesitance, as if she were somehow unworthy of the person she's meeting.

"Pleasure to meet you. Marco Rondano."

I hand her the envelope.

"Here it is, Signora Teresa. Inside this envelope are the documents I told you about. Just tell Paolo to sign where I marked an *X* in pencil."

She repeats it back to me, just to make sure that she understood correctly.

"He should sign where there's an *X* in pencil."

"Exactly. Thanks very much, Signora."

220

I take a couple of steps backward, as if I'm about to turn and go. I stop and interrupt her words of farewell by lifting my wrist to check the time. I put on the worried face of someone who's just remembered something important.

"Could I ask you a favor?"

"Of course."

"There's a person I have to call and I need to catch them now, before they leave the office. Would it be too much trouble if I asked to use your phone? It's a local call."

Many people who are getting along in years are very cautious about their phone bills. I added that last detail to reassure her that the call won't cost her a cent.

"Well, if it's a call here in the city, certainly. Paolo pays my phone bill, and I wouldn't want him to spend too much money."

I feel like telling her that her son loses more money at the card tables in five hours than she gets from her retirement payments in five years. But it would just be gratuitously unkind and a waste of time: there are myths that are completely bulletproof.

Signora Teresa ushers me into a hallway that's so clean it looks like a painting. There's a slight scent in the air that's reminiscent of eucalyptus cough lozenges. The furniture is worn but gleaming, probably furniture that was new the day she was married. On the walls hang ordinary paintings, purchased at the fair or won at a charitable drawing. A framed photograph of her son with his class at school, surrounded by a crocheted passe-partout, hangs above the phone. A caption is embroidered into the doily-like mat under the glass: *Third Grade*. I'm surprised to learn that Daytona even made it that far in school. When I see the phone, I heave a sigh of relief. It's one of those black ones, with a circular dial. It's sitting on an otherwise nondescript piece of furniture, with two shelves one above the other, and a cabinet under the shelves with two little doors.

I lay the desk diary on the lower shelf.

I dial my own phone number and pretend to have an intense conversation with a nonexistent client, leaving a long message on my answering machine, well beyond the beep that indicates that the message has gone on too long. I end the conversation as if the person I just spoke with had told me something worrisome.

"Don't worry, I'll be there in just ten minutes. Piazzale Maciachini, right?"

I leave a pause for an answer that would never come.

"Number six, I've got it. I'll see you in just a bit."

I turn to look at poor Signora Teresa, who has been listening to my end of the conversation from the kitchen, where the table is strewn with chopped and as-yet-unchopped vegetables for eventual use in a future minestrone. A time-consuming, labor-intensive, health-giving recipe: and, most important of all, an inexpensive one. I act like someone with the devil on his tail.

"There, all done. Thank you so much. Unfortunately I have to run now. Say hello to Paolo and tell him to get in touch."

She takes a step toward me.

"Don't bother, I know the way out. Take care, Signora."

She calls out *arrivederci* when I'm already at the far end of the hallway. Oh, she may say "until we meet again," but she has no idea how soon it will be. If everything goes as it should, I'll be back in fifteen minutes.

I close the door behind me and I hurry away, afraid that I might hear the door swing open any minute and her voice summoning me back. Luckily, that's not what happens. I slip into the first bar I pass. I order an espresso and smoke a cigarette, leafing through the *Corriere della Sera*, which is lying alongside the *Gazzetta dello Sport* on the ice cream freezer.

On the newsprint pages there are words and pictures. All of them related to the events that occurred in a wealthy home in Lesmo, outside Monza. Facts and suppositions, stories of individuals, the smiling faces of pretty girls, the serious faces of men in official settings, bodies sprawled on the ground, covered with bloodstained sheets transformed into black-and-white splotches. Whatever the nature of a life, death should afford a little privacy.

There's nothing about a woman with hazel eyes who was supposed to be in that house but wasn't. She wasn't in any of the places where she told me that she'd been. And she wasn't in any of the places where she told me she'd be. Only in my apartment and on my skin, here and there.

I glance at my watch. It's been twenty minutes. That should be plenty.

A few seconds later I'm downstairs, pressing the same buzzer again. Her voice takes the exact same amount of time to issue from the intercom.

"Who is it?"

"Signora, I'm sorry to bother you, it's Rondano again. I forgot my desk diary. Can I come up and get it?"

The door clicks open. I walk in and hurry up the steps. She's standing at the door with the object of my all-too-intentional forgetfulness in her hand.

"I'm just getting everything backward today. I don't know what's come over me. As they say: If you don't use your head, you'll have to use your legs."

I take the leather-bound volume with its gold clasp lock from her hands.

"It certainly is heavy!"

"Well, that's the leather binding that makes it so heavy. It was a gift from my girlfriend, otherwise I would have already gotten something lighter."

We say good-bye again, and as I hurry downstairs this time my haste is genuine. As soon as I'm out in the street I pull a small brass key out of my pocket and I insert it into the lock on the clasp that secures the desk diary. I open it and I'm reassured by what I find inside. I've cut a space into the paper just big enough to conceal the portable tape recorder that is still turning, before my eyes. In succession I push the stop button and then the rewind button. With a faint whine the tape whirs back to the beginning. I wait to get back to my car before listening to it, and I've never walked a longer three hundred yards in my life.

I get behind the wheel and slam the car door shut. I heave a sigh that amounts to an auditory crossing of fingers and I push the play button. For a little while you can hear, faint but comprehensible, the conversation between me and Daytona's mother. My whole performance right up to when I say good-bye and hurry offstage.

Finally, I hear what I'm most interested in.

In the silence of the apartment, the sound of a telephone rotor being dialed. Loud and clear. Even though it's being recorded through the cover of the desk diary.

Trrr . . . trrr . . . trrr . . .

Then Signora Teresa's voice.

"*Ciao*, sweetheart, it's me."

Silence.

"I know I'm not supposed to call you, but somebody came

to see you. It's your insurance agent. He brought you some documents you're supposed to sign for a reimbursement."

Silence.

"I don't know. They're in an envelope."

A pause. The woman becomes increasingly anxious as she openly avows her inadequacy.

"Now, you know I don't understand anything about this kind of thing. I'll put it in your bedroom and you can open it when you come home."

Another short silence. This one's not to listen but to screw up her courage.

"Will you be here soon?"

I imagine Daytona hiding somewhere, anxious and on edge, his comb-over disheveled and his face red as a beet. I imagine his mother's face as she accommodates her son's lies. I consider that if she had decided to open the envelope, my own lies would have been uncovered.

"All right, darling. But take care. And call me now and then."

The sound of the receiver being hung up and then steps fading away. Back to the kitchen, I imagine.

I stop the tape recorder. From the brief conversation that's recorded on the tape, I have a confirmation of two facts. The first is that, whatever's going on, that bastard Daytona's in it up to his neck. The second is that I may have a way of finding out where he's hiding.

I rewind the tape to the point where Signora Teresa dialed the number. I pull out a sheet of paper and I start a process of deciphering the numbers that I hope will prove to be effective. I start marking down the numbers after counting the whirring clicks of the telephone dial. The system is catch-as-catch-can and I have to rewind the tape a number of

225

times before obtaining a result that strikes me as reasonably certain. If there's a god who watches over sons of bitches, I pray that he'll rest his hand on my head and remove his hand from Daytona's.

Trrr . . . trrr . . . trrr . . . trrr . . . trrr . . . 5.

Trrr . . . trrr . . . trrr . . . trrr . . . trrr . . . trrr . . . trrr . . . 7.

Trrr . . . trrr . . . trrr . . . trrr . . . 4.

Trrr . . . trrr . . . trrr . . . trrr . . . trrr . . . trrr . . . 6.

Trrr . . . trrr . . . trrr . . . trrr . . . trrr . . . 5.

Trrr . . . trrr . . . trrr . . . trrr . . . trrr . . . 5.

Now I have a phone number: 57 46 55.

The next thing I need is an address to go with it. Of all the people I know, there's only one I can turn to. I start the car, drive for a short distance, and stop at the first phone booth I find. I could call the phone company and ask Information, but I'm afraid that service is available only from a home phone. I have only one alternative. I can't deny that the finger I use to dial the main switchboard of the police station on Via Fatebenefratelli is a little shaky.

I ask the switchboard operator to put me through to Detective Stefano Milla. She puts me on hold, and a few seconds later I hear his voice.

Very professional, and therefore with a sharp edge of irritation.

"Detective Milla."

"This is Bravo."

The leap in tone is sudden. I'd have to imagine it corresponds to a leap off his chair.

"Have you lost your mind, calling me here?"

"Mabye so. But I have a problem."

"I know you do. You want me to have one, too?"

"No, not if you give me a hand with something."

That last phrase sounds like a threat. Maybe it is, maybe it isn't. The important thing is for Milla to think it is.

"What do you want?"

"I have a phone number. I need to get the address that goes with it."

"Why?"

"It's a long, murky story. The minute I figure it out, you're the first person I'll come to with the details."

"Bravo, don't fuck around."

"That's the last thing I would do. Which is why I need your help to find that address."

In the end he gives in. It's partly out of fear and partly out of that inborn curiosity that makes a man want to be a cop.

"All right. Go ahead and give me the number."

I repeat the numbers one by one, giving him plenty of time to write them down.

"How long will it take you?"

"As long as it takes. Where can I reach you?"

"At home. If I'm not there, leave a message on my answering machine."

"That's a risky thing to do."

"I'll erase it the minute I listen to it."

The silence that ensues indicates hesitation. He's trying to weigh how much trouble he might be getting himself in by helping me. He doesn't need to think too hard about the consequences: he knows them in detail. You always have to know how to count your steps when you dance with different pairs of shoes.

I try to tip the board in my direction.

"Stefano, I really don't know what's going on. All I know is that I have nothing to do with all this crazy bullshit. I sent

227

three girls over to Bonifaci's house for a party, just like I've done dozens of times before. And that's all."

For the moment, I decide it's best not to give him any more information. There are things I need to find out and understand before I share them with anyone else. My position is already sufficiently precarious, and I have no intention of giving anyone any information that they might use to destabilize it further, tipping me over the edge once and for all.

In the end, Milla gives in.

"I'll get it as fast as I can."

I thank him, for what that's worth. I hang up and find myself all alone, waiting for an address where my last slender hope resides. I look around. The weather seems to be particularly kind these days to humanity. A springlike blue sky and beaming sun, a cool breeze that pushes away the city's smog. Busy people up and about; the rough customers still in bed, sleeping off the hangovers of their vicious pursuits. If it was a normal day, maybe that's where I would be. Or else I'd be kicking around Milan, shooting the shit with people and making my deals, having lunch at Santa Lucia or eating a panino at Bagi.

But that's not the way it is. It's impossible for it to be that way again anytime soon.

A number of people are dead now. I helped three of those into a car and sent them to their deaths. I stood to collect 30 percent of the money they earned. I have a sneaky feeling that I'm about to collect 100 percent of the guilt that attaches to whatever happened.

I look around.

Without paying attention to where I was going, I'd driven around Milan's Monumental Cemetery, and I'd wound up on

Via Cenisio. A hundred yards or so from where I parked my Mini is Pechino, a Chinese restaurant where I eat fairly often and which serves Milan's finest grilled wontons.

I decide that, as little appetite as I have, one place is as good as another. As I walk toward the restaurant I feel a stab of discomfort in my groin, a faint burning sensation that I know all too well. Inflammations of the urinary tract, with my anatomical condition, are fairly frequent. I also feel an occasional shiver, though I don't know whether it's due to stress or a degree or two of fever.

Tac. Got you! Feverish and on the lam.

That's what Godie would say as he jabbed his two fingers in a scissors-grip against my neck. But those times are gone now, and I'm not sure they'll ever come back. I'm in too much of a hurry to waste time lingering over my own misery or letting tears drip down my shirtfront. I'm finally keeping pace with the city that surrounds me, where haste reigns uncontested, where everyone runs, even when it's time to go to sleep. In the middle of all this feverish bedlam, my life is at stake. Now I have nothing to do but kill time waiting for a corrupt cop to give me the information I need and then go to clear up a couple of matters with my friend.

Fifty yards from the restaurant is a pharmacy. Behind the counter is a pharmacist I know, a woman dressed in a white lab coat, with the glasses and acne of the grind that she is. The discomfort is getting worse but I have no wish to discuss it with anyone, especially not with a woman. I ask for a box of Furadantin, and after a little back-and-forth, even though I have no prescription, the pharmacist agrees to sell me one.

I leave the pharmacy and toss back a tablet without water. I don't want to be seen at a table in a restaurant taking certain pharmaceuticals. It's a learned sense of caution that goes with my handicap. I open the front door of Pechino and walk into a little restaurant decorated with red lampshades and other Chinese bric-a-brac. The place is usually pretty empty at lunchtime. In fact, right now only one of the tables is occupied.

The proprietor of the restaurant, who knows me well, comes beaming to welcome me. He's a competent and jovial guy. He speaks perfect Italian and equally perfect Milanese dialect. It's odd to hear Milan's distinctive dialect—*meneghino*— spoken by someone with his distinctly non-Italian features. The restaurant is successful in large part because of his likable personality, as well as the first-rate food.

We exchange greetings and I think he sees from my face that I'm not in the mood. He wastes no time in chitchat. He shows me to my table, takes my single order, and heads off to the kitchen, where his wife does the cooking.

I sit down at an angle to the counter of the bar, which is on the right side of the restaurant, just inside the front door. A young Chinese man is working the espresso machine and watching a small portable television set that he has placed, with the sound turned down low, on the marble countertop.

The evening news is on, and I imagine to myself the panic of the producers as they try to keep up with the flood of news pouring in from all directions. But the chief news item right now is what happened outside Monza. From where I sit, I have a fairly good view of the screen, which is showing a stream of images that one way or another I'd already glimpsed in the newspapers I've read.

I stand up and walk over to the television set.

The young man, a guy whose voice I've never actually heard, goes on with what he's doing and says nothing to me. I ask if he could turn up the volume a little.

He does, and even turns the television set in my direction.

On the screen I see a man get out of a long dark car. He's immediately surrounded by a cohort of police officers to protect him from the frenzied mob of reporters. Behind the swirling crowd I can see the front entrance of the Hotel Principe e Savoia in Piazza della Repubblica. The man at the center of attention is tall and powerfully built, his thick head of hair marked by white patches at the temples, and he has the determined expression of a man who knows where he's going and exactly how to get there.

I know him well.

Everyone knows him well.

He's Amedeo Sangiorgi, a Sicilian, a parliamentary group leader in the Italian senate, and a leading figure in his party and in Italian political life. His much younger brother Mattia was one of the men found murdered in Bonifaci's villa. He was a member of the Chamber of Deputies and one of the rising young figures of the Christian Democratic Party, seen by many as a potential future prime minister of Italy.

The fact that his brother was found dead in the same house with two other men of his same social milieu and three beautiful young women, all likewise dead, does not appear to have left any marks on the face of Amedeo Sangiorgi. Without a doubt, deep inside he's seething with fury at the way this aspect of the matter has become a topic for public debate, instead of remaining safely concealed in the folds of judicial secrecy. But he's too experienced and consummate a politician to reveal his emotions and not to know that we live in a strange country, where certain foibles are forgiven and forgotten with extreme ease. With a little help from your friends, as someone once said. I'm sure that, after the initial leering speculation in the press, and with the proper pressure applied judiciously in the appropriate venues, Cindy, Barbara, and Laura will simply become three dedicated and unfortunate secretaries who paid too high a price for attending a business dinner that day.

An RAI journalist approaches Amedeo Sangiorgi with a microphone in his hand, followed by a cameraman with a television camera on his shoulder. The senator waves away the policeman who's about to block the journalist's path and agrees to issue what is commonly known as a brief statement.

He then proceeds to do so in a deep voice, steeped in grief and indignation.

"This act is the product of an unprecedented savagery, the kind of barbarity that is an expression of total contempt for the sanctity of human life. It leaves us aghast and grief-stricken, wondering what sort of men can harbor such ferocity deep inside their souls. We weep over the loss of brothers, husbands, sons. These are moments in which our hopes and our faith in the institutions of the state seem to waver and fail us, along with words themselves. But it is precisely in moments like these that it is our right and our duty to react. We must be certain of only one thing. Wherever this cowardly attack may originate, whether it is a terrorist plot or the work of some organized crime family, it will not go unpunished. The police are hard at work trying to lay their hands on the guilty parties, to bring them to justice and to mete out the punishment that they so richly deserve."

His voice wavers slightly as he comes to the end of his statement. A shadow of grief passes briefly over his face. It's a perfect performance: the very image of what people expect from a man in his position—a resolute dignity capable of transcending the tempest of emotions.

The screen goes back to the news anchor in the studio, who begins to explore the question of how many men were in the squad that attacked the villa where the massacre, as everyone now refers to it, took place.

The words of Chief Inspector Giovannone surface in my mind.

You haven't the faintest idea of the tornado that this latest twist has unleashed . . .

Oh, I have a very clear idea. A politician of Aldo Moro's stature, held captive by the Red Brigades; another one of equal prominence lying dead on a slab in the morgue, slain by persons unknown. Add to that the strain of ongoing terrorism trials and the chilly veil of fear that touches everyone and everything.

Right now, every police and Carabinieri officer in Italy must be on high alert, along with all the operatives of the DIGOS intelligence service and the other intelligence agencies, as well as who knows who else. In the various ministries, all the most important politicians in the country must be tearing their hair out, wondering what the hell is happening in the Bel Paese, sending their men—and there are never enough of them—from one point to another on the map, like tin soldiers in a war game.

I see the proprietor emerging from the kitchen with the dish of wontons that I ordered, which he sets down at my table. I go back, sit down, and eat in silence, and the burning sensation in my groin increases instead of diminishing. I force myself to finish my food, hoping fuel will produce energy.

I look at my watch. Maybe Milla has already found the information I need. In any case I no longer have the patience to sit here, waiting, doing nothing, the victim of events, with the growing impression that I'm not the master of my own existence.

I pay the check, leave the restaurant, and go back to the phone booth near where my car is parked. I drop a token into the slot and I dial my home number. I listen to my own voice announce my absence and ask me to leave a message for myself. I wait for the message to end and I pronounce the sequence of sounds that activates the remote control.

After a few clicks and hisses, the answering machine plays back the entire sequence of messages. A couple of phone calls from clients who have no idea how much trouble they could get in just for leaving a message on that strip of tape. Sandra, one of my girls, asking me to call her. A phone call from someone who hung up without leaving a message. My phone conversation with no one from the house of Signora Crippa, Teresa. Then, last of all, the voice of Stefano Milla, who provides me, without any further comment, the address I'm looking for.

As soon as I get back in the car I make a note of it, even though I'm sure I would never forget it. I pull out into traffic, thinking to myself that it's going to be a long drive to San Donato Milanese. The burning sensation, in the meantime, has become a red-hot wire that someone has twisted around my groin and through my stomach.

CHAPTER 15

My small dark blue car is racing down the road at the top legal speed, heading in the direction of the metropolis that everyone knows as San Donato Milanese, an outlying development that in the past two years has risen to the rank of a full-fledged township. A satellite city, with everything that this term implies. It's a strange place, an ENI company town, where a considerable number of the inhabitants work for that large, state-owned oil company. Two structures in one. One half industrial plants and office buildings, the other half a bedroom community, equipped with all the services that a settlement of that kind demands and requires. A classic instance of hardworking Lombard enterprise, which I will never entirely be able to wrap my head around.

As I drive, my mind continues to wander through the twisting labyrinth that someone has decided to force me to explore. The characters that crowd into this story—whose beginning I can't understand and whose end is nowhere in sight- are all sitting in the car with me.

Tano Casale, with his familiar voice, who's waiting to collect his winnings on a counterfeit lottery ticket so that he can double his money thanks to my brilliant idea. Laura, who should have have been a happy, free woman with a cabaret artist boyfriend but who wound up dying in a place she was never supposed to be. Carla, who was supposed to be there instead, and who has now vanished into thin air like a ghost after pretending to be something and someone she never was, possibly under a name that was never hers. Daytona, who did everything he could to make sure I met her and then, after all hell broke loose, took to his heels. And last of all me, a member of that category of the stupid or the innocent who wander through stories like this one without the protection of an alibi.

I can feel the fever chills racking my body. The pain has stabilized at a tolerable level, but it's no fun to live with. I leave the beltway and turn onto Via Rogoredo. I continue on for a while, passing the various factories that have sprung up over time like warts on what was once farm country. I keep driving until I find a place where I can pull over and park the Mini.

I pop another tablet and pore over the street map of Milan and surrounding territory that I always carry with me in my car, looking for the address that Milla found for me. The house where the phone company installed the phone that Daytona's mother called is number 106 of Via dei Naviganti Italiani, and the service is in the name of a certain Aldo Termignoni. A name that's new to me. But with all the connections and business dealings my friend is constantly juggling, it would be hard to keep up with all the people he knows and sees.

It's stop-and-go driving for a while, as I pull over frequently to double-check my route on the map. I leave the city and the directions steer me farther and farther away, out into genuine countryside. Buildings arranged around a square courtyard, the last outposts against the onslaught of progress and development. As I drive, the roar of low-flying airplanes coming in for a landing at Linate Airport glides over my head and over the houses around me.

At last I turn onto the street I've been looking for. There's a small cluster of houses and a road that continues straight toward a stand of trees in the distance. I check the street number of the last house on my left and discover that that side of the street is odd-numbered. I drive on slowly until I come to other buildings. The street numbers seem to come one by one out of a bingo tumbler cage.

There's no one in sight. The cars are parked in the courtyards or else along the side of the road, and the people are all inside their houses. A little boy plays alone in a yard. He doesn't know how that loneliness can grow over the years. Everyday life, everyday words, everyday deeds. An alarm clock rings, a child to take to school, paydays that never seem to come in time, two weeks of vacation every year, polkas in the local dance hall, sex in a car with your girl until you can get married.

Or, if you're not that lucky, a five-thousand-lira streetwalker on the Via Paullese.

The stabbing pains in my groin and the intermittent shivering both continue. And now I have bouts of nausea to keep them company. I emerge from the trees into what I would call open countryside, if it weren't for the fact that on the horizon the bastions of yet another industrial plant loom over a field of amber wheat. Maybe this is the kind of dystopian postindustrial place where the Old Man and the Little Boy from the Francesco Guccini song will stroll together one day.

I pull up to an isolated farmhouse that has seen better days and that still, all these years later, carries a whiff of the postwar era. The appearance of the farmhouse is one of general decrepitude; the courtyard looks more like a junkman's warehouse than part of a working Italian farm. A rusted-out refrigerator is leaning against a tree; the gutted carcass of an automobile stripped of license plates and tires is perched forlornly on four stacks of bricks. A roll-down shutter is jammed to one side so that the window looks like the half-lidded eye of a dog. In the background I catch a glimpse of a low building made of panels of rusted sheet metal nailed to wooden poles driven into the soil.

Weeds sprout up here and there, sowing their intermittent chaos at random, and one side of the house can be reached only by wading through a full-fledged plantation of stinging nettles. Numbers and letters daubed inexpertly with a paintbrush and black paint on one of the two pillars flanking the little entry drive inform me that I've reached my destination.

I stop the Mini in the courtyard. Maybe it would have been smarter to drive on, park some distance away, and walk back to the house quietly. But I'm in too much pain and in too much of a hurry.

The door in the front of the house is fastened by a padlock on a chain that runs through two holes drilled through the wood of both panels. On the ground floor, all the wooden blinds are rolled down completely. I skirt the house and reach the back. A walkway of shattered, crumbling concrete runs the entire length of the building. Through the door of the shed in the back, left half open and concealed from the road, I can see the orange tail of Daytona's Porsche. I proceed up the sidewalk, past windows protected by metal grates, and come to a halt before a wooden door.

The door is ajar.

I shove the door, instinctively apprehensive of the squeak that might follow.

What an idiot I am.

My arrival has been amply announced by the sound of my Mini pulling into the courtyard. I step inside and glance around at the dark, filthy room, to all appearances completely uninhabited. I take a quick look around the ground floor. Nothing but bare, empty rooms, crumpled paper on the floor, a dusty blanket, a stack of chipped dishes in what seems to be a kitchen. Everywhere, the dank smell of dust and saltpeter. I wonder to myself who could live in such a pigsty. And yet someone must, since someone pays the electric and phone bills.

I start up the stairway that runs from the landing just inside the front door and climbs back up to the second floor, a typical architectural feature of these country houses. When I get to the top of the stairs, I find myself in a slightly better kept part of the house, where signs of cleaning and tidiness point to a human presence. A hallway runs the whole length of the house, with the open doors of the bedrooms looking out along the wall like so many gaping mouths.

It looks as if the area to the right has been pretty much neglected, and so I turn left. I go past a room with two cots with bare mattresses on them. A closed door with a pane of frosted glass might be a bathroom. Then there's another room with a half-open door, through which I can make out a double bed with rumpled sheets.

Finally I step through a door and into the last room on this side of the building.

A quick glance around the room gives me a clear idea of the place. The paint on the walls had been applied in broad, messy stripes with a paint roller; there are some swaybacked armchairs, newspapers and glasses on a small round table, canned food on a shelf, dirty dishes in a bucket, a gas hot plate connected to a propane tank, a telephone attached to the wall.

While I was walking upstairs, I wondered why no one came to see who was in the house.

Now that I'm here, I can see the reason.

Daytona is stretched out on the floor, on one side, his head lolling on his extended arm. The whole front of his shirt is soaked red with blood. As a result of the fall, the comb-over that he so zealously kept in place has split in half. One part is draped lankly over his rolled-up sleeve, while the other sags over his ear, baring the bald spot that he worked tirelessly to conceal. Hearing my footsteps, he moves his eyes without turning his head. When he recognizes me, his alarmed glance relaxes slightly, replaced by a look of relief.

"B . . . avo."

His voice is faint and weak, and in fact I guessed more than heard him utter my name. I kneel down beside him. His breathing is labored, with a hissing rattle that seems to be coming from somewhere other than this room.

He's crying, and I don't know if it's from pain or distress. A sob turns into a spurt of reddish foam emerging from between his lips to greet the world. From the corner of his mouth it slithers to the floor, where it turns into a red tear of disappointment.

"Fr . . . gv . . . me."

Forgiveness does not belong to this world. But I have the pretty strong impression that soon neither will he, so I don't think twice about giving him what he wants.

"Of course I forgive you, you ugly idiot."

As if prompted by his weeping, tears well up in my eyes too: I cry for him, for myself, for all the idiots just like us, for the whole world that an imperfect god has relegated to the space outside these windows with their filthy glass panes. For all those who made us the way we are, and for us, who allowed them to do it. For this pain that twists my guts, which must not be all that different from what Daytona is feeling.

"What happened?"

"Stabbed . . . in . . . chest."

Each word seems to cost him an infinite effort. He's at the end of the line, and he knows it. He's counting his breaths, waiting to draw the last one, the breath that no one can ever fix in their memory, because after that last breath comes nothing. Maybe he's wondering if it was smart to muster all the venom in his soul in pursuit of the killing he thought would finally make him rich. Or maybe he's wondering if he made the right decision when he chose this miserable life. Instead of a paycheck for honest work, this: to die like a dog, all alone, bleeding onto a filthy floor in a shithole of an abandoned house. And what does he leave the world as his last bequest? The total nothing that his whole life has amounted to.

"Who did it?"

Making an immense effort, he lifts one hand and raises it to his head. He touches the lank lock of hair and does his best to arrange it on top of his head, in a last clumsy impulse of vanity. I reach out and help him to put his comb-over, glistening with hairspray and dye, back into place.

I repeat the question.

"Who did it, Daytona? Where's Carla?"

He stares at me without seeing me. He seems to be reliving a scene I never witnessed. Perhaps the scene in

241

which someone killed him. Maybe, the way people say, he's reliving his whole life. Then he shuts his eyes.

"White . . . ice . . ."

They're his last words.

A surge of nausea rushes up from my stomach and into my throat. I stand up, walk a step or two away, and then I fold over like a switchblade knife snapping shut.

I vomit.

Long, painful bouts of retching that seem to turn my stomach inside out and split my head in two. When I'm done throwing up, I'm covered with a film of clammy sweat. I'm sorry that my funeral eulogy for Daytona was nothing more than a noisy regurgitation that brought back the fried wontons transformed into an acid porridge.

I pull out my handkerchief and wipe my mouth.

I see that he still has his precious gold Daytona Rolex on his wrist, the watch that kept time through the ups and downs of his life—a watch that formed a larger part of his identity than his own first and last names in a certain Milanese milieu. I slip the watch off his wrist, with the thought that the only part of him that's still ticking is this timepiece. I drop it into my jacket pocket. As soon as I can, I'll get it to that poor woman who was his mother, with whom I share this unenviable fate: finding out in the worst way possible just who her son really was.

My last few remaining shreds of intelligence urge me to get out of this place as quickly as possible. I can't help thinking that if I'd managed to get here just a few minutes earlier, I might be lying on the floor next to Daytona right now, with all warmth and color slowly seeping out of my body. I take one last look at the corpse of a man who I once thought was my friend, forgetting that in reality no one ever truly is poor pathetic two-bit loser but, in spite of everything, maybe someone who didn't deserve what happened to him. I turn to go, abandoning him on the floor of that shithole, as his body's blood seeps into his clothing. Perhaps tonight will be the first night in many years that he'll spend without staying up till sunrise.

And without waking up later that afternoon.

I head downstairs and retrace my steps back to the Mini. I get in, start the engine, and pull away from this house that smells of decreptitude, neglect, wasted time, and death. My shivering is worse, the burning pain keeps flaming away in my groin, and the fact that I vomited does nothing to lessen this nausea that seems to fill my stomach with foam.

I press my hand against my forehead. It feels hot. Maybe it's just an impression, maybe it's a fever, maybe it's my body's reaction after watching Daytona in his death throes. It's the price of the anguish, of feeling my way along without any clear idea of what's going on around me.

This isn't one of the pastimes that Lucio and I share, a puzzle passed back and forth between a couple of minds held prisoner by bodies that house them against their will. I have the feeling that this is a final, terminal enigma, a puzzle whose solution might be worse than the puzzle itself.

I'm a pathetic warrior, alone and frightened, scared of dying in the dark.

I take the road along which I came and continue in the same direction out to the beltway, without returning to the city. It strikes me as the safer alternative to avoid retracing my route, not to pass the same windows and the same courtyards twice. For the rest of the ride home, Daytona's last words keep tormenting me, last words that were murmured in a voice that was already no longer that of a living creature.

"White ice." What is "white ice," and what does it have to do with anything?

I say the words over and over in my head, as if I were solving a cryptic clue, and finally, as I drag out the final *s* sound of *ice* while I make a tight right turn, it occurs to me that Daytona might not have finished the word. A sign flashes before my mind's eye: the White Isis.

What does the White Isis have to do with anything?

It's a public bath and day hotel located under Via Silvio Pellico, in the Galleria del Duomo. There's another one in Piazza Oberdan, at Porta Venezia. It's a place where you can take a shower or a bath, find a barber or get a manicure, make a phone call, stop at the bar, or leave your luggage. It's part of a chain of similar facilities set up by an industrialist in the early twenties in many large Italian cities: Milan, Bologna, Turin, Rome, and Naples. At the time, since bathrooms in private homes weren't all that common, they were used as public baths. Still, the use of expensive materials and fine furnishings made them relatively refined settings, a gathering place frequented by a high-end clientele, traveling for business or pleasure.

I wonder just what role can be played in this whole story by an institution that, given the development of Italian society and the Italian economy, is destined to vanish, a place that will someday be a distant memory, a curiosity, a piece of social archaeology to be looked back upon as an artifact of a way of life and an era that are gone forever.

What does a public bath serving hundreds of people every day have to do with the murder of ten or so human beings in a luxurious villa outside Lesmo? It strikes me as decidedly unlikely that such an overtly public facility could become a hiding place for anyone. Or else I'm completely missing the point and the answer to this question can be found in the old saying that the best place to hide something is in plain view.

I turn off the beltway onto the exit that puts me on Via Vigevanese, heading for my house. On the far side of the exit ramp are various buildings and industrial sheds housing retail outlets and businesses. High atop one of those buildings is the sign of an extermination service. Once, after the umpteenth all-nighter with Daytona and Beefsteak, I took this exit and as I did, I heard Beefsteak's voice pipe up from the backseat.

"Ehi, chì ciapen i danee per masà i ratt."

Remembering that I'm not from Milan and don't understand the dialect, he repeated it in Italian, for my benefit.

"Over there they make their chips by killing mice."

He thought it over for just a fraction of a second, that tiny interval that is more than enough for a genius to translate intuition into words.

"You want to know the company's slogan?"

He went on without waiting for my answer.

"I hate those meeces to pieces!"

We laughed like three idiots when we heard that perfect imitation of the furious exclamation uttered regularly by Mr. Jinks, the Hanna-Barbera cartoon cat from the *Huckleberry Hound Show*. Wisecracks, jokes, and laughter that seem to belong to centuries past, when we moved through time without understanding what was going on around us.

Safe in bed after watching the evening television shows that always ended with the ten-minute block of kid-friendly ads and sketches known as Carosello.

But after twenty years they shut Carosello down, leaving us without landmarks or stars to steer by and the long hours of the night ahead of us, demanding to be filled. During my ride in Tulip's car I remember I thought, as I looked out at the city lights, that for many people it would be a rude awakening to discover that the party they were promised was actually already over. I hadn't expected that moment to come so soon. I hadn't expected it to come for me.

Some kind of rage makes me set my jaw and increases my nausea.

I wonder what the people who knew Daytona will say when they hear about his death. I wonder what Detective Stefano Milla will think and do when he learns that a man was found dead, murdered, at the address that he gave me under the table. There's one thing for sure: I can't sit on the sofa in my apartment like an idiot, waiting for him to come ask me to explain just what happened, either in his official capacity or otherwise.

This time I drive through the front gate and park right outside the glass doors of the front lobby. I'm going to come back out immediately with a travel bag in my hand, and I feel too ill to carry it all the way outside the enclosure wall.

I walk upstairs, hoping I don't run into Lucio. The meeting I fear doesn't take place and I'm relieved. I don't want to get sucked against my will into a battle of wits that has become a routine over time, to the point that the banter has eliminated any form of communication between us aside from cryptic puzzles and puns of various kinds.

Now that the stakes are higher, everything strikes me as stupid and infantile. Death is a prima donna: it manages to focus all attention on itself. And the attention that it attracts is all the more hypnotic the stranger the circumstances in which death makes its appearance. At the same time, one way or another, death has a way of making everyone a star.

I'm learning that at my own expense, now that everywhere I turn I seem to find bloody bodies strewn around me. And apparently every one of those bodies is pointing a finger straight at me.

When I get up to the apartment I'm ready to rush into the bathroom and throw up again. In my haste, a splash of vomit stains the hem of my jacket. I take it off and throw it into the dirty laundry hamper.

I wash my face and glimpse myself in the mirror.

What I see before me is no longer the face of the man I once knew. There are circles around my eyes; my complexion is yellowish; my lips are dry, chapped, with flakes of skin here and there. There are traces of cobwebs in my hair, which I must have picked up without realizing it as I explored the farmhouse.

Gone is the handsome and useless young man who used to make women say *If it was you, I'd do it for free* . . . and who failed to understand, despite his cynicism and egotism, that it was a lie. That young man must be stretched out dead on the floor next to Daytona back in that shithole. The man looking at me now is someone else. Now it's my job to find out just how different he is, before the others can make it clear.

I take off my shirt and send it to join the jacket in the hamper. I pull a clean shirt out of the armoire in the hallway and grab a travel bag. I lay it out on the bed and turn on the television. I flip through the channels in search of a news program. The first and second RAI channels, Telemilano, Antenna 3, plus a couple of other channels that the newspapers describe as local networks. All I find is programs for kids and other crap of that sort.

I turn off that useless device and turn on the clock radio on my nightstand.

I start filling the travel bag with clothing and other necessaries for a short trip. The whole time, from the radio's tiny speaker, Claudio Baglioni's voice sings to me about Tunisia and suggests going away, far far away. I wish he was in the room right now, singing to me, so I could tell him how happy I'd be to do as he says.

When the travel bag is full, to the notes of an old song by the Dik Dik, I start to open my special safe, the one that the police were unable to find when they searched the apartment.

The bed is made of wrought iron, with round legs on either side of the headboard and footboard. They're a little taller and fatter than average and are topped by brass knobs. I kneel down by the first leg and give a ring on the base a 360-degree turn; at first glance the ring looks like nothing more than a decorative touch. That turn releases the brass knob, but it can be unscrewed only by turning it clockwise, in the opposite direction of a normally threaded object. Simple enough but, to judge from the results, highly effective. Inside the leg is a light cylindrical container made of transparent plastic, attached to the knob with a length of twine. I extract it and remove the plug that closes it. I lay it on the bed and spill out the rolls of cash it contains. I repeat the operation with the three other legs, and now I have all my cash and the 490 million lire that, for the moment, is represented only by a Totocalcio lottery ticket.

I've always thought it was better not to entrust all my money to the banks. First of all, a steady and significant inflow of cash, without any plausible justification, might be hard to explain in case of an audit. In the second place, there might very well be cases in which it would not be advisable to leave a trail of checks and credit card receipts.

Events have proven my caution to be eminently justified,

even though there were times when I wondered if I wasn't taking it a little far. Still, folk wisdom suggested that being too cautious never killed anyone, and who was I to argue with folk wisdom?

I slip the cash into the bag and the lottery ticket into my pocket. I leave the pager on top of my nightstand: it might prove to be a booby trap. I pick up the bag, feeling the tortured emotions not of an emigrant about to leave home forever, but of a wanted man. The musical program comes to an end and the news broadcast begins. About to depart on a journey of unknown duration and possibly no return, I stop in the middle of the bedroom to listen.

I turn it off without even waiting for the newscast to end.

The newscaster's voice has just entered my house and, word by word, shattered the world around me into pieces. As I walk out the door, driven no longer by haste but by fury, I wonder if the time I have left to live will be enough to put the pieces back together again.

CHAPTER 16

I brake the Mini to a halt with the nose of the car pointing straight at the bars of a gate with flaking paint, on Via Carbonia, in the Quarto Oggiaro section of northern Milan. I get out of the car and it takes me a minute or two to find the correct key on the key ring in my hand. After a few attempts I manage to get the lock to click open. I swing the gate wide and get back in my car. I have to stop and get back out immediately, to close the gate behind me. Inside me is a lurking sense of panic that drives me to move as quickly as I can, with a rising feeling that daylight is my enemy and that everyone in the street behind me has eyes only for me.

During the drive from Cesano I took plenty of detours, making left turns and right turns and checking my rearview mirror each time to see if I was being followed. When I felt confident that everything was okay, that there was no suspicious car dogging my trail, I made a brief stop at a newsstand. I picked up the evening edition of all the news-papers, a few magazines, and a couple of weekly puzzlers. I got back in my car and drove off. I turned on the car radio, twisting the dial through a succession of voices suddenly snuffed out and songs instantly cut off, in search of a radio news broadcast that could confirm the report that I'd just heard, luxuriating in that fine-edged masochism that seems to surface along with the sense of anxiety in people in trouble.

At last I settled on a special RAI news broadcast, devoted to the latest developments of the mass murder in the Villa Bonifaci. A couple of hours earlier, an anonymous caller had contacted an office of the Italian wire service ANSA; the authenticity of the call was still being determined. The man had claimed credit on behalf of the Red Brigades for the murders at the villa in Lesmo, describing them as a new and victorious operation in the armed campaign against the Italian state and its representatives, a further success on the heels of the kidnapping of Aldo Moro and the annihilation of his security team. Next came a prerecorded statement from the Italian Ministry of the Interior, emphasizing the extreme gravity of the situation and at the same time the firm stand of the institutions of the state in the face of this growing terrorist threat. A special cabinet-level meeting of the government was now in progress.

That's more or less what I had already heard at home. It's what made me decide to get out of there fast, before Giovannone or someone like him decided that there were plenty of good reasons to swing by and pick me up for a little preventive detention until they could figure out just what my role was in this tangle of events.

Then the newscaster announced a new development, which might represent a turning point in the investigation so far. Something that on the one hand opened my eyes to a shaft of light and on the other hurled me down into a dark and slimy pit. An eyewitness, a young man coming home from a discotheque on the night of the mass murder, saw two cars carrying a number of people exiting the front gate of Villa Bonifaci. One was a large Volvo station wagon, the other was a small dark vehicle, either dark blue or black, which the eyewitness identified as either a Mini or possibly a Fiat 127.

That last item froze me to the spot. My shivers turned into an uncontrollable tremor, so bad that I had to pull over until it went away. Then came a ratlike frenzy to get to my destination, to find out whether the suspicion that had begun to blossom in my mind was realistic or not. The confirmation, when it came, wouldn't solve anything: it would just transform a series of unpleasant questions into so many frightening answers.

The horn of a car waiting behind me wakes me up to the here and now.

About fifty feet away is a cement ramp leading down to a row of garages that line the basement. I turn down the ramp, clearing the way for the car behind me to move off toward the other outdoor parking spots in the courtyard of the building. When I reach the bottom of the ramp I turn right, heading for the garage marked with the number 28.

In the dim light that filters down from the grated windows up high, I park the Mini parallel with the long sequence of garage doors. I get out and open the garage in question. Inside, a brown Fiat 124 is parked. A nondescript, ordinary car, both in terms of model and color. The perfect car for me, in this context. I open the door and get in, and I find the keys tucked behind the sun visor. The engine turns over almost immediately, spouting a dense cloud of smoke from the exhaust pipe. I've kept the battery charged on a regular basis, and I bless the foresight that made this small miracle possible. I emerge into the open air with my new means of conveyance. I park the brown 124 in one of the parking spots marked in paint on the blacktop around the complex.

Every time I'm out in the open, the same obscure sense

of danger sweeps over me again. My precarious physical condition amplifies the fear to an extreme degree. I hurry back into the half-light of the garage and the cool air.

I walk back to the Mini and pull it into the garage, where there's more than enough room for it. I pull down the swinging garage door and I switch on the hanging lamp, which creates more shade than light in this tiny space. I add the glare of the car's high beams on the dreary walls. I pull a flashlight out of the trunk. I get back into the driver's seat and open the glove compartment. I pull out the registration booklet and then pop open the hood.

As I'm getting out of the car I say over and over to myself that I'm an idiot, that what I'm thinking is bullshit, that nobody could ever . . .

It doesn't happen often in life, but there are certainties that, when they surface, are more devastating than any ignorance could be. That's what I think, and that's what I feel, at the instant in which I turn the beam of the flashlight on the chassis number and see that, this time, it matches the number in the registration booklet.

Suddenly a rancid taste floods my mouth and my breath seems to infect what little dank air there is in this concrete box, this stable for automobiles that suddenly seems to have been transformed into a cell on death row.

I begin a fine-tooth-comb search of the Mini. I tilt the seats forward, I pull up the floor mats, I check the side pockets on the doors and the contents of the glove compartment and the dashboard shelf, I empty the trunk. And as I'm searching, I tell myself that it won't be that easy. If my suspicions are even partially true, whoever it is that put this whole thing together has certainly been more zealous and more imaginative than me.

253

I grab a pair of electrician's shears and a screwdriver from the tool kit. I start with the trunk, pulling the spare tire out of its housing and lifting the upholstery of the compartment. There's nothing unusual in there. I move on to the interior of the vehicle. I tip the front seats forward and I use the shears to cut into the upholstery of the rear bench seat, uncovering the fibrous padding concealed under the upholstery and then pulling it out too.

I stop only when I've completely gutted the backrest and the seat and I've found nothing out of the ordinary. I'm covered with sweat. My head is throbbing and it feels as if someone's inside my skull trying to shove my eyeballs out of their sockets from within. The burning sensation is back, and now it's a flaming ribbon wrapped around my guts.

I move on to the front seats.

I slide the driver's seat forward until it comes free of the rails. I set it on the garage floor in front of the beam of the car headlights and I inflict upon it the same methodical punishment as the rear bench seat, again with no results. I get back in the car and aim the beam of the flashlight onto the floor. There, like a novelty item on the floorboard, is a stain—dark red in color. I don't have to be a doctor to know just what that is. Blood is a calling card that everyone knows how to read. I don't know whose blood that is, but I'm certain that a lab technician would be able to tell me that the blood group matches one of the victims of Villa Bonifaci.

I continue searching like a maniac, and all the while I hear voices whispering incomprehensible words in my ear. Or maybe they're just in my mind and it's the fever and the panic that are making them seem so real.

I cut, I rip, I dismantle. And finally I find it.

Strapped into place with duct tape, inside the passenger-side door, is a pistol equipped with a silencer. It pops into the flat-white beam of the flashlight like a sudden threat. An inert and silent stowaway, and at the same time, a sinister and menacing unwanted passenger. Once again, I feel pretty sure that this is the weapon that one night, not long ago, in the open countryside, dug three bullet holes into the body of Salvatore Menno, aka Tulip, with no more noise than three arrows whipping into a target.

Pfft . . . pfft . . . pfft . . .

Even without the verification of an expert, I'm equally sure that this gun did additional work elsewhere, specifically at a villa near Lesmo, outside of Monza.

I pull it out of its constrained housing and take its full weight in my hand. It's a Beretta, though I couldn't say what model. I know a little something about handguns because my father owned a couple. I've never fired one, but I watched him while he handled them. I release the clip and examine it. It's full of cartridges. Whoever put it here wanted to make sure they did things right and didn't leave me defenseless. Or else give the impression, to whoever might happen to find it, that I was armed, dangerous, and ready for anything.

I check to make sure the safety is on and I slide the gun into my bag. I'm pretty sure it's a mistake, but right now I feel just a little safer having it with me. Whoever hid this gun in my car did it to fuck me. If I ever find myself face-to-face with whoever did it, I'd rather not be emptyhanded. I'm up to my neck in shit, but I'd just as soon not dig my own grave in it.

I open the garage door and a gust of fresh air allows me to breathe decently again, after the damp heat of the garage. I pick up the bag and seal the remains of my car in its vault.

I head for an elevator built into a bare cement wall on the far side of the entry ramp down to the private garages.

I push the button for the fifth floor and hope I don't run into anyone. The apartment building I'm in is a beehive shaped like a giant letter *C*, on the outskirts of the city and the law. Quarto Oggiaro is a quarter of Milan that organized crime has colonized to its considerable profit, making this neighborhood a dangerous place to spend time—somewhere you would be ill-advised to stick your nose into other people's business.

As usual, the devil's not as black as they paint him and the situation in Quarto Oggiaro isn't as dire as it's described. But, given the circumstances, I'm fine with it: it's a good place to hide out, especially now that the devil's on my tail and he's looking a lot uglier than any illustrations I've ever seen.

The elevator comes to a halt. I leave behind me the graffiti carved into the elevator walls, to inform posterity and the various passengers that Luca is a faggot and Mary is a whore. With corresponding phone numbers. Another message carved into the wall, and half erased by a hasty hand with a differing opinion, states that the Inter soccer team is a piece of shit. These little acts of vandalism, which once annoyed me, now strike me as evidence of normal life, life with time on its hands, life with no thoughts other than these kinds of trivial secrets.

I leave the elevator and find myself in a hallway. Long and silent: the plaster walls emanate a faint smell of moisture. The door immediately to the left is the apartment I'm heading for. When I finally get inside, I heave an instinctive sigh of relief.

I drop the bag and lean against the door.

My head is throbbing. The pain in my eyes has subsided. But the burning sensation hasn't.

I pull the bottle of Furadantin out of my jacket pocket and I slip another tablet into my mouth. I gulp it down, again without water. Then I kneel down and extract a case with a reserve supply of medicines from the bag. While I was rummaging through the bag in search of it, my hand repeatedly touched the inert metal of the handgun. Instead of making me feel uneasy, that contact gave me a sense of reassurance. I walk to the kitchen and pull a glass out of a dish rack in a cabinet over the sink. I rinse the glass and I pour some Novalgin into it, a drug that serves both to bring down the fever and to relieve the headache. I pour in a little water and drink it, accepting the bitter flavor of the medicine, which seems to cut through the taste of bile in my mouth.

I go back to the living room and take in the apartment at a glance. It's just a little larger than my apartment, with an eat-in kitchen and one extra bedroom. The furnishings correspond to what you'd expect in an apartment building and a neighborhood like this one.

Run-of-the-mill furniture, run-of-the-mill paintings, run-of-the-mill fabrics.

There's a smell of confinement and a sense of neglect in the air. There's a layer of dust on everything that I have no intention of cleaning up. Nor am I going to call anyone to do it for me. Until a year and a half ago, a man lived here who is now in a cell in the San Vittore Prison.

Carmine Marrale is one of the ugliest men in the world. He also has one of the biggest cocks on earth. I know that first fact about his anatomy because I have eyes and I can see; I know the second fact because one of my girls told me so in complete confidence. She was the only one who was willing to have carnal relations with him after two others refused in horror.

I met him under very particular circumstances, the kind of circumstances that will either make two people lifelong strangers or else create a strong friendship, no matter where it may lead in the future. To be specific, he and I are the protagonists of a classic story, the one about push and what happens when it encounters shove.

The irony of lives based on power.

I was in the countryside outside of Milan, not far from Motta Visconti, in a rural trattoria well known for its frog's legs. Frog-leg frittata, frog-leg risotto, fried frog's legs. For people who are fond of that particular cuisine, it's a place worth knowing about. Back then, it was very fashionable to sit down at those bare, unadorned group tables, eat whatever the waiter served you, and drink wine from bottles without labels. It wasn't uncommon to run into members of the Milan that matters there, along with the Milan that thinks it matters. I wound up there that night with a group of people whose names and faces I've long since forgotten, people I've fallen out of touch with. The only things I still remember are a girl I liked and my own bad mood, which slowly evolved from physical desire to a desire to be someone else and somewhere far away. When I decided that I'd had enough, I got up and made half of my wishes come true.

I stood for a moment in the doorway and lit myself a cigarette. A car with three people inside left the parking area behind the trattoria, peeling out from the corner on my right. I watched as the taillights moved off and vanished into the darkness, lost in the murk of the dust kicked up from the dirt road. By one of those odd twists of fate, of the eyes, and of the mind, I happened to memorize the license plate number.

I walked out to get my car, parked at the far end of the lot. Halfway there I sensed, more than saw, the figure of a man stretched out on the ground.

He was flat on his back and was trying unsuccessfully to roll over onto his side. I knelt over him. I helped him sit up as he uttered a stream of curses under his breath. It didn't take a lot of light to see that whoever had tricked him out this way hadn't pulled their punches.

He had a broken nose and a split lip. The dim light prevented me from counting all the various bruises. I figured his body was in worse shape than his face. Now that he was sitting upright, the blood was dripping from his chin onto his shirt. I pulled a handkerchief out of my pocket and handed it to him.

"No broken limbs?"

He moved his legs and answered me through the thin cloth pressed to his lip.

"I don't think so."

"What happened to you?"

"They gave me one hell of a beating. Bastards outnumbered me: there were three of them."

"Did you recognize them?"

"They were wearing ski masks. Chickenshits."

"You want me to call an ambulance? You might have some internal bleeding."

"No, I don't want an ambulance. I don't want the emergency room."

Reading between the lines, that last statement had a second meaning: I don't want the police.

"Can you drive?"

Before answering me, he made a quick survey of his energy level.

"No."

Then he evaluated me.

"I'll give you a hundred thousand lire if you drive me home."

I replied promptly.

"Two hundred."

His answer was just as prompt.

"You're a turd."

"Yes, I am. But I'm a turd who can drive. Otherwise, you can always call an ambulance."

"Fuck you. Help me up."

I helped him up until he was more or less steady on his feet and I listened to a new and fanciful litany of vulgar twists on religious concepts. I eased him into the car and then I headed for his house, or the address that he gave me, anyway. During the ride, I couldn't keep my eyes off his swollen face, in the intermittent light of the street lamps. I remember a faint smile he gave me, immediately replaced by a wince at the pain of his cut lip.

"There's no point in you looking at me. I guarantee you that before they beat me up I was even uglier than I am now."

I brought him here, to the apartment that I'm in right now. I helped him get cleaned up and get comfortable on his bed. I watched as he tried to get into the best position his body could offer without demanding too much pain in exchange. Finally, I put a bottle of water and some aspirin I found in the bathroom on his night table.

"Do you want me to call anyone?"

"No."

"Sorry to remind you, but you still owe me two hundred thousand lire."

Without a word he pointed to the drawer of the night

table next to the bed. I pulled it open. Inside was a pile of money. I counted out what he owed me and pocketed the money.

The comment followed immediately.

"You're a vulture."

"Maybe so. But I'm going to give you a little extra something for that money, along with the ride."

I pulled a ballpoint pen out of my inside jacket packet and, on a magazine next to the table lamp, jotted down an abbreviation followed by a number.

"I don't know if it's of any use to you, but this is the license plate number of the guys that beat you up."

A couple of months later I happened to run into him at the Negher de Milan, a club on the Navigli. He came over to say hello. He offered to buy me a drink and made it clear that it wasn't to thank me, because as far as he was concerned the two C-notes I put in my pocket were more than adequate thanks. It was strictly to toast to the success of a punitive expedition against the three crooks who had given him that beating. He'd managed to track them down from the license number I left on his bureau.

We became friends in a way, the kind of friendship that could develop between a couple of mice who'd fallen into a glass demijohn by accident. I knew his story, which wasn't really all that different from that of plenty of others who never seem to get tired of getting thrown back into jail almost as soon as they're released. He basically grew up on the street, with plenty of bad friends, a history of petty theft and stupid risks. The next step was breaking and entering, and finally armed robberies. With a few intervals of working as a *rebongista*, street slang for a coke dealer, to pick up a little cash when things were tight. His wife left him when

261

she finally realized he was never going to go straight and that she was going to have a baby. Carmine came home one day and found the apartment empty, all her clothes gone from the hangers and drawers, and the box with what little money they had dry as a bone.

And a note on the bed.

In which she clearly stated that she had no intention of letting their son grow up with a father like him. He never saw her again. One day he received an envelope postmarked Germany, with nothing in it but a photograph of a little boy, about two. On the back of the snapshot, written with a ballpoint pen, was a name: Rosario.

When Carmine pulled his umpteenth armed robbery, two people got killed. A plainclothes policeman who tried to interfere and a female bank customer. He was arrested thanks to a police informer and the judge sentenced him to twenty-two years. That's when I decided to go ahead and pay the condominium fees on his apartment, thinking that if things went south, it might prove useful, along with the car. Now I feel that it was money well spent and that, at least for a little while, Carmine's apartment can serve as a safe haven. That is, until the lawsuit brought by the families of the victims results in an order of confiscation. It was an arrangement Carmine and I made privately; nobody else knows about it. I pay the condominium fees every month in his name with a postal money order, and as far as anyone knows he's paying them himself. Same thing for the utilities.

I pick up my bag and go into the bedroom. I set it down on a chair. Luckily, my friend has the same habits as I do. In front of the bed is a dresser with a Saba brand television set and a VCR next to it. Hoodlums and crooks always seem to be at the cutting edge when it comes to technology. Next to the VCR and piled on a shelf are plenty of videocassettes, but unfortunately for me nearly all of them are porn.

Not my favorite type of entertainment.

I'm reminded, sourly, of a joke by Giorgio Fieschi that doesn't seem funny right now: sex is like sports—the important thing is to participate.

I turn on the television set and check to make sure it works. I leave it turned to RAI 2 with the volume down low. I step into the bathroom, slide my trousers down, and sit down on the toilet. A couple of involuntary *Madonnas* that might reasonably compete with those uttered by the actual owner of the apartment escape my lips. It feels as if I'm pissing flaming matches.

I flip the switch that turns on the hot water heater, and as I wait to be able to take a shower, I go back and lie down on the bed. I shove aside the rough cover on top of the bare mattress and the pillows without pillowcases. I take off my shoes without unlacing them. The pictures on the television set are blurry and the words belong to a nonexistent language.

I feel like shit.

I grab the dirty-looking horse blanket and pull it over myself, like some pathetic character in *The Godfather*, when the families are at war and everyone goes to the mattresses. A sudden wave of exhaustion sweeps over me, keeping me from thinking and making me forget that, just as I'm starting to understand, I'm losing the ability to believe.

Sleep looks like the only refuge available to me.

I sleep.

CHAPTER 17

When I wake up, my eyes are all crusty.

Though I've never actually eaten any, it strikes me that my mouth tastes like rabbit shit. I'm a little dopey, but the burning sensation is almost completely gone and one night's lead-weighted sleep has brought me back into the ranks of the human race. Thought shows up a few seconds later, punctual as always, to remind me of the dire situation I'm in. Human beings don't have police searching their apartments, and they're not afraid to walk down the street. Human beings do whatever the fuck they feel like without having to look over their shoulder or keep an eye on oncoming cars, without the constant thought that one of them might turn out to be police or the Carabinieri and suddenly screech to a halt and make a U-turn to come after them.

Human beings don't run, they walk.

I get out of bed and determine that my bones have returned to the interior of my legs, where they belong, and that my head is no longer spinning dizzily. I strip and toss my clothes on the bed. This time, I make no particular effort to avoid the mirror on the door in the middle of the armoire. My naked body is an anatomical wisecrack, and someday I'll be strong enough to think it's funny. Right now, though, my mutilation is the only asset I possess, the one source of true anger I can draw on to react to what's happening to me.

To what someone's doing to me.

I head for the bathroom.

The little room is a triumph of dark brown, with odd tiles with geometric patterns that impart a somber impression, perfectly suited to my state of mind. It's a clear warning that, wherever you may hide, you can't escape dark brown tiles.

Here, to make up for that, I find another mirror, a smaller one.

It offers me the detail of the face—the scraggly beard, the bleary eyes, the greasy, disheveled hair. Maybe I'm not completely sane, but in spite of everything, there's a thought that makes me smile. The idea that this surface, accustomed as it is to presenting the ogrelike features of Carmine, might feel a sense of relief at reflecting a wrecked face but still one that belongs to the category of normal human beings.

A face that, by personal choice, has practically never been photographed. Anytime I've found myself in front of a camera, which is something that happens from time to time when you're out with friends, I've always made a point of covering my face or turning my head so that I can't be photographed head-on. In my drawers, unlike Lucio's, there are no pictures commemorating my past life. Which I've done my best to forget and successfully wiped away, along with my name.

I consider my physical appearance and evaluate how I can work on it.

I decide not to shave. My whiskers grow fast, and in a couple of days there'll be enough of a beard to constitute a pretty good disguise. My long, wavy hair is recognizable, but I can find a solution to that problem. I start going through the drawers of the Formica cabinets. Among the various items, some of them distinctively feminine, I find what I need. I'd have to guess that after Carmine's wife left him, he couldn't bring himself to throw out all the things she left behind in the bathroom. I take a fine-tooth comb, a hairband, and a pair of hairdresser's scissors. I would never have expected a man like Carmine to be so vain that he'd trim his mustache. But I'm pretty sure that if Carmine heard about the situation I'm in now, he'd say that he never would have expected me to be so stupid as to let myself be framed like this.

I turn on the water, put my head under the faucet, and wet my hair. Then I comb it out, pulling it straight up, and grab it close to the top of my head, forming a sort of ponytail in the center of my scalp. I wrap the hairband around it to secure it, twisting and retwisting and then sliding it firmly to the very base of the ponytail.

I take a look at myself. With my scraggly beard and this barbarian hairdo, I look like an extra in a sword-and-sandal movie from the sixties. The effect would be comical if it weren't the product of a situation of such dire necessity.

I take the scissors and cut the ponytail off clean, just an inch or so above the elastic band. When I pull the band away, the hair tumbles down, nicely layered. I mentally thank my friend Alex, who unintentionally taught me this trick one time when I was in his salon. I snip and trim here and there with the scissors, neatening up my hair with the aid of a hand mirror I found in another drawer.

When I'm done, I consider the results in the mirror. Now I'm a man with short, layered hair, and probably a cheap hairdresser; I may need a shave, but I'm definitely not the same person I was before.

I gather the shorn hair from the floor and the sink and toss it into the toilet. Maybe, long ago, Delilah did the same thing. I flush the toilet and the rush of water carries my hair away, and with it, my strength.

I extract some reasonably clean towels from a cabinet. My appearance seems to be an acceptable modification. In my situation, I can't be too choosy about things. I get into the shower and stay there until I run out of hot water. When I step back out, I'm once again in possession of my physical and mental faculties, for what they're worth.

With a towel wrapped around my waist and a pair of slippers a size too small for me on my feet, I head for the kitchen. Over time I've stocked the kitchen with pasta and canned foods of all kinds. The refrigerator is full of mineral water, and there's oil, vinegar, salt, and sugar.

And above all, coffee.

After turning the gas on at the wall, I fill the espresso pot with water and coffee, give it a twist, and set it on the flame. I sit down to wait for the gasping wheeze of the espresso pot. As I wait, I think through all the elements of this tangled story. All the characters that I saw moving around me like so many puppets without realizing that the only real puppet was me.

Everything starts with Carla, and everything leads back to her. Somebody, somewhere, must have learned that I had a special relationship with Lorenzo Bonifaci and that I was one of the few people who could get people into the villa.

Pretty girls, to be specific.

That someone got Daytona working for him, certainly by offering him money. From what I know of Daytona, he hardly strikes me as the type to be roped in by ideological considerations. My miserable friend arranged for me to meet Carla, manipulating me by flattering my pride. He dared me to talk her into going to bed with him and, like an idiot, I fell for it. Then he sang the praises of her physical beauty and her performance in bed. He threw in the fact that the girl was money hungry by mentioning her demand for a higher fee if there was a next time with him. When I rejected his offer of her phone number on the way back from the gambling den in Opera, he dropped me off in Piazza Napoli, and that was no accident. Carla was immediately informed of my lack of interest and she decided to speed things up by waiting for me outside the Ascot Club.

She knew perfectly well I'd show up there eventually.

There was someone following me the whole time. Whoever it was saw Tulip kidnap me at gunpoint. We were followed all the way to Trezzano, and I have only my guardian angels to thank for the fact that I didn't wind up in an unmarked grave in the countryside near a quarry. Though the only reason they sent Menno straight to hell was to avoid seeing their safe-conduct pass into Lorenzo Bonifaci's villa torn to shreds right before their eyes. They saw me abandon the dead man's car and set off on foot for Via Monte Rosa. When all was said and done, I played right into their hands. I handed my car keys to Carla and asked her to drive me home, allowing her to walk through my front door and into my life.

At this point, heaven-sent and anything but an accident, comes Laura's defection. Carla emerged from her cocoon as the radiant butterfly that she was and I had already shown a certain weakness for her. Given no other options, the decision to send Carla in Laura's place was inevitable, the only possible alternative.

All the same, it was crucial that for the evening of the murder I should have no alibi. Which is why Daytona, who I just happened to run into outside the Cinema Argentina, sent me with an envelope filled with bundles of newspaper strips in my pocket to a rendezvous where he knew no one would show up.

Next comes the sleight of hand of the switched cars. They used my car for the raid on the villa in Lesmo, replacing it with an identical vehicle designed to ensure I wouldn't notice a thing. Unfortunately for them, I noticed. After the killings, they made sure to smear some blood on the floor of my Mini, they concealed the handgun in the door panel, and then they put the car back where it was originally.

Apparently quite complicated, but in practical terms, very simple.

I'm also reasonably certain of one thing.

The minute the police really did put out an all-points bulletin on me, I wasn't going to be arrested. I was going to be found somewhere, in a Red Brigades lair set up especially to deflect the investigators, with a bullet in my head and a pistol in my hand. And on the table next to me a raving suicide note in which I openly declare my guilt and state that I refuse to give the Italian government— so brutally and victoriously wounded by my deed—the satisfaction of taking me alive.

End of story.

The one thing I don't entirely understand, and can do no more than theorize, is the reason they included Laura as one of the victims in the massacre. Probably, even if she was in cahoots with them, they did it for two reasons. First of all to eliminate an inconvenient witness who they were going to have to kill sooner or later anyway, just as they did with Daytona. In the second place, to make sure that the numbers added up in what was, after all, an orgy: three men and three women.

The numbers would add up, and Carla's presence at the scene of the crime would be erased. Once I was eliminated, and, with me, my version of what happened, even if Carla was somehow linked to me, she could just claim to be a poor defenseless girl who fell for me, only to run away in disgust once she discovered that my only interest in her was to turn her into a prostitute.

I consider my situation.

If I'm thinking the whole thing through correctly, then not only do I have the police on my trail, but also whoever it was that organized this whole elaborate prank. I could opt for the lesser of two evils and go to the police, but I don't think that's the right way. They'd throw me in solitary confinement so hard I'd bounce, and then they'd lose the key while they checked out my story. And it might not check out at all, in the end. Whatever happened, it would certainly mean an open-ended stint behind bars, given the gravity of the charges and the general dislike that cops and judges feel for people in my line of work.

The only solution that strikes me as acceptable, now that I know more or less how and why, is to try to find out who. I have to do it myself and I have to do it fast, before Tano Casale finds out about the trouble I'm in and goes to cash the counterfeit lottery ticket that I fobbed off on him. Instead of being in trouble twice over, my problems would multiply threefold. Unless he decides to pull the caper I suggested to him on his own, in which case I'd have a little breathing room.

The espresso pot huffs and puffs to let me know that the coffee is ready. I pour myself a cup and drink it, even though it's the world's worst, because the pot hasn't been used in so long. I should force myself to eat something, but I just can't do it. My stomach is in the clutch of an iron fist, and it won't stop squeezing.

270

I get up and go back to the bedroom. I get my things out of the travel bag and get dressed. I find a reasonably secure hiding place for my money and lottery ticket, reassured by the thought that generally thieves don't break into other thieves' apartments.

After thinking it over, I pull the silencer off the gun and stick the gun down the waistband of my trousers.

I might be making a mistake, but I can't bring myself to leave the apartment unarmed. The people I've interacted with for so many years have taught me that in certain desperate cases, the only satisfaction left to you is to take someone with you on your trip to the afterlife. I've always considered this school of thought to be utter crap, but I have to say that recent events have given me a new appreciation of its worth.

Right now, there's only one handhold I can seize on in my attempt to make some sense of all this.

The last words Daytona uttered before he died: *White Isis*.

I have no idea what the White Isis has to do with this whole story. I have no idea whether it's something or someone inside the public baths or if it's something in the surrounding area. To make matters worse, the company has two locations in Milan, though the best known and most popular location is in the Galleria.

That's where I decide to get started.

I put on a pair of sunglasses and take a look at my new appearance in the mirror. Anyone who knows me as Bravo would take a minute or two to link my name to this brand-new image. The people who are looking for me? Less than a second. I just hope I don't meet anyone from either of those crews.

I leave the apartment without giving the key the final double twist for added security.

271

The hallway is empty, and in the elevator Luca is still a faggot and Mary is still a whore. The comment about Inter has been erased completely. Miracles of the soccer fan's faith.

I head downstairs and walk toward the parking spot where I left the Fiat 124. It's lunchtime and there's nobody in sight. My stomach is starting to rumble and it may be necessary, once I get to the center of the city, to feed it a panino. I get in, start the engine, pull out, and head for the main gate.

The gate is wide open, so I'm not forced to get out of the car and fool around with keys and locks.

Once I get out in the street, I suffer an attack of agoraphobia. I have to make an enormous effort to keep going and resist the temptation to turn around, leave the car wherever I happen to be, and run headlong back to the safety of the apartment. I tell myself it's only an anxiety attack, like the ones you get when you go scuba diving, when the air from the tanks doesn't seem to be reaching your lungs. I force myself to breathe normally. Little by little, the fear subsides and I follow the traffic to the first Metro station I happen to find.

Today is Saturday, and there must be a huge crowd heading downtown. I'm more likely to go unnoticed. With my usual excessive caution, this time I double back and make multiple turns, twisting across the face of the street map of Milan, just to make sure nobody's following me.

I decide to go and catch the Metro at the QT8 station, in Piazza Santa Maria Nascente, where there's an adjacent parking lot. It's a fair distance from Quarto Oggiaro, and just in case someone happened to recognize me, it would throw them off my track because they'd assume I was hiding out somewhere nearby. All this overthinking, all these precautions I'm forced to take, all these obsessive-compulsive rituals, are enough to drive me into a fury.

I tell myself that perhaps, in a way, that fury has been there all along. The events I've become entangled in are nothing more than a lens that has enlarged everything. A lens with a sharpshooter's crosshairs etched into it. I've been maneuvered like a puppet, shoved this way and that like a piece of furniture, fucked up the ass without even the benefit of a joke or two, a little cajoling, and all with the clear intent of destroying me. They yanked me like a molar out of my indifference toward the world and toward myself.

Now that I've thought it through, ascertained the state of things, and accepted facts as they are, I'm armed and seething with fury. And I'm determined to take this thing as far as it goes. Which may mean I'm taking it straight to my grave, but at this point I don't fucking care.

Now I want to know a name. I want to see a face in front of me.

What happens after that, for now, is a problem I choose to ignore.

I leave the 124 in the parking lot and I head for the Metro station marked by a familiar white logo: *MM*.

In the past, these two letters have been the object of fanciful interpretations by one and all. Daytona, Beefsteak, Godie, and the cabaret artists from the club. Now they seem like nothing more than an acronym for Mortal Misstep.

I walk down into the underground tunnel and discover to my relief that there are very few people. That's good. I head over to the newsstand to buy a few Metro tickets and when I get there, I turn into a pillar of salt.

What I'm seeing isn't Sodom and Gomorrah in flames, but a special edition of *Il Giorno*, with an identikit on the front page that does a stunningly good job of reproducing my features.

The banner headline is significant.

be on the lookout for this man

It's lucky for me that in the sketch my hair is long and I'm clean-shaven, so I venture to approach the news vendor and ask for a copy. I also take the latest issue of *La Settimana Enigmistica*. The man hands it to me and takes my money without so much as glancing at my face. I've never felt such pleasure at the way people ignore other people.

I turn away and retrace my steps.

Shit.

That was the last thing I needed. I thought I'd have a little more of a head start. The fact that they've identified me comes as no surprise. The people behind this whole intricate plot have shown they're not stupid. For that matter, the police aren't stupid either, especially not when they're handed such a carefully constructed chain of clues.

Now I don't know what to do.

Maybe going downtown right now, when all the newsstands are filled with newspapers emblazoned with a reasonably good sketch of my face, might not be such a good idea. I don't know how far along the investigators might be, but if by some chance they've figured out a link to the White Isis, rushing down to hang out near the place strikes me as a bad move.

The tiny gleam of light that had flickered into a flame now appears to belong to a candle stub that immediately died out. Now it's pitch-black again and I'm stumbling around in the dark.

I decide to go back to my car and read the article.

When I open the door, a wave of heat pours into my face. I sit inside without opening the windows, as if those panes of glass were a barrier against the treachery of the outside world.

I start reading. At the same time, I start sweating without realizing it.

The investigation into what is by now generally referred to as the Massacre of Lesmo, for which the Red Brigades have claimed responsibility with an anonymous phone call that is still being checked out, seems to have come to a crucial turning point. This comes in sharp contrast to the investigation in the case of the Moro kidnapping, still apparently at a dead end. The murders at Monza seem to have been the work of one specific person, a man with a name and a face. That man is Francesco Marcona, also known by the moniker he uses in the milieu of the Milanese underworld: Bravo. He is currently a fugitive from the law. A search conducted in his residence in Cesano Boscone, in Via Fratelli Rosselli 4, turned up no evidence or material linking him explicitly to any subversive plots. Nor have the police found any photographs allowing them to work with a clear image of his face. Still, the investigators did find, in the pocket of a jacket he hastily abandoned in his escape, a gold watch believed to be the property of Paolo Boccoli, also known as Daytona precisely because of the watch in question. Boccoli's dead body was found in an abandoned farmhouse on the outskirts of San Donato Milanese. He had been stabbed to death. The bloody murder of this major figure in the Milanese underworld comes on the heels of the killing of Salvatore Menno, another notorious ex-convict, murdered

275

just a short time ago with one of the weapons that was later used in the mass killing in the villa of Lorenzo Bonifaci. All this leads the police to theorize that they were working as confederates in the . . .

This major figure in the Milanese underworld . . .

I note bitterly that the description affords Daytona a qualitative leap in status that he was never able to achieve while he was alive. I go back to reading the article, which adds nothing new, doing nothing more than rehashing the facts, offering a clumsy reconstruction of the murders, emphasizing the importance of the victims, and theorizing with many a nudge and a wink just what the presence of the young women at the villa might signify.

I fold up the newspaper, open the car window, and light a Marlboro. I can feel the sweat dripping under my armpits. On my forehead, it's turned into a crown of thorns.

I never dreamed I was so hopelessly cornered, that the frame could be so thorough and so complete. All my best and worst intentions have collapsed pathetically. The handgun I'm carrying is no longer a guarantee of anything: now it's just a heavy object tugging at my belt and hurting my hip.

I decide to head back to Carmine's apartment, and I just hope that no one recognizes me. I repeat to myself that in Quarto Oggiaro people mind their own business, but it's fleeting comfort, gone out the window with my cigarette smoke.

I start the car and perform my various turns and switchbacks while checking in the rearview mirror, even more carefully this time. As I drive, I think. The smartest thing for me to do would be to call my lawyer, Ugo Biondi. Then go turn myself in, accompanied by him, in the hope that they'll believe my story. Leaving aside the fact that today, on a Saturday, I wouldn't know how to get in touch with him, there's another aspect to the matter that holds me back. I'm afraid that this move might strike the police as a way of further muddling their investigation and creating confusion in a case that's already sufficiently tangled.

In any case, the consequences would remain unchanged. Until proven otherwise, I'm involved in a terrorism case and I'd be held as a prime suspect until my innocence could be demonstrated categorically.

Which might take months or years. Or might never happen at all.

I spot the familiar silhouette of the massive apartment building in which I've taken refuge. I drive through the front gate and leave the car in the courtyard. There are a few people on the grass, but they're far away and pay no attention to me. I walk into the lobby, and even though I've never done any fighting, I feel like a combat veteran after a battle: I hopelessly ride up in the same elevator I rode down in with such confidence.

This time I don't bother to give the graffiti so much as a glance.

I walk back through the apartment door and close it behind me just as the hallway echoes to the sound of a door lock clattering open. It could be a woman taking her dog out for a walk or just a kid going downstairs to play. But I'm happy I made it inside without being seen.

Now the apartment in which I'm a prisoner and guest strikes me as even more bare and dreary. I take a step or two, take off my jacket, and go over and sit down on a couch that's still encased in a slipcover. My back immediately adheres to this temporary upholstery and becomes warm and sticky. I lean my head back and look up at the pink ceiling, certainly a design decision of Carmine's ex-wife.

A thousand thoughts alight and immediately flutter away again. At a certain point, maybe just to bring me back to earth, my body pipes up to remind me that I'm also a living organism with specific physiological requirements.

I pick up my copy of *La Settimana Enigmistica* and I head for the bathroom. There are things you do that, once you've repeated them a sufficient number of times, simply become conditioned reflexes. The bathroom still shows traces of my recent shower and haircut. There's no Signora Argenti here, making sure that when I get home everything is neat and tidy and the floor has been swept.

I drop my trousers and sit down on the toilet. I light a cigarette and start leafing through the magazine. The first thing I see when I open it is the Page of the Sphinx, with a cryptic clue that I don't even try to solve. I read on, looking only at the jokes and the curiosities. I get to a section called the *Edipeo Enciclopedico*—the Oedipal Encyclopedia—a series of questions of all kinds that allow the reader to test his general knowledge.

I run quickly through the questions, checking each one against the answers, which are given at the bottom of the page. I absorb them as simple facts, without giving too much importance to them. I'm halfway through the section when a question catches my interest. I check the answer and, as is always the way with lucky hunches, the solution comes to me at the speed of thought. In my mind all the letters of the Scrabble game are suddenly present on the board, forming a series of words with a complete meaning.

Actually just two words.

A first name and a last name.

CHAPTER 18

I push the button and hear a bell ring inside. It's a familiar sound. After what seems like an eternity, a voice issues from behind the door. It's familiar too.

"Who is it?"

"It's me, Bravo."

The door suddenly flies open. An alarmed expression is stamped on Lucio's face. The lenses of his dark glasses reflect the ceiling lamp on the landing. He gropes for my arm and drags me inside. He slams the door behind me as if he were trying to keep out the devil. His tone of voice is that of someone who believes that in spite of everything he's done, the devil has still managed to get inside.

"Have you lost your mind? What are you doing here? Every policeman in Milan is looking for you. They've even come by to question me."

"I know. But I need your help."

Lucio takes a step back.

"Christ, are you trying to get me in trouble, too?"

"No. I've been forced to learn how to be careful. I checked to make sure no one was following me before I came up here. Don't worry, no one saw me."

He relaxes, but not so much that the tension is gone entirely. Perhaps, just as with Laura, he's a little bit afraid of me.

He's brusque and dismissive.

"What do you want?"

"I need you to help me solve the mystery."

Astonishment. Resentment. Rage.

"Which one? *Starlets going incognito in an opera libretto*? You're willing to risk prison for yourself and for me for a piece of bullshit like that?"

"No, that's not what I was talking about. That's easy. The solution is *sunglasses*—that is, *sung-lasses*. I'd even forgotten about it, think of that. I meant the other one, the mystery that you've posed all this time and that was far more difficult to decipher."

"I don't understand."

"Lucio, how long have you been a member of the Red Brigades?"

He was walking over to the table. His uncertain gait suddenly comes to a halt, and he turns in my direction with a helpless, incredulous smile.

"Bravo, are you crazy? Me, in the Red Brigades? How on earth could I do it, in my condition—"

I interrupt him, with my voice and with a wave of my hand. So that he can hear me and see me.

"You're not blind, Lucio. You never have been."

He sits without speaking. He watches me from behind his lenses. Now I know that he can.

I go over and pull open the drawer and find the pictures of Lucio together with the other members of his alleged band. At this point I have to wonder if there was ever a musical group that called itself Les Misérables. I pull out the photographs and study the figures captured on the matte paper. Not to make sure—I have no need. Just to confirm that all our tricks and wiles, however refined they may be, one way or another, ultimately demand payment, perhaps with a twenty-year journey back to Ithaca.

Or a twenty-year prison sentence.

I toss those colorful rectangles onto the table, next to him.

"The photographs you showed me. The ones of you playing with your group, when according to you your eyes were already shot."

Instinctively I wave my hand at the pictures.

"Your eyes are red in the picture. If there's a red dot in the middle of your eye in a photograph, it means your eyes are perfectly healthy. Isn't it ironic? I found the solution in my weekly puzzler magazine, of all places."

Lucio sits there, lost in thought for a minute.

Then he smiles.

At last, with a resigned gesture, he removes his glasses, revealing the glaring sight of his pupils covered with a white film. He cups a hand under one eye and lets the first contact lens fall into it. He does the same thing with the second lens. He squints both eyes a couple of times, finally free. He lays on the table that slight contrivance that has offered him enormous shelter for so many years now.

As if our movements were synchronized by a fate imposed from above, I extract the pistol from my waistband, with the silencer screwed on again.

Maybe that's why Lucio recognizes it immediately. And he understands that, in this case, I'm quite willing to use it.

"Ah, so you found it, after all."

His voice is relaxed, untroubled, and when he says it he's simply acknowledging an obvious fact. It doesn't seem to bother him a bit that the eye of the barrel is pointing straight at his belly. He's a cold-blooded creature. I could hardly expect any other reaction from him.

"That's right. As you can see, I found it."

He crosses his legs. His movements are more fluid, now that the masquerade is over. Now that he can use his eyes and look reality in the face without having to hide.

"How did you figure it out?"

I shrug modestly.

"A series of details. Various minor oversights. Errors, marginal ones if you like, but add them up and it amounts to an ironclad case."

"Such as?"

"Substituting another car for mine was a brilliant solution. The only problem was that it didn't smell of tobacco inside. Whereas my car was driven by a regular smoker. At that point, I think you'll agree, checking the serial number on the chassis was a brilliant idea on my part."

He gives me that point with a complete absence of commentary. His irony, which once seemed like the armor of an otherwise defenseless man, seems to have vanished into thin air.

I'm in the presence of a hard, emotionless, pitiless person.

A murderer.

"Go on."

"Error number two: in the envelope that Daytona gave me to hand over there was nothing but a stack of cut newspapers."

Lucio leaps to his feet, his features tense and drawn, showing that he actually does possess a nervous system.

"That chicken thief was a greedy, slippery idiot. There was supposed to be real money in that envelope. He stole it, thinking that no one would ever know."

I wave him seated with the muzzle of the handgun. By the time his ass is flat on the chair again, he has regained his composure.

"You killed him, didn't you?"

His calm becomes nonchalance.

"Yes, I did. And I enjoyed it, I have to say. That piece of shit was a menace to everyone he came into contact with. In the end, he was only a menace to himself."

That's what I'd figured. I should have guessed from the start that the White Isis had nothing to do with it. That poor devil was gasping for his last few breaths. When I asked him who it was, when I asked him where Carla had gone, *White ice* was the last thing he managed to utter. What he was actually trying to say was: the guy with white eyes.

Or something of the sort.

It makes me mad to hear Lucio talk like that about Daytona. It makes me mad to think that he's responsible for the death of three beautiful young women. It makes me mad to think that he killed the men of the security detail, who were guilty of nothing but doing their job. It makes me mad to think that he's played with me like a toy. My fondest wish is to pull the trigger and lodge a bullet in his skull, two bullets, three bullets . . .

With the comfort of a silencer, capable of transforming three gunshots into three hushed arrows.

Pfft . . . pfft . . . pfft . . .

Maybe I'll do it. But not right away. There are still things he needs to tell me.

And he knows that.

His irony surfaces again, except that now it's veering over into the spiteful realm of contempt.

"It's hard to resist, isn't it?"

"Resist what?"

"It's hard to resist the temptation to pull the trigger when you're looking at someone you hate."

"What do you do in those cases?"

"The only way to get rid of temptation is to yield to it."

"Oscar Wilde."

He looks at me with some surprise that I knew the source of his quote. His eyes are dark; they seem to be trying to enter into me.

"Who are you, Bravo?"

"Somebody who wants information, sitting across from someone who can supply it."

I give him a moment to think it over, so that he can fully appreciate the roles that have been assigned.

"Let me tell you a few things. I'm just going to ask you to interrupt me when I get something wrong."

Step by step I lay out my reconstruction of events for him, as I composed it in my head during my time in Carmine's apartment. The role that Carla played, Daytona's part, the murder of Tulip, Laura's defection, the maneuver to deprive me of an alibi, the elimination of witnesses, right up to my own suicide as the epilogue of a story that began and ended in total delirium.

I get to the end without being interrupted even once.

Then he deigns to give me the luxury of his consideration.

"You're smarter than I thought."

"It's not that I'm smarter than you thought. It's that you're not as smart as you thought you were."

"Is that what you think?"

"That's what I think."

"We'll see about that."

He smiles at me and for just a second I see Lucio's old expression, the one he used to put on when he made a wise-crack. It's there for only an instant and then it's gone, like all pleasant memories when they're replaced by the present.

After which he looks at a point somewhere over my shoulder.

"Take his gun."

The moment he utters that word, I feel something small, round, and hard press against the nape of my neck. It doesn't take me long to figure out that it's the muzzle of a pistol. From behind my back comes a voice that won't take no for an answer.

Chico's voice.

"Throw the gun on the couch. And put your hands up."

Then I hear another voice. I know this one too.

"And don't get any funny ideas. There are two of us."

I toss the gun on the couch, hoping it might go off and kill someone. As stupid as I feel right now, it'd be fine with me if the one it killed was me. The first rule is to inspect the apartment, and I ignored that rule because I was so anxious to glory in my idiotic triumph.

Shit. Shit. Shit.

The pressure on the back of my neck lightens.

"Move over to the wall."

I move as instructed. Giorgio Fieschi walks into my field of view and reaches down to the couch. He picks up the Beretta, making it the second gun pointing at me. Seeing him here, for some reason, doesn't surprise me all that much.

"So you're in on this, too."

"As you can see."

There's nothing left of the clean and naïve young man who used to hang out at the Ascot Club. He has the determined face and the brisk motions of a professional. This is an evening of revelations and transformations. I look at him and I see him on the stage. Young, talented, with the world in the palm of his hand. If it's true what I thought at the time—that the other artists were afraid of his skills—I think now how astonished they would be to discover how much more afraid of him they should have been.

I realize to my astonishment that I'm not afraid of him. I'm just disappointed. The way you are whenever you see a missed opportunity.

"You're good. You're brilliant, I have to say. You could have done important things."

He looks at me the way you'd look at a mental defective.

"I'm doing them."

"Was Laura one of them?"

He shrugs with indifference.

"Laura was a whore. She sold her ass to the highest bidder. No better than you. We're at war, and in terms of the goal we're fighting for, she was nothing but a pawn we were willing to sacrifice."

Lucio breaks in. He's still sitting where he was, expressionless as he watches his comrades reduce me from threatening to threatened. I too have undergone my own little transformation.

"As you have no doubt figured out for yourself, so are you."

Without a word, I wait for the rest.

He stands up and takes a step toward me. We look each other in the eye, which is something we could have done a long time ago if he weren't he and I weren't I.

"Bravo, I don't believe that however much I might explain it to you, you can ever understand what's happening in this country. You belong to the category of people who don't pay attention to what's around them. People who could walk through a concentration camp without noticing its horrors because they're on their way to get an aperitif at the Bar

Tre Gazzelle. While you were sleeping your days away and fooling yourself that you were living by night, the world changed and none of you noticed. There was 1968, then 1977, class warfare, armed battles in the streets. All of them things without meaning for you. Worse still, things you knew nothing about. You're nothing but a faint mist, a stretch of nothingness between good and evil."

"It strikes me as obvious that you believe evil is the people you kidnap, hurt, and kill. I think it's equally obvious that you believe that good is the things that you do."

He shakes his head, bitterly.

"No. We're only an armed force in the service of good, willing to resemble evil in order to become strong enough to defeat it."

"You're insane."

He replies as if this were the real solution to every puzzle.

"No, Bravo. I'm a dead man. Just like you are."

Chico breaks in to interrupt this secular confession.

"What do we do now?"

I take a look at him. He's a young man, a little shorter than average, with curly hair and sideburns that make him look like a hippie at Woodstock. The civic-minded volunteer serving as a companion for a blind man has just tossed a practical question onto the table.

Giorgio Fieschi puts in his two cents, with a hint of impatience in his voice.

"We've got to get out of here. And fast. I'm not comfortable in this place."

"There's a car with two plainclothes policemen watching the front entrance. How can we get him out of here without them seeing us?"

Chico has just confirmed a problem that I had already

identified and worked around myself, in the path I took to get into the apartment building. Behind the shelter of a stand of trees, I'd climbed over the enclosure wall at the corner of its longer perimeter, opposite the building, where it borders a field overgrown with bushes. Then I walked along the wall, crouching low so as to remain out of the line of sight of the two plainclothesmen sitting in the suspicious-looking Alfa Romeo.

I was counting on the fact that the watch that the police put on the apartment building would probably be reasonably perfunctory, since no one really thought that I'd be stupid enough to try to come back to my own apartment. But obviously that same route can't be taken more than once, and certainly not by a group of people.

Lucio studies me as if this were the first time he's laid eyes on me. His eyes remain on me while his mind goes somewhere else. When he returns, he brings the spark of intuition with him.

"I've got an idea. You all wait here."

Lucio leaves the room and vanishes down the hallway.

The three of us sit in this living room without sharp edges or corners, each of us with a deep and abiding certainty. The two of them that they're in the right. Me, that I've come to the end of the line. This time there won't be any guardian angels to protect me, the way they did when it was Tulip holding a gun on me. Now those angels have become the threat, the mortal danger.

We wait in silence, because everything we could say to each other in the same language has already been said. Going any further would be nothing more than a pointless journey to Babel.

The sound of footsteps in the hallway announces Lucio's

288

return. He comes in carrying a guitar. He's shaved off his long and unkempt beard. He's got a long brunette wig on his head and a fake mustache of the same color. It's not the most realistic looking getup, but it's nighttime and he can rely on the fact that all cats are gray in the dark.

He smiles at the expression on my face.

"We all need to be actors in life, don't you think?"

He walks over to the coatrack and pulls down his jacket and the hat he usually wears. He tosses them over to me, forcing me to reach out and grab them in midair.

"You made things easier for us when you cut your hair and left your face unshaven. It makes us look very much alike, if you take into account the fact that we both have roughly the same build. The plainclothes officers out there are expecting to see a blind musician leave the building with his usual volunteer companion. And that's exactly what we'll give them, but this time with an extra fan in the entourage."

Chico understands and smiles. He holds the pistol out to Lucio, who makes it become part of his hand in an entirely natural way.

"I'll bring the car around. Then I'll come up to get you and the guitars."

He leaves, opening the door just wide enough to squeeze through. Giorgio Fieschi asks for instructions for himself.

"I came on my motorcycle. What should I do?"

"Wait fifteen minutes after we leave. Then catch up with us in the place you know."

Lucio has the confidence of a born leader, and he's capable of transmitting it to his men. I'm pretty sure that this whole masquerade is amusing him, as well as giving him a surge of adrenaline. When he notices that I'm still standing motionless in the middle of the room with the jacket and hat in my hand, he waves the gun at me impatiently. In fact, he repeats the exact same gesture that I employed when I told him to sit down.

"What are you waiting for? Get dressed."

I shrug on the jacket and clap Lucio's hat on my head. He steps over to the table. He gathers up his contact lenses, looks at them with a faint smile, then slips them into his pocket. He picks up the dark glasses and tosses them to me. I put them on, losing a little light and a few details in the bargain. There are no mirrors in the apartment to check the results, but I'm pretty sure that the rule governing cats and the dark applies to me as well as Lucio.

My impression is confirmed by none other than him.

"You're perfect. I don't have time to give you guitar lessons, but I don't think you're going to be asked to play."

The car must have been parked nearby because it's only a couple of minutes before there's a knock at the door. Giorgio walks over and lets Chico in, but only after cautiously opening the peephole and checking to make sure it's him.

"We can go."

Chico comes close to me and locks arms with me, holding me on his left. His voice lacks the tone of kindness he used when he did this with Lucio. His gestures are harsh and powerful. His right hand jams the muzzle of the pistol against my side.

"Walk nice, short steps. Don't look where you're putting your feet, just look straight ahead of you. I'll guide you."

To emphasize the order he jams the barrel of the gun roughly into my ribs.

"Is that clear?"

I nod my head yes.

Giorgio opens the door. The first ones down the stairs are

me and Chico. Lucio walks down the stairs with the guitars in hand, bringing up the rear. The night air is cool and there's no one in sight. It's a last little scrap of winter, discouraging loiterers and open-air conversations. The car, a white Opel Kadett, is parked directly outside the glass doors.

One guitar is placed in the trunk, the other is propped up in the backseat, behind the driver and next to Chico. I'm in the passenger seat. There's a handgun discreetly aimed at me the whole time. As soon as Lucio starts the engine, I feel the muzzle of the pistol rise back up to tickle the nape of my neck.

We pull out.

Without any unexpected problems, we leave the Quartiere Tessera behind us, with all its police surveillance and all its indifference. I wonder to myself whether Lucio will ever be able to get over this part of his life. I look at him as he drives wordlessly, curious to see him for the first time doing something that I thought was forever forbidden to him.

He'd be surprised to know just how similar we are, how much time we've both spent hiding, pretending to be something that we've never been, while waiting to understand something that we'd never become.

I think it's too late now anyway. None of it would change a thing. Now that everything's been unveiled, there's only one thing that Lucio can devote the rest of his life to. The thing that makes his gaze harden, the thing that persuaded him to abandon the world of words and conversation and to take up arms. Every revolution has its victims and its martyrs. I have the feeling that I'm going to leave this life without any idea of which role I've been assigned.

As we pull onto the beltway heading east, I take off my sunglasses and look out the car window at the lights of

Milan. I'm not wearing a blindfold, which means that my captors aren't worried about letting me see where they're taking me. In any case, it'll become obvious immediately, as soon as they stage whatever it is they intend me to take part in. If you stop to think about it, it's all just theater. Though in this case the show will end after opening night, because death never sticks around for a repeat performance.

CHAPTER 19

We exit the beltway at Viale Forlanini, in the direction of Linate Airport.

Lucio drives, his face illuminated intermittently by the lights of oncoming cars and streetlamps, his eyes riveted to the road. He's taken off the wig and false mustache and he's gone back to being himself. Which is to say, someone that I don't really know at all. He's lit a cigarette, and that gives me a clear gauge of his chilly self-control. There was never the slightest whiff of tobacco in his apartment—never a trace of this addiction. Which means he never smoked, even when there was no one there to see him.

I wonder what his life would have been like if he'd dedicated his considerable gifts and determination to something constructive instead of all this destruction. I answer myself with the thought that maybe he tried, pursuing an ideal that day by day shrank to an idea, until music stopped being his refuge and turned into his hiding place. I answer myself that maybe he is wondering the same thing about me.

We come to the end of the boulevard and our way is cleared by a green traffic light allowing us to make a quick left turn, down toward the Idroscalo. We leave the lights of the airport behind us, where at this time of night there are few passengers and infrequent flights. The dull roar of a plane taking off promises a new horizon, but instead it's just one more trip toward identical situations and different people. The illusion lasts no longer than the time between takeoff and landing, with the sole comfort of a fitful sleep in an uncomfortable seat. We drive around the outskirts of the Luna Park. The amusement park is closed: the stalls where you can win a goldfish have their shutters pulled down, the skeletal attractions stand immersed in the darkness, and the flying saucers are all covered with canvas tarps. The next ride, the next thrill: they're all done for the day, and it'll be tomorrow before there's another chance to knock down the pyramid of milk bottles.

For the duration of the trip, no one has spoken. Chico, in the backseat, has relaxed, and the pressure of the pistol muzzle on the back of my neck is gone now. Still, I'm sure the gun is in his hand, aimed straight at my head. One false move on my part, a light tug on the trigger, and

pfft . . .

with the sound of an air rifle, my skull would shatter like a plaster target at the shooting range. What I once was would be nothing more than the red spray of blood on the windshield, in a macabre airbrushed pattern.

And yet I feel strangely chilly and remote.

I'd been afraid to ask the only questions that I really cared about getting the answers to. Why ask questions that would only make me more helpless and defenseless?

What happened to Carla?

What role has she actually played in this whole thing?

I can't imagine her with a gun in her hand, pulling the trigger and eradicating the lives of people that a twisted ideology identifies as her enemies. Wiping out the lives of girls with whom she had been laughing and kidding around just a few hours earlier, masking her contempt and her intentions. I can't bring myself to envision her in the garb and the mind-set of someone who looks at the world around them and sees only dead bodies sprawled in puddles of blood and considers what they've just done to be something normal.

Perhaps that's because every time I try, those sequences in my mind are overlaid by her eyes, too beautiful to be true, too beautiful to be false. Maybe because, in spite of everything that's happened, I never really moved away from that sidewalk, cool with the dawn air, and from the warmth of her words.

If it was you, I'd do it for free . . .

I look at Lucio and remember his body clinging to the body of Carla. As I sat there watching them, it was as if their pleasure was mine. Suddenly I feel a wave of resentment and self-pity sweep over me. Not because I'm a prisoner, not because I'm about to die. But because when it's all said and done, the only thing I really want to know is whether that night, in a nondescript apartment in the Quartiere Tessera, that act of love was a gift meant for me or for him.

We drive on along Via Rivoltana, past Segrate. At a certain point we take a right turn. A couple of kilometers later we come to a small, isolated house. A gate, a low enclosure wall topped by a metal railing, a small patch of lawn dotted with rock-spray bushes and a pine tree in the distance.

No lights in the windows.

Lucio gets out to open the gate. Seeing him move so easily still seems odd to me.

In the glow of the headlights that open out like a curtain after clearing the gate, the house is nondescript, white, two stories high. The house that little children draw in their notebooks in elementary school, if it weren't for the garage alongside the building, on the right. The little driveway ends right in front of a lowered metal garage door.

Lucio gets back in the car and we pull up to the panel of sheet metal painted green, which reflects and tinges the glow from the headlights. The garage door is opened by someone inside, alerted to our presence by the sound of the engine.

We pull in and come to a stop next to a Volvo 240, just as the noise and the Cyclops eye of a motorcycle burst out of the darkness of the road.

A Kawasaki 900 brakes sharply alongside the Kadett. In the same motion, Giorgio Fieschi extends the kickstand and dismounts from the motorcycle. He pulls off his helmet, revealing a head of curly hair that, if he let it grow, would make him look like Donovan. He unzips his leather motorcycle jacket and he could be any kid coming home from a night out with his girlfriend, if it weren't for the fact that a pistol butt is protruding from his waistband.

Lucio gets out of the car. There's no anxiety in his voice, just the confidence of someone who's used to watching his plans work to perfection.

"Everything okay?"

"Everything's fine. After I left the apartment, I hung around for a few minutes to check things out. Nothing fishy."

"Very good."

Lucio speaks to one of the two people waiting for us inside the garage, the one who opened the metal door. He's a short, squat guy, about thirty, with dense eyebrows, fleshy lips, and a powerful bone structure. His head, which protrudes from a turtleneck sweater, seems to be attached directly to his torso.

"Alberto, close the gate and make sure no one followed us."

Without a word the guy walks out and heads off with a slight limp to obey his orders. From the expression he shows the world he must not be particularly bright, just a thoroughly indoctrinated brain and a reliable hand.

I look around, by the light of the two fluorescent bulbs hanging from the ceiling. The garage is actually something on the order of a warehouse. Inside it is everything that you could hope to find in a space of this kind.

A bicycle hanging from a hook, a workbench with a vise against the wall on the right, a tool panel with a drill and other equipment neatly arrayed. A steel tool chest that must contain wrenches and other tools. A shelf filled with canned foods. An old pair of skis propped up in a corner, next to a mimeograph machine. On the floor, a pile of printed leaflets bearing the logo of the Red Brigades. I feel certain that all through the rest of the house is scattered material that will identify it as an authentic terrorist hideout.

The set is ready, and the screenplay has been written for a long time. The star of the show has just arrived.

Lights, camera, action.

Lucio speaks to the other person, a tall young man who looks as if he were still a student. At first sight, you'd place him outside a high school, with an armful of books, talking to a friend or a girl he likes. Instead, in all likelihood, he was one of the passengers in the two cars that set off to carry out a mass murder, convinced that those murders were not crimes but acts of some higher justice.

"How's everything here?"

"Everything's quiet. We're all ready."

"Perfect."

297

Lucio glances over at me. It strikes me that he wants to see whether this demonstration of his authority has had the proper effect on me. Every man has his weaknesses, his vanities, small or large though they may be. If I'm here in this situation, it's because I yielded to my own weaknesses.

So I ask.

"Do you really think that all this is going to change anything? That it's really going to bring about something new?"

"I don't know. All I can say is that I've been living for years in something old and I don't like it."

Giorgio breaks in.

"Don't waste time on this collaborator. How could he understand in ten minutes what he's failed to see in a lifetime?"

I look at him. I see him in my mind's eye on the stage as he was giving a crowd of people one of the most beautiful gifts that one man can give another: a hearty laugh. I remember the desolate tenderness of his face as he delivered the closing line:

Having ruined our childhood . . .

Whatever it was that ruined his, it's too late to fix it now. Or else that's just the bullshit that psychiatrists love to spew and there's no real reason. Maybe nature alone is responsible and he's just one bad apple in a bushel of good ones.

There are those who can spot them and avoid them.

And there are those who can spot them and know how to use them.

I answer him in the same tone of voice.

"There's one thing I've figured out, in all this mess."

"Yeah, and what's that?"

He plants himself in front of me, waiting. Arrogant, with a challenging look in his eye.

"There are people who plant bombs because they believe in something. And there are people who plant bombs because they like to hear the boom and the screams of the dying and the injured."

I let the concept sink in.

"I'm just trying to figure out which category you belong to."

The burst of rage explodes from somewhere very close, because in a flash it's in his eyes. He whips the pistol out of his waistband and jams it under my chin, forcing me to tilt my head back.

"You lousy piece of shit, I ought to—"

I don't have time to find out what he ought to, because Lucio intervenes.

"Giorgio, stop it! Put that gun away."

The rough pressure of the muzzle slackens, but the fury remains intact. He reluctantly obeys the orders given by the man in charge. So Lucio is just like Tano Casale, and Giorgio is just like Tulip. As if I needed any further confirmation, I can see that everything's the same wherever you go.

It's the illusion of the airplane. It's the places that change. Not the people.

The gun slides back into the belt and he takes a step back.

Alberto, the guy who went to close the front gate, comes back to the garage. He pulls down the garage door and leaves the cool of night locked outside. Now we're shut up in this box of bricks, roof tiles, and sheet metal, under pitiless lights, each of us a prisoner in his own way.

The door at the top of the short staircase on the left swings open.

Carla walks out and stops on the landing to look down at the men standing beneath her, who have all instinctively turned their heads to look up at her. She comes down the steps with her lithe, fluid gait, and I have the impression that when she walks down those few steps it's happening in slow motion, so that I have all the time I need to relive moment by moment the hours we spent together. All her expressions, all her transformations. From cleaning woman to ingenue full of disbelief at her own beauty to grown woman well aware of her power over men and determined to take the world by the horns. Right up to the Carla I'm looking at now, a stranger with a hard gaze and a grim twist to her expression.

Not even the fluorescent lights can dull her beauty. Nor can the cheap jeans and sweater that she's wearing. Nor the fact that she approached me with the clear and specific idea of luring me into something from which I'd never get out alive.

She ignores Giorgio and Chico, who's still right behind me, just one step and a pistol muzzle away. She goes straight to Lucio, wraps her arm around his waist, and presses her lips to his. Then she jerks her head in my direction.

"I see we have company. How did you manage to find him?"

Lucio glances at me with a half smile. But I don't find his irony funny anymore.

"Bravo was true to his nickname. Unfortunately, I have to say he was just *bravo*, and not *bravissimo*! He figured out almost everything all by himself, though he made the mistake of turning himself in to me instead of to the police."

Carla makes no comment and turns to look at me.

He eyes aren't friendly or flattering.

"So here you are."

A flat statement. She says it as if it were the most natural thing in the world for us to come face-to-face again in this situation, with a gun in Chico's hand as he warily monitors my infrequent movements.

"Yeah. Here I am."

What can I add that hasn't already been said or would be pointless to state? Is there an emotion I could express that she hasn't already seen stamped on my face or implicit in my gestures?

I look at her and she looks at me. Once again, as with Lucio, I'm still the same person.

She's not.

And as if there were any need for it, her words make it crystal clear to me.

Harsh, precise, merciless.

"You disgust me, Bravo. I wanted to tell you that the minute I met you. Because of what you are. Because of how useless you are. Because of the filthy rotten world you represent and that you serve in your slimy way."

There's only one thing that I can say. So I say it.

"I've never killed anyone."

"Neither have I. Only people who deserved it, but they don't count."

The others have listened in silence to this exchange. It's not hard to figure out whose side they're on and who they're agreeing with, in their hearts.

Lucio intervenes.

"This is exactly what you're never going to be able to understand, my friend. We have no opponents, no adversaries—we have only enemies. Politicians can talk about their opposition as a cover, a way of disguising a series of frauds and connivances, abuses of power and state-sanctioned murders. To the point that the word *adversary* has become a synonym for *accomplice*. What strengthens

301

us in our convictions is the knowledge that nothing is irremovable, ineluctable, irreplaceable. When you believe in something, that puts not only the lives of others, but your own life into the background. Carla has agreed, like so many other comrades, to lower herself to acts that disgusted her, in order to attain the goal that we have set for ourselves. She didn't close her eyes, no, she kept them open, looking far into the distance, while she was letting you fuck her."

He caresses her hair. He smiles at her.

"The world of tomorrow owes you a debt of gratitude."

Carla watches me. On her face I can see an expression that confirms the chilly words she spoke to me just a short while ago. But all I can hear are Lucio's words.

While she was letting you fuck her . . .

That means she didn't tell him anything about me, about my pathetic mutilation, which would have created an outburst of wisecracks and giggling if it were tossed like a bowling ball at the pins of the Ascot Club. It would have been a source of sarcasm and derision among these men, capable as they are of snuffing out lives in the name of nothing and then vanishing suddenly into that same nothing.

She let him believe that she and I . . .

"I think it's time to get moving."

The young man who looks like he's still in high school has just broken into that moment. Words spoken aloud because that's the way life is and other words left unspoken because that's the way people are.

All important words, all useless words.

Lucio takes command again. He extends the gun that I found hidden in the door panel of the Mini to Carla.

"Here, leave it on the workbench. They need to find this in the house. Leave a couple more of the ones we used in

302

Lesmo: it'll make the whole setup look more convincing."

Carla grips the handgun as if she'd never done anything else in her life. She's steady, strong, a born liar. I wonder once again why she bothered to lie about the two of us. I'm afraid I'll never know the answer. While I still have some time, I can only try to imagine one.

Lucio gestures with his head toward the door at the top of the stairs.

"Is he upstairs?"

"Yes."

"Perfect. Let me go talk to him, then we'll grab the stuff and we can go."

We can go.

I'm reminded of Daytona and the way I used to kid him. This time I wish I was included in the plural. But I'm pretty sure I'm not.

Chico lets me hear his voice again. The pistol barrel jabs my ribs.

"Through there. Get moving."

We follow Lucio over to the steps. On the other side of the door is a hallway wallpapered with geometric patterns. We walk in Indian file, man-man-gun-man, until we enter a living room where the wallpaper clashes with curtains that need to be washed thoroughly and hung out on a clothesline until the end of time. The area on the right is concealed from view by a bookshelf that serves as a partition. On the left are several pieces of walnut furniture, with a sofa and two armchairs in Naugahyde in front of a television set. On the floor, next to the sofa, are a number of bags, the fugitives' luggage.

Sitting in one of the armchairs is Gabriel Lincoln. I've seen him only once in my life, but he's one of those people you never forget, both because of his features and because of the circumstances.

"*Buona sera, Mister* Bravo."

His perfect Italian and his British accent are as distinctive as his cologne. He's a man of certainties, a conservative. The elegance of his suit is like the screech of a fork on a china plate in this roomful of ordinary mortals.

"As you can see, it's a small world. A small, nasty world, I should add."

I couldn't say why, but I'm not surprised in the least. Gabriel Lincoln is a logical answer, a tile that fits into the mosaic entirely naturally. The man who was always one step behind or two steps ahead, the faithful assistant, the Judas Iscariot with his many, many pieces of silver all deposited in an offshore bank account.

"I can't say it's a pleasure to see you again."

"To tell the truth, neither can I. It's really just, let us say, one of the duties of the job. Unfortunately for you, this time it's not your job, but mine."

"Just out of curiosity, do you work for the intelligence services?"

He smiles and pretends to ward off a compliment, feigning modesty. Still, I doubt that modesty is one of his strong points.

"To put it that way smacks overmuch of James Bond. All the same, let us say that the field in which I operate could be described in that way."

"So why me? You were Bonifaci's trusted assistant. Why did you need to use me?"

He stands up and smooths out his gabardine trousers.

"Regrettably, Lorenzo dismissed me a few months ago. A minor stumbling block. I know everything about him but I was no longer able to interact with him. Villa Bonifaci was off-limits to me."

He makes a gesture with his hands that explains everything, including the reason I'm going to take a bullet to the head in just a few minutes.

"The only person who could get us into that house under those circumstances was you. Nothing personal, just a matter of opportunity."

He pauses. Then he gives me a sign of sympathy.

"So sorry."

From the hallway I hear the sound of the door that leads into the garage. The sound of footsteps on the floor and a few seconds later Carla walks into the living room. She has a gun in her hand. A funny smell trails after her. It takes me just a moment to recognize it, at the exact instant that it overpowers Gabriel Lincoln's French cologne.

It's the smell of gunpowder.

Lucio takes a step to one side.

"All done?"

She does two things practically at the same time. First she nods her head yes, then she lifts her right hand and

pfft . . . pfft . . .

two tiny spurts of blood right above Chico's heart stain Mister Lincoln's fine suit. Lucio moves fast, as if in his mind's eye he had already envisioned the sequence of what was about to happen. Before Chico's falling body hits the floor, he's already torn the gun out of his lifeless hand.

So this time there's no silencer. The shot rings through the cramped space and out into the broad silence of the night like an explosion. A hole appears in the center of Gabriel Lincoln's forehead. A thousandth of a second later, his blood and his brains are flung against the curtains over the window right behind him.

He tumbles backward with the expression of someone who fails to understand why they're dead. No one who's killed ever really understands why. His limp body is made up of broken lines and it forms a strange geometric pattern contrasting with Chico's.

Carla has joined us now and stops, looking at the two corpses. Maybe that's how it happened at Lesmo. With that cold gaze she checked that all life had been expelled once and for all from the bodies strewn on the floor, ready if necessary to fire a final kill shot.

Lucio asks.

"The others?"

Carla answers.

"All gone."

"Get the suitcases. I'll finish up here."

Carla walks quickly past the sofa and through a door at the far end of the room. Through the open door, once she turns the light on, I can see a bedroom. She vanishes inside and the only living souls left in the room are Lucio and me.

He raises the handgun and places the barrel against my temple.

"Sorry, Bravo. The real puzzle was much more complicated than the solution you found."

"That is to say?"

"What we found in that house made us change plans. Now our plans have nothing to do with our comrades, the struggle, the day of victory that may never come. Now our plans concern only Carla and me."

A few terse words from Carla block my next question before it leaves my lips.

306

"I'm afraid you've got one name too many in your future plans, Lucio."

We both turn our heads toward her voice. Just in time to

pfft . . .

see a small burst of flame emerge from the muzzle of the handgun that Carla is aiming in our direction and carry off a fragment of Lucio's head. A light spray of blood splatters my jacket and my face. The pressure of the barrel against my temple disappears. Another body joins the other two already sprawled on the floor.

Carla points the gun at me. She waves me to a corner of the room with the barrel of the handgun.

"Get over there and no funny business, unless you want to wind up like him."

She moves fast. She pulls a rag out of the back pocket of her jeans and she wipes down the handgun she just used to shoot Lucio. Then, holding it by the barrel through the cloth, she kneels down next to the body of Gabriel Lincoln and squeezes his fingers around the handle, to impress his fingerprints upon it.

Then she lets the gun fall to the floor and stands up. All this time she has kept one eye on me. And all this time I've been keeping an eye on the second pistol that's sticking out of the waistband of her pants.

She looks at me. There's no anxiety in her voice, just the urgency of practical considerations.

"Did you touch anything?"

I shake my head.

"Good. Wait here."

She disappears through the bedroom door again and reemerges dragging two suitcases. She sets one down next to me.

"Take this one. We have to work fast. Someone might have heard the shot."

It all happened so fast and without explanation. Lightning, thunder, hail, and suddenly the downpour was finished before I had even realized that water was falling from the sky. Except it wasn't water, it was blood. I'm stunned by the noise and the smell of the shots, the relief that I'm not one of those bodies lying motionless on the floor.

The only thing I know for sure is that I'm still alive.

We walk back down the hall. The door is still open, the wallpaper's still ugly, the pungent scent of cordite is still strong. When we walk out onto the landing I can see at a glance what the garage has become. Giorgio is on the floor next to his motorcycle, the front of his shirt soaked with blood, his leather jacket gaping open above his heart. The high school boy is sprawled out on his side, his eyes staring. A red puddle is spreading across the cement from his head. He seems to be looking at Alberto, flat on his belly, even more stout and awkward in his inelegant way of death.

Carla doesn't give them so much as a glance, as if they formed part of a scene that her mind recorded in the moment and then immediately archived. We walk fast down the stairs. My suitcase is heavy. I don't know what the fuck's inside but it's heavy. Though it's only a short distance, I'm already panting.

Carla is stronger, leaner, calmer, more efficient.

The word *lethal* comes to my mind, but I dismiss it immediately.

We get to the Kadett and she opens the trunk. She pulls out a pair of work gloves and tosses them to me, one at a time.

"Put these on. Lift the garage door just partway and check

308

to make sure there's no one out there. Then go out and open the gate."

I do as I'm told while she puts the suitcases in the car. I find myself outside, in the odorless air of the night, which is already a blessing. I walk up the little concrete drive, guided toward the gate by the violet glow of the city in the distance.

The minute I swing open the metal gates, the engine of the Opel starts up and the car pulls out in reverse. The beams of the headlights glance over the bodies on the ground and then recoil, as if they were disgusted. Only the neon lights on the ceiling remain to illuminate the scene.

The car pulls out onto the road and stops, its headlights pointing in the direction from which I arrived, either a few minutes or a few hours ago. For a second or two, I expect the car to keep going. I expect to be left all alone here in the courtyard of this house filled with corpses, to try to figure out what happened and then have to explain it to the people who would be questioning me.

But the passenger door swings open. In the faint glow of the dashboard I see Carla gesturing for me to get in. With a sigh of relief I sit down beside her, finally allowing my arms and legs to tremble freely. We drive fast to the highway and turn left. Once again, the Luna Park, once again, the Idroscalo, once again, Linate Airport. At the traffic light, as we turn left and head for the city, there's a prefabricated wall made of cement panels along Viale Forlanini. Someone took a can of black spray paint and left us a graffiti message.

What the fuck is Nelson doing on our ship?

CHAPTER 20

We park outside Carmine's apartment building. Above the roofs there's a vague promise of light. A new day is dawning and Carla and I are together again. I indulge in the luxury of a dream, a chimera, the only one available to me in this particular moment. I wish I could go back to a morning like this one and hear her tell me for the first time

If it was you, I'd do it for free . . .

and believe that it's all true and answer yes, Jesus Christ yes, from here to the last light my eyes can see yes, for what I am and for what I'm not yes, Goddamn it yes, anywhere you name yes, anyhow you want it yes . . .

In any world you care to name yes, just not in this one.

Carla's hand turns the key and kills the engine.

I gave her the address of the apartment in Quarto Oggiaro when she got back in the car after making her phone call.

Toward the end of Viale Forlanini, she stopped outside a phone booth. She got out and I watched her through the windshield as she walked around the hood and then through the car window as she lifted one hand and dropped a token into the slot, dialed a number, waited for someone to answer. Then I watched as she spoke with someone, a short conversation, during which she seemed to be blocking and cutting short questions that the other person was asking.

She hung up and got back in the car. She drove off without haste, her eyes carefully watching the road. Too carefully for me to fail to understand that she was deciding what to do next.

Not what to do with me.

What to do *about* me.

I was the one who broke the silence. I had lots of questions. I wondered how many of them would be answered. I started with the first question, the one prompted not by curiosity, but by surprise.

"Why didn't you kill me too?"

Immediately after asking that question I turned away and stared at the road ahead of us, for fear of seeing from her face that she had just been asking herself the same thing.

I went on, challenging her intentions and her silence.

"It would have been perfect. Everything would have fit into place. According to the logic of this whole frame-up, my dead body's the only one missing in that house, on the top of the pile."

Carla rummaged around in the glove compartment. She held out a package of Kleenex to me.

"Wipe off your face. And take off your jacket, it's all covered with blood."

I understood that this was just one of many ploys she had at her disposal to delay answering my question. Or for making me understand that there wasn't going to be an answer at all. I took off my jacket and tossed it onto the backseat. I turned the rearview mirror toward me, turned on the dome light, and began to wipe spots of Lucio's blood off my face.

"Where have you been hiding for the past few days?"

I answered without looking at her.

311

"In a place."

"Is it safe?"

"Yes."

"Let's go there."

I turned off the light and let Milan illuminate Carla instead. She took my silence for uncertainty.

"When I stopped back there I called the police. I told them I'd driven by the house and I thought I'd seen some bodies flat on the floor in the garage. I played the part of a frightened citizen doing her duty but anxious not to get involved."

She looked at me.

"You need a place to stay until the police find the bodies and reconstruct what happened. The presence of Gabriel Lincoln, Bonifaci's former assistant, fired without notice, and the discovery that Lucio wasn't blind, as he wanted the world to believe, will shore up the theory that in this mess you've been made the victim of a plot, that you were framed."

"A lot of points are going to remain murky."

"In cases like these there are always plenty of murky points. Left murky or intentionally made murky."

"No. There are other moments for which I have no alibi. And anything I could say or do would only look like an effort to construct one for myself."

Carla sat in silence. Maybe she'd already thought the same thing and my words were nothing more than a confirmation. Through the windows of the car come the images of a city that just a few days ago I had the gall to consider as something like my own private property. Without realizing that in reality no one owns anything. You can only choose to belong to something. Skill and luck are great aids in making that decision.

Love does the rest. Love can fool you sometimes, but it's not for sale and it can't be bought.

Ever.

After giving her the address, I slumped back against my seat. Until we reached our destination, I didn't say another word. I just sat there, replaying the course of events in my head. I told myself that over the course of just a few days I'd had some unbelievable strokes of good luck. One was when I was saved from Tulip. The other was when I walked out of a house, alive, leaving five corpses behind me. I'm afraid I've completely wiped out any credit I might have had with the bank of good luck.

I avoided putting together any theories on why on earth this whole mess was assembled in the first place. The Italian state, the intelligence services, the Red Brigades, various ideals, the class struggle, the armed struggle, were all just so many meaningless clues. I knew that however good my imagination and my skills at solving cryptic enigmas and puzzles, this one was too tough even for me. I had the key to everything sitting next to me. And I still didn't know whether to expect an explanation from Carla or a bullet in the head.

We get out of the car. I toss the bloodstained jacket into the Dumpster. I doubt that Lucio will have a much more dignified burial. My back aches and my eyes are burning. We walk around to the back of the car and we get out the suitcases. Carla also pulls a travel bag out of the trunk.

I wave my hand at the Kadett.

"Is it okay to leave the car here, in plain view?"

"Yes, it's clean."

I walk ahead of her to the elevator. The suitcase seems even heavier than before. But maybe it's just my exhaustion and the black cloud extending over my future that makes the load seem like such a burden.

While we ride upstairs, my eyes happen to light on the graffiti again. Now they strike me as testimonials to life, a prank played on time rather than on other people. I tell myself that when I get out of prison, Mary and Luca will be adults and I'll be an old man. A smile escapes me that's so bitter that it would arouse compassion, a smile that my fellow elevator passenger fails to notice.

Once we're in the apartment, after dropping her bag on the floor, Carla looks around. Nothing has changed, except for one minor detail. The grim squalor is wiped away completely by the feeling of safety.

"It's not the Ritz."

"No, it's not. But it's a place where for now nobody's going to come looking for us."

"Who lives here?"

I conjugate the verb in the proper tense, to put her at her ease.

"The person who *used* to live here is in San Vittore Prison. It's the apartment of a friend of mine who was sentenced to twenty-two years."

She takes in the information without further comment. She moves her head, as if to stretch her spine.

"I need a shower."

I point down the hall.

"The bathroom's that way. I'll make a cup of coffee in the meantime."

Carla has an odd expression on her face, as if she's sorry for what she's about to say.

"I'd prefer to have you stay with me."

I understand and eke out a smile. The smile from before,

on the elevator, was a sugar cube compared to this one. There's nothing morbid, no exhibitionism in what she just suggested. She's not trying to give me any visual pleasure. She just wants to be able to keep an eye on me the whole time, because she doesn't trust me. The rule followed by people who kill other people is that no one, ever, for any reason, must be given the chance to kill you.

In silence, I walk ahead of her to the bathroom. I wonder when it will be time for us to talk. Time for the words that will tear away dark shrouding veils and allow a little light to shine in.

I pull open a cabinet and lay a couple of towels on the sink, next to the shower. She pulls the handgun out of her belt and lays it on the towels. The black metal stands out like an insult against the threadbare whiteness of the terry cloth.

I sit down on the can and indulge in a cigarette.

Carla begins to undress. There's nothing provocative about it. She's simply a person getting out of her clothes with brisk, asexual movements. She pulls her sweater over her head and underneath she's not wearing a bra. Her breasts are firm and full. Her nipples are swollen from rubbing against the wool. She leans against the sink and, one at a time, pulls off the *camperos* that I gave her at my house. She unbuckles her belt and with a single motion slips out of jeans and panties.

She's nude.

She's stunningly beautiful.

She's a woman who's murdered people.

Only now does she look at me. Her eyes are full of something I can't place. Regret, grief, or perhaps just exhaustion. Whatever it is, it fades in the presence of another gaze, the one-eyed glare of a pistol watching me from its perch just inches from her hand.

The gaze lasts only a brief moment, then Carla swivels around to turn on the water. Her buttocks and her hips are perfect, despite the faint outline left by her leather belt and the rough denim of her jeans.

She finds the right temperature and then steps into the spray jetting down from above. She doesn't pull the shower curtain. She begins soaping herself and the water that pours over her body is no longer the ordinary product of pressure and pipes and mechanisms. Instead it's rain falling from the sky to outline and blur her beauty, only to restore it intact to my gaze. I watch her until she closes her eyes and tips back her head. With both hands she pulls back her hair and lets the spray cleanse it of the suds.

Then she walks to the edge of the stall and gestures to me. A few drops of water fall from her hand onto the floor.

"Come on in."

A yearning for the soft touch of her hand stirs within me. As I stand up I know that that touch will become a talon and that with her razor-sharp claws she'll hurt me. But I don't care anymore. For the first time in a long time I strip off my clothing in front of another person by my own choice and my own free will. I ignore my mutilated body. I'm aware only of her perfect body.

I take a few steps and then I'm next to her, under the shower spray.

She wraps her arms around me and clings to me and the water glues us together and I find her tongue and her mouth. I explore her with my hands. I find her and I open her and she welcomes me with a moan. In some fashion she finds me and I am and I exist, and in her pleasure something comes to me too that I can't describe and there's no more slashing talon and the pain has vanished.

Afterward we remain locked together under the spray of water that has gone back to being an ordinary shower, but it's perfect for that very reason. The things it was supposed to carry away have whirled down the drain and the things it was supposed to remind us of are now emblazoned on our flesh.

I move away first. She turns off the faucet and the rush of water is replaced by silence. I step out of the shower, move the pistol, and hand her a towel. She rubs it over her hair and then wraps it around her breasts.

I don't have the nerve to look at her.

There are too many things I'm afraid I'll see in her eyes.

There are too many things I'm afraid I won't find there.

I run the other towel over my body briskly, then I gather my clothing and leave the bathroom. I finish drying off in the bedroom and put on a clean pair of slacks and a shirt.

I go into the kitchen and start making a pot of coffee. The espresso maker is gurgling away when Carla walks into the living room. She's barefoot and still has a towel wrapped high around her chest. She squats down on the floor and rummages around in her bag. She pulls out a lighter and a pack of cigarettes. She lights one and takes a drag as if it were the source of life. Finally she pulls out a pair of panties, a pair of pants, and a light T-shirt.

She disappears back down the hall. She returns fully dressed just as I finish pouring the espresso into the demitasse cups. She leans over her bag again and I see her slip the handgun into it. Then she joins me at the table. We don't talk about whatever it was that just happened. I don't know what it meant to her. For me, it was the answer to a question. And I choose to believe that it was exactly what I think it was.

She takes a sip of her coffee, unsweetened. Then she sits there, staring at that cup of steaming black liquid. The time has come to say things. And she knows it.

She starts talking without raising her gaze.

"Bonifaci was a very powerful man. More powerful than you could ever possibly imagine. Over time he had built up dossiers that he used to control most of Italy's political and business elite. Photographs taken during the orgies at his villa, documents that gave proof of involvement with organized crime, evidence of corruption and malfeasance in the administration of public funds, illegal financing of political parties."

Carla looks up at me.

"There was more than enough evidence in those dossiers to send an embarrassing number of people to prison for years. The kind of thing that would have decimated this country's governing class. Bonifaci manipulated everyone for years as if they were so many puppets on strings. To his own advantage, of course. Then he decided to take things a little too far, push a little too hard. Somebody decided that the time had come to uproot the source of his power once and for all."

"How?"

"It's obvious. By getting the dossiers that he possessed."

She drinks the last of her coffee and lays the cup down on the table. There are no coffee grounds at the bottom in which to read the future. The future is a child of the present, and for the two of us there may never be one.

But that's not the point.

Right now I just want to understand the past.

Carla knows that and deep inside she has decided that it's a fair request.

"There was a massive coalition of power and wealth ready to move against Bonifaci. Gabriel Lincoln, his right-hand man, had been corrupted with an astronomical bribe and was willing to cooperate. Unfortunately, Bonifaci fired him. Maybe he got wind of something. Or else perhaps it was nothing more than a manifestation of that sixth sense that certain individuals seem to possess."

"I understand all that. What I don't get is how the Red Brigades fit in."

"We needed a cover organization to carry out the operation. The Red Brigades are in a very tough situation right now. The police are breathing down their neck because of the Moro kidnapping and they need support and money. In exchange, they were willing to supply men. The person who organized all this arranged to obtain contacts inside the organization. He made certain promises in exchange for other promises."

"Are you telling me that there are people in the panorama of Italian politics who would be willing to abandon Moro to his fate just to get help in laying their hands on those documents?"

"That's exactly what I'm saying. The outcome would be mutually beneficial. On the one hand, it would give the Red Brigades a new victory in their armed struggle. On the other, Bonifaci would be eliminated as a danger to those who feared him most."

I stand up and light a cigarette.

"But who would guarantee that once they got their hands on the dossiers and found out what was in them, the terrorists wouldn't use them as a weapon and make them public?"

"Me."

She said it with disarming simplicity. As if it were the most obvious thing in the world.

"I became involved in this operation for two reasons. First of all, because I work for a sector of the SISDE and I'm thoroughly trained. Second, because I'm a pretty girl. I was

319

the contact with the Red Brigades, and at the same time I was the right person to gain the trust of the only man who had access to Bonifaci's villa."

"Me."

I too utter that one-syllable word with disarming simplicity. An inevitable consequence of the fact that it's the most obvious thing in the world.

"That's right. You."

Carla allows herself a mirthless smile.

"When I found out that you lived across the landing from Lucio, I couldn't believe it. It wasn't planned. It was coincidence, pure and simple."

She pauses, still incredulous at the way that chaos and chance govern the world.

"The one person who was indispensable to us in getting to Bonifaci lived just a few steps away from one of the people who was assigned the job of getting to him."

Everything seems so simple and innocuous, in Carla's calm and methodical account, now that it's no longer real life but past history. Still, she's explaining the reason she left a trail of murdered people behind her. There's no gore in her words, just descriptions and memories.

"We learned about you from Lincoln. He told us that from time to time you sent girls to the villa in Lesmo."

"And so you lured that poor devil Daytona into your camp."

"That's right. It seemed like the softest way of introducing myself into your circle of acquaintances. Getting to you through someone you trusted. From that moment on, you were under surveillance day and night."

I break in.

"I know this part."

I explain to her briefly how I figured out the truth. How I

was rescued from Tulip, how she waited for me outside the Ascot, what happened with the car and its replacement, how I figured out where Daytona's hideout was, the handgun in the door panel. As I tell my side of the story she watches me, focused, attentive, as if she were trying to puzzle out aspects that extended well beyond my words.

She doesn't know it, but there are more wrinkles to it than she could ever imagine.

But that's another story. Now there are other things that I want to know. I ask the question that most fills me with fear, the question that has been tormenting me ever since I heard the first news report about the massacre. With the certainty that if there is an answer, it will haunt me till the end of my days.

"What happened in Bonifaci's villa?"

Carla lets her eyes wander the room. Maybe she's gauging the difference between the bare space in which we're sitting and the opulent luxury that surrounded her that night. Maybe there are images unspooling before her eyes that she'd just as soon forget. What I can only imagine, she has to remember, and she will have to deal with those memories for a long, long time to come.

"Can I have another cup of coffee?"

I stand up, go into the kitchen, and start to rinse out the espresso maker. I think I understand why she asked me for another espresso. She'd prefer not to have anyone see her face while she's telling this part of the story.

Her voice reaches me as I fill the little aluminum basket with ground espresso.

"During the party I had left a French door open. When Lucio and the others arrived, bringing Laura with them, I was already holding a gun on the girls, Bonifaci, and his guests."

I press down on the fine dark brown powder with the little espresso spoon.

When Lucio and the others arrived, bringing Laura with them . . .

That means that the men in the security detail were all already dead. And that the poor girl was dragged out there to be a human sacrifice to the Gods of Political Expediency. Perhaps by the very man for whom she'd decided to begin a new life.

Carla goes on. I twist the Moka pot shut.

"Gabriel Lincoln told us that the vault was hidden in the cellar. Lucio and I went down with Bonifaci. He insisted there was no such thing as a safe room and a vault in his cellar, so I shot him in the leg to convince him to open it."

I light a match and turn on the gas. The pale blue flame licks at the base of the espresso pot.

"At that point Bonifaci gave in. He told us where the vault was and gave us the combination. When we opened it, Lucio shot him."

The flame flickers and undulates with a hypnotic power, as do Carla's words as they waft in from the other room.

"Inside the vault we found what we were looking for. We packed up the dossiers and then we went back upstairs. When we got there, there were only corpses in the drawing room."

I see that the dark liquid is beginning to bubble up, under the tilted-back lid of the espresso pot. I lower the lid. I wait for the sound of the last spurts gurgling in the throat of the percolator. I turn off the flame, pick up the pot, and go back to the other room.

Carla is motionless, her arms flat on the table, her gaze

lost in the middle distance. I pour espresso into the cup on the table in front of her. I fill my cup too.

"Chico and Alberto went straight to your apartment building to replace your car. I went with the others to the house on Via Rivoltana with the dossiers."

Carla reaches out and picks up the demitasse. She sips her coffee.

I realize that I don't want my coffee. I just want Carla to finish her story.

"Tell me about Lucio."

Actually, I want to ask her about that night. The night she . . .

Her voice breaks into my thoughts.

"Lucio was tired. I could see that he really couldn't stand the life he was leading. He was sick of living in hiding, of being a virtual prisoner, a captive of his disguise. All of his ideological discourses were concocted to use on other people, just so much smoke and mirrors. A life in hiding and on the run just wears you down, and sooner or later you look for an alternative. Any alternative, whatever the price, as long as you can hold your head up and live in the light of day. I started sleeping with him and I won him over, because I was certain of one thing."

"What was that?"

"That once he got his hands on those documents, he'd recognize that they offered him the alternative he'd been dreaming of. And so I pretended to be his accomplice in exploiting them."

"Which means?"

"Keeping the documents for ourselves. With those papers in our possession, we would have as much power as Bonifaci. They would become our insurance policy and a bottomless

323

well of cash."

She finishes her second cup of coffee. I light another cigarette.

"Everyone's dream. Freedom, immunity, money."

She looks at me.

"There was just one problem."

I wait in silence for her to confirm what I had already guessed.

"I was equally certain that Lucio would use me to eliminate the others and then, once he'd achieved that objective, he'd get rid of me too. So I had no choice. Either him or me."

I tap the ashes from my cigarette into the coffee cup. They sizzle faintly when they hit the liquid. There's one more thing I want to know.

"What motivated you to take part in this thing?"

"The same reasons that everyone does everything. Money. A chance at power. Take your pick."

She looks at her hands.

"A lot of things that don't make any sense now."

She pauses and then her eyes are on me again. I don't know what she's looking for in my face. I don't know what she's finding there. I take a last drag on my Marlboro and then douse it in the demitasse.

There's one last question, the most important one of all.

"What do you plan to do now?"

Carla shifts uneasily in her chair.

"I don't know exactly."

In silence, my eyes follow her as she stands up and walks over to the suitcases lying on the floor. She points to them with one hand.

"But one thing I do know is that if I do hand over this material to the person who sent me to get it, within the hour

I'll be a dead woman."

I look at her. I get back the exact same look.

We've become twin mirrors.

In her eyes is a foreshadowing of the only certainty available to every human being. I see the weariness and disenchantment you see in combat veterans, in people who have snuffed out the lives of others and now realize that it was all pointless. But who still have to fight for their own lives.

Carla suddenly regains the decisive tone of voice of someone who's just made a decision.

"Give me a six-hour head start and then go to the police."

"What am I going to tell them?"

"Everything that happened."

"They'll never believe me. I have no alibi and I don't have a scrap of evidence."

"You'll have both."

Carla leans over and snaps open the lock of one of the suitcases. It's filled with rigid file folders of different thicknesses and colors, each one closed with an elastic fastener and bearing a label on the front. She flips through a number of them before she finds the one she's looking for. She pulls it out, opens it, skims it rapidly. She lays it on the floor. She relocks the suitcase and takes a jacket out of her bag. When she stands up, she's holding the file in her hand and is wearing the jacket.

"This file contains documents and evidence that will get the person who organized all this dead to rights. There's enough evidence here to nail him to whatever wall happens to be closest. This is your new life insurance policy."

She walks over and lays the file on the chest of drawers. Then Carla goes back to the suitcases.

"The other files will be my policy."

"Where will you go?"

"The less you know, the better."

Her face tells me that where she's going is a mystery to her too. I hope that wherever it is, it's a place where she can be at peace. But I'm certain it won't be.

"Do you have money?"

"Yes. There was plenty of money in Bonifaci's vault. That man didn't trust banks. Not even the banks he owned."

There's not much left to say. Carla comes over to me and brushes my lips with hers.

"I wish I were a different person with a different life, I wish I'd met you in a different way. It could have been so nice."

From the smell of her skin and the warmth of her lips a question springs spontaneously. A question I regret the instant I utter it.

"Will I ever see you again?"

She lays a finger on my lips, to keep me from saying anything more. Her eyes are a wish and, at the same time, a verdict. Then she turns around, opens the door, picks up her bag and the suitcases, and drags them out onto the landing. The door closes behind her, erasing Carla's figure until it becomes a wooden panel and nothing more.

And now I'm alone.

The sound of the elevator coming up to my floor means the beginning of a trip. Which in Carla's case will mean being on the run for the rest of her life, in a way that will make the rest of her life a curse. And I'm equally cursed, if not more, because I can't muster the slightest remorse over the pity I feel for a murderer.

CHAPTER 21

The exhaustion washes over me the instant I realize that it's all over.

Here I am, still on my feet, finally immobile. The tension, fear, and excitement have all vanished suddenly, and now that the typhoon has stopped gusting, I feel hollow as a reed. There's not a milligram of adrenaline in my veins, and perhaps there's not a drop of blood either. I feel certain it's spattered all over a floor somewhere else in this city. While here, in the middle of this room, I'm only kidding myself that I'm still alive.

That's why I feel such a strong need for sleep. Because sleep is the natural state of the dead.

I look over at the file on the chest of drawers, lying there full of secrets. I don't even feel a twinge of curiosity, an urge to open it up and find out a name. What happened in the past few days belongs to the past, and like everything in the past I'm certain it holds no lessons for me or anyone else. All I know is that I had an opportunity and I let it slip through my fingers.

Chaos and chance, remember?

I walk into the bedroom. I stretch out on the mattress and stuff a pillow without a pillowcase under my head. Almost the second I have the pillow in place, I fall asleep. My last thought, before dropping off, is that Carla asked me to give her six hours.

First hour.

I sleep.

Carla drives through the streets of Milan, on a radiant Sunday morning. A lazy day for the rest of the world. Breathless with urgency for her. She parks her car in any of the thousands of parking places at Linate Airport. She knows that she'll never come back to pay her parking bill. She doesn't bother to wipe the car clean of fingerprints. The way things stand, it turns out it was a waste of time to have wiped the house on Via Rivoltana clean of fingerprints. A few miles away, in a small isolated villa full of dead bodies, photographers are taking snapshots to record the location and position of the corpses on a roll of film. The flashbulbs emit light for scant fractions of a second, searching in vain for a reflected glint of life in those dead eyes. Technicians from the police forensic squad are conducting tests to determine what kind of gun fired the shots, how many shots were fired, where they were fired from.

Second hour.

I sleep.

Carla pulls a luggage trolley from the rack and piles it high with suitcases, thinking to herself that sometimes survival can be a heavy thing. She walks into the terminal and looks up at the departures panel listing times and flights. Buenos Aires, Rio de Janeiro, New York, Caracas. One place is as good as another. It doesn't matter where the flight's going, what counts is when it's leaving. A few miles away, in a small, isolated villa, cars pull up, escorting other cars that transport the people who count. The people who decide right then and right there what to do, what to say, what to leave unsaid. Men wander around, point, make guesses, check papers, utter names. One of those names is mine.

Third hour.

I sleep.

Carla has purchased a first-class ticket on the first plane with a seat available. She paid cash, which is something she'll get used to doing from now on, and for a long time. Perhaps she showed a false passport in which the only thing left of Carla Bonelli is the photograph. Assuming that's actually her name. She's checked her bags at the ticket window and now she's walking through the gate with a boarding pass in her hand. She's hoping the luggage isn't lost on the flight. There's a risk of that happening, but there's always risk in life. Especially in her life. She boards the shuttle, takes a seat at the far end, and waits for the rest of the passengers to do the same. In the travel bag at her feet is clothing and cash. She threw the handgun into a trash can in the parking lot. A few miles away, in a small isolated villa, a medical examiner authorizes the removal of the dead bodies. When they're gone, what's left is the chalk outlines of the bodies and the tape markings where shell casings were found. Outside, journalists are clustering around the gate. As always, thanks to their unnamed sources, they're on the trail of something big, and now they want information. Just a little information, a few scraps, enough to trigger that personal hand grenade that is a reporter's imagination.

Fourth hour.

I sleep.

The airplane's in line for takeoff, awaiting authorization. Carla has placed her travel bag in the overhead compartment, with the helpful assistance of a stewardess. A few passengers give her knowing glances. Glances that contain the history

329

of the world, but not the history of Carla. If they knew that story, they'd immediately dive back into the newspapers they're holding in front of them. Other passengers are ignoring her, but they're doing it ostentatiously. Perhaps they hope she'll notice them for it. A few miles away, in a small isolated villa, a few men remain on guard until seals have been placed on doors and windows. The people who count are leaving, heading for meetings where they'll have to report to people who count more than they do, people who in turn will have to report to the people who count most of all. The staircase goes straight up, and it appears to be endless, but the important thing is to be careful of that last step, because after that one you plunge downward into the void. A few miles away, an underworld criminal named Tano Casale is turning a Totocalcio lottery ticket over and over in his hands; he believes it's a winning ticket and he's wondering what to do. My suggestion has intrigued him, captured his imagination. The fact that I'm a wanted man has caused him a slight problem, but he's decided to wait and see how things turn out. He's coming to the conclusion that he can do it all by himself, that after all he doesn't need anyone else. After all, he's the king of the world as well as the boss of part of Milan.

Fifth hour.

I sleep.

By now the airplane is a dot in the distance, as seen from the ground. A trail of smoke at takeoff that will be the same as the trail of smoke on landing, only scattered into a different sky. Carla shivers slightly with cold, the aftermath of tension and fatigue. Her mind is blank and her body demands rest. She has decided to put off until her arrival all planning, all thoughts for the future, all hypothetical strategies. She's

330

tilted her seat back into the most comfortable position, she's tucked a pillow under her head, and she's covered herself with the thin blanket provided by the airline. The engines are buzzing in the tail and it's easy to drift away. Many miles away, meetings are being held to determine the official version of events and what items to leave out, under cover of personal or state secrecy. A police detective named Stefano Milla is trying to decide whether it's worth the risk to buy the Alfa Romeo Spider roadster he dreams of. He can imagine himself driving it, the wind in his hair. He can afford it, and he doesn't feel the slightest remorse for the way he got the money. The only problem he has is explaining his sudden prosperity.

Sixth hour.

Carla is asleep.

I wake up.

My wristwatch tells me a time that means nothing. I think of turning on the television set but immediately dismiss the idea. I'd be looking at Corrado on *Domenica In* or Arbore's band on *L'altra domenica*. There's no television news at this hour on a Sunday. People want entertainment: some people decide not to know, others decide to forget. It's a deeply human application of the commutative property. Whichever you choose, the sum remains unchanged. In any case, the only thing I could learn from any public news outlet is how fragmentary the reports are that I already know in complete detail.

I get up and go into the bathroom. I do the usual things, as if it were an ordinary rise-and-shine. I pee. I wash my face. I brush my teeth, and as I do, I think to myself that it's been an awful long time since I've had anything to eat. Food is for the living, and I therefore have no right to it.

Chaos and chance. Now I remember.

I look at myself in the dim light that filters through the slats of the blinds. The mirror imparts an image that doesn't belong to me. I myself don't belong to me, because I wear a name that can no longer protect me and that can't be fixed. It's like an old shirt, and as such, it needs to be thrown away.

I step out of the bathroom and walk into the living room. The floor is cold and filthy under my bare feet. Hygiene is always the first thing to deteriorate when you're wanted by the law and on the run. I saw the house where Daytona died. I saw the house where Lucio and the others died.

It must have been cleaner in Bonifaci's villa.

But they're all just as dead anyway.

I pick up the file from the chest of drawers and sit down on the couch, which welcomes me with the rustle and crinkle of the plastic slipcovers. On the cover of the file there's a white label. Someone's hand wrote a hasty script with a fountain pen and black ink: *Daedalus and Icarus*.

I think it over for a minute, but the phrase means nothing to me. I unhook the elastic fastener and open the cover. I fold out the three flaps. Inside I find a pile of photographs and a stack of papers. I extract them and leaf through, slowly at first and then frenetically. When I get to the end I go back to the beginning and pore through it more calmly. Those sheets of paper and those snapshots are a traveler's guide to a subterranean world, a tunnel carved out yard after yard by a complete lack of scruples, guided in the proper direction by unbridled ambition. It's enough to unhinge a person's sanity just to pass through it once, because it's hard to absorb the depths to which human abjectness can sink. There's enough evidence in this folder for a magistrate to order a series of arrests, with handcuffs and preventive detention—that is, as long as the magistrate in question isn't ordered to desist by his superiors.

I close the file and lean back on the couch.

The ceiling becomes a screen upon which my mind projects images. I see familiar faces, places, and colors again. There is a succession of streets, people, seaside settings, children's games, grown-up love affairs, inadequate hiding places.

Then, suddenly, without warning, I start laughing.

I laugh for myself, for all these years spent with a suspicion that has now become a certainty. I laugh for that razor blade that condemned me to spend the rest of my life as nothing more than a spectator, while I in my utter stupidity believed that I had more than a few strings to pull. I laugh for Carla and for all the planes that, sadly, have to land sooner or later. I laugh for Barbara's breasts and Cindy's white flesh and for Laura, who fell in love and was betrayed. I laugh for Lucio and his soulless music and his pointless years of pretense. I laugh for Giorgio Fieschi, who could have spent the rest of his life listening to the roar of the crowd but instead died in the faint hiss of a gun with a silencer. I laugh for Daytona and his expensive watch and his comb-over that, even at death's door, his hand was rising up to pat into place. I laugh for Tano Casale and his all-too-familiar voice. I laugh for men who took the job of defending others but when the time came found no one to defend them. I laugh for the ideals that deal death and the death of ideas. I laugh because only the stupid and the innocent lack an alibi. I laugh because chaos and chance aren't governing the world, they're destroying it.

I laugh and laugh and laugh.

I laugh so hard that my lungs start to ache because I can't catch a breath. I laugh so hard that I'm afraid someone is going to pound on the wall to make me shut up in here. I laugh so hard that I find myself sprawled out on the couch with the plastic slipcover glued to my face, wet with tears.

When I'm done laughing, the tears are all that's left.

Tears of liberation, grief, and farewell.

I recover and get to my feet. I know what to do now. The first thing I have to do is track down my lawyer, Ugo Biondi, as quickly as possible. I try his office, but just to cross it off my checklist. I know that it's highly unlikely that I'll catch him there on a Sunday, but I can't overlook any possibility. His phone rings and rings without anyone answering. I was hoping he might be in the office to prepare for a case in court on Monday, but no such luck. Ugo's no workaholic. The day that the Italian government decides to issue knighthoods for minimal effort, I'm pretty sure that he'll be on the first year's list of honorees.

I dial his home number, but with the same result. I imagine a phone ringing in an empty apartment, the sound bouncing off the walls. Off the furniture and lamps and carpets and books on bookshelves.

There's only one other place I could find him. I know that he has a vacation home on Lake Maggiore. Whoremonger that he is, he sometimes spends weekends there with his latest Lady Quack-Quack. Once or twice I sent one of my own girls there with him. Free of charge out of loving-kindness, and entered on the balance sheet as a PR expense.

I even think I remember the name of the town.

I dial the number for Information provided by the Italian phone company, SIP. I ask the operator for a phone number of a certain Ugo Biondi in Arona. My doubts about the name of the town are immediately swept away by a voice giving me the number requested.

Now I dial that number.

Every movement is clear and precise. Every sound is crystalline. My finger in the holes of the rotary dial, the sound of the rotor as it clicks back into place. Now I'm clear-headed and determined, as if I'd just snorted a line of coke.

The phone rings on the other end of the line. It rings for a long time, without anyone coming to pick up the receiver. The answering voice catches me by surprise, just as I'm about to hang up.

"Yes, hello?"

He's a little out of breath, as if he'd run to pick up the phone in time.

"*Ciao*, Ugo, this is Bravo."

Now he's completely breathless. I'd have the same reaction, if I were him.

"Fuck. Where are you?"

"In a place."

He doesn't mince words.

"You're up to your eyebrows in shit."

"Not anymore. I've taken care of everything."

"What do you mean, you've taken care of everything?"

"I'm innocent and I can prove it. I'm planning to turn myself in and I want you to be there as my legal counsel. I think this will get your name in the papers. It might be a fairly complicated case, but what is there in this life that's simple?"

He takes a second to think it over. Another second to answer.

"I'm at the lake."

I have to smile. My phone call must really have caught him off guard and flustered him for him to say such a ridiculous phrase.

"Umm, I know that. I called you there."

"Jesus, of course, obviously. What I mean is, it's going to take me some time to get back to Milan."

"Take as long as you like. Nobody's chasing *you*."

There's another short silence on the other end of the line. He's probably wondering how on earth I manage to make jokes, given the situation I'm in. He doesn't know that I'm about to experience one of the happiest moments of my life.

I take advantage of this opportunity to get practical.

"How long do you think it'll take you, more or less?"

"Depends on traffic. An hour and fifteen minutes, maybe an hour and a half."

"We'll see you in an hour and a half in your law office."

I hang up the phone without giving him a chance to answer. I'm pretty sure that even if he was in the middle of having sex, he's going to leave his lady love sprawled on the bed halfway to paradise, jump into his trousers, and drive straight to Milan as fast as whatever car he owns can go.

Now I cross my fingers and hope for another stroke of luck. I rummage around in drawers and cabinets until I find a phone book. I lean on the table and look up Stefano Milla's name in the directory. He could be on duty, which is very likely, considering that all hell has broken loose, but I'd prefer to put off a phone call to police headquarters until it's my last resort.

He picks up on the sixth ring and answers in a sleepy voice. He probably worked the night shift and I just woke him up. I need hardly add that I couldn't care less.

"Hello."

"Hello, Stefano. This is Bravo."

Silence. I know that he can't believe his ears. Then I hear the rustle of sheets, the sound of someone suddenly sitting bolt upright in bed.

"Hello?"

"I said, this is Bravo."

"Unfortunately, I understood you the first time. I just wanted to make sure."

I breathe my most ceremonious voice into the mouthpiece.

"How is everything?"

"You piece of shit. Do you have any idea how many people are out on the street, trying to find you?"

Nobody recognizes a piece of shit like another piece of shit. I have to hand it to him.

"I know that. Don't worry, they'll be able to relax soon enough. I'm planning to turn myself in. But first I need your help."

"Have you lost your mind? I've already run enough risks for you."

"I'm going to give you two alternatives. The first is, you do what I ask, you get a bundle of money, and you even make a good impression on your superior officers."

"What's the second?"

"Be an asshole and show up with your bullyboys at the address I'm going to give you. Do that, and I can guarantee you that we'll make the trip back to police central together, both of us in handcuffs. I don't know if that's clear enough for you."

His voice changes. Suddenly he's turned into a good cop. Maybe now he's not even being a cop.

"Bravo, you can't do this to me. I've always been a good friend to you."

"You're nobody's friend, Stefano. I'm pretty sure that there are days when you can't even stand yourself. All the same . . ."

I leave the phrase hanging. Just long enough to dangle

337

him over the hot coals. The coals begin to roast him and he prods me.

"All the same?"

I repeat the words I said to my lawyer just a few minutes ago.

"I'm innocent, Stefano. And I can prove it. I have documents that are so explosive they'll leave a hole as deep as the craters on the moon."

"How the hell did you get into this mess in the first place?"

"I really had no say in the matter. But I do have a say in how I get out of it. If you give me a hand, I'll make sure you're one of the people who get full credit. And, just to reinforce the concept, a fat bundle of cash."

The last few words seem to calm him down.

He wouldn't feel so calm if he knew the names of the people I just read in that file. If he knew what's about to happen to Tano Casale.

"What do I have to do?"

"Wait at home. I'll call you later and tell you where you need to go."

"How much later?"

"Fifty million lire later. Does that work as an approximate time?"

Once again, I hang up without giving him a chance to reply. I'm positive that he'll do what I tell him to, now and later. In the first place because he's shitting his pants with fear, and in the second place because he's never seen, much less laid his hands on, fifty million lire in his life. He wouldn't know how to write the number out, even if he were copying it directly.

Now all I have to do is wait.

I'm relaxed, now that time is no longer barreling straight

at me like an oncoming collision. In my mind there's still a plane in the sky, carrying a sleeping woman, and with every minute that passes it gets farther and farther away. Now it's time to think about the plane that will carry me away. Where? I'll make that decision at the last minute, too.

I go into the bathroom, and there I find the copy of *La Settimana Enigmistica* that I had left sitting on the towel cabinet. The issue that unveiled Lucio's masquerade and allowed me to unmask him. I pick it up and go back to the living room. I sit down at the table and leaf through it, in search of a cryptic clue. I find one on the Page of the Sphinx.

Accommodation that's barred for flappers (8)

I smile. I like the imagery, and considering my current residence, it's even somewhat topical. It's one word, eight letters long. I light a cigarette. The coffee cups are still sitting on the table. One of them still has the taste of Carla's lips on the rim. The other one is full of coffee that's cold now, the coffee I never drank.

I work on the cryptic clue. It takes me a while to work it out, but I come up with the solution.

Birdcage.

It wasn't really that hard after all. Every puzzle shows its weak point, once you solve it. Sometimes it's enough to read a little-known fact in a weekly puzzler; sometimes it's enough to find a hidden pistol, if you know where to look for it. Sometimes all you have to do is open a stiff cardboard file. Unfortunately, there are many things and

339

many people that you lose along the way, and you can never get them back.

I extinguish my cigarette in my coffee again. The sizzling hiss is drowned out by the sound of a key turning in the lock.

I swivel to look at the door.

The latch clicks open and the door swings toward me. In the rectangular frame two figures appear, a canvas suitcase on the floor beside them. A woman with a cloth jacket stares at me in astonishment and fear. At her side stands a pale little boy with dark hair, about five years old. Their appearance and their clothing indicate that they've just arrived here after a long journey and are trying to make up their minds whether the place they've arrived is worse than the place they left.

CHAPTER 22

When I get to the end of Via Carbonia, Stefano Milla's Alfa Romeo Giulietta is pulled over to the sidewalk on the opposite side of the street. All around me, a working-class Milanese neighborhood is experiencing the tail end of a springtime Sunday afternoon. Saturday is a fading memory, Monday is an unwelcome prospect. But for just a few more hours there's still something left. A soccer game, a movie, a pizza, a pinball machine, music in a bar or a disco. A man, a woman, the backseat of a car, a bed, a hand job in the darkness of a movie theater, teenage kisses without tongues and practically without saliva. A joint, a line of coke, a shot of heroin, a glass of bad wine, a glass of Coca-Cola, a glass of mineral water with a slice of lemon. Everyone is standing in line to order or to pick up whatever most helps them to be or not to be. What a pathetic loser Hamlet was after all. I have nothing in common with the people who surround me. Neither past nor present nor future. Not my clandestine name. I'm not even showing them my face, covered up as it is by my raised collar, my dark glasses, my unshaven beard, and one of Carmine's hats, which I found in an armoire. My Saturday in the village was punctuated with gunshots and dead bodies in a villa a little way beyond Segrate. The party ended early, as is so often the case. Even though I scrubbed and scrubbed, I can still feel Lucio's blood spattering my face.

I remember the words he said to me in the Quartiere Tessera, the night I went and fell into his trap.

No, Bravo. I'm a dead man. Just like you are . . .

But it turns out I'm still alive. I hope I don't wind up regretting it.

I cross the street. On the opposite sidewalk coming toward me is a young couple. The boy is very skinny, long-haired and wearing an olive drab combat jacket, a perfect substitute for a parka in this season. The girl has frizzy hair and pimply cheeks, and she'll never be skinny.

Laurel and Hardy, walking arm in arm.

They strike me as beautiful.

Right after we pass one another I come even with the car. I pull open the rear passenger-side door and toss my bag onto the backseat. Then I pull open the front door and get in, next to Milla. He turns his head to appraise my disguise, perhaps making a mental comparison with an identikit that no longer matches my current appearance. He's wearing a pair of sunglasses, too. He's tense and nervous. He wishes he were someone else, and somewhere else, and he's not trying to hide it.

Or maybe he is, but he's not doing a very good job.

"Jesus, Bravo. Do you have any idea how much trouble you're getting me into?"

I shake my head.

"I'm not getting you into trouble at all. Quite the contrary."

I take off the hat and toss it into the backseat. I run my hands through my hair. I'm not used to it being so short.

"When this is all over, in the eyes of your superiors you're going to be the heroic police detective who talked me into giving myself up to the law. You'll have plenty of money. And if you do as I tell you, you'll even be set free."

"Set free from what?"

"From your love story with Tano Casale."

Something flickers across his face and then it's gone. So fast that I can't figure out what it is.

"I don't know what you have in mind, but if that guy ever decides that I'm plotting something behind his back, I'm a dead man."

I take off my sunglasses and look at him.

"I've been one for a while now. As you can see, it's really not so bad after all."

He makes up his mind and starts the engine.

"Where the hell are we going?"

"Piazza Amendola, number five. Next to the taxi stand."

The car pulls away from the curb. I put my sunglasses back on and get comfortable. We turn left into Via Arsia, heading for the Fiera, Milan's trade fair. I tell myself again that it's all over. That nothing can hurt me now, nothing can do me any damage. With what I've got in my bag, I'm ready to start doing the hurting.

And I plan to do plenty of damage.

We stop at a red light. At the corner is a pharmacy open on Sundays. A woman with a little girl is pushing the door to go in. My thoughts go back to two people I just met a few hours ago, standing at the front door of an apartment that was a safe haven for a few days. Now it's just one of the many addresses on the street grid of the city of Milan.

The instant I saw them, I stood up and walked across the room toward them.

The woman didn't move, she just reached out her hand

343

and pulled the child over to her. I saw her stiffen. Her initial fear and surprise had given way to firmness now. The same firmness that made her leave her husband when she understood that he'd never change. When she decided that her son wasn't going to grow up in the same home as a convicted felon.

"Who are you, Signore?"

I stopped about an arm's length away.

"I'm Bravo, a friend of Carmine's. I assume you're his wife, Luciana?"

The woman paid no attention to me. Her eyes were searching the interior. Being referred to as Carmine's wife stopped bothering her years ago. Now it's just a regrettable fact of life, like the dust on the furniture and the deplorable condition of the apartment. Maybe she's reliving a time when that furniture belonged to her and the apartment was a little cleaner but her life was a little dirtier.

"Did Carmine rent you the apartment? Why didn't he change the locks?"

I extended my arms in a gesture that encompassed apartments, door locks, decisions in life.

"I didn't actually rent it from him. When Carmine . . ."

I looked over at the little boy as he stood switching his gaze back and forth between me and his mother. At that age kids are vacuum cleaners. They understand much more than we imagine. And the things they don't understand sometimes remain stamped on their minds and concealed somewhere deep inside. Over time, those things can do much greater damage. So I decided not to utter the word *arrested* in front of him.

"When Carmine had his problem, I just took over the payments on his utilities and condominium fees."

"Why?"

"Sometimes there are things you do for no good reason."

"Even if it doesn't seem like it at first, there's always a reason."

She turned disenchanted eyes on me. In them I saw days spent coldly evaluating every person she encountered, to gauge whether they were a hoodlum like her husband or a policeman. Without ever being able to say which of the two categories was more dangerous. But with one rock-solid certainty: both were her enemies. Just a week ago I would have put her away on the shelf of her own fucking business and gone my own way. Now my certainties were undermined by deep fissures and the shelf in question was starting to look precarious. Her certainties, in contrast, however, seemed to have endured very well, because they had been borne out by time and experience.

She didn't let me add anything more.

"Are you hiding here?"

I shook my head.

"Not anymore. I had some problems, but that's all taken care of. I was just about to leave."

"Are you armed?"

"No."

She must have decided that my voice was sincere and so were my eyes. For that matter, she had surely adopted as her guiding tactic in life not to stick her nose into other people's business. A rule that is usually only partly a choice and partly something that is imposed upon a person. She picked up her suitcase and pushed the boy into the apartment ahead of her. Then she leaned over him and began tugging his overcoat off. The coat was a little heavy for the season.

"I'm sorry, but I didn't have anyplace else to go. We just

got here from Germany. Another tenant in the building who I've stayed in touch with told me that the apartment was unoccupied. I've always wondered why I was holding on to this key. Now I know."

The little boy, liberated from his jacket, now felt free to speak.

"Mama, I need to go to the bathroom."

She took off her jacket and tossed it onto the couch. She was wearing a skirt and a sweater with colors combined according to a lack of better alternatives, rather than a matter of personal taste. I could see she was a little overweight, but she had a nice shape to her. She must have been a pretty girl before life decided to give her some shock therapy.

"We'll go right now. Come with me."

She took her son by the hand and led him down the hallway. I waited a few seconds; then I picked up the file folder and followed her. I went into the bedroom. As I listened to the sound of running water, I put on my socks and shoes and pulled my leather jacket out of my travel bag. I did the reverse with all the clothing I'd carelessly scattered around the room. I removed the cash and the lottery ticket from their hiding place and put the cash in the travel bag and the lottery ticket in my wallet. The file was the last item packed into my bag. When mother and son emerged from the bathroom, they walked past my door without a glance at me. I idiot-checked the room, to make sure I hadn't forgotten anything. There wasn't a sign I'd ever been there, aside from the body-shaped hollow on the bed. That would be gone soon enough.

I went back into the living room and set my travel bag down next to Luciana's suitcase. Someone arrives and someone else leaves. The usual story. With just one difference. The

346

suitcases are always heavier when you come back than when you depart.

I went over to the kitchen door. Luciana was at the sink, filling a glass of water for her boy from the faucet. The child looked at me with dark, joyless eyes. It's incredible how the melancholy of certain journeys spares nobody.

I spoke to the woman.

"Have you had anything to eat?"

"A sandwich on the train."

I pointed to the cabinets and pulled open the refrigerator.

"There's plenty of food here. It's all canned, but there's enough for a few days or so."

Luciana began to inspect the cabinets, examining their contents. The little boy left us and went back to the sitting room, to take possession of this new space.

After she was finished with her inspection, Luciana looked at me. She had a nice face and eyes that must have once been lively.

"Are you hungry? I'd be glad to make a bowl of pasta for you."

"No, thanks. I'm in a bit of a hurry. I have some things to take care of. I'll have plenty of time to eat after I'm done."

The child's voice came wailing down the hall from the other room.

"Mama, I'm having a nosebleed."

"Oh, Rosario, not again."

The woman stepped around me. She hurried to the boy, who was standing with his head tipped back. A rivulet of blood was trickling from his right nostril. She went over to her bag and rummaged around until she found a handkerchief, already dotted with red stains. She squatted down and held it against the little boy's nose to compress the nostril.

Then she turned to look at me. Her eyes were brimming over with tears. The unmistakable tears of a grieving mother.

"I came back here because the boy is sick. He's a hemophiliac and he can't get medical care in Germany because the health service won't pay for the therapy. He needs injections, and they're expensive. I don't have the money."

She paused. The grit was back, and she was in fighting form again.

"But I'll get it. If I have to make Carmine sell this apartment. Buying this place was the only smart thing he ever did."

Another pause. That period must be difficult to think about. Just as certain decisions are difficult to make.

"When I left, I promised myself that I wouldn't take anything from him ever again. But now things are different. Now I have responsibilities and I'm not really in control of my own life."

I was afraid to tell her that there was no way that anyone could sell the apartment. The victims' survivors were civil plaintiffs in the case. The lawsuit for restitution would probably go on indefinitely, but ownership of the apartment was, in practical terms, frozen solid.

Luciana lifted the handkerchief slightly to make sure the nosebleed was over. She wiped away the last traces of blood from her son's face. Then she hugged him.

"You see? It stopped."

"Oh, it always stops, Mama."

"Now that we're here we're going to make you all better, so it won't ever come back again."

She stood up. Rosario followed her every movement with his eyes.

"Mama, I'm tired. Can I go lie down on the bed?"

"Yes, sweetheart, go lie down. Have a nice nap while Mama makes us something good to eat."

Luciana took the child by the hand and together they disappeared down the hallway again. Before leaving, the little boy looked me straight in the face for the first time. Then, with a very serious expression, he gestured at me with one hand. I didn't understand exactly what it meant. But there are times when it doesn't matter what certain communications mean. It's enough that they exist.

I went to the phone and called Milla. I gave him the address and told him to be there in one hour. I hung up the phone on his fears and worries. I was sick of being the only one to sow seeds in that field. From now on I'd have company when I did it.

I took some money out of my travel bag and counted out three million lire. I set the bundle of cash on the chest of drawers, exactly where the file folder had been. Maybe Luciana would have turned up her nose if she knew the source of my savings. But she couldn't afford to be too finicky when she remembered why she needed it. The woman's voice caught me by surprise, while I was still arranging the bundle of cash.

"Poor little thing, he fell fast aslee . . ."

She saw the money and fell silent immediately. She looked at me quickly. Her astonishment slowly seeped into her mistrust. Or maybe it was the other way around, I really couldn't say. Maybe she'd never seen that much money all in one place at the same time. I'm certain that she'd dreamed about it, ever since she discovered that her child was sick.

"That should be enough, at least for the first little while. After that, I'm pretty sure that Rosario is going to get good medical care and you won't have to sell the apartment."

Luciana was relieved and afraid at the same time. The way a woman always is when she receives a gift from a man who asks nothing in return.

"Why are you doing this?"

I smiled at her.

"Believe me, there's no point in your asking me that question. I'm already wondering the same thing."

She picked up the money, folded it in half, and went to put it in her jacket pocket. I looked at my watch. There was time, all the time I needed. Suddenly I was starving.

"Now, if the offer is still good, I'd be glad to accept that bowl of pasta."

A sudden jerk corkscrews me out of my thoughts. A guy on a bicycle ahead of us just made a sudden turn without a hand signal. Milla was forced to jam on the brakes to keep from hitting him.

"Would you just take a look at this asshole."

So I take a look at this asshole. Who hasn't even noticed that he came this close to having his balls crushed under the tread of a fast-moving whitewall tire and is just placidly pedaling onward, toward the next set of screeching tires and the next furious string of curses. Milla starts up again. With his foot on the accelerator and his litany of questions. I really didn't expect it to take him this long.

"Bravo, are you going to tell me what happened? A lot of people have been murdered."

"I know. But I swear to you, I didn't kill even one of them."

He waits for more. But I just don't have it in me.

"Give me a break, Stefano. It's a long story and I'm pretty sure I'm going to have to tell it over and over again when we get to the police station. If you'll just be patient, I feel certain you're going to be sick of hearing it before long."

"At least tell me where we're going."

"To my lawyer's office. I want legal counsel when they question me."

This last detail seems to set his mind at rest once and for all as far as my good intentions are concerned. He's not as sanguine about other developments. And I don't mean in my life, I mean in his. He knows that he has both testicles perched in the jaws of a bear trap and that I have the power to make those jaws snap shut. I know that sensation all too well, and I know how deeply unpleasant it can be.

While we were talking, we've driven around the perimeter of the grounds of the Fiera and now we're in Piazza Amendola. I point out the place and Milla stops his car in front of the large wooden doors of an old-fashioned seven-story building. On the fifth floor is the office where my legal eagle awaits me. I open the car door, and before getting out I issue appropriate instructions to Stefano.

"Wait for me here. It might be a while. There's one thing you could do for me, while you wait. Get hold of Tano. Tell him that I'll have things straightened out pretty soon but there might be too many people watching me for quite some time. It's too dangerous for us both to get me involved directly in the operation that we talked about. I think he'll agree with me."

"Is that all?"

"That's all. He'll know what I'm talking about."

I stick my leg out of the car but his hand grabs my arm just as I set my foot down on the asphalt.

"Bravo, I'm risking my ass for you. What about my money?"

351

"What money?"

"Don't be an asshole. My fifty million."

I smile at him. The same smile I might give a child with a nosebleed.

"You haven't earned that money yet."

"What do you mean, I haven't earned it yet? I'm here, aren't I?"

"Being here earns you my silence. The money, on the other hand, is to buy your silence."

"Bravo, I don't understand."

"For right now, you don't have to. When the time is right, you'll understand."

"But who guarantees me that I'll get the money?"

I put on a face that expresses just how uncertain the future is for us all.

"So sorry, detective. I'm afraid you're going to have to trust me this one time."

I get out of the car and pull my bag out of the backseat. I close the car doors, and as I do I leave him sitting at the same time on both ordinary automobile upholstery and a bed of nails. A few quick steps and I ring the doorbell marked law firm of ugo biondi, esq.

The street door clicks open almost immediately.

I walk into the lobby. The light filters softly through the frosted glass of a massive courtyard door across from the entrance. In the dim light, the decorations on the walls appear even more austere. I walk up a couple of steps and I'm on the elevator landing. Inside the cabin of the elevator there is no graffiti. The wood paneling glistens with a handsome sheen. The scent of wax is in the air. I smile at the sight of a velvet-upholstered bench for added comfort during that short journey upstairs.

I push the button for the fifth floor and ride up. Ugo's waiting for me at the door.

"Ciao."

"Get in here, quick."

He closes the door behind him and leads me through an office that smells of paper, ink, and leather. All the doors are closed, so I have no visual cues to remind me of what functions the various rooms lining the hallway serve. But the room we wind up in is unquestionably his own office. I have to say that my lawyer treats himself nicely, and it stands to reason that as a result, he treats his clients very well. Few enough of them deserve it, of course, since he's a criminal lawyer.

His desk is an imposing American antique from the turn of the twentieth century. The other furniture and bookcases, groaning with books and bound legal codes, covering almost every wall, are in keeping with the style of the occupant of the office. The paintings look like some pretty decent artwork.

Ugo points me to one of the two Poltrona Frau office chairs standing in front of the desk.

"Have a seat. Would you like anything to drink?"

"No, thanks."

My lawyer sits down at his proper place. I'm already sitting at mine. Despite everything, this is nothing more than a dress rehearsal for what usually follows meetings like this. A chair in the dock for the defendant, a throne on a raised lectern for the judge.

He picks up a pencil. He starts to fiddle with it. This must be something he usually does when he's meeting with a client. The stories that a criminal lawyer has to sit through would make anyone look around for a distraction.

He's tense, no question. He's sitting with Milan's most wanted man. And he wants to make sure I know it.

"No two ways about it. You've become a celebrity. I don't think I've seen this big an uproar as long as I can remember."

"Just think what it looked like from inside. An entirely different point of view, I can assure you."

He lays his forearms on the desktop.

"I'm all ears."

"Where should I start?"

"Starting at the beginning has always seemed like a good tactical approach."

I tell him everything. As I talk, I'm amazed at my ability to unspool such a complicated story line without getting anything tangled. With every word, Ugo's eyes widen a little more. By the time I'm done, he's stopped fiddling with his pencil.

"Fuck a duck."

I decide to stretch the concept a little further to make it fit the facts.

"A rather large, fat duck. But that's not all."

I reach into the bag that I set down on the floor next to my chair and toss the file folder onto the desk.

"Take a look at what's in there."

He takes the file and unhooks the elastic: he doesn't yet know that he's pulling the pin on a hand grenade. It takes a little longer than the classic count from one to ten to go over the various documents, several times over. Then the wrecked expression on his face must look more or less like the expression I had when I first saw them.

"Jesus, Bravo, this is an atom bomb."

"And there's a real danger it might not detonate at all."

We both know the meaning of what I just said. This is such

a major scandal that the possibility of it being buried very deep is anything but remote. *State secrecy* is a magic phrase that can close door after door instead of opening them. But there's another possibility. He's the first to put it out there.

"Or it could go off right under our asses."

The moment he saw those documents, he knew that our lives might now be worth less than the loose change in our pockets. There are things that you might think could happen only in the movies. But no one stops to think that the reason they put those things in the movies is that they've already happened in real life.

I decide to take a practical step to make some of the murky confusion swirling through our heads settle.

"Do you have a copy machine in the office?"

"Yes."

He looks at me. Perhaps a thought had already begun to form in his mind. Now he waits, curious to see if that thought has already become fully formed in my mind.

"Do you have a safe?"

"Of course."

I shift forward to the edge of my chair.

"Here's what we could do. A series of envelopes, each with a copy of the documents, and each addressed to the Milan newsroom of a major national daily: *Il Corriere della Sera*, *La Repubblica*, *La Stampa*, *Il Giorno*, *La Notte*. Put them in your safe and leave a note for your secretary to take them tomorrow morning and deliver them personally to all those newspapers."

He thinks it over for a minute.

"We can do even better than that."

He picks up the phone and dials a number. He gets an answer after a few rings.

"*Buona sera*, Federica. This is Biondi. I know it's Sunday, but I have a very big favor I'd like to ask you. This is something of the greatest importance."

He waits for a positive answer. He must have received it, because he continues.

"An hour from now there are going to be several envelopes with Milan addresses on my desk. Would you be so kind as to come by and hand-deliver them yourself?"

On the other end of the line, a logical objection is raised in an attempt to rescue the remaining shreds of the holiday.

"I'd really prefer you do it this evening, not tomorrow. I'll explain everything later."

The person he's talking to must have realized that this is a very serious matter.

"I knew I could count on you. I'm sorry to bother you, but this coming week I'd like you to take a day off, the day of your choice. And I'd like to give you two tickets to La Scala."

The conversation ends with a formal *good evening*.

"*Buona sera* to you too, Federica. And thanks again."

Ugo hangs up. He points to the phone as if it were the person he just spoke to. Even though I didn't ask, he provides me with her references.

"Federica Isoardi is my secretary. She's smart, reliable, and capable of keeping a secret. She's also very cute, but she's such a good worker that I've never even winked at her. I'm afraid of losing her."

He looks me in the eye with a meaningful glance, both hands resting on the file.

"It may be excess caution, but I'd just as soon not leave this kind of material in the office overnight."

He sighs. The world really is a terrible place. A terrible, filthy, dangerous place.

As if it took a considerable effort, he gets to his feet.

"Outstanding. Let's get to work."

I stand up, too.

"There's another thing I'd like to ask you to do for me."

"Which is?"

I put my hand in my pocket and pull out my wallet. I open it and extract the lottery ticket and the newspaper clipping with the scores of the soccer games on that lucky Sunday.

"I want you to cash this in, when I give you the word."

He takes it from me, holding it gingerly between two fingers. He studies it with some curiosity.

"What is this?"

"A winning soccer lottery ticket worth 490 million lire."

He looks up suddenly. I have to say that Ugo Biondi, Esq., has a fairly narrow range of exclamations of surprise.

"Fuck me."

"Well, for once that would be you, not me, is all I can say."

He compares the scores on the newspaper clipping with the numbers on the lottery ticket to make sure they match up. I knew he'd do it. Partly out of personal curiosity, but mostly because that's what he does for a living. If his own mother had given him that ticket, he would have checked it out, just to make sure. Check box by check box, he runs down to the thirteenth matching score.

At that point an exclamation bursts from his lips.

"Wow: 490 million lire. Nice win."

Holding the slip of paper as if it were the most fragile thing on earth, Ugo steps over to a painting on the wall to my left. He swings it open to reveal the wall safe behind it. Not even a successful lawyer like him, with all the authoritative experts he must know, has been able to come up with a less clichéd hiding place. He dials the correct combination and the safe clicks open. The lottery ticket is placed carefully inside.

"While you're at it, could you add these?"

I lean over and pull out all the bundles of cash my bag contains. I walk over and put the money in his hands. My increasingly astonished lawyer walks the money over and places it next to the lottery ticket worth half a million dollars. The painting is considerably more valuable when he swings it back into place.

We go back to the desk. Ugo picks up the file.

"I'll write you a receipt for everything you just gave me. But now I think we have some more important things to do."

"Agreed."

I follow him out of his office to a cramped utility closet where there's a copy machine. We work together, without speaking, at a steady rhythm, until we have all the copies we need. When we're done, a series of dark brown envelopes are laid out on the table. Each has an address written clearly on the front.

All but one. That's for me.

We go back to his office, where we pile the envelopes on his desk. Ugo sits down and promptly handwrites a few lines on a sheet of letterhead stationery. He adds a date and a signature and then hands it to me.

"Here's your receipt. I'm sorry, but I don't know how to use a typewriter."

"I'll manage somehow."

Another sheet of paper, with a few lines of instruction for his secretary, is set carefully on the stack of envelopes.

We exchange a glance. We know there's nothing more to do here.

Ugo swivels around and picks up a leather valise from a

small table on his left. He opens it and places the file with the original documents inside. Then he stands up with the eyes of a man ready for a fight. Only during the battle will he know if he's fighting against giants or windmills.

There's one last thing to add. And I add it.

"Ugo, there's a police detective in a car downstairs."

"What?"

"Don't worry. I asked him to come. We're going to come up with a convincing story of my arrest. I wanted him to bring us in to the police station."

Ugo studies my face. Suddenly he's a lawyer looking at a fugitive from the law.

"Why him in particular?"

"Because I know him and I want him to get the credit for this. And because he's the only cop who'd be willing to make another stop before taking us to police headquarters."

"To do what?"

"To tell an old friend good-bye."

Ugo, as a human being and as a lawyer, cannot stifle an instinctive question.

"Who?"

I look at him and smile.

"Francesco Marcona, better known as Bravo."

I turn away and head for the front door.

Successful lawyer Ugo Biondi, with his leather briefcase, standing next to a desk that cost several million lire, in his centrally located and beautifully decorated law office, is disconcerted.

I, with my dark brown envelope in my hand, am happy.

CHAPTER 23

The Alfa Romeo Giulietta hums along Viale della Liberazione at a reasonable speed.

All around us Milan is lit up and ready to celebrate yet another nocturnal ritual. The usual characters of the night will be on the move. The wealthy, the misfits, the cops, the crooks, the artists, the whores. Sometimes the faces change, but the roles remain the same. It's always hard to tell just who's who. I'm the slight exception to that rule. Things in my life have hurtled forward at the speed of light. For the rest of the world, one short week has passed. For me, years have sped by.

Too much blood, too many dead bodies, too much naked reality.

Which is exactly what I'm going to confront.

The whole way, Stefano Milla has driven almost as if he were practicing for his learner's permit, as if he were afraid to commit some minor infraction that might attract the attention of one of his fellow policemen. The presence of the lawyer made him decide not to tell me any details about his phone call to Tano Casale. The unexpected side trip, which I told him about only when Biondi and I got in the car, added to his existing anxiety.

The nails he was sitting on have now been transformed into daggers.

We turn onto Via Cartesio and we stop at the corner of Piazza della Repubblica. On our right are the trees that screen the main façade of the Hotel Principe e Savoia like a small verdant park.

I open the car door.

From the backseat, Ugo expresses a thought out loud that I know has been echoing through Milla's brain.

"Bravo, are you sure you know what you're doing?"

"Oh, yes: one hundred percent."

The actual percentage of confidence that I feel is much lower than that. But there are things you've been waiting your whole life to do. Sometimes even a lifetime isn't long enough. When the time comes, there's nothing for it but to go along for the ride. This is one of those times. And, after all, the future is in the hands of the gods, which isn't actually much of a guarantee.

I get out of the car and I walk unhurriedly up the ramp to the main entrance of the hotel. There's plate glass and wood and stucco. The lamps inside the hotel pour their light out onto the roundabout where cars stop to unload travelers' luggage. The air is filled with the scent of playthings and perfume. In places like this hotel, when evening falls you always have the impression that you're living in a perennial Christmas.

On either side of the entrance a couple of police patrol cars are parked, something that always happens when an important person is staying at the hotel. The policemen are sitting in their cars on upholstery of pure boredom. One officer glances at me through his open window as I walk up to the front door. A bored look, then he goes to back to his conversation with his partner.

Maybe they're discussing the violent events that have put

law enforcement officials and the police on red alert across the country. Or perhaps they're just calculating that even if they took a whole month's salary, they couldn't afford to spend a weekend in the hotel they're guarding.

As I walk through the front door, I muse that there are two things in the world that are difficult to master: boredom and fear.

I go over to the reception desk, where a clerk in uniform is gazing with some distaste at my rumpled clothing, my leather jacket, and my scraggly beard. All the same, he's still courteous and formal. Not out of respect for me, but respect for himself.

"*Buona sera.* Is there something I can do for you?"

I can read in his eyes the words that he'd really like to use.

Why don't you turn your ass around, stop scuffing up the carpet, and get out of here, you filthy bum?

It's typical of small people who are given small powers. Strong with the weak, weak with the strong. Kiss up, kick down. He would be dismayed if he could read my mind and find out how little I care about him. As far as I'm concerned he can go fuck himself, but I'm still courteous and formal. I'm being ironic toward myself, not toward him.

"There certainly is something that you can do for me. I know that Senator Sangiorgi is staying here. I have an envelope to deliver to him. Personally."

He looks me up and down as if I'd asked him to heft my travel bag and guess its weight.

"Signore, I'm afraid that won't be possible. I'm sure you can understand why. If you'd like to give it to me, I'll make sure it reaches him. The senator has—"

I break in. I guess I'll never know what the senator has.

"Call the senator or his assistant right now and tell him

that Nicola Sangiorgi is in the lobby and would like to come up."

The name causes a slight shift in attitude. Still, it might be a case of a simple coincidence, involving identical surnames. He takes care to make sure that such is not the case.

"Do you have family ties with the senator?"

"Abundant family ties."

I let a pause fall, a pause that's more than ten years long.

"I'm his son."

It's been a lifetime since I uttered those words. To my ears, they land on the marble counter with quite a thump. Evidently to the ears of the clerk, too, because he suddenly puts on a new expression.

"Could you excuse me for a moment?"

"Why, absolutely."

He moves away to the far end of the counter. He picks up a receiver, dials an extension, and talks to someone. It must be an important person, because he keeps bobbing his head submissively.

When he comes back all that's left is courtesy.

"Would you care to be so kind as to wait right here, Signore Sangiorgi?"

"Certainly. I would indeed care to be so kind as to wait right here."

I believe that he's so caught up in his exquisite manners that he doesn't even notice that I'm mocking him brutally. I walk a short distance away. There's a nice scent in the air, the warmth of velvet on the sofas, and the glittering pomp of gilt paint is everywhere. But there's the sense of the ephemeral and fleeting that no hotel, even the finest hotel in the universe, can ever completely disguise. Whatever the thread count of the sheets you sleep between, the variety of hardwood in the

363

chairs you sit on, the price of the champagne you sip, and the hourly rate of the women you invite upstairs, a hotel room is still just a hotel room.

A middle-aged man of less than average height, with salt-and-pepper hair and beard and a dark brown suit

My God, how I hate dark brown

emerges from behind a column and clearly scans the room for me. He spots me and moves across the lobby in my direction. A cluster of foreign visitors leaving the hotel cross his path, and he slows his pace. The women are dressed in evening gowns, the men are dressed in tuxedos. Maybe they're going to La Scala, or maybe they're just going to get fucked in the ass somewhere, for all I care. I wish I could throw a water balloon full of shit at them, big enough to turn all of them, including the face of the guy walking toward me, dark brown.

When he reaches me, he's forced to tip his head back to look at me. He doesn't seem too pleased about that. His voice has a Sicilian accent, which I'm not accustomed to hearing used in the pronunciation of my name anymore.

"Are you Nicola Sangiorgi?"

"In the flesh."

He extends his hand.

"A pleasure to meet you. My name is Enrico Della Donna. Your father, the senator, does the honor of bestowing his trust on me."

Which is to say: I'm his secretary and personal assistant and I lick his ass every time he tells me to.

I shake the extended hand without much enthusiasm. I'm practically certain that he's even less enthusiastic than I am.

"You're a little different than the pictures I've seen in your father's home. You're grown up, you've become a man."

I don't think he expects an answer. In any case, I wouldn't have given him one.

"If you'd care to follow me."

I would care to follow him. So I do.

Della Donna leads the way down a hallway lined with soft carpeting. The wallpaper is seemly and bright.

He walks like a servant. I walk like a confident fugitive who is no longer afraid.

"I was told by the senator that you now work in Latin America. It's certainly commendable to try to make one's way in the world through one's own efforts. There aren't many people who would have had the courage to choose the more daunting path, in your situation."

We reach the end of the hallway. The man upon whom my father the senator does the honor of bestowing his trust completes another of his important tasks. He pushes the elevator button.

And he goes on talking.

"I imagine you hurried back to Italy when you learned of the terrible fate that was visited upon your uncle. Such a horrifying thing. We are staying here in Milan until the judicial authorities issue a clearance for his burial. If we'd had advance notice, we would certainly have sent a driver to pick you up at the airport."

I have no idea how much he knows about my personal history, because I don't know the extent of the trust that has been bestowed upon him. The general logic of the things he says is leaky as hell, but there's no one on earth quite like a politician's personal assistant when it comes to believing things he has a vested interest in believing.

We step into the elevator and, in accordance with that odd ritual that seems to govern elevators all over the planet, we ride in complete silence. The walls of the cabin are sheathed in wood, with darker moldings that appear to be briarwood. The back panel of the elevator is a mirror, to greet and welcome the reflections of the passengers.

The elevator stops at the floor requested.

Della Donna steps out into the hallway to show me the way.

I stay in the elevator. I raise a hand to beg his pardon.

"Please excuse me for a moment."

"Of course."

I reach into my pocket and pull out a bunch of keys.

I choose the sharpest one.

Then, with utter calm and a steady hand, I carve two phrases into the beautiful glistening wood:

Luca is a faggot.
Mary is a whore.

Anyone who reads it will just have to trust me, because I've forgotten the phone numbers.

Della Donna refrains from commenting. I feel sure he's commenting in his head. He's free to do so, it doesn't cost a cent. If we were to lock up all the people who ever dreamed of murdering someone, we'd have to turn the Italian boot into one giant maximum-security prison.

We walk down the hallway until we stop outside a door without a number. That usually means that it's a suite. The man knocks discreetly and then enters without waiting for an answer. He ushers me in and immediately closes the door, remaining outside, silent and discreet as ever.

My father is standing in the middle of the room.

He's tall, erect, and solid. I'm looking at what might very

well be my own portrait when I reach his age. His dark eyes gaze at me without curiosity, the same curiosity that I fail to feel about him. I ought to be experiencing emotions, a flood of memories, fragments surfacing from the past. I ought to extend my hand to him, or spit in the hand that he extends to me, if he happened to extend his hand. But I feel absolutely nothing. I've seen too much blood spilled in the last few days to have any desire to see more. This isn't a meeting between a father and a son. It's just a chance encounter between two people who were bound to run into each other sooner or later.

We're separated by only a few yards, but it's an unbridgeable gulf.

His tone of voice is the same as ever. He doesn't ask. He demands to be told.

"Where have you been?"

"Are you trying to tell me that you care?"

I've recovered my Sicilian accent and I address him with the old-fashioned formal that uses the *voi*, just as he so often told me he used to do when speaking to his father. He has no reaction. He steps closer to me. Now he's only inches away. The slap arrives without warning and it covers the whole side of my face. But I'm not a little boy anymore and I feel no pain.

I straighten my head and at last I smile.

"It's quite easy to hide from someone who isn't looking for you."

Senator Amedeo Sangiorgi maintains his composure. His attitude remains unchanged. His tone remains entirely unruffled. He still demands information.

"Why did you leave?"

"Because I was afraid."

"Of whom?"

367

"Of everything and everyone. But especially of you."

He listens to my words without seeming to take it too hard. As if it were just another of the gratuitous attacks leveled on the floor of the Italian parliament by a member of the opposition. He walks over to a small round table where a bottle of mineral water stands in an ice bucket. He pours himself a glass of water. He drinks it and then carefully sets the chalice back down on the table, as if he weren't too sure of its structural integrity.

"That begs the next logical question. Why have you come back?"

"I've come back to tell you about chaos and chance."

When he lifts his gaze to meet mine, there's a question mark in his eyes. But that doesn't yet rise to the level of curiosity. He's just wondering whether his son has perhaps lost his mind. He walks over and sits down in the middle of a crimson velvet sofa. He extends both arms and rests them on the back of the sofa.

I continue. It's my turn now. Now I'm the one who's demanding information.

"I've come back to tell you about the way that those two factors took Nicola Sangiorgi by the hand and transformed him into another person."

I walk around the room. I happen to notice a painting hanging on the wall, a fairly good imitation of Utrillo's *Moulin de la Galette*.

I can feel his eyes boring into the back of my neck.

"A short while after I left, I was holed up in a cheap pensione in Rome. I met a poor devil, a man who worked in the office of vital records in a small town in the province of Perugia. His wife had cancer, and he'd spent every penny of his savings on her treatments. The two of us were born to get along. He needed money, I needed a name. So I found money for him and he found a name for me."

I turn so that he can see my face. But especially so that I can see him. It's a show I wouldn't miss for anything in the world.

"He made me a member of the family of a married couple that had just moved to Australia to live with their relatives there. Unfortunately for them, the two poor souls died almost immediately afterward in a plane crash. The chaos and chance I was telling you about were working hand in hand, as you can see for yourself. Just consider the irony of fate. I'd only just come into the world and I was already an orphan. And think of poor Marisa and Alfonso Marcona, summoned to their maker without ever meeting their only child, a son: Francesco."

It takes him a few seconds to put together first and last name. Then, all at once, he gets it.

The newspaper headlines; the identikit that, he suddenly realizes, matches me perfectly; the police reports about the hunt for me that, in his position of power, he has certainly read.

"Then you're that . . ."

I can't tell if his voice fails him or whether I've simply interrupted him.

"Yeah. I'm the guy they set up to get to Bonifaci. Didn't Carla tell you that, if that's really her name?"

I give him some time to try to guess how much I know. I'm going to savor the pleasure of letting him realize little by little that I know everything.

"Or did she just vanish without a trace, and without bringing you and your friends what you sent her to get from the villa in Lesmo?"

369

He leaps to his feet. There are sparks in his eyes. But they're useless flames, flames that can burn only him.

"My brother's body is still warm in his casket and you come here to bother me with this paltry nonsense?"

"Your brother's in his casket because you put him there."

I use the same tone of voice with which Someone first questioned Cain about what he had done.

For the first time in my life I see a sword pierce the invulnerable armor of Senator Sangiorgi. His voice cracks slightly as he walks over to the telephone and lifts the receiver.

"What are you talking about? Have you lost your mind? I'm going to call the police and have you arrested."

"What for? The minute I leave your hotel room I'm going to turn myself in."

I throw the dark brown envelope onto the sofa where he was just sitting.

"But first I wanted to make sure you had this. You've earned it."

His eyes follow the trajectory of the envelope as it sails across the room. He slams the receiver down on its hook, leaving it slightly askew. He walks over to the envelope, his eyes never leaving that paper wrapper perched on the velvet sofa like a worthless jewel.

He sits down, picks up the envelope, and opens it.

Inside it is everything.

His own story and the story of Mattia Sangiorgi.

Photographs of my uncle naked in bed with a girl I've never met. Documents that prove both my father and my uncle were collaborating with the Mafia, specifically with Turi Martesano, the most powerful capo in all Sicily. The help that the Mafia boss gave the two brothers, elevating them to the highest political offices. After that, the rigged contracts, the wheeling and dealing, the bribes, the murder of citizens who failed to cooperate, the election fraud.

Documents that represent many years of life, as well as many years of prison.

When he's done examining the dossier, my father looks up. There's not a trace of the man who was there until just a moment ago. Which scatters to the winds every trace of the man I used to be.

There's only one question I can ask.

"Why?"

He looks at me.

Suddenly, memories line up in my mind to claim their due. The beach house in Mondello, the smell of the soil, the blue of the sea, long walks through the streets of Palermo, the dog that used to run to greet me when I came home from school, dinner parties with my parents' friends, and the way I'd make the rounds of the festive table, saying good night to each of our guests.

My father's inflexible personality; the people who came to see him in his office; his face, which we saw less and less at home and more and more on the election billboards. My mother's face, her cautious diplomacy with her husband and her staunch complicity with me. Her funeral, which I missed, because I'd already become Bravo and I cared more about myself than about the woman who had brought me into the world.

Then everything begins to spin and fade. The faces turn into blurred images and then into nothing but patches of color, while the words become indistinct sounds that all take shelter in the question that I ask him again.

"Why?"

My father stands up and goes over to the window and looks out. He's wearing a white shirt, no tie, a suit vest, and dark trousers. Before, he was tall and erect and he emanated a sense of solidity. Suddenly his clothing looks a little loose on him.

His shoulders sag slightly, and his step is less brisk and determined. Now I'm looking at what could one day have been my own portrait if I hadn't decided to come here today.

His voice has come back to earth. It's the voice of a man now.

"When I first went into politics, everything was so clear. There was a point of departure and an ultimate objective and that was the point toward which I would strive, without wavering or making concessions. I had a thousand new projects, a million ideas. Important projects, the kind of thing that could change the course of history and the lives of people everywhere."

There's a pause, bowed down under the weight of regret. Or maybe that's just me, believing he's still capable of such a feeling.

"But then you're faced with the first obstacle, the one you can't overcome without giving up a tiny part of yourself. It's nothing much, just a minuscule compromise. You tell yourself it's for a good cause, that it's just a minor detour on the way to something bigger, for the common good. But a compromise is a compromise. There aren't big ones or little ones. There's only the first compromise, which you always accept with the illusion that it's also the last compromise."

He breaks off, thinking how deceptive numbers can be.

"Until one day you stop counting them."

He turns. Now we're face-to-face. This is the longest conversation we've ever had.

"It's been said that power erodes the soul. It's not true. What eats away at the soul is the fear of losing power. Once you've tasted power, it's not something you can easily do without. It's just that much harder when the people who helped you to achieve that power are no longer willing to do without you."

He walks over to the table and pours himself another glass of water.

"People like Bonifaci gain their strength from the weakness of other human beings."

He takes a long drink. Then he sets down the chalice, but this time hard.

"That man held us in his grip. He had an enormous and diffuse power, touching people in every party, in the world of finance, and even in the Vatican. He had to be stopped, somehow. And we finally found the way."

"And you didn't hesitate to sacrifice your own brother."

He rubs his face with his hands. He too has to deal with the exhaustion of the past few days.

"Mattia was clearly beginning to crack up. We could no longer rely on him. With the things he knew, he could have done just as much damage as Bonifaci, if he decided to talk. When he was invited to the villa in Lesmo, we saw that this was an opportunity to rid ourselves of two threats with one blow."

"What about all the people who were murdered? Did you ever think about them?"

He looks at me the way you look at the most obstinate kind of deaf person, the one who refuses to hear.

"You still don't get it, do you, Nicola? In the face of interests of this size and scope, there's no one who's not expendable. No one."

An image surfaces in my mind. The picture of a man, utterly alone, kidnapped and locked up in a room, sentenced to death by a band of terrorists and by the Gods of Political Expediency.

"Is that true for Aldo Moro, too?"

In his eyes I glimpse the irrevocable certainty of a verdict before it's uttered. His voice is an icy gust of wind, and I'm surprised not to see a cloud of frozen mist emerge from his mouth.

"Aldo Moro is already a dead man."

We sit in silence. A pointed, sharp-edged silence, a silence that wounds and draws blood. The time has come to sum it all up, now that hidden thoughts have become words and intentions have become irrevocable acts.

In a flat, toneless voice he asks a question, though he already takes the answer for granted.

"What will you do now?"

"I told you. I'm going to turn myself in. I'm going to hand over to the police the originals of the documents I just showed you. And to make sure there is no chance of a cover-up, this evening the newsrooms of all the major dailies are going to receive a complete copy of their own."

He nods his head, without a word. Then he goes over to sit on the sofa. He takes his head in his hands and rests his elbows on his knees. What I'm looking at now is nothing but his body. His mind is already long gone. It's already abandoned the useless luxury of that hotel room.

But there's still one thing I have to know. To complete the picture, to make sure that nothing I've done or am about to do is unjustified. That everything should have its specific point of arrival, because everything had its point of origin.

"I have one last question for you."

He waits in silence. He's drained of energy. He has no words, he has nothing.

As I ask the question, I can't keep my heart from racing.

"When Turi Martesano gave the order to do what they did to me, did you know about it?"

The silence that comes as the only answer to my question is a chilling confession. I take a deep breath, because my lungs need all the air that I can manage to give them. I don't know how this man feels right now. I can't imagine what room he's shut himself into, where he's taken refuge from the ghosts of the people whose deaths are on his conscience.

I don't know and I don't give a damn.

I walk out of that hotel room, leaving on the floor behind me the shattered pieces of the Almighty Senator Amedeo Sangiorgi.

As I close the door behind me, a bitter thought runs through my mind.

I wonder if God felt remorse when He gave them permission to kill His son.

CHAPTER 24

The taxi is heading for the airport.

The driver is a woman, which is something you don't see that often. She's nice to look at, about forty, blond, and shapely. She'd be much more attractive if she were willing to compromise and apply just a hint of makeup. When she came to pick me up, in response to my call, at the Quartiere Tessera, she gave me the once-over as I walked toward the car. I must have passed some sort of test just then, because during the drive to the airport she started telling me the story of her life. Maybe she felt she needed to explain why she was driving a cab. How her cabdriver husband was in bad health, too sick to drive; the financial problems that ensued, with the hack license going unused; how she decided to take over.

"I couldn't very well go stand in the street and build a fire in an oil drum to warm my hands, could I?"

"Of course not."

I gave her the answer that she wanted to hear. I skipped over the fact that a woman with her looks, if she was to take the correct approach and do things right, could find a much more remunerative line of work than driving a taxi. She might take that as a somewhat risqué compliment, without realizing that it was nothing more than a clear-eyed market analysis.

*

Now she's done talking and, as she drives, she gives me a curious glance in the rearview mirror every so often. From the way she felt called upon to explain why she was driving a cab, I doubt she's the type to make a pass at a passenger. So I have to guess this is nothing more than a creature of the female persuasion studying a creature of the male persuasion that she finds attractive. In a way, this too could be considered a market analysis, so I take it as a compliment. If I told her my life story, on the other hand, she'd probably have to pull over more than once to fix her hair, because I know certain details would make it stand on end.

I look out the car window, watching people, cars, and fleeting scraps of this city. I took this trip once before, not so long ago, with the barrel of a pistol pressed against the nape of my neck, on a night when I felt sure I'd never again see the light of the morning sun. I realize that every breath I've drawn since then has been a gift. A gift that I owe to a woman who could be anywhere on earth and whom I know only as Carla.

After I turned myself in, my ordeal in the police station on Via Fatebenefratelli lasted four days. Milla's chest swelled with pride as he accompanied me and my lawyer into the office of Chief Inspector Giovannone. The version that we'd agreed on during the trip from the Hotel Principe e Savoia to the police station was very simple and, therefore, highly believable.

In short, here's how our version went:

Milla couldn't believe his ears when I called him at home and told him that I wanted to turn myself in, to him of all people. He hopped in his car and sped to pick me up at Ugo's office. Because I was accompanied by my lawyer and because I'd voluntarily contacted him in order to turn myself in, he decided there was no need to handcuff me. The lawyer and I both agreed to confirm this version of events. In any case, we all knew that what was going to happen after my arrest would completely and immediately drown out all other considerations in the uproar, including the fact that the detective had failed to contact his immediate superiors.

Chief Inspector Giovannone froze with shock when he saw me. The ice that gripped his limbs and face turned even more solid and motionless once he heard my story. After he had a chance to leaf quickly through the dossier that Ugo Biondi, Esq., placed on his desk, he appeared to be carved out of marble.

I think the same thing has happened to every person who has held those documents in their hands.

I told my version of events over and over, dozens of times. To the chief inspector, to the chief of police administration, to investigating magistrates, and to high officers of DIGOS, the special operations and investigations branch of the national police. Then the mayor wanted to hear my story. Then I had to recount everything that had happened to people who listened without telling me who they were or where they worked. I'd guess they were probably from the intelligence services. These people were especially eager to hear more about Carla, and they asked me to tell them anything I could remember about her. What she said, what she did, even vague impressions I might have had. An undersecretary from the Ministry of the Interior even came to see me. He told me that he'd be reporting back to the minister himself, who had asked him to come. This undersecretary seemed to be especially interested in knowing whether there might be more documents similar to the ones I had handed over to the authorities.

I spent the first night in a high-security cell in the police station. Ugo Biondi demanded, successfully, that he be allowed to spend the night in the cell with me, his client. A few hours later a massive police sweep was carried out, resulting in the arrest and detention of a hundred or so people, in Sicily, Rome, and Milan. Political leaders, members of the Mafia, important members of the branches of government. It was a volcanic eruption of unprecedented devastation, triggered by documentation unlike anything that had ever surfaced before. Ashes and pumice would continue to rain down on the ruling class of Italy for the foreseeable future. No one could say how long the black cloud that had been unleashed upon the world would continue to darken the skies.

The next day a number of things happened.

The front page of Italy's newspapers blared out headlines in banner type. Emboldened by the sequence of arrests still under way and confident of the documents in their possession, *Il Corriere della Sera*, *La Stampa*, *La Repubblica*, and in time all the other papers in the country vied to print the most stunning reports. In the midst of all these drumrolls and trumpet fanfares, nobody really paid much attention to the report of the suicide of Senator Amedeo Sangiorgi. Public opinion seemed to consider it relatively unsurprising that he should have chosen to throw himself out the window of his hotel suite, unable to face the looming scandal that was sure to destroy his career. Nobody seemed to notice that he killed himself several hours before the police sweep even began.

I was taken to the house out on Via Rivoltana for some on-site testimony and questioning. I explained in detail exactly what had happened. Who fired, where from, how many shots. I believe that, as I spoke, it was impossible to miss my relief at not having become part of the pile of corpses. I'm almost certain that some of the people I was speaking to, on the other hand, would have seen that outcome as a godsend.

The major success in the battle against terrorism and the massive blow that was delivered to organized crime, however, helped to sugarcoat that bitter pill. The authorities were anything but pleased that I should have decided on my own initiative to release such important information to the press. There was a protracted series of negotiations between the police, representatives of the judiciary and the executive branches, and Ugo Biondi to find a satisfactory settlement. In the end, the version that was agreed upon met with general satisfaction. It was decided to report that the discovery of the Red Brigades lair had led to the recovery of the dossier that incriminated so many prominent citizens. It was ordered that there should be no further attempts to identify the blond woman who had delivered the envelopes to the newsrooms of the various papers.

This version would help to shield me from the vendetta of people who wound up in prison, who put the blame or the credit on me, depending on your point of view. For many leading figures in that world, revenge is considered a delicacy. Delicious either cold or hot, it really doesn't matter which.

Roughly speaking, that's the way it went.

The son of Senator Sangiorgi managed by and large to escape notice in all that bedlam. No reporters came chasing after me. There were plenty of more important people than me to try to track down. The president of the Italian republic, the prime minister, various cabinet-level ministers, and so on, moving down the political food chain. I had never even set foot on that particular ladder of ambition. Here, too, I'd preferred to stay hidden away in the cellar, where I'd lived comfortably for many years.

Little by little, the names of Francesco Marcona and Nicola Sangiorgi would fade from everyone's memory. A number of the people who knew Bravo won't even realize that they were the same person.

There's one more small but meaningful curiosity. There were two eyewitnesses to back up my incredible story, along with the dossier I turned over. The cleaning women from the offices of Costa Britain, the ones I spoke to one night on Via Monte Rosa, thought they recognized me from the identikit that was published in the newspapers. They went to the police and reported that they had met me and that I had asked them about a mysterious and imaginary coworker of theirs.

By the name of Carla Bonelli, they thought they remembered.

I'm willing to bet that they added that it was obvious from my face that I was either a lunatic or a crook.

Or both.

I had to smile when I heard about it and I arranged to send a sumptuous bouquet of red roses to each of them at home. After all, every woman should have a secret admirer.

The taxi stops under the sign reading international departures. I get out of the car. It's a beautiful day to fly away. I'm leaving the fine weather of late spring, with a memory of sunshine and blue skies, before summer comes to spoil everything. I knew that this moment was bound to come sooner or later. The moment when I would look up

381

at a departure board. Things were actually a little better for me than they'd been for Carla. No one was chasing me and I wasn't forced to take the first open seat on the next plane out.

I'm pretty sure that along with the plane ticket I'll be buying an illusion and that wherever I wind up, I'll find the same men and the same women, with different faces and speaking different languages. But what does that matter, really?

All that matters is takeoff.

What I find when I land is part of a whole different story.

My taxi driver gets out and opens the trunk. I pull out my travel bag, pay her fare, and add a thousand-lira tip. Before she gets back in her cab, she shoots me a meaningful glance. Maybe I misunderstood. With that pinch of vanity and narcissism that lurks in everyone's heart, I tell myself again that she's not the type to make passes at her passengers.

But she might have made an exception for me.

I feel something like the onset of happiness as I walk into the terminal. I spot the big black departure board listing the times of the various flights. I walk over and scan the list of airlines, abbreviations, and destinations.

There's an Alitalia flight for Rio de Janeiro departing in just three hours. I picture myself on the beach of Ipanema and I like what I see. I go over to the ticket counter and ask the young lady if there's a first-class seat for Brazil.

There's room. All you have to do is pay for it.

I pay in cash, pulling a wad of bills out of my inside jacket pocket. I wonder when I'll pay for something in lire again, whether I ever will. It's nice not to know. I like the idea of belonging to nothing, of being able to make a decision and change my mind a minute later.

I walk over to the check-in. It's still too early for that flight.

I spot a newsstand and go over. I choose a book, two newspapers, and a few magazines. I spot a few copies of *La Settimana Enigmistica* stacked next to the cash register.

I hesitate for a second, but then I decide against it. I'm done with puzzles.

That time is over. The last puzzle I solved had the name Bravo as its solution. It's a good outcome, and you can't ask too much of fate.

I sit down, put my bag on the seat next to me, and open *Il Corriere della Sera*. The first few pages of the paper are still full of the aftermath and continuation of the events to which I was witness and of which I was a leading protagonist. I dip in here and there, because I'm just curious to see how much was reported and which things were left out, sandbagged, or twisted in the hallowed name of freedom of the press.

The story that has all Italy holding its breath drags on. Aldo Moro remains a prisoner of his kidnappers. I hope that among the many lies my father told over the course of his lifetime, one of them had to do with the fate of that man, abandoned and alone. I hope that the words he uttered in his hotel room weren't true, that they were nothing more than a final manifestation of his delirious conviction that he was all-powerful and all-knowing.

All I can do is hope.

I turn the page. In the crime section there's an article about Tano Casale. A headline covers half the page.

the number 13 brings bad luck
*Counterfeit Lottery Ticket Leads to the Arrest of
Notorious Milanese Gang Boss*

I smile. I don't even need to read the article. I know exactly what happened. And I know exactly what's going to happen next.

Once my testimony had been written out, checked by a dozen or so people, and then signed, I was declared a free man. Ugo Biondi and I, our faces lined with exhaustion and with bags under our eyes that looked like tree rings, said good-bye in the courtyard of the police station.

We were exhausted, shattered, numb. My voice was hoarse from talking.

"I'll call you tomorrow about that other matter. Right now I just need to get some sleep."

I shook his hand. He gripped mine in return.

"Me too. You have no idea."

Through the front gate to the street outside we saw his taxi pull up. Biondi ran to get in and I climbed into Stefano Milla's Alfa. The detective had offered to drive me to the motel in Settimo Milanese where I'd decided to stay for a few days until things calmed down a little. The offer wasn't meant as a gesture of any particular kindness. It was just a chance to have a private conversation that had been impossible in the days leading up to my release.

He must have felt like he'd been standing on hot coals. The car hadn't even entirely pulled out into traffic when he came to the point. He had a message to deliver and it was worth fifty million lire to him.

"I talked to Tano."

"What did he say?"

"That he agrees with you. He thanks you for the idea but he thinks it's best for you to stay out of it."

If he expected to see a reaction on my face, he was

384

disappointed. I didn't give a damn whether I was in or out. The day I took the lottery ticket to Tano, I'd proposed another plan. It was risky but feasible. I'd laid it out to him as another con game, just a new way of doing what he already did all day every day: make a mockery of the law.

In fact, I'd asked him that day if by any chance any of the patrons of his clandestine gambling den happened to work for a bank. We needed a patron who happened to be in hock up to his neck with Tano. Someone who would cooperate with anything Tano demanded, and without having to be asked twice. It would all be very simple. The day that Tano cashed in the lottery ticket, he'd go to deposit the money in the bank where his man worked. His man would arrange to accept the deposit personally. He'd sign a receipt in exchange for an empty briefcase. Just then, a band of bank robbers would burst into the branch office, take all the money from the tellers' windows, and grab the briefcase while they were at it.

Like a game of three-card monte. Like a shell game.

It would be Tano's fault in a small way, for having crowed too openly about his lucky win in the Totocalcio soccer lottery, thus attracting the attention of a band of bank robbers. Understandable and all too human: Who can withstand the temptation to celebrate a stroke of good luck? He might look like an idiot for a while, but to make up for that he would have a valid bank receipt and the 490 million lire in cash winnings still hidden under his mattress.

I smiled when I thought back to how Tano's face had looked when he first heard my plan. The cunning move, the idea of being there in person, the surge of adrenaline. These were all aspects he knew intimately and whose allure he couldn't resist. Most of all, greed, which is what I was counting on. And vanity, so much more powerful in men than in any woman. I was sure that he would proceed on his own. That he would recruit his own gang of thieves for the knockover. And even if he was too shrewd to go for it, I'd still have gained my main objective.

Which was to stall for time.

Milla jerked me out of my reverie.

"What idea? What the fuck are we talking about here, Bravo?"

He still called me Bravo, even though by now he knew everything—or almost everything—about me.

I turned to look at him.

"Tano's going to be arrested."

In his reply there was a distinct note of alarm.

"When?"

"Soon."

His eyes were back on the road. He was probably imagining something bad coming straight at him, through the line of cars, the pedestrians, the traffic lights.

"Jesus, what have you done? Have you gone crazy? Do you want him to have us both killed?"

"That's not going to happen."

I did my best to impart a sense of confidence to my voice. I'd need a lot of it, to help him get over his fear. To convince him that it was a good idea to do what I was suggesting.

"Let me tell you what you're going to do. You're going to take fifteen days off. You'll go have a good time at the beach, or in the mountains or on the lake. Or in the farthest-flung armpit of the world, wherever you want."

I waited for a few seconds, so he could envision himself on vacation.

386

"When you get back, you'll find a cashier's check for fifty million lire on my lawyer's desk. You're going to take that money and forget that we ever had this conversation or that I ever met Tano Casale."

"But what about him?"

"Don't worry. I'll take care of him."

A voice on the loudspeaker reminds me that I'm at Linate Airport, with a plane ticket in my pocket for South America. I look up and see that the check-in counter is open now. I walk up and hand my ticket and passport to the young woman in uniform.

"Buon giorno."

She looks at me and smiles with pleasure. I feel the same pleasure and smile back.

She checks my name on the ticket.

"Buon giorno to you, Signore Sangiorgi."

Even though it could be considered a piece of carry-on luggage, I decide to check my travel bag. I want to be free, unburdened by any excess baggage, however light. I've carried the weight for far too long. I receive directions to the boarding gate, the departure time of the flight, and my boarding pass. I move off with the line of people heading for Security.

I spent many days holed up in that motel, feasting on the television news until I was cross-eyed, leaving my room only to eat and buy the daily newspapers. I watched the fire grow until it was a towering inferno. I told myself that in time it would dwindle to a bonfire and then the only ones who would remember the scorching heat of the flames would be those who were actually burned. I was also confident that many of them would pass through the flames and emerge completely intact.

The day I decided to emerge from my lair, I went to see Ugo in the office of the notary two floors above his law office. I gave him instructions for cashing in the lottery ticket and I won his eternal gratitude by offering him a fee of a hundred million lire, both for what he had done and what still remained to be accomplished. I took delivery of the permit to visit Carmine in San Vittore Prison. Last of all, I signed papers giving the notary all the authorizations he would need to perform a number of financial transactions on my behalf.

Afterward, as I was leaving his office, Ugo shook my hand and made me smile. Because he asked me the same question I had asked Carla.

"Will I ever see you again?"

I didn't think this was the time to kiss him and tell him that everything could have been so different between us. I limited myself to a phrase that included all possibilities.

"Who can say?"

A police officer examines my brand-new passport, processed in record time, a friendly gesture of the Milan police headquarters. He hands the passport back and looks past me to the next passenger. I walk by the duty-free shop and decide to go in and buy a pack of cigarettes. I'll need them for the plane trip, which promises to be long and dull. With my two packs of Marlboros in hand I head for the cash register. I show my boarding pass and I pay. I continue at a leisurely pace to the gate marked rio de janeiro. I take a seat. The article about Tano's arrest takes me back to my last meeting with Carmine, in the visiting room at San Vittore Prison.

*

He entered the room, accompanied by a guard. The guard then moved off just far enough to give us a chance to speak privately but still be able to keep an eye on us. Carmine's physical appearance hadn't improved. He was still one of the ugliest men I'd ever seen. I felt pretty sure that the other distinctive aspect of his physical makeup hadn't changed either. I had to guess that it had won him a lot of bets during his time in prison. Men never really grow up, deep down. No one can help it, in certain situations: they always wind up competing to see who's got the biggest dick.

He sat down across from me. The expression on his face was what you'd expect from a man deprived of his freedom.

"*Ciao*, Bravo."

"*Ciao*, Carmine."

He turned to make sure that the guard was far enough away that he couldn't overhear.

"Luciana came to see me. She brought me pictures of the boy."

"He's a good-looking boy."

There was a father's pride on his ugly face when he agreed.

"Yes, he is. He's a good-looking boy."

He immediately fell silent. He was certainly thinking about his son's condition. His wife must have come to visit him in prison primarily to inform him about Rosario's health problems. But Carmine had made no mention of it, as if not speaking about a tragic event helps in some way to exorcise it a little.

"She told me what you did for them."

"It's nothing."

"No, it's a lot. It's what I wish I could do, if I weren't locked up in this fucking prison."

I glimpsed the frustration at his forced state of helplessness stamp itself on his face. The mortification over the mistakes he'd made, mistakes that his son's illness were making him pay for in a much more painful way than mere imprisonment could ever do.

"Carmine, there is something you can do for your family."

He lost his temper. Understandable, for a man in his situation.

"What the fuck do you think I can do, locked up in here?"

I lowered my voice, to make him lower his.

"Your boy is sick. He needs medical treatment. And that treatment costs money, a lot of money."

I felt like a monster as I twisted the knife. But I thought that this summary of the situation was necessary, in view of what I was about to tell him.

"I'm willing to give your wife a cashier's check for 250 million lire. That's enough money to pay for Rosario's medical treatment and ensure he has a good future. Steer him away from certain influences, allow him to live in a healthy environment, make sure he can study."

I increased my distance from him slightly by leaning back against my chair. As much as was possible in those tight quarters, I left him alone to think it over, to imagine a shred of potential future for his son. The answer was that of a man who'd never been given anything for free in his lifetime.

"What do I have to do?"

I lowered my voice even more.

"Do you know Tano Casale?"

He didn't bother to answer. Everyone knows Tano Casale. In silence he waited to hear the rest. I gave it to him.

"In a few days he's going to be arrested. It's going to be a minor charge, but the police are going to take advantage of the opportunity to convert his arrest into detention and bring him here."

There was curiosity in his glance, even though he'd probably already understood.

"So?"

I looked him in the eye. Rarely in my life have I been so calm. Or so happy at the idea of something happening.

"I want you to kill him."

The voice of the stewardess announcing my flight drowns out the voice of Carmine as he called the prison guard to take him back to his cell. I stand up and get in line with the other passengers waiting to board. I scrutinize the faces of the people around me. There's no one I know. When it's my turn, I hand my boarding pass to the young woman in uniform and I receive in exchange a beaming and pro forma *Have a good trip*.

Before I walk out of the terminal and head down to the shuttle that will take me to my plane, I turn around to look at the place and the people I'm leaving. I'm leaving all alone, a condition that at times can be a burden, at other times a form of liberation.

Bravo didn't even come to say good-bye.

May 1998

EPILOGUE

Pilar moves in her sleep, extending her leg so that it touches me.

I wake up and open my eyes. The morning light filters through the openings in the blinds. It never really gets dark in this room. In the half-light I turn my head and watch her sleep, with my head resting on my pillow. The sheet has slipped off her and she's completely naked. Her hair is short and glossy, her breasts are small, her ass is nicely shaped, her legs are long.

She's tall, slender, and strong.

In the middle of the night she left the boy she'd just made love with in the other bedroom. For a little while I sat with them myself, seated in an armchair at the foot of the bed, watching those young bronzed bodies, in the full blush of a youth I no longer possess, writhe and coil in an exchange of pleasure. Every time that it happens, I can't help but remember; every time I remember, I can't help it happening again.

At a certain point I got up and came back to my bedroom. I lay there facedown on my bed until I heard the *thump thump* of bare feet on the floor coming nearer. Then I felt the sheet move and Pilar slipped into bed next to me.

She drew close and slipped in between my arms. Her breath was hot on my cheek.

"Are you asleep?"

"No."

I felt a hand rise up to caress my face. Then her soft voice in my ears.

"I love you."

"I love you too."

With a fluid movement, she stretched out on my body and began moving on top of me. I felt the warmth of her flesh against mine and her breasts against my chest. She began kissing me and kept on moving until I felt something that had been oppressing my belly melt and flow so far away that it almost fooled me into believing that it would never come back.

I turn onto my side. In the half-light I stretch out a hand and stroke her thigh. Not so she can feel my presence, but in order to be certain of her.

Last night we went out on our own. We hadn't had a night out to ourselves for a long time. We dined in a restaurant at Playa El Yaque, near one of my hotels. After dinner, attracted by the voices and the light of a bonfire, we wound up at a surfer party on the beach. There were guitars, boys and girls, and beer. Sitting on a rock, with a cold can in my hand, I watched Pilar by the glow of the fire as she talked with one of the surfers, a young American with blond hair and freckles on his tan face. They were laughing, and in the bright white flash of their laughter I understood that they liked each other. By the shimmer of the flames I watched Pilar turn around to catch my eye. I smiled at her and when we left for home, the young man was in the car with us.

I get out of bed. I'm naked. I've learned not to be ashamed of my body. I'm discreet, but I'm not ashamed. I didn't think it was wise to tell Pilar who taught me that. There are things that belong to me alone, and if I share them with someone else I have the impression that I've given part of them away.

I give her the same freedom.

I walk barefoot to the bathroom. I open the French door and walk out onto the terrace that it shares with the bedroom. My house is isolated and no one can see me. Stretching out before me is the vast reach of Ensenada La Guardia, an inlet that lets my view of the ocean extend endlessly. Today the sky is clear, and bluer than the human mind can conceive or absorb.

A warm morning wind caresses my skin.

I'm still not used to this sense of peace.

I go back into the bathroom with its rough walls and decorations that are reminiscent of Moorish architecture. Fastened to a wall is a full-length mirror in which I seek myself, see myself, and accept myself. My eyes are unchanged, even if there's a little gray creeping into my hair. I've gone back to playing sports fairly regularly and my physique has improved markedly. I'm lean and muscular enough to look younger than my forty-five years.

I turn on the shower and jump under the spray. I soap up and let the scent of sex slide away with the foam. I stand under that stream of water until not even a drop of memory is falling from above.

Then I step out of the shower stall and put on my bathrobe.

I go back to the bedroom. Pilar is still asleep. She hasn't moved since I left. She's a patch of golden amber against the white sheets, in the middle of the wrought-iron bed frame. But this bed doesn't have any hiding places in the legs. It's been a long time since I needed to hide my money.

I walk into the closet and put on a pair of linen trousers,

a shirt, and a pair of comfortable shoes. Here on the island everything is designed with simplicity, personal comfort, and freedom in mind. With that concept seamlessly incorporated into my mood, I decide I'm ready to start my day.

I step out of the sleeping quarters and walk across the large living room, full of sofas and coffee tables looking out over another terrace that also serves the kitchen. Feliciana, my housekeeper, has set the table outside for breakfast. I sit down and pour myself a glass of orange juice. The view from here is more or less the same as the view from the bedroom.

The sun is rising, painting a beautiful May day, minute by minute.

It's not yet time for the cloudbursts, especially the nighttime cloudbursts that characterize the island's climate from June to August. The downpours are exactly like all of life's adverse experiences ought to be.

Rapid, violent, sudden.

Then everything turns clear again, including your mind.

When I first left Italy, I traveled around the world. South America, Asia, the United States, and Canada. I had plenty of money. The money in my family was on my mother's side. Even though I'd left without saying good-bye, and despite the fact that I'd never gone to see her when she was sick, she still made me the sole heir to her estate. That is and will always be something that I regret and mourn. I discovered it only after my father's death, and I gave orders to liquidate all the property. Scorched earth behind me, a carpet of flowers ahead of me. I was suddenly a wealthy man: to the tune of twenty-eight billion lire. That was a considerable sum ten years ago. It still is today.

I never touched the estate of Amedeo Sangiorgi. During my last meeting with Ugo Biondi in his law office, I authorized the notary to give all his money and his property to certain charities. With special attention to the victims of the Mafia.

Feliciana walks in silently from the kitchen. She's a stout middle-aged woman, with an olive complexion. She has been taking care of my house and me for seven years now, with the assistance of a local girl who doesn't live with us, but commutes every day from Piedras Negras. We also have a gardener and jack-of-all-trades named Cristóbal, who does the various small maintenance jobs required in such a large house. Impossible to guess his age: he is the father of four kids and the husband of two wives, unfailingly cheerful and smiling. He lives in La Guardia and drives up every other day with his truck full of tools and equipment. There is often wine on his breath, and his mouth is missing more than a few teeth.

He's a man who never utters a cross word, as Beefsteak might have quipped about those puzzle-like gaps in his teeth.

Feliciana lays a couple of newspapers on the table.

"*Señor*, here are the newspapers from Italy. Cristóbal brought them from Porlamar."

I reach out to pick up a copy of *Il Corriere della Sera* that has traveled a long way to be here this morning. As I unfold it, Feliciana reminds me that she is a cook, as well as a housekeeper.

"What would you like to eat today?"

"Scrambled eggs and toast. Then coffee and a slice of your coconut cake, if you've baked any."

Feliciana looks at me, stung to the quick.

"Of course I baked it. There is always Feliciana's cake in this house."

I've lived here for eight years and my Spanish has evolved over time: from pathetic to not bad to what I'd now describe as excellent. My unequaled housekeeper, however, is

399

impervious to any curiosity about foreign languages and she doesn't speak a word of Italian.

She understands it, but she refuses to speak it.

For that matter, now that I think about it, why should she?

She bustles off, slightly indignant that I should have dared to doubt the availability of her masterpiece of confectionery. I plunge into the newspapers, reading about things that all these years later don't even arouse my curiosity. Sometimes I have the impression that if you took the newspapers from ten years ago and substituted new names, you could just publish the same articles. Political squabbles, the underdeveloped south that refuses to grow, the working class that never went to its worker's paradise. Still, in spite of everything, I am and I remain an emigrant. A pinch of nostalgia, tiny but tough, is still there.

Here on Isla Margarita, the Italian newspapers always arrive a couple of days late.

Today is the eleventh of May.

On the copy of *Il Corriere* that I'm holding, the date is the ninth of May.

Ten years ago, on that very same day, the lifeless body of Aldo Moro was found in the trunk of a Renault R4. That desolate image appears at the center of an article on the third page, the editorial page in Italy, retracing the stations of his calvary.

I remember a few chilly words in a hotel room.

Aldo Moro is already a dead man . . .

The state funeral had the scale and imposing gravity that a person of his stature, killed in such tragic circumstances, deserved and required. The funerals of my father and my uncle were carried out with the furtive haste usually employed in sweeping dirt under the carpet. No one was interested in being seen attending them and no one cared to say farewell to either man. Now they're nothing but a couple of names and a photograph on a headstone and, in certain circles, a lingering awkward moment whenever they are mentioned.

Just like everywhere else in the world, in Italy we sometimes choose to remember. And we sometimes choose to forget.

The scrambled eggs and toast are served at the exact moment that Pilar emerges in her bathrobe through the glass door of the living room. She's barefoot and her hair is glistening with water, which means she just took a shower. She takes a look at the view and stretches before coming over to sit next to me.

"*¿Cómo estás, mi hermoso italiano?*"

I take her hand and kiss her skin, which smells of bubble bath and pretty woman.

"Wonderfully well. How could I be otherwise?"

Pilar points to the eggs and speaks to Feliciana.

"Could I have the same?"

As the woman heads back to the kitchen, Pilar steals a slice of toast from my plate. She starts chewing it, pretending to be a hamster. I laugh, the way I always do when she pulls that sight gag. She pours herself a glass of *coco frío* from a pitcher.

"What are you doing today?"

"I have to go to El Pueblo del Viento. There's a meeting for the development of a new shopping center and they're wondering whether I have intentions of investing any money."

"Do you have any?"

"Intentions or money?"

Instead of eating her last bite of toast, she throws it at me.

"Estúpido."

I spread my arms out wide, like someone faced with the undeniable.

"The problem isn't ideas, it's money."

She reaches out and embraces me. She presses her forehead against mine.

"My poor penniless darling. I hear there's a rich gentleman from Switzerland in a hotel in Pampatar who's very generous with the pretty girls. If you like, I can get you some money there."

Those words take me back in time. To when I used to say them and the roles were reversed. A small cloud passes over the May sky, and I do everything I can to make sure Pilar doesn't see it. Unsuccessfully.

"I don't think that'll be necessary."

She looks at me, nonplussed. Then she bursts out laughing.

"You're jealous. *Madre de Dios*, you're jealous. *Hermoso y celoso.*"

She stands up and comes over to sit on my lap. She hugs me. The moisture of her bathrobe, the moisture of her hair, the moisture of her lips.

"Te quiero."

"Yo te quiero también."

It's the second time we've said it to each other in the past few hours. And that's something I didn't mind even a little bit. Pilar fell into my life as an unexpected gift. She was a tourist with plenty of money who flew from Spain to Playa El Agua, either because she was looking for something or because she was running away from something. We met and she decided to extend her stay on the island. At first, it was supposed to be for another month. That turned into an extra two months. Then she moved into my house. Finally, the

402

idea of a departure date was simply dismissed entirely. I told her only what I felt like telling her about me. She did the same. I explained to her what I was, what I wasn't, and what I'd never be. She did the same thing. Since then, we've had a mutually comfortable relationship that's lasted for more than five years. Like anything involving human beings, there's no saying how long it will last. We may not be a family. But we're the closest thing to it that we've been able to assemble.

Our moment of union is over but not forgotten.

I lift Pilar out of my lap and march her back to her chair. There's a damp patch on my trousers where she was sitting. I brush a few bread crumbs off my shirt.

"I have to go. What are you going to do today?"

Pilar points inside the house.

"Howard invited me to go surfing with him, in the afternoon. We thought we'd go down to El Yaque too. As soon as he wakes up."

Howard is the boy who followed us home. After the hard work he did last night, I have my doubts as to whether he'll wake up anytime in the next couple of hours. From Pilar's expression, I see that she feels the same way.

"That's fine. In the afternoon, after the meeting, I'll stop by the resort village. There are some things I have to work out with the manager. We're planning to renovate a few of the bungalows."

I forestall any possible reaction on her part.

"Let me reassure you, there are no money problems. So you won't really have to call your wealthy Swiss gentleman."

She laughs again.

I turn to go. Her voice reaches me as I'm about to head down the steps that lead from the terrace to the ground floor, past the pool, and to the garage in back of the house.

"I need the Patrol. Take the Mercedes."

Without turning around, I give her the thumbs-up sign.

I walk around the pool toward the garage; the water is bright, reflecting the blue of the sky and absorbing its color. The garden is filled with trees and short palms; flowers are blooming everywhere, thanks to the expert care of Cristóbal.

A Mercedes sedan is parked next to a Nissan Patrol. The keys are in the ignition. I climb in and start the engine. I drive along the lane that leads out of my property. I turn onto Avenida 31 de Julio and continue until I reach the highway that runs across the island and takes me to Porlamar. At a fork in the road I lean right and take the road that runs around the airport and continues down to Playa El Yaque.

Every time I drive around this island, I'm forced to congratulate myself once again for the decision to live here. When I first got here, after an initial period of adjustment and giddy astonishment at the sheer beauty of the place, I took a good hard look around. I could sense a potential for tourism in the air that would certainly turn into a boom before long. That's exactly what happened and what continues to happen. Here was a chance to live in a secluded place without having to feel like an exile or a fugitive. A chance to work while leading a relaxed life at the same time. I bought three hotels and I invested in a number of businesses: restaurants, shops, and agencies providing services of all kinds to tourists.

I'm not doing all that badly.

I turn on the radio. From the more or less paved asphalt road, a trail of dust kicks up behind the car and the cloud almost seems to be swaying to the rhythm of the music. When I get to the beach, I park in the courtyard, in a space reserved for staff of El Pueblo del Viento, one of the resorts that I own.

It's a series of bungalows built in wood and masonry, carefully designed to appear primitive and still offer all the modern comforts. They're arrayed around a clubhouse that contains the reception desk, the restaurant, and a number of services that I was the first to offer tourists on the island, such as massages and beauty treatments for the body.

The resort village takes its name from the fact that it's just a short walk from a windy beach that is a paradise for windsurfers on Isla Margarita. In fact my clientele is for the most part made up of fanatical windsurfers who can't believe they've found a place where they can walk out of their room, pick up their board, and minutes later be skimming over the waves in a steady wind. Of course, all that comes with a price tag. But then, everything comes with a price tag, in the world of men.

The people I'm scheduled to meet today agreed to hold our little war council in one of the conference rooms at the resort village. It was a gesture of respect, as well as a way of making it as convenient as possible for me to join them. After all, I am one of the most sought-after investors in this latest venture. In the presence of money, trousers have a way of sliding down around ankles, all over the world. The line about money and ideas isn't exactly the way I recounted it to Pilar.

There's plenty of ass, it's the money we lack. That's the original version.

Godie *dixit*.

I head for the clubhouse and walk in through the front door. I'm immediately in a large five-sided space, illuminated on three sides by large plate-glass windows.

405

On the left is the bar and the lounge. On the right is the restaurant, which extends out onto a terrace overlooking the beach.

Across from the front door is the reception desk.

A group of new arrivals is standing in the lobby, waiting to be directed to their various rooms. Next to them sit the colorful patches of their suitcases, which will be carried to their rooms by the staff. I walk over and notice the manager, a man of average height with a beard and an aggravated bald spot, busy talking to a family of three.

Standing perpendicular to me, so I see him in profile, is a tall man with a receding hairline, an athletic build, and a square jaw. He has no need to wave an American flag for his nationality to be unmistakable. Next to him, with their backs to me, are a little boy about seven and a tall, slender woman with honey blond hair. She's wearing a pair of jeans and a light denim shirt.

It strikes me from their posture that there's some tension in the air. As the manager talks, he dry-washes his hands, a typical nervous tic of his in difficult moments. When he sees me coming, a look of relief spreads across his face and he gives me a sign. The three guests turn all at once, in response to his glance.

The woman is Carla.

My heart stops for a second. I manage to keep from lurching to a halt myself. I keep walking toward them, hoping that my face is just as smooth and untroubled as the face of the woman I'm seeing again after all these years.

"Buenos días, Guillermo. ¿Qué pasa?"

"There must have been a misunderstanding of some kind. The McKays tell me that they made a reservation but I see no sign of it in our records. Unfortunately, the resort village is completely booked and I have no way of giving them a place to stay."

The manager spoke in English, so that everyone could understand. My theory about their place of origin has proved correct.

The little boy grabs his father's waist.

"Oh, Daddy, this place is so pretty. Look at all the surfers. Can we stay here?"

Carla pulls the boy away from his father and pulls him close to her.

"Wait and see, Malcolm. I'm sure everything's going to be fine."

I extend my hand. The man returns a firm and vigorous grip. Since English is the official language of this conversation, I go along.

"Mr. McKay, my name is Nicola Sangiorgi. I'm the proprietor of this establishment. Let's see what we can do today to make your son happy."

Carla jerked imperceptibly in shock. I was the only one who noticed it, because I was the only one who knew to look for a reaction when she heard my real name.

I walk away, leaving them to wait expectantly. I check the reservation ledger and see that Guillermo Castillos, the manager, told the truth.

The resort village is fully booked.

I see on the list of arrivals for today a French couple, regular clients so faithful that they could be considered friends.

I point to their names.

"Please inform the Tourniers that there's been a mistake and that we won't be able to have them as our guests here. To make up for this regrettable mishap, they'll be

407

transferred to La Fortaleza and there will be no charge for their stay."

La Fortaleza is the name of another hotel I own. It's in Juan Griego and it's unquestionably my finest property. The French couple will have nothing to complain about.

"But the Tourniers . . ."

"The Tourniers don't care about windsurfing. They'll be delighted to spend their holiday free of charge in accomodations that are perhaps even finer than these. Do as I say and you'll see, everything will turn out perfectly."

"As you like, Señor Sangiorgi."

His expression is so unmistakable that I can practically hear the words he's thinking.

Do whatever the fuck you want. You're the boss and as long as you're happy . . .

And I am happy, and so he'd better be happy too.

The manager goes back to his work. I go over to the family of three who are waiting to learn the outcome. I assure them that it's just as they'd hoped.

"Everything's taken care of. As soon as you've registered, the porter will help you with your luggage. Have an enjoyable stay at El Pueblo del Viento, Mr. and Mrs. McKay."

The child throws his arms in the air in a sign of victory.

"Yay!"

The man smiles at me. A smile that evokes baseball games, barbecues with friends, family camping trips, a well-paid job.

A lawyer, I'd guess. Or a doctor.

"Let me thank you. And let me introduce myself properly. My name is Paul McKay. You've already met my son, Malcolm."

He points to the woman standing beside him.

"And this is my wife, Luisa. She's Italian, as are you, I'd imagine."

I shake the hand that Carla extends. In my mind, Luisa is the name of a stranger.

"A pleasure to meet you, Signora. I must say that our country is honored to be represented by someone like you."

Carla responds only with a nod and a tight smile.

I take a step back.

"Now, if you'll forgive me, I have a few things to see to."

I walk away and head for the reception desk.

I ask myself how I feel.

Who can say?

I certainly can't, not now that I've just had one more confirmation of the fact that it really is a small world. At a moment when chaos and chance have just paid a call to remind me that they never sleep and that the same rules as ever still apply. You can try to decide what you want to do with your life, but often it's life itself that decides what it wants to do with you.

I step up to the reception desk. I ask one of the girls at the desk to hand me the phone. I call my secretary. She answers on the first ring.

"Rosita Seguro."

"Rosita, do me a favor, please. Immediately inform Helizondo, Manzana, Cortes, and Llosa that I've run into a scheduling problem. Ask them whether it would be possible to postpone today's meeting and find out the date that would be most convenient for them."

"As you say, Señor Sangiorgi."

I hand the receiver back to the young woman and I turn to go to the office that I had built across from the kitchens. As soon as I'm safely inside, with the door closed, I go over to pour myself a glass of water.

I swallow it all in a single gulp. I remember my father taking a long drink of water, many years ago. I still don't understand that man, but I do understand the need for a glass of water at certain times in your life. I sit down behind my desk and sink back into the comfort of the leather swivel chair.

I canceled my meeting because I'm certain that I wouldn't have the necessary focus to talk about business. I wouldn't be able to look at the faces of those men, utter words and listen to the words of others, be with them in the conference room. I couldn't do it, just minutes after the past had come to find me and I found myself looking into Carla's eyes.

If it was you, I'd do it for free . . .

It's been years and yet it's all so vivid in my memory that I feel as if it's all still happening to me. Daytona's comb-over, the cool morning air outside of the Ascot Club, Tulip's flashlight somersaulting through the air in the darkness, Tano Casale's voice, Lucio's dark glasses, Carmine's face . . .

There's not a detail, a word, or a color missing.

Especially the red spatters of blood.

In the silence of my thoughts, I hear a knock at the door.

"Yes?"

The door opens partway and the face of a boy on my staff pokes through.

"Señor Sangiorgi, there's a woman who wishes to speak with you."

I sigh. I didn't think it would be so soon.

Something somewhere is beating in a forbidden way. However much time may pass, my heart will never be a reliable accomplice.

"Show her in."

I stand up and wait until Carla has come into the office. I point to the chair in front of the desk. As soon as she's seated, I sit down myself.

I look at her. Ten years have only refined and softened her beauty. In her I sense that restless gentle hush of the hour just before sunset, when the sun shines warmer and brighter to make us forgive the darkness that will fall once it leaves. Her hair color and style still match the line that Alex first set, many years ago.

Her eyes are the same as they always were. And, I imagine, as they always will be.

I wish I were a different person with a different life, I wish I'd met you in a different way. It could have been so nice . . .

But it wasn't.

"*Ciao*, Bravo."

I can't help but smile.

"No one's called me that in years."

"I always thought that nickname suited you so well."

I say nothing. She continues.

"But instead, after all these years, here you are with a name that can't be easy to carry."

"It's my name. There was a time when I thought one name was as good as another." I allow myself a pause. "I was wrong."

I pull out a pack of cigarettes. I offer her one. To my surprise, she refuses.

She flashes a smile at the sight of my baffled face.

"Time passes, and resisting bad habits becomes easier."

I light my cigarette alone, thinking to myself that that's not always true.

"Your husband seems like a very nice person."

411

"He is."

"And your son is a lovely child. Smart, I'd say."

She smiles. The smile extends to her eyes this time.

"Oh, he's smart all right, maybe too smart."

"How are you?"

There's no real curiosity in my question, only a hint of regret.

"You summed it up nicely. I have a husband, a son. They help to keep me from thinking."

I lean my elbows on the desk. I know what she means. Sometimes, thinking can be really unpleasant work.

I change my tone of voice.

"What can I do for you?"

She searches for the words.

She finds them.

"When I left, there was no time to talk. But I did tell you a story."

Her memories aren't enough for her. That happens sometimes, when they aren't nice ones.

"Now you owe me a story too."

I wonder if she really has been thinking about it all these years. The answer is that I would have thought about it myself, if I were in her shoes.

"A story, you say?"

I minimize with the look on my face, and for an instant I turn my head away.

"It's a simple story to tell. I can sum it up in a few words."

She looks at me. And waits for the words.

"I was young, handsome, and wealthy. I had all the girls I could ever wish for. In the city of Palermo I had become a minor celebrity. During my last year in law school, I fell in love with the wrong girl. A girl that Turi Martesano's nephew

412

had already decided was the girl for him. Turi Martesano was a big gun in the Mafia. They warned me that I was running a big risk. But I thought I was untouchable, that I was protected by the shield of my father's political power."

I can't help but smile at the thought of how naïve I was, and how helpless.

"She was in love, as much as I was. Perhaps more, because if I'd had any idea what was going to happen to me, I would have run away immediately. We went on dating. One night, on my way home, I was grabbed by three men. They threw a hood over my head and shoved me into a car."

I give her time to conjure up images corresponding to my story. She certainly has experiences in her own past that should help her do so.

"They took me to a place. I think it was a farm. I could smell the countryside. I heard the voice of the man talking. A rough, gravelly voice, he told me to hold still, that if I was good he wouldn't hurt me as much, and he kept telling me Bravo! Bravo! . . . Then they pulled down my trousers and he sliced off my dick."

Even I am forced to use my imagination for this part. There was a hood over my head. All I saw was blackness. I remember the yellow flash of pain before my staring eyes.

"Then what happened?"

"They threw me out of the car in front of my house, an isolated villa at the beach, at Mondello. I was immediately sent to a private clinic for treatment, where I had emergency surgery and was cared for in conditions of absolute discretion. Absolutely no one was to know that they had kidnapped Amedeo Sangiorgi's son and cut his dick off."

My voice must sound to her the same way it sounds to me.

Choked and still filled with disbelief.

"Once I recovered, they transferred me to Rome and I was put into a psychologist's care. To come to terms with the trauma, they said. The sessions did one useful thing: they made me suspicious. It had all been too well orchestrated to have been a lucky chance. The way they dropped me off in front of my house, the fact that I was given such prompt medical care, the fortuitous presence of the right surgeons in the clinic, as if my father had been warned in advance of what was going to happen."

I look her in the face again. I've watched as this woman killed people in cold blood. But now there's a bottomless grief and pity painted on her face.

"And in fact that's pretty much what had happened. He confirmed that to me himself. He knew, but he lacked the courage to do anything about it. Or there was nothing he could do, which doesn't really change matters much. By this point he was in too deep and he was too determined to climb to the top of the ladder of power."

I allow her to reflect on the tragic irony of the whole story. The fact that, of all the files, she should have chosen to put into my hands the one that dealt with my father. The fact that the only person who could have helped Senator Amedeo Sangiorgi to recover a dossier that he'd fought so ferociously to track down was his son, whom he'd sacrificed to the laws of the Mafia.

"That's why I ran away. That's why I lay low and used a fake name. I took diction lessons to conceal my accent. I was afraid of the world, and I felt only fear and contempt toward everyone. Toward other men, who could be what I could never hope to be again. Toward women, who had the power of exciting me but not of satiating me."

414

She looks at me in silence. There's not much left to say. And what little there is, it's up to me to say.

"And so, in memory of the words spoken that night, Bravo was born. A pimp."

"Did you ever find out the name of the man who mutilated you?"

I smile. Despite the effort it costs me.

"Certainly. He was a professional killer hired for the occasion. I met him again in Milan. He'd risen through the ranks, and now he was a gang boss. But I had a clue. I remembered his voice. He didn't have any way of recognizing me, not even my face, because my head was covered with a hood."

"What ever happened to him?"

"He died in San Vittore Prison. He was killed by another prisoner in the exercise yard."

It takes her a second to make the connection. But she gets it almost immediately.

"Did that prisoner by any chance live somewhere near Quarto Oggiaro before winding up in prison?"

My silence is equivalent to confirmation. And it strikes me as the right moment to venture a small additional observation about myself.

"As you can see, I'm no better than you are."

My story is done. As I'd promised her, it wasn't long. There will be other stories for both of us. But each of us will experience them on his or her own. Now there's not much left to say, only a short time left to spend as best we can.

Carla stands up.

"I think I'd better go rejoin my boys. Officially I came in here to thank you properly while they took a dip in the ocean. But now I have to go."

I accompany her to the door. Her voice stops me short.

"Now let me ask you a question. The same question you asked me. How are you?"

"I have a woman. Just one. I let her see other men. But not for money."

I open the door for her. I follow her down the short hallway.

"I've wondered more than once what that life would have been like."

"What life?"

"Working for you."

We walk through the door and we're in the lobby. Beyond this wooden panel is another world. The world of people who don't know and in this case would certainly prefer not to.

"I told you, one day in my apartment, when you asked me to bring you into the business. It's not a road you can't come back from. But if you do, you'll be bringing some unpleasant memories with you."

"Who doesn't have them already?"

"Right, who doesn't?"

A few more steps and we're outside, on the patio from which we have a view of the beach and the sea, abloom with colorful sails. From here, it's impossible to identify Paul and Malcolm McKay, but I feel certain that down there somewhere they're enjoying themselves like any father and son on holiday. And they're waiting for a wife and mother whom they know as Luisa to rejoin them.

I'm tempted to ask her her real name. But I refrain.

Whatever that name might be, to me she'll always have just one name: Carla.

Carla Bonelli.

Just as we're about to say good-bye, Pilar catches us by

surprise. She must have left the Nissan Patrol in the parking lot and walked around the building, so I didn't see her coming. She stops just a step or two away.

She looks at us and, with the instinct that all women seem to possess, examines us.

"Pilar, this is Mrs. McKay. She's going to be our guest at the resort village with her husband and son for a couple of weeks."

Pilar walks over. The two women shake hands and study each other the way that only women know how to do. Then Carla . . . no, *Luisa*—decides that the time really has come to get back to her family.

"Have a good day, Mr. Sangiorgi. Thanks very much for your kind help. You have a good day too, Pilar."

Without waiting for a reply, she turns and walks away, with a gait that has lost none of its grace. I follow her with my gaze as she stops to take off her shoes and then walks off barefoot across the sand.

Pilar's voice summons me back to her side.

"That woman likes you."

I realize that she was watching my eyes, without understanding what was reflected in them. Certainly a number of things, all of them easy to misunderstand.

"Are you going to leave me for her?"

I take her face in my hands. I can hear something solid in my voice, something definitive in my words.

"No. I'm not going to leave you for her."

I take off my shoes. I want to feel the sand under my bare feet too. It's been far too long since I last did it. I step off the wooden boards of the patio and sink into the sand. I look at the woman who's lived with me for the past few years. She's wearing a pair of olive drab shorts and a black

417

T-shirt beneath which her breasts are free to be themselves and allow others to imagine them.

"Come here."

Pilar walks over and I pull her toward me. I wrap an arm around her shoulders. I feel her skin, soft to my touch.

"Let's take a walk. You want to?"

We walk off toward Punta de Mangle, without haste or purpose.

Pilar wraps one arm around my waist.

"Didn't you have a meeting?"

"Didn't you have a date to go surfing?"

She laughs and her teeth are the white of a young female shark.

"Oh, that boy was so dull, so *barboso*. I have more fun getting bored with you."

From that moment on, we walk, arms around each other, without speaking, heading somewhere we know perfectly well we'll never reach. But we feel this progress, this walking together, this new thing pushing us step by step to move beyond our footsteps. We'll find them there on our way back. If they're mingled with other footsteps and we're unable to recognize them, what does it matter? We're on an island, and everyone here is a survivor in his own way, of one shipwreck or another.

Here the spring lasts a long time and summer, when it comes, doesn't spoil anything.

ACKNOWLEDGMENTS

This novel contains the story of a world that no longer exists. It vanished as people went away, as years passed, and as society changed. It faded with the numbers that mark the years of my life, when in the tens column a three replaced the two, and then came a four, followed by a five, and that's where I stop, because six is Satan's number.

Milan was not yet a brand you could drink, and the night was still a noble adversary to face in single combat. Sleep was our true enemy, and sunshine at dawn was part of the routine. Indifference was the only sin, unappreciated talent the harsh hair shirt we wore.

In that world and in those years, an adventure began that continues today. I would like to thank all the people who made those years unforgettable, with their kindness or their rejection. Both helped me to become the man I am today, for better or for worse.

But to do this, I'd have to write a hundred pages and mention a thousand names. I'm happy to name just one out of the many: Beefsteak. He left behind a trove of unforgettable, outsized wisecracks, the kind of witticisms that only genius for its own sake could engender. I like to think that I paid him due tribute and endowed him with just a smidgen of the immortality that his creative flair deserved.

Then there are people I should thank for their help in writing and editing this book. They are people who brighten my life with their friendship and esteem, and I return those sentiments in the most complete manner imaginable.

Let me therefore thank:

Claudio Giovannone, who ensured that a person he loves would be transformed into a chief inspector. And he did it in the best possible way: by doing good.

The Lavazza family, who gave me the same opportunity.

Dario Tosetti, for serving as an enthusiastic middleman in this exchange of good wishes.

Dr. Cesare Savina, an outstanding pediatrician, who took a short time off from treating the illnesses of real children to provide me with one for a fictional child.

Dr. Franco Bardari, director of the Department of Urology at the Civic Hospital of Asti, who enlightened me, while I shuddered, on the surgical ordeal that Bravo endured.

La Settimana Enigmistica, in the person of Alessandro Bartezzaghi, who helped me out with the cryptic clues contained in this novel.

Piero Tallarida, historian of and devoted waiter at the legendary Derby Club, the avowed inspiration for the Ascot Club.

Claudia Zigliotto, an assistant deputy commissioner of police, a dear friend, and at the same time a ruthless protagonist in the battle against crime in the city of Milan.

Andy Surdi, spectacular drummer and vocalist.

Michele del Vecchio and Furio Bozzetti, old friends who have surfaced safe and sound.

Giovanni Bartocci, a young businessman and my companion in New York City nights of revelry. Two different ages, the same blues, the same beer.

Last of all, let me mention the group of people I work with, men and women who are my coworkers and at the same time my friends. And work and friendship have never interfered.

Here are their names:

Alessandro Dalai, the man of the clouds.

Cristina Dalai, the young lady of the clear blue sky.

Lorenza Dalai, my favorite elf.

Antonella Fassi, who has a good word for everyone.

Mara Scanavino, who has a good color for everyone.

Chiara Moscardelli and Elisa Montanucci, who have a good press release for everyone.

Stefano Travagli, who is impervious to the siren song of the lap dance, not something you can say about everyone.

Francesco Colombo, who edits me like no one else can.

Piergiorgio Nicolazzini, who encourages me like no one else can.

Roberta, who does all these things put together and more besides.

If I can consider myself a lucky man, they are all fundamental factors in that good fortune.